I0730585

LAST TRAIN

TO

KENGIR

STEPLAG, KENGIR, KAZAKHSTAN, 1954

ROMAN ALEXANDER GERUS

Copyright © 2025 Roman Gerus.

All rights reserved. No part of this publication may be reproduced, distributed, or transmitted in any form or by any means, including photocopying, recording, or other electronic or mechanical methods, without the prior written permission of the publisher, except in the case of brief quotations embodied in critical reviews and certain other noncommercial uses permitted by copyright law. For permission requests, write to the publisher, addressed "Attention: Permissions Coordinator," at the address below.

ISBN: 978-1-7348951-6-2 (Paperback)
ISBN: 978-1-7348951-7-9 (EBook)
Library of Congress Control Number: 2025911293

Any references to historical events, real people, or real places are used fictitiously. Names, characters, and places are products of the author's imagination.

Cover and Typesetting by Stewart A. Williams.

Printed in the United States of America.
First printing edition.

Roman Gerus, LLC.
1321 Terrill Road
Scotch Plains, NJ, 07076
https://romangerus18.wixsite.com/mysite

I dedicate this book to my parents, my baba Nilya and to the men and women fighting for Ukraine against Russian aggression since 2014 and full-scale invasion on February 24, 2022.
Героям Слава

Glory to Ukraine's Heroes

PROLOGUE

Less than ten years after World War II, the world was embroiled in a new type of war—the Cold War between the Communist East and Capitalist West. Eastern Europe was still smoldering from the greatest devastation, where Nazi Germany and its allies had killed over thirty million people, including the majority of Holocaust victims. Although the war officially ended in Western Europe and the Soviet Union in 1945 on May 8th and 9th respectively, peace still eluded the east.

Immediately after the end of WWII, hundreds of thousands of people from western Ukraine, Poland, and the Baltic countries of Lithuania, Latvia, and Estonia were executed, imprisoned, or deported to the infamous Soviet penal system, *Glavnoje Upravlenije Lagerej*, better known by its abbreviation: Gulag. The vast majority of these people fought with the Soviet Union against the Nazis, but many also fought against the Soviets for their independence, including a significant minority who fought alongside the Germans. True to his name, the infamous "Man of Steel," Soviet Premier Joseph Stalin cemented his will over these people with an iron fist.

These new strangers pouring into the vast Soviet penal system were pushing the state to a tipping point. The Gulag had never held such an organized, fanatical wave of "politicals." The original "politicals" still alive in the gulags were mainly intellectuals, teachers, and artisans swept up in the Great Purge of the late 1930s that had also left hundreds of thousands dead. These older inmates were equally amazed and afraid of the new arrivals flooding into the prison system.

These contrasting feelings were not misplaced, as these strangers were battle-hardened anti-Soviet partisans and their equally as devoted families. They sent fear down the ranks of the once-untouchable *urka,* the criminal class who often worked with the guards for favors. *Urka* harassed the older, meeker politicals with impunity, until their good times finally ended.

Despite the deaths of Stalin and his hangman Lavrenty Beria in 1953, millions were still locked away in this "ice guillotine" that had claimed nearly two million lives since its inception by the Soviet Union's founder, Vladimir Lenin, three decades prior. That was all about to change. The latest Soviet premier, Nikita Khrushchev, wanted to reopen the Soviet Union in a campaign later known as the "Thaw" as a departure from isolationist Stalinism. However, like everything else in that frozen wasteland, progress moved slowly.

Starting almost immediately after Stalin's death, gulag uprisings roiled the Soviet Union, from the "frozen hell" of Arctic camps in Vorkuta and Norilsk, to the massive Kolyma prison camp system in the eastern Siberian region of Kamchatka near Japan. In response to the revolts, the Soviets decided to segregate the various partisans from the general population, which would have fateful repercussions for the Gulag overall. It is said that Russia's history is like a great pendulum, swinging between tyranny and reform. When that pendulum swings, many are struck.

This is the story of those that struck back.

1

FEBRUARY 23–24, 1954:

LAST TRAIN TO KENGIR

Z/K VOLODYMYR ANDRIYOVICH'S chains scraped against the rusty hull, rattling his aching bones. He was pressed shoulder to shackle with his fellow captives in the large metal sarcophagus of the *Stolypinka* car. They were fresh from an overcrowded *osobye lagerya*, a special prison camp for political prisoners. He might be in hell, but it was too cold.

The *Stolypinka*, irreverently named after Tsar Nicholas II's assassinated prime minister Pyotr Stolypin, was originally designed to transport peasants and their livestock throughout the Russian Empire. The Soviets showcased their ingenious cruelty when the cars were adapted to deport masses of prisoners throughout the Soviet Empire. There is a Ukrainian proverb Volodymyr remembered from his *dido*, or grandfather, with fresh chills: "A master is not as cruel as a servant would be in his place." In a system that supposedly banned all masters, they were servile to a crueler code.

Volodymyr looked over his brothers-in-arms. Each man bore the years of suffering on his furrowed brows and hollow eyes that stared at the frozen, crusted blood on their wrists and ankles, or stared out into space in quiet contemplation. Whatever they were before, they were now *zeks* (from the Russian abbreviation *z/k* for *zaklyuchennyi*, or locked up).

A KGB bear of a man loomed over the zeks. The KGB (the Russian abbreviation of *Komitet Gosudarstvennoy Bezopasnosti*, or Committee of State Security) was the most recent succession of the notorious Soviet secret police. Beside him sat a morose *nadziratel*, or armed guard, cradling his iconic WWII Soviet Mosin rifle. The authorities sat rival partisans next to each other in an attempt to sow division. These disparate parties, such as the Ukrainians and Poles, had put their differences aside and banded together as a new multinational army.

They were all lost in the Great Eurasian Steppe of Kazakhstan. Each zek was another speck in the great "Gulag Archipelago." They had left countless hours ago from the closest city, Karaganda, several hundred kilometers and a world away.

Weeks between railyards were spent in the endless expanse of desolate steppes and arctic tundra. They had fallen off the face of the earth. Even Soviet citizens irreverently referred to Karaganda as "Karagan-*Hde*"; a Russian play on the ending, meaning "Karagan-*Where*."

The camp where they were headed, known as Steplag No. 3, or simply "Kengir" (located near the closest Kazakh village of Kengir), had a reputation that preceded it. All the men had served hard time, but Kengir still sent chills down their spines. Kengir was a maximum *katorga*, or forced labor camp regime. Each guard was said to be more sadistic than the last, and there was no outside authority to guide their already limited moral compass. The zeks were all condemned to the miserable last train to Kengir.

Volodymyr Andriyovich Zaluzhniy, Z/k 22422, was referred to by his call name Baran, or *ram*, by his brothers-in-arms. He got his name after he rammed the head of the *troika*, a group of Soviet officials used to try prisoners in lieu of court, reading out his sentence when he was captured. Although not particularly large or striking, Volodymyr had an indelible spirit. He fiercely defended himself and his comrades when cornered.

Volodymyr, Baran, or Vlodko to the few friends and family he had left, was a Ukrainian Hutsul shepherd from a long line of shepherds in the village of Pechenizhyn. The Hutsuls are a rugged breed born out of the rocky, eastern Carpathian region bordering Romania that bears their name: Hutsulshchyna. Volodymyr's village was also famous as the home of the "Ukrainian Robin Hood": Oleksa Dovbush. Dovbush had led his band of legendary Ukrainian mountain warriors known as *Opryshky* against their foreign adversaries. These tales had partly inspired Volodymyr to join Ukraine's largest resistance army at the time: the Ukrainian Insurgent Army (*Ukrainska Povstanska Armia*), or UPA, when he turned eighteen in 1943.

Volodymyr's *Hoverlia* detachment of UPA, named after Ukraine's highest peak of the Carpathians, was one of the last regular units to surrender to the Red Army in 1949, although some localized UPA units continued to resist Soviet rule into 1954 along with the Baltic partisans. Volodymyr now realized too late, along with thousands of his brothers- and sisters-in-arms, the naivety that they would be treated as legitimate prisoners of war under the Geneva Convention held that same year. Volodymyr cursed learning how to read in the army, just to know how much they had been cheated. These prisoners were now, ironically, the last ones carrying on the torches of their movements in captivity.

Before Kengir, Volodymyr spent time in the infamous Mordovia camp, which was about five hundred kilometers southeast of Moscow. Thousands of dissident Ukrainians, including the major archbishop and cardinal of the exiled Ukrainian Greek Catholic Church, Josyf Slipyj, were held there. Volodymyr once defended *Otets*, or Priest, Slipyj from an urka. For Volodymyr's bravery, Slipyj had given him a gold chain with a beautifully engraved crucifix and a promise to let Volodymyr's family know of his whereabouts. Volodymyr still clung to his faith, though it was getting harder.

The sad herd of human chattel reminded Volodymyr of his poor flock of sheep he had left behind in the green and amber mountain meadows, or *polonyna*, of the Carpathian Mountains in western Ukraine. He quickly shook off such painful thoughts. He wasn't a shepherd boy anymore.

Up to fifty zeks were crammed into rows snaking around the eighteen-meter-long, three-meter-wide boxcar. Their condemned caravan held ten cars, around five hundred souls, making this a particularly large haul of prisoners. The *nadziratel* watched over them like hawks. There was barely enough room to breathe. Every time a man moved, the entire column would have to readjust. Woe to the poor devils in the center of the car that didn't even have a cold steel wall to lean on.

The train hit a bump and listed. Everyone swished around the slippery metal floors. Volodymyr's arm slipped and knocked into his neighbor.

"Watch it, Vlodko," said Stas. "I'm trying to get some beauty sleep."

"You'll need more than that," said Volodymyr.

"Have you seen yourself?" asked Stas.

"Stubborn Pole." Volodymyr smirked.

Volodymyr's good friend Stanislaw, or Stas, hailed from the Polish city of Rzeszów on the Polish side of the Carpathians known as the Tatra. They both shared personal reasons for joining their resistance forces. Volodymyr and Stas would squabble and tease each other about many things, especially about which side of the Carpathians was better, but it was all in good humor.

"The Tatra are much better for skiing," Stas would say.

"*Tak* but they're too sparse. Give me the sprawling *polonyna* of the Beskydy any day," Volodymyr would say, referring to the Ukrainian Carpathian slopes.

After spending a stint as a miner, Stas had put down his pick and picked up a rifle to join the Polish resistance force *Armia Krajowa*, or Home Army, after the regular Polish army was defeated by Germany in 1939. He was rounded up in a mass arrest after WWII, around the same time as Volodymyr, after he was betrayed by an undercover Soviet agent. Their friendship would have been unthinkable only a few years ago. Many Poles and Ukrainians had fought each other as ferociously as the Nazis and Soviets over western Ukraine, or what the Poles called the Kresy lands. The struggle was a continuation of historical grievances.

After fighting each other from 1918-1919 in the Polish-Ukrainian War, Ukraine and Poland fought together against their common Russian enemy from 1920-1921 in the Polish-Soviet War. Ukraine was divided afterwards in the Treaty of Riga between Russia and Poland, leaving Ukrainians bitter. The tenuous truce between these two rival armies was another result of their strange and terrible circumstances. After WWII, UPA and Armia Krajowa cooperated again in some operations against their common enemies: the Soviets and their Polish and Ukrainian communist allies.

Stas had been separated from his Polish platoon and his commander, Jerzy Pulaski. Over the past few years, he had spent more time with the Ukrainians. Volodymyr and Stas had met on one of these hellish rides. At first, they were both appalled by the other, carrying on their armies' bitter rivalry. Along the way, though, they began to bond over their love of their mountainous regions and hatred of their common enemy: Russia. They learned to communicate in Russian from their years of captivity, but they also both spoke Polish, as Volodymyr was from western Ukraine where Polish was widely spoken. Then, as is inevitable on these desperate journeys, Volodymyr and Stas had been cornered by a gang of urka.

Volodymyr's and Stas's mutual experience fighting the Nazis and Soviets worked wonders when they taught the urka a new bloody sense of humility. Sometimes the worst brings out the best in people. Volodymyr watched Stas drift back off to sleep.

Volodymyr leaned back against the cold steel frame and listened to the whirring tracks. He was stirred from his trance by someone humming a Ukrainian folk song, "Verkhovyno, Maty Moya," or "Mother of Mine," about a famous region of the Ukrainian Carpathians. He wiped away a tear. Volodymyr's dido would sing him to sleep as a child before he was killed.

Volodymyr's dido was killed in the Vinnytsia Massacre of 1937 during the Great Purge, when thousands of Ukrainian prisoners were executed by the Soviet secret police then known as the NKVD near Vinnytsia in central Ukraine. His dido's death politicized his father, Andriy Anatoliyovich. Andriy was killed, in turn, by the Soviets three years later in the L'viv Prison Massacre in June 1940.

Andriy had been imprisoned under trumped up charges of sedition for belonging to the Ukrainian cultural organization Prosvita, which had been founded in the Western Ukrainian city of L'viv in 1868 and shuttered by Stalin's paranoid policies in 1939. Andriy was killed by a gunshot to the back of the head when the retreating Red Army was ordered to "empty" the political prisons in western Ukraine to prevent collaboration in the wake of the Nazi invasion of the Soviet Union: Operation Barbarossa. Andriy's older brother, Yurko, took in Volodymyr and his devastated mother. Yurko had never remarried after his wife had died during childbirth. He took over as Volodymyr's father figure, especially after his mother, Marusia Serhiyivka, succumbed to typhus she had contracted from helping an escaped Jewish family from L'viv.

Stas had lost his father, a Polish officer, in the Katyn Massacre of 1941 when the Russians executed thousands of Polish officers in the Katyn forest of present-day Belarus out of paranoid fear of an uprising. Despite his defiant demeanor, Volodymyr knew Stas was still traumatized by the loss of his dear father. He heard Stas call out to him in his sleep. Stas's mother was still alive when he was arrested after the war, but like the rest of them, he had no contact with the outside world.

Volodymyr was lucky enough to be seated at the end of the car nearest to the barred window. He looked out in humble silence at the vast stretch of the Great Steppe. It was an overcast day and the scene was disorienting with the light dusting of snow over the gray grass and rolling hills sinking into oblivion. It was hard to tell where the sky ended and the earth began. These endless wild fields that stretch thousands of kilometers from Mongolia to Ukraine along the ancient Silk Road had been the playground of the great khans.

Every so often, strange specks appeared to be moving in the distance. They got closer, and Volodymyr saw a wayward herd of surreal saiga antelope munching on spindly saxaul trees. They pawed at the rough bark of the traditional Turkmen firewood, sniffing with their proboscis snouts. The male saiga had the distinctive long, twisted horns coveted by hunters. He was surrounded by his harem of about a dozen females. He was oblivious to the iron beast snaking by and its miserable cargo. He thought only about his meal and his females.

"Lucky guy." Volodymyr smirked.

Volodymyr soon began to see strange grassy knolls rising out of the steppes. He looked closer and realized they were mangled huts from abandoned villages. Volodymyr understood something terrible also happened to these people, like in Ukraine.

They were indeed memorials to the forced collectivization in Kazakhstan that killed over a million and a half people around the time of the Holodomor in Ukraine. Ukrainian for "death by hunger," the Holodomor was the Soviet Russian genocide of Ukrainians under Stalin. Between 1932 and 1934, over four million Ukrainians deemed *kulaks,* or wealthy peasants, died of state-engineered famine in Soviet-controlled Ukraine.

The burden of history weighed heavily on all of them. These cataclysmic events were not just pages from a history book; they were fresh in their minds and tormented their souls. Volodymyr would at times fantasize about a nuclear strike from America, but then he thought about all those terrible pictures from Hiroshima and Nagasaki. He imagined the calcified corpses of Yurko and his wife Ma. *How did we come to this?* Volodymyr thought. He finally started to doze off when the train started screeching to a halt.

"What the hell is it now?" asked Stas, knocked out of his sleep again.

The train halted after a few minutes. The heavy steel door shrieked as it opened. Their *nadziratel* laboriously stood up, shaking his sleeping limbs.

"Central Steppe Station No. 3," said the conductor.

It was the changing of the guards. Their *nadziratel* was only too happy to get off. How the zeks prayed they could be so lucky.

The station was a simple mud-and-brick hut in the middle of nowhere, surrounded by *nadziratel* and a few lowly Kazakh shepherds with some scrawny sheep for market in Karaganda. The Kazakh civilians looked at the train and ran in fright once they realized its cargo. The new guards looked even meaner and more haggard.

"Hey, wake up, Kolya," said one of the prisoners, shaking his neighbor. "Kolya?"

A guard pushed his way through the mess of men and shackles. He moved the other prisoner aside. The guard put his ear to the unconscious man's mouth.

"Dead man, coming through," said the *nadziratel*.

He briskly unshackled the deceased. Kolya was one of the older UPA men. Volodymyr knew him from when he was first deported to Mordovia. He was a humble farmer from the Western Ukrainian city of Sambir near the Polish border.

The brutish *nadziratel* made Kolya's comrade haul him out without even fully unshackling him. Zeks didn't have the luxury of grieving. Death was a part of their lives.

"His troubles are over," Volodymyr sighed.

"*Balanda*," said a shrill voice.

The zeks were confronted by an old babushka slinging the dreaded cabbage stew. The *nadziratel* quickly passed around crude bowls of soup. The lukewarm liquid spilled on the zeks and on the floor, those in the back of the wagon hardly receiving any at all. Volodymyr swirled around the gray broth and closed his eyes, swallowing his grief, imaging it was his *baba*'s homemade *borshch*.

Volodymyr looked at the guards; they had drifted off to sleep. He could see a flask poking out of the KGB guard's pocket, so he knew that they would be out for a while, giving the zeks some breathing room. Their UPA *sotnyk* Oleksa Zalizniak, call name Sokil, or falcon, also noticed the unconscious guards and began rallying the men.

Sokil was a World War I veteran of the Austro-Hungarian army and the elite Ukrainian Sich Riflemen, who took part in the Ukrainian War of Independence from 1917-1921. Less than twenty years later, after Nazi Germany invaded Poland, he had worked with the short-lived Ukrainian Carpathian Republic that declared independence in late 1939 before it was annexed by Nazi-allied Hungary.

He had then fled and joined the founder of UPA, Stepan Bandera, on the killing fields of WWII.

Sokil was a shrewd commander who took opportunities where he could, even among former enemies. They had worked out a simple enough code among Armia Krajowa and the Baltic partisans. Sokil whispered to the Jewish doctor Nacham Lyman, his second-in-command.

Nacham barely escaped Ukraine's capital Kyiv after it fell to the Nazis in 1941. He had survived the three-day Babi Yar Massacre, during which Nazis shot over 30,000 of Kyiv's Jews in what would become part of the "Holocaust by Bullets." He had survived by playing dead for two days among scores of corpses. He'd then walked hundreds of kilometers through hostile territory to the Carpathians.

Being a former doctor made Nacham's skills priceless. Sokil personally intervened in saving Nacham, and they became inseparable. Though uncommon, Nacham's case was not isolated, as UPA made use of Jewish doctors fleeing Nazi-occupied Ukraine.

Any antisemitism in their ranks was quickly quashed after seeing Nacham's bravery and dedication. He had been swept up in the mass arrests after the war for acting as a UPA medic. He now held the role of a *feldsher*, or a medic in the Gulag.

Sokil tapped out his message. All the prisoners understood, despite their language barriers. The word went down to the last man in line, Volodymyr: *Cargo Status*. This was meant to gather intelligence on who or what was in the car next to him.

They had established the car next to Sokil was filled with urka. There was word that the female UPA combatants were somewhere on this train. This fact particularly excited the men, having not seen anything resembling a woman besides the old babushka that fed them balanda.

Volodymyr gingerly poked his head up to the door, pressing his cheeks against the frigid metal. It was so cold that the steel stuck to his skin, but he ignored the pain. He craned his neck and squinted into the next car.

Volodymyr inched forward, and nearly fell off the train. He was struck by a pair of the most beautiful evergreen eyes and wavy golden hair, like rays of sunshine over a *polonyna*. The world stood still.

"Vlodko, what do you see?" asked Stas.

Volodymyr quickly put his hand over Stas's mouth. One of the guards fidgeted and moaned but went back to sleep. Volodymyr leaned into Stas.

"You almost got us caught you loudmouth *Lyakh*," said Volodymyr, using a Ukrainian slur for Poles.

"Ah, you stubborn *Ruthenian*," said Stas, using a defunct Austro-Hungarian term for Ukrainians.

Volodymyr shrugged him off. It was the green-eyed angel. Moments later, another female face poked into the barred window.

By this time, Volodymyr could feel Stas breathing down his neck. He conceded for Stas to have a look. Stas leaned out and the four of them made eye contact. The two women whispered excitedly. Stas quickly covered his mouth, squealing like a piglet.

"You finally had something interesting to show me, Vlodko," said Stas, playfully nudging Volodymyr. "Shepherd and miner's daughters, eh?"

By that time, the men were getting restless seeing the commotion at the end of the car. Volodymyr sent the message down the ranks: *Female Zeks.* The men then did something they hadn't done in months, if not years: they smiled.

Suddenly, the party was over as quickly as it began when someone yelled "*katorga*" in the other car. The two angels disappeared back into their hellish reality. The men's own intoxicated guards awoke. The KGB behemoth stood up shakily.

"What's going on?" he asked, cocking his pistol. "The next sound I hear will be followed by a coup de grace!"

The zeks sat back and stared at the floor in one choreographed motion.

"That's better," said the KGB officer, plopping back down onto the pallet to sleep.

"That was close," said Volodymyr.

"*Tak*," agreed Stas. "We almost stepped in some real shit."

"*Parasha*," said a Kazakh guard.

"Oh shit," said Stas, turning his cheek and pretending he hadn't heard the guard. Volodymyr wasn't so lucky. The young, angry Kazakh shoved the putrid pale of waste into Volodymyr.

The stout, burly Kazakhs, many of them former nomadic herders not unlike many of their Western Ukrainian prisoners, had been forced into such glum services to escape the drab, hard life on the *kolkhoz*, or collective farm. They hated their Slavic masters and took it out on the prisoners. It was not a pleasant journey for them either.

The amenities for the rank and file guards were often barely above the zeks. They too were sometimes forced to use the same rancid, overflowing *parasha* to relieve themselves. Crude toilets had to be shared between several cars to reserve the better latrines for the officers.

Volodymyr gingerly stood up, praying he didn't spill any of the foul contents. The smell was burning his nostrils and eyes. He made his way, dragging his shackles to the edge of the train when he saw the angel peering through the bars. She waved to him.

Volodymyr smiled from ear to ear, until the train jerked forward and he was splashed with days-old urine and feces. Volodymyr tossed the *parasha* like it was on fire, gagging and coughing. The angel blushed and covered her mouth, ducking back down. He rushed back inside.

"Jesus, Vlodko, you smell worse than you look," said Stas, covering his nose.

Volodymyr ignored him. He was still thinking about his angel. She was the most beautiful woman he had seen in years, ever since his wife. He closed his eyes and shook off more unhealthy thoughts. *Had he dreamt it?* It was getting dark and the car was quieting down. Eventually, Stas and the rest of the car drifted off to greener pastures. Volodymyr was still restless. He quietly rose up to look out at the dark prairie night.

Night on the steppes was like nothing he had seen before. The constellations were an immense bright panorama swirling in every direction. The dark abyss devoid of natural barriers made it feel like they were shooting through outer space.

He wondered about the heavenly body in the next car. Staring out at the night, he lost track of time. He was so exhausted that he fell asleep leaning against the barred window.

Volodymyr opened his eyes and realized he had left the sprawling steppes and was rolling through the towering Karpaty. Dawn was rising over the mountains. The train abruptly stopped. The doors opened and he stepped out. He looked around and saw a desolate village. It was eerily quiet, like death. He then heard something coming.

Volodymyr didn't know exactly what it was, but it didn't sound right. He tried to get back on the train, and saw the angel. He called out to her, but the train had taken off, and it was going too fast. The noise was getting closer. Volodymyr began to run, but the figure was getting closer. He turned around to face his demon when a little lamb stumbled out of the bushes. Volodymyr picked up the lamb, and a hungry wolf pounced.

Volodymyr realized he must have been out for a while when he awoke with a terrible neck ache. Twilight was creeping over the Kazakh steppes. That angel had struck him hard. He wondered how she was doing.

Volodymyr casually looked over to her car. To his amazement, there she was staring back at him. She smiled. He wondered how long she had been there.

They were too far away to speak, so they just looked, basking in each other's light outside space and time. They gazed at a thousand worlds watching the sun rise. It got brighter and their cars started waking up. They both nodded adieu and sat back down.

The guards looked at their watches and started getting animated. The KGB officer started giving his underlings orders, and they quickly got up. The zeks started getting nervous. Sokil sent the message down the line: *Arrival.*

2

ARRIVAL

THE TRAIN SCREECHED to a halt. The zeks were shoved hard side to side, banging into the hull. The heavy steel doors opened. The light seared their corneas after days of darkness. Several gang-planks were rolled up. A cacophony of screaming guards, barking dogs, and squealing whistles exploded in their eardrums.

The zeks were mauled by the dreaded camp guards, known irreverently by the zeks as *vovki*, or wolves. The *vovki* lived up to their names. They clawed and kicked the zeks down the ramps.

Several zeks tumbled down into a melee of flailing shackles, chains, and limbs. The giant snarling hounds, steppe wolf-dog hybrids, went into a frenzy. The camp regime had adopted this dynamic of man and beast quite well from the infamous German concentration camp.

A mounted officer rode up cursing and kicking, trying to part the sea of zeks. It was another KGB officer judging by his oversized epaulets and britches too high for his horse. He wore a sinister scowl and a distinct wart on his cheek that moved with his speech.

"I am *Kapitan* Belyaev," he said. "I am in charge of keeping order in this camp. You are here because you are enemies of the state and you will be rehabilitated through *katorga*. If you wish to ever make it out of here, you will obey your comrade guards to the letter!"

Volodymyr scoffed and rolled his eyes. A *vovk* caught wind and struck him with his rifle butt. Volodymyr fell to his knee.

Belyaev cut his tirade short and trotted over. He stopped just short. His horse snorted in Volodymyr's face. Volodymyr stood up and met Belyaev's menacing gaze.

He looked over Volodymyr and saw Slipyj's cross hanging from his neck. Belyaev bent over and yanked the cross from Volodymyr's neck. It happened so quickly Volodymyr didn't even have time to react. Belyaev looked it over and scoffed.

"Useless relics for *duraki*," said Belyaev, calling Volodymyr a fool.

Belyaev tossed Volodymyr's cross by the gang-planks.

"Move out," Belyaev barked.

"Alright, you heard him," said the *vovk*.

The prisoners started shuffling along, but Volodymyr stood firmly.

"I have to get that cross," said Volodymyr.

"Are you crazy?" asked Stas. "Wait until later. They'll split your skull!"

There was no stopping him. Baran charged back into the crowd with Tatra in tow. He bumped and knocked into the other prisoners and guards, desperately clawing at the ground.

He then felt a tap on his shoulder. He expected another swift strike of Soviet justice when he made contact with the angel's eyes. She held out her hand

"Is this yours?" she asked in a Western Ukrainian accent, holding out Slipyj's crucifix.

"*Ta-tak*," Volodymyr stammered. *Yes.*

She smiled and placed it into his shaking hands. They stared into each other's star-gazed eyes. She was about to say more when she was cut off by a female guard.

"Men to the right, women to the left!" she shrieked.

The women guards sounded even worse than the men. Volodymyr grabbed her hand. They held onto each other for as long as they could before they were yet again pulled apart. Each car formed its own columns with a line of guards between them.

Dozens of heavily armed *nadziratel* spread out and trained their Degtyaryov infantry machine guns on the zeks. Some might say it was overkill, but it felt just right to the trigger-happy guards. They were in it now.

"*Vnimaniye, vnimaniye,*" a sinister voice crackled over the loud-speaker, Russian for "attention." "You have arrived in Steplag No. 3, Kengir, Karaganda Sector, Kazakh SSR. This is a maximum security *katorga* camp, and as such, *zaklyuchennyi* will abide by strict proto-cols including, but not limited to . . ."

The announcer's ramblings were increasingly drowned out by a commotion ensuing in a group by Volodymyr. An unconscious old man was roughly dragged out of line by a guard. The unfortunately familiar scene reminded Volodymyr of poor Kolya just yesterday.

Unlike yesterday, the reaction from this group was as surprising as it was bold. Furious Chechen voices drowned out the loudspeak-er. Their heavy Caucasian accents gave them away, as did their long beards, which they kept in practice as devout Muslims.

Emotions were especially raw among the Chechens. From 1944 until Stalin's death, the Chechens and Ingush peoples of the *Kavkaz*, or Caucus Mountains, had been deported from their mountain homeland in southern Russia to the most inhospitable reaches of the

Soviet Union. This act of genocide, known as Operation Lentil, was carried out on behalf of Stalin's paranoid delusions of mass "collaboration" with the Axis forces, even though the majority of his fellow Caucasians had fought with the Soviets. It is estimated that up to a third of their population had perished from hunger, disease, exposure, and abuse.

"You leave him be, you godless infidel," a burly Chechen told the guard.

The guard dragging the old man raised his rifle to the Chechen, but the Chechen didn't budge. Belyaev raced over. He pulled out his own pistol and waved it around wildly. Some more guards followed close behind him like lapdogs.

"What in the hell is going on?" Belyaev asked.

"Comrade Kapitan, this man is abusing a very sick old man with no cause," said the Chechen, pointing at the abusive guard.

"You see, no respect from these swine. They don't even address me as comrade," said the guard.

The guard then kicked the old man. That was too much for the Chechen. He struck the guard so hard that his boots flew off.

A spontaneous burst of cheers erupted down the line of zeks, including Volodymyr and Stas. The guards fired several warning volleys into the air to restore order. The crowd eventually quieted down, but it was more out of respect for the Chechens than fear of the guards.

"Goddammit, just get them out of here," Belyaev shouted, grabbing the guard by the collar.

The Chechens calmly followed the guards when they finally carried the old man away on a stretcher. *Incredible*, Volodymyr thought. That would've been an execution on the spot in the past. The other guards blew their whistles and tried to prod the zeks along with extra resolve to remind them of their authority, but Sokil wouldn't have it.

He turned to his men.

"*Uvaha*," said Sokil. *Attention.* "*Kurin, marsh: ras dva, ras dva . . .*"

For the first time in years, they felt a surge of pride as they marched forward in military formation to show the guards they were also a force to be reckoned with. The screaming guards and barking dogs and crackling loudspeakers strained to be heard, making them sound almost comical. They marched forward as a military unit once again. Their mettle would soon be tested.

They reached a processing center within the *zona*, or the restricted area within the inner barbed wire. There they stood in a long line near the large *vakhta*, or guardhouse. It was an imposing structure surrounded by barbed wire, trenches, and watchtowers manned by menacing *nadziratel*. The guards were armed to the teeth, awaiting the next Operation Barbarossa.

The zeks entered a large hall. Volodymyr and Stas were used to the routine. The guards unshackled the men.

The zeks had lost all feeling in their atrophied limbs. It felt like a surge of prickly needles as the blood poured back into their swollen hands and feet. They split up the men into groups of five and sent them to a table.

"Zeks for processing," said the guard.

A stocky officer scoured over some papers. He wore the iconic pointed *Budenovka* cap with a prominent red star in front and oversized epaulets. He looked up impatiently at the guard. Then, he looked over the zeks.

"No room," he sneered. "Outside."

A harsh steppe zephyr picked up.

"Move it, zeks," another guard yelled.

The guards prodded them along. The officer pushed himself away from the table and followed. They lined up the prisoners in the freezing cold. The officer slowly walked down the line, seemingly enjoying watching the zeks shiver and squirm. He stopped.

"Strip," he said.

The zeks grudgingly took off their clothes. The biting wind stung their flesh. Each second was agonizing. The guards continued to wait until the men were shivering uncontrollably.

"Bath time," the officer laughed.

The guards opened a large nozzle and hosed the zeks down in the stinging cold. Then without warning, they threw lice powder all over them, including their eyes and mouths. It felt like cold fire. One of the men collapsed. The guards howled like jackals, shoving new prison clothes into the zeks' red, burning arms.

"Processing," said the officer, "we want you to look nice for your pictures."

"That'll teach 'em," said another guard.

They reentered the inhuman Soviet prison system "naked and barefoot," as another Ukrainian adage goes. The prisoners shuffled over to an enclosed room with a large glass screen. They were just glad to be inside. A glum old man waited with a large camera and tripod. A guard handed Volodymyr a placard to hold up. It read in Cyrillic: *Z/k #22422: Volodymyr Andriyovich Zaluzhniy.*

"Hold," the old man murmured.

A huge flash blinded Volodymyr.

"Turn," said the old man.

Volodymyr turned left and right for his profile.

"Next," said the old man.

Volodymyr was pushed along to make room for Stas. He unraveled his clump of a uniform with his trembling, numb fingers. He eventually got on his scruffy, cotton *bushlat* jacket, thick floppy *ushanka* hat, and finally his stiff felt *valenki* boots.

The drab zek clothing still felt foreign after all these years. He longed for his old UPA uniform. It seemed silly with everything he had been through, but one of the hardest parts about surrendering was giving up his uniform. It had become a part of him.

His uniform had survived the horrors of World War II and its aftershocks, such as the Famine of 1947, which killed thousands across the Soviet Union. Ukrainians, especially Hutsuls, took great pride in their clothing. He remembered how warm and snug his mother's thick woolen sheepskin vest felt. He had still worn her vest, which warmed his body and spirit, the first few months of zek life before a greedy KGB officer took it.The zeks plodded along to their barracks. It was a sorrowful sight to say the least. Several emaciated *dokhodyagi*, or "walkers," passed by. These miserable creatures were like ghosts. They were zeks too far gone from hunger, disease, despair, or a mixture of all three, but continued to walk the earth knocking on death's door. The urka would circle them like vultures, waiting for them to keel over to rob them. Often, they wouldn't even wait.

They finally reached their pitiful barracks. The flimsy tin roofs and rotted wooden walls looked like they could tip over and collapse with the slightest breeze. The guards organized them into groups of ten for each barrack. Volodymyr and Stas lead their group.

A *dokhodyaga* opened the door. He didn't even react to the zeks. His empty, dead eyes made Volodymyr shiver more than the cold.

They entered one by one and, to their surprise, the barracks were already crowded with other zeks in rows of crude wooden bunk beds. They were a miserable-looking bunch that didn't even lift their heads when the new prisoners entered. The *dokhodyaga* slowly closed the door behind them, sealing them in their tomb.

All of the prisoners suffered from various ailments caused by malnutrition, exposure, and abuse. Scurvy, pellagra, and dysentery were rampant along with diseases unique to each camp system. The bubonic plague that originated in these steppes was still endemic.

An older man walked over to them. His skin was tough and

weathered like the soles of his *valenki* boots. He placed his hands over his mouth.

"*Vnimaniye, vnimaniye*," he said, mocking the announcer.

Volodymyr and Stas didn't know what to think.

"Lighten up," he said. "Did they rob your sense of humor too?"

Volodymyr and Stas smiled politely.

"My name is Leonid Ilyich Kotlin. I'm the *starosta* around here. I just turned fifty-four last week, can you believe it?" He looked twenty years older. The *starosta*, or elder, was someone in the barracks that had been there for a while. He had clout and knew how things worked. He gave the orientation to the new zeks.

"I'm sure you've met our dear comrade warden, Kapitan Belyaev, or the Wart, as we call him," Leonid smirked, pointing to his cheek. "He may seem nasty at first, but once you get to know him, you realize he's a real sadist."

Volodymyr and Stas looked to each other nervously.

"Oh, but don't fret, I've been here for about three years now," he said. "I was in the Kolyma gold mines in Kamchatka before this. That's where I developed these fine beauties."

Leonid smiled a big, toothy, yellow smile. Experience told Volodymyr and Stas to be polite, but guarded. Volodymyr figured he would tell Leonid the bare basics, at first.

"We just came from Karaganda," said Volodymyr.

"Ah, so you do talk?" asked Leonid.

"We bark and do tricks too," said Stas, still cranky.

"I like it, as long as you're *vovki* and not *suki*," said Leonid, warning them to be wolves not bitches. "You two have funny accents. Where are you from?"

Volodymyr and Stas shut up. They were not native Russian speakers. Russian was not widely spoken in Poland or western Ukraine.

They still had Ukrainian and Polish accents after all these years despite their efforts to blend in. They figured the jig was up. He seemed harmless enough, but what would happen now? They would go to jail? If he was a hidden agent, he would find out anyway.

"I'm from *Ukraina*," said Volodymyr.

"*Polska*," said Stas.

They were a little nervous how Leonid would react. He was silent for a few seconds. Eventually he nodded solemnly.

"While I can't say I support Armia Krajowa or UPA, I can't pass judgement either," he said. "I met some fine Ukrainians and Poles over the years. What's happening here is a crime. This is not the People's Republic I fought for, or that my father died for in Kronstadt."

They were all surprised by his response. The Kronstadt sailors, who were among the first Bolshevik rebels, had led a heroic albeit futile rebellion against the Bolsheviks in 1921 known as the Kronstadt Rebellion. The sailors at the Kronstadt naval base near St. Petersburg held out against the superior Red Army forces for several months before eventually being overrun. Many of the survivors were sent to the Gulag or executed.

"I'm originally from Leningrad when it was still *Sankt Petersburg*. I was captured by the *Niemtsi* in 1941 in Kiev," said Leonid, using the pan-Slavic slur for Germans. "I almost died in Sachsenhausen before Stalin threw me in here. I was even friends with his son Yakov over there before Stalin left him for dead too. Some father! But enough about me; let's meet the rest of our motley crew!"

They were stunned by his candor. If he was a spy, he was either very good or completely mad. Leonid walked them over to a humble, lanky man tidying up the *vagonki*. Despite his gauntness, he held himself with poise unlike the other zeks.

"This here is the Evangelist," Leonid chuckled. "We've called him that for so long we practically forgot his original name, but it's all as well. We're all different people here, no? He's our *dezhurnaya*."

The *dezhurnaya* was a type of concierge that would take care of the barracks and protect the zeks' belongings from the urka and guards.

"Welcome to our humble abode," said the Evangelist.

His pleasant demeanor was a welcome departure from their miserable surroundings.

"*Vnimaniye, vnimaniye,*" the loudspeaker crackled.

"Oh God, what now?" asked Volodymyr.

Leonid grabbed a tin cup and rusty old spoon.

"Dinner," he smiled.

The new arrivals hardly had time to catch their breath before a *vovk* was huffing and puffing, blowing their barrack down.

"Line up for dinner, zeks," the *vovk* howled.

The irony was not lost on them. Indeed, they were lead out like sheep to slaughter. The herds of emaciated zeks were led to an imposing brick-and-mortar slab of a building. It was the same drab, efficient Soviet design built for a sparse land with few trees for timber.

"New arrivals, approach to receive utensils," said a guard.

The most recent arrivals stepped forward. A stone-faced guard stood over a long table manned by urka. One by one, the zeks were pushed forward like on a conveyer belt. The urka handed each prisoner a tin cup and a spoon.

"These utensils are property of the state," said the guard. "If either the receptacle or eating utensil is damaged or lost, there is no guarantee of a replacement."

"God, even dinner is a state affair," said Stas.

Volodymyr stared into his rusty tin and wondered how many other diseased mouths had been on it. They were corralled into the mess hall. The doors opened to a cavernous room. There was hardly any light with only the slightest of windows high up on the stone walls. A few frazzled young Kazakh guards were trying to stem the tide of starving zeks clamoring to get to the food counter.

"One at a time, you miserable zeks," a *vovk* barked.

Volodymyr and Stas felt overwhelmed until they saw Leonid.

"Come over here, *tovarishchi*," said Leonid, using the pan-Slavic for *comrades*.

Volodymyr and Stas took their chance to get a better spot in line. They stepped over an unconscious *dokhodyaga* just outside the door, as if they needed anymore motivation. Cheating was the unwritten code of the Gulag. It was survival of the fittest.

"This is our grand ballroom," Leonid snickered.

Again, Volodymyr and Stas didn't know what to make of Leonid's offhanded remarks.

"You must think I'm crazy, but you need a sense of humor in a place like this, or you will surely go mad," said Leonid.

"I understand, I was in a *psikhushka*," said Volodymyr, solemnly referring to a psychiatric ward often used to punish disorderly inmates.

Stas looked over his souring comrade. He knew a little of the episode, but not enough to fully understand. Volodymyr didn't like to talk about it; he didn't even know why he had brought it up.

"It's best not to dwell on these things," said Leonid.

After some time, with the occasional push and shove to assert their place in line, the three men reached the counter. They were greeted by a grimacing urka. They held out their tins and each received a piece of moldy bread and some salted fish from God knows where, topped off by a hardy plop of balanda soup with some measly vegetables.

The balanda splattered on their clothes and onto the floor. To their horror, several inmates dove down onto the floor desperately slurping up whatever broth they could salvage. Some guards shooed them away. Volodymyr and Stas stared disappointedly into the bottom of the meager stew.

"Next," said the urka.

"Come on," said Leonid, pulling them along. "There's a seat over here with our lot."

They sat down with some people from their barracks. Guards discouraged too much mixing. The zeks found a way around this, of course. They also used a series of codes and signals known as *blatnoi slovo,* or thieves' talk. A zek walked by and slyly passed something to Leonid. Leonid looked over his shoulder before opening the small package. It was a package of *makhorka,* strong tobacco cigarettes. Leonid sniffed them and smiled.

"These are worth their weight in gold around here."He then tasted his food.

"Hey, not bad. It's not the smelly fish this week."

Volodymyr stared at their measly meal. The starving zeks wolfed down their meals before they were forced to depart. The loudspeaker crackled in the background, adding to the cacophony.

"Lucky you didn't come on a bad day," said Leonid. "There was a rockslide in the quarry two days ago. Killed a *zek* and maimed a guard, but they'll be open first thing tomorrow."

A bell rang and dinner was over just as it began.

"Proceed to your barracks," said the loudspeaker. "Work will begin at 5 a.m. tomorrow."

"What did I say?" said Leonid.

The zeks quickly packed up, nervously holding their tins and spoons close to their bodies lest someone steal them. Everybody shuffled out single file, trying not to move too slowly or too quickly. The urka and guards ominously roamed the perimeter, looking for prey.

Finally, they made it out the doors into the frigid night. They could see their breath, some stronger than others. They had all become more attuned to their primal instincts singling out the strongest and weakest in the herd. The older and sicker zeks stayed close to the center with the relatively healthier zeks like Volodymyr and Stas forming the outer ring. Leonid kept up his pace with them, always eyeing the *dokhodyagi,* urka, and *vovki,* knowing not to get between their dance of death.

They made it back to the barracks unscathed. Leonid opened the door for them. Volodymyr and Stas looked into the room and were pleasantly surprised. It was actually neat and tidy. They even saw their beds were made. The Evangelist stood proudly over his work.

"Not a single urka or *vovk* tonight," said the Evangelist.

He looked over his shoulder and unfurled a rag, unveiling a bar of soap.

"Well done," said Leonid, passing him some *makhorka.*

Leonid turned to Volodymyr and Stas and laughed, "Five-star service!"

The rest of the zeks shuffled in, heading straight for their beds.

"Get some sleep, boys," said Leonid. "It's going to be a long day."

Volodymyr and Stas knew all too well what that meant. They had spent their share of time down the shaft. Despite its barren appearance above, these desolate plains were rich with metals like copper, manganese, and iron ore.

After a while, it began to quiet down. Volodymyr stared out the window, thinking about what had transpired that day; about the angel. Eventually, his eyes got heavy, and he began to drift off when his heavenly dreams were disrupted. He was awoken by a loud thud. He sat up in his bed. A wave of panic came over him. Anything that went bump in the night in the gulag wasn't good.

His hands started to get clammy with his adrenaline pumping. He listened intently like on patrol duty. Volodymyr waited several moments, his heart and thoughts racing. It happened again, this time twice in a row. He frantically scanned the room. He squinted hard into the dark. His imagination ran wild. After his eyes adjusted, he calmed down. He saw a faint figure in the corner of the room.

It was a *dokhodyaga* trying in vain to find his way in the dark. He had contracted night blindness from malnutrition. Volodymyr heard the ghostly figure go bump in the night a few more times before he abruptly stopped.

"God rest his soul," Volodymyr whispered.

3

FEBRUARY 26–28, 1954:

DESCENT INTO HELL

"*Vnimaniye, vnimaniye,*" the loudspeaker blared.

Volodymyr was jolted awake in a cold sweat. The zeks scrambled to put on their clothes lest they be thrown naked into the cold. The fresh arrivals were still exhausted from the train ride, but they had to get up and go. They were running on gulag time. Being veteran zeks didn't make things any easier. Volodymyr grabbed his puffy *bushlat* and threw on his thick *ushanka* cap. He then pulled up his *valenki* boots not a moment too soon. A guard threw open the door.

"*Vnimaniye, zeki!*" said the guard. *Time to work!* The zeks quickly assembled into a single-file line. Volodymyr looked over at the *dokhodyaga* slumped over in the corner. He and the other zeks tried not to draw too much attention, but the guard was adamant. He turned to the corner of the room.

"What's wrong with you?" the guard asked the unconscious man.

The guard jabbed him with his rifle butt. He then stuck out his wristwatch next to the man's mouth. They all looked at the shiny watch surface. If the *dokhodyaga* was still breathing, his exhale would've appeared as steam on the watch face. The guard turned back to the group.

"Get him out of here," he said.

Two zeks walked over and dragged him out. He was so light, so pale. They handled him like they were just pulling out an old carpet. His foot bumped Volodymyr's shivering leg.

"He's better off than us," said Stas solemnly.

They didn't have time to reflect. They were hardened to camp cruelty, but this place was rough. They felt the sting of their new harsh environment.

"Move out," said the guard.

So began their arduous march. They counted off one by one, stepping over the nameless corpse. They shuffled out of the barracks into the chilly February air. They joined the stream of zeks flooding out of the other barracks headed towards the quarry.

"Just stand by me, and we'll survive this," said Leonid.

Volodymyr and Stas nodded absentmindedly, looking at the lines of *vovki* and *nadziratel* flanking them with their rifles drawn. They pressed forward before stopping at the main gates, an imposing hardwood and barbed-wire mesh. The guards in the watchtower opened the giant gates and forward they moved.

They marched on for almost half an hour. The grueling march reminded Volodymyr of when he was first captured in the forests of western Ukraine so many years ago. Just as quickly as they began, they stopped.

Volodymyr's heart sank. Huge mounds of earth surrounded an enormous abyss of rock and ash. He couldn't even see the bottom.

The walls of shale and granite were lined by shafts and shelves carved into the rocks that spiraled down into oblivion.

Hundreds of men worked precariously along the edges of the pathways with no safety nets. The rhythmic strikes of the pickaxes and hammers against the hard rock chipped away at the zeks. *Vovki* stalked them from above. Volodymyr instinctively rubbed his hands, knowing they would be worked to the bone.

"*Da*, there it is," said Leonid solemnly. "Just remember: Don't stand out, bad or good. We don't need more *dokhodyagi* or *Stakhanovites*."

Stakhanovites, named for the miner Aleksei Stakhanov who allegedly cut over one hundred tons of coal in one shift in 1935, were workers that over-fulfilled their quotas. The myth's claims were dubious at best, but its purpose was clear cut. The idea of the *Stakhanovites* had been pounded into all of their heads, mutating from an ideal to an imperative.

They stopped in front of a small hut. A *naryadshchik*, the camp clerk responsible for assigning work, appeared from the woodworks. The nervous, bespectacled man scoured over a pile of forms without even looking up at the men. He signaled for some other zeks. They came over with several large bundles. They placed them on the ground and unfurled them, revealing an array of ancient mining equipment.

"Here are your state-issued tools," said a guard. "You will be replacing the previous shift at the bottom pit by the excavator. Be like Stakhanov! Redeem yourselves through your work!"

The tools were rudimentary: long, awkward pickaxes that were as battered as the pulverized rocks. Stas got a splinter as soon as he touched his. Volodymyr's was little better.

"Back in the day, we had to make our own tools," said Leonid.

This fact was little consolation. Volodymyr and Stas stared at their pitiful tools and the enormous rock pit. Their task would make

Sisyphus weep.

"Work smart, not hard," said Leonid. "Only when the guards are looking."

The zeks they were replacing appeared from the pit like Lazarus rising from the underworld. These creatures that looked somewhat like men laboriously hobbled by. It looked as if many would meet the Lord soon.

Some of the zeks were so weak that they had to be held up by the others. They were walking skeletons. They looked right past the new crew as if they had already crossed over, except for one who looked at Volodymyr. He didn't have to say anything. His glazed eyes told the story of their suffering. A whistle shrieked. The new shift began.

"March," said a *vovk*.

They began their descent into hell. On the way down, a small flash caught Volodymyr's eye. He saw an odd crevice. He looked closer and found a tiny yet distinct Orthodox Christian shrine, complete with a three-barred cross carved into the rock and a small icon of the Virgin Mary.

Stas said a Hail Mary in Polish. All around them, zeks of all denominations prayed to God. Despite the Soviet state's hard line against religion, the "opiate of the masses" had breached the façade of this seemingly godforsaken place. Volodymyr closed his eyes and briefly prayed for hope. A harsh steppe wind sent dust into his corneas. They were always exposed to the harsh elements of this miserable environment.

They kept their pace with each step, descending further into the abyss. It was a panorama of misery like something they had imagined in the biblical times of the pharaohs. The open-pit quarry looked like a great inverse pyramid tearing into the heart of the earth.

The further down they got, the pings of the pickaxes dissipated, being replaced by a great whirring sound. There it was: a monster of a machine with a great conveyer belt. Multiple claws tore into the earth like a giant bear. A gang of urka stopped them. The largest stepped forward.

"*Stakhanovite*," Leonid whispered.

"Alright, listen up," said the urka.

He was a burly fellow with heaving shoulders. His uniform was in better shape than theirs and his cheeks were full, suggesting far better rations. He had a comically large red star pinned to his *ushanka*, which protruded from his large forehead. An underling picked up a large pan.

"You will follow closely behind the excavator to pick up the rock and dirt in this pan like so," he said, gesturing toward the other urka, who scooped up a pile of debris. "Then you will bring it over to the sifter, where you will look for any copper, manganese, or iron ore such as these."

Another urka brought them an example of each rock to pass around. When Stas received his rocks he quickly turned them over to Volodymyr with disgust. Stas knew these rocks like the back of his pick from his mining days. Volodymyr felt the heavy red iron ore, silvery manganese, and green copper. Their shapes and colors intrigued him, but his scholarly interest was tainted by the fact that he would have to excavate these rocks by the ton.

"You will do this until your shift ends, or you drop dead, whichever comes first," the urka laughed. "Godspeed!"

A screeching steam whistle sounded from the excavator and they began. Volodymyr and Stas scooped up a huge mound each and rushed it over to the sifter. Leonid nudged them.

"You want to be buried under this dirt?" asked Leonid. "Not so much. Like so . . ."

He carefully lifted up a modest haul. It was just enough to cover the bottom of the pan. He then gently placed it into the sifter, looking peripherally to see if the guard was watching. It was such an inefficient system, but there was no rhyme or reason to this place.

"You don't rise through the ranks honestly," said Leonid bitterly. "True *Stakhanovites* don't exist here. Hard work only leads to your grave."

They followed his lead and paced themselves, but it was still back-breaking work. They were quickly caked in muck. Volodymyr looked around; they all looked like the same miserable heaps of dirt around them.

"Well, you can't say the Soviet system doesn't make everyone equal," said Stas. "Equally miserable."

Volodymyr solemnly nodded.

They had been at it for hours when Volodymyr thought he heard someone calling his name. It was hard to tell against the raging machine.

Baran. Volodymyr shook it off as overactive nerves. *Baran!* He turned around.

"*Sotnyk*," said Volodymyr, excitedly shooting up a salute.

"At ease, Baran," Sokil said hurriedly.

Volodymyr quickly put his hand down, feeling foolish. Both Sokil and Nacham were there. Volodymyr could hardly believe it. Sokil turned to Stas.

"Your captain sends you greetings, Tatra," said Sokil. "What's the status report?"

Sokil then stopped, looking warily at Leonid. Leonid returned the cautious gaze.

"He's alright," said Volodymyr. "His name is Leonid. He's our *starosta*."

"You still have a *starosta*," said Sokil.

"I meant no disrespect, sir." "I understand. Pay me no mind," Leonid interjected. "I'm not about to join UPA or Armia Krajowa, but I respect good discipline from my own army days."

Sokil scrutinized Leonid, unsure of what to make of him, but he had little time to think. They heard a terrible screech and crash. Clouds of smoke billowed from the excavator.

"Watch out!" someone yelled.

A bloodcurdling scream immediately followed. The excavator knocked down a ridge filled with zeks above them. A zek fell down, nearly crushing them too. A large boulder rolled on top of him, smashing his legs. Volodymyr could hear his bones break. The engineer stopped the machine and jumped out.

"You idiot," said a guard, walking right past the screaming zek to the engineer. "Do you know how much it is going to cost to repair this? We're going to wait forever before we hear from Karaganda!"

The zeks had grown numb to cruelty, but this callous indifference to the injured man chilled them even more than the bitter cold. Volodymyr had seen much combat, but he had never seen someone in so much pain. Nacham ran over to the man and went into medic mode.

"Someone grab me a tourniquet!" he yelled. To the man he said, "Don't worry, you'll be alright."

The man completely ignored Nacham. He was overwhelmed with pain. His eyes started rolling back into his head. Nacham helplessly pushed on the boulder.

"Someone, please help me pull this rock off his leg," Nacham shouted desperately.

Before anyone could react there was a quick loud bang and the man's head fell back, blood squirting onto Nacham. He froze. He was undoubtedly having flashbacks to Babi Yar. Nacham turned around. A *nadziratel* was standing over him with smoke still emanating from the barrel of his pistol.

"We could've saved him," Nacham cried.

"There was nothing we could do. I did the decent thing," said the *nadziratel*.

"You monsters don't know the meaning of decency," Nacham replied.

Everyone stopped what they were doing. They waited to see what would happen next. The guard even stopped for a moment, shocked by someone having the audacity to speak back to him. He raised his rifle.

"Don't forget your place, *zek*. Unless you'd like to join him?"

"What in the name of Marx, Lenin, and Stalin is going on here?" a man yelled.

A KGB officer appeared out of the woodworks. He stormed over to them. He was fuming. His big green cap and bright red epaulets reminded Volodymyr of copper and iron ore.

"What's the meaning of all this?" asked the officer, his hands flailing wildly. "Why has work stopped?"

He looked at the dead zek under the debris, the smoking excavator, the guard, and then Nacham.

"Who are you?" he asked Nacham.

"I'm a *feldsher*, comrade officer," said Nacham. "I was trying to help this man before—"

"Before what?" the officer interrupted.

The guilty guard stared at Nacham menacingly.

"Did you do this?" the officer asked the guard.

He stammered. "Well, sir, I mean—""Do you speak Russian?" asked the KGB man. "You're relieved of duty. I'm going to get to the bottom of this. As for you, *feldsher*, get some men to clean up this mess and bury him up top."

The KGB officer stormed off. Nacham knew better than to turn and face the guard. The less he saw of Nacham's face the better.

"This isn't over," the guard said to Nacham before he left in turn.

Nacham shook off his words. He was used to threats. He was more concerned about the crushed *zek*. He looked at the men with the same pain in his eyes.

"Let's be better than these beasts and give this man a decent burial," he said.

No one moved. They were still in shock. Only the rhythmic clinks and bangs of the ceaseless background work could be heard, like nothing had happened.

"I'll help," said a man from behind.

They saw the unfortunate excavator driver get out. He took off his cap and walked over. His face was red and puffy.

"It's the least I can do," he said solemnly.

He turned the excavator around and lifted the rock off the poor *zek*. Nacham, Volodymyr, Stas, and Sokil each grabbed a limb and hoisted the man into a coal cart. The man was slowly rolled up on a trolley over the top like another load of rocks.

The driver followed them up with a drill to help break through the frozen earth. His face hung like death. He limped along like a *dokhodyaga*. The four of them picked up their spades when the driver lifted his hand.

"Allow me," he said.

He thrust the drill into the ground and went to work breaking the frozen earth. Once the initial hole was dug, they chipped in, although the driver still insisted on doing most of the work. They picked up the light body of the emaciated zek and lowered him into his early grave. They didn't have enough wood for a coffin, so they wrapped him in a thick sack. They all watched on in silence. The engineer lit a *makhorka* and tossed them the rest of the pack.

"Keep it," he said. "This very well may be my last smoke."

"What's your name?" asked Volodymyr.

"Dima," he whispered.

"We're all in the same hole, Dima," said Volodymyr.

Dima looked out at the rows of unmarked graves.

"How did we come to this?" Dima asked, shaking his head.

They didn't know. They didn't want to know. They filled in the grave, and didn't ask questions.

"Well, that's it then," said Dima.

They walked back to the pit. Volodymyr did finally stop to reflect when he looked back and sighed. *Is that the only way out of here?*

They heard the harsh shriek of the whistle. Their shift was over for the day. They fell glumly back in line with the rest of the miserable zeks.

"March," said the *nadziratel*.

They marched forward, greeting the next miserable crew. They were the ones now climbing the walls, rising from the dead. Volodymyr met a younger *zek*'s gaze. The young man froze in terror. Volodymyr did too. He was now the dead man walking.

They kept up their solemn march back to the barracks. Volodymyr stayed behind a little. Nobody noticed. The zeks were too exhausted, and the guards were too focused on the accident.

A wind picked up and Volodymyr caught a fading glimpse of the waving steppe in the last rays of light through the wire. His thoughts drifted to the woman from the train. He was startled by something that tapped his shoulder.

He looked down and saw it was a little tied-up bundle of cloth. Volodymyr untied it, and saw it was a small handmade cross in the design of Slipyj's.

He heard a whisper.

"Over here." Volodymyr looked and saw a figure standing by the wire of the women's prison in camp. He looked around to make sure it was clear and cautiously approached. The figure waved at him.

"What are you waiting for?" she asked. "You're already in jail!"

Volodymyr came up to the wire. He waited for his eyes to adjust to the darkness. He followed the moonlight shining onto the figure and lit up. It was her!

"It's you," said Volodymyr.

"*Tak*, it's me," she smiled, "but you can call me Kateryna."

"I'm Volodymyr," he stammered, "or Vlodko."

"*Pryjemno*, Vlodko," Kateryna laughed. *A pleasure.*

"Where are you from, Kateryna? *Nashi*?" asked Volodymyr, the word Ukrainians used to refer to their fellow countrymen.

"*Tak*, I'm from a village called Polonyna near Verkhovyna. "Volodymyr couldn't believe it.

"Kateryna from Polonyna?" he said. Her name glided off his tongue. Finally, he could put a name to her face. He wanted to say it as much as he could, lest she disappear again.

She laughed. It was a simple act, but Volodymyr had been deprived of normal human interaction outside his close group of comrades, especially with the opposite sex. It sounded like an angelic choir. She leaned in.

"Are you a Hutsul?" she asked.

Volodymyr was surprised by her intuitiveness.

"*Tak*, from Pechenizhyn," he said.

"Oh my, like Oleksa Dovbush yet."Her knowledge continued to amaze him. He was starting to wonder. The years of looking over his shoulder, sizing up the man next to him, made Volodymyr—everyone, really—paranoid.

"*Tak*, you know a lot," he said. "How does that happen?"

"My father and mother were teachers; they were involved with *Plast*," she said, referring also to the Ukrainian scouting organization.

Volodymyr couldn't believe what he was hearing. His miserable luck seemed like it was finally turning. They talked and talked until they realized it was getting late and they had to return to their barracks.

"Dobranich, myla," said Volodymyr, suddenly blushing at letting his tongue slip. *Good night, darling.*

There was a pause before Kateryna said, *"Dobranich, kokhanna."* *Good night, beloved.* They parted for the night. Volodymyr floated away light as a feather. The horrors of the day slipped his mind. He approached the barracks and saw the Evangelist outside smoking.

"Beautiful night isn't it, Evangelist?" asked Volodymyr, still in bliss.

The Evangelist smiled and raised his hand in greeting. He turned to go back inside when a loud crack rang out. The Evangelist crumpled over and fell next to the door. Volodymyr's heady state of mind slowly unraveled, trying to contemplate what just happened. Everyone inside came to the window.

"What's going on?" asked Leonid.

He looked down and realized it was his good friend lying on the ground.

"The bastards!" he cried, clutching the Evangelist's head.

One by one, the lights turned on. The other barracks woke up. The zeks gathered.

"Is there a doctor?" asked Leonid helplessly.

Nacham appeared on his way back from his hospital shift, which seemed like an amazing coincidence. He put his head to the Evangelist's chest. People from their barracks, including Stas, crowded around. The recently killed zek and *dokhodyaga* were fresh in their minds.

"Give him space," said Leonid.

Blood was pooling around the Evangelist. Nacham looked pale. He patted Leonid.

"I need to get my things," said Nacham. "I'll be right back."

Nacham got up and ran to the hospital. After a few hundred yards, he was stopped dead in his tracks. The shooter smiled menacingly with his rifle drawn.

"I thought I'd draw you out of your hole, *feldsher.*" It was the guard from the pit.

He lifted his rifle to Nacham's head. Nacham closed his eyes and said the Shema prayer. The floodlights started turning on. More people started gathering. The guard saw his cover was blown.

"This isn't over, *feldsher*," he said, before disappearing back into the shadows.

Suddenly, several flares rocketed into the sky, illuminating the whole courtyard. Packs of *vovki* appeared. Belyaev rode out like one of the Four Horsemen.

"What's going on here?" he asked.

"My friend has been shot," said Leonid, still cradling the Evangelist.

The crowd was growing. Some of the zeks were holding makeshift bats and various hammers and wrenches from the workshops. The guards weren't used to such a united front by the zeks, and neither was Belyaev. He was visibly shaken, trotting his horse round and round in nervous circles.

Belyaev turned to his men. "Well, don't stand around like a bunch of dumb cattle! Get these people back to their barracks and get this man out of here before this gets out of control!"

The guards went to work frantically corralling the zeks back into their pens.

"We'll investigate what happened here," Belyaev said gruffly.

"How?" someone yelled in another extraordinary outburst.

"We will contact Karaganda," said Belyaev irritably. "Now everyone back inside, or I swear to God there will be more of you lying here by the end of tonight!"

The zeks eventually made their way back inside. The mood in Volodymyr's barracks was unsurprisingly tense. Leonid was still fuming, covered in the Evangelist's blood.

"By the way of the Old Testament: Vengeance is mine, I will repay," he said.

Volodymyr sank his nails into the wood planks beneath his bed. He was so angry that he could tear out the floorboards. Then, to his amazement, he did.

4

EARLY MARCH 1954:

TASTE OF FREEDOM

OVER A WEEK passed by and, not surprisingly, nobody was indicted for killing the Evangelist. Tensions came to a head between the camp regime and the zeks when the Chechen who had struck the abusive guard by the train was found riddled with holes in the zona while being transferred to the SHIZO, or punishment cell. The men's camp was placed on lockdown for three days after several clashes broke out between the guards and inmates.

Further straining relations was the surprise decree by Khrushchev, first announced on the front page of the Soviet state newspaper *Pravda* on February 27, that the Crimean Peninsula was being transferred from the Russian SFSR to the Ukrainian SSR. The move was intended to celebrate the "300 years of Rus" on the 300th anniversary of the Treaty of Pereiaslav in 1654. This fateful treaty had joined most of

Ukraine, as an autonomous state, with Russia for the tsar's aid in the Khmelnytsky Cossack Uprising against Poland.

This act was considered a day of mourning for many Ukrainians, especially Crimean Tatars who had been thrown out of their homeland exactly ten years before. Beginning in May of 1944, like the Chechens and other Soviet ethnic minorities, Crimean Tatars were deported from their homeland to the sparsely populated parts of Central Asia, mainly to the Uzbek SSR. Thousands died from exposure, disease and abuse. The removal of the Tatars, known as the *Sürgünlik,* or *Exile* in Tatar, was recognized as a Stalinist crime. Despite official condemnation, the vast majority of Tatars were still unable to return home.

It was another cruel day, and the zeks were lined up for the daily grind. A harsh steppe zephyr picked up, stinging their skin. March had roared in as a lion. The guards were making their usual roll call when a man collapsed. Volodymyr recognized him as a fellow Ukrainian.

"Get up!" yelled the guard.

He prodded the man, who moaned in pain.

Sokil stepped forward.

"This man is ill, and not fit for work," he said. "He is entitled to medical treatment under Soviet law."

The guard raised his rifle to Sokil. Sokil didn't flinch. Everyone watched intently.

"I'll check him," said Nacham. "I'm a *feldsher.*"

There were several moments of tense silence. It reminded Volodymyr of the mine disaster. Just like then, the browbeaten zeks didn't know what to do when Nacham had enough.

"Go ahead then, just don't do anything stupid," said the guard, not taking his eyes off Sokil, nor Sokil him.

Nacham bent down to examine the man. The man's face was

contorted in pain as he held his leg, but he stubbornly refused help. Nacham patted the man reassuringly.

"Let me have a look, *brat*," said Nacham. *Brother.*

The man relented. Nacham carefully lifted his pant leg. Nacham tried to keep his composure, but his nauseated expression told the full truth.

"This man has a seriously infected wound," said Nacham. "He needs to be taken to the infirmary immediately."

"The infirmary's full; he'll have to wait," said the guard.

Nacham pulled the man's pant leg up. Everyone looked down and was immediately revolted by the oozing mess. The guard gagged, but remained firm.

"He'll be put on light duties until we find room for him," said the guard.

"He's not going anywhere except the infirmary," said Sokil, stepping in front of the man.

Nacham stood up next to Sokil. Volodymyr had seen enough, and he too stepped up, followed by Stas and several other Ukrainians. Leonid joined in too. The guard stepped back.

"What's this?" asked the guard, nervously brandishing his rifle, "insubordination?"

Then, amazingly, the other ethnicities started joining in, including the Chechens and Tatars. They formed a protective ring around the man. The guard was wide-eyed with horror. He frantically blew a whistle.

"I need backup!" he yelled. "We have an insurrection!"

Several *nadziratel* and *vovki* surrounded the zeks, drawing their rifles and machine guns. The wind seemed to have instinctively picked up with the rising tension. There was dead silence.

Sokil and the original guard were staring each other down with searing hatred in their eyes. The guard was losing the staring contest, which was a dangerous development. Finally, after several long minutes, a KGB *polkovnik*, or colonel, arrived.

"What in the hell is going on here?" he asked. "Lay down your arms!"

The guards parted for the gruff KGB man. He briskly made his way to Sokil, the guard, and the unfortunate man. The KGB man looked Sokil up and down.

"Somebody better tell me what's going on here right now or there will be hell to pay," he said.

"These zeks are causing all kinds of trouble," said the guard frantically.

"This man is seriously ill, and he is being refused medical attention," said Sokil.

The KGB looked down at the injured man. The man was moaning, rocking back and forth. The KGB man then looked to Nacham, having slightly softened his stance.

"Let me see," he said.

Nacham gently lifted the man's pant leg. The KGB officer leaned in. He quickly started coughing and shaking his head.

"Alright, I've seen enough; take him away," he said.

"I'm a doctor," said Nacham. "I'd like to make sure the proper care is taken."

"And I am the man's commanding officer, as prescribed under Soviet articles for prisoners of war. I am entitled to oversee his care,'" said Sokil.

"*Da,* just get out of here," said the KGB man briskly.

The guards, Sokil, and Nacham picked up the injured man. They carried him off to the infirmary. The KGB man turned back to the rest of them.

"As for the rest of you: You all know this insubordination cannot go unanswered," said the KGB man forebodingly. "Let's get back to work!"

"You heard him! On the double, zeks! *Davay!*" said the guard.

The guards marched them forward double time to the pits. The zeks knew there would be hell to pay, but they were glad they had stood up for themselves. After another miserable, back-breaking day in the mines, they went back to the barracks wondering what their fate would be.

"That was awful. Do you think that was it?" asked Stas.

"What more can they possibly do?" asked Volodymyr. "We're already beyond pain!"

"You don't know what pain is," said Leonid solemnly.

The loudspeakers blared extra loudly the next morning. Guards breached their barracks before roll call. The zeks weren't even fully awake.

"Get up, zeks," barked the *vovk*.

The guards harried them along. They pulled men out of their beds. Some of the men didn't even have all their clothes on when they were thrown out into the cold.

"Early bird gets the worm," a guard cackled.

They were quickly corralled to the food hall. There were many more guards than usual. They entered the cavernous hall and lined up for their breakfast. Several of the guards snickered as the prisoners passed by.

They stepped up to the kitchen counter one by one. The usual urka servers weren't there. Volodymyr, Stas, and Leonid saw, to their dismay, the guard from yesterday's standoff.

"Bon appetit," he winked, handing Volodymyr his meal.

Volodymyr, Stas, and Leonid looked down at a single piece of moldy bread. These were punishment rations served to people in the SHIZO. Leonid shook his head.

"Reminds me of Sachsenhausen," said Leonid glumly.

Leonid noticed one of the orderlies walking by. He grabbed his arm. The man was startled, like he had just seen death.

"Hey, what happened to the zek with the rotten leg?" he asked.

"He won't suffer anymore," the man said, shuffling away.

They all knew what that meant. They wondered when it happened. Sokil and Nacham must have known and certainly not been happy about it. Sokil was up in line. He realized who was serving him and his expression soured. The guard pursed his lips and shook his head.

"None for him! Now move along you *khokhol* dog," he sneered, using a Ukrainian slur.

"If we can't eat, we can't work," said Sokil firmly.

The guard's head cocked back. He looked as if he had been physically struck. Sokil's simple statement sent shockwaves down the lines.

"Did you hear me?" the guard said, raising a kitchen knife to Sokil.

As usual, Sokil stood his ground. The guard stood there in his ridiculous pose. The whole mess hall had been brought to a standstill.

Volodymyr stared at his mealy bread, turning it round and round in his hand and head. He stood up, fed up with their treatment, and proceeded headfirst toward the kitchen, throwing his bread at the guard's head. The guard was so startled he dropped the knife.

"That's our Baran," said Sokil proudly.

The rest of the Ukrainians began *returning* their meals, pelting the guards.

"Go ahead and starve!" the guard yowled.

Stas and Leonid joined in, then more zeks. The rest of the zeks rose from their tables in a mass wave, clinking their pots and pans. The guards stepped back nervously before one of them fired into the ceiling. The zeks stopped, seeing if anyone was shot. Then, seeing nobody was hurt, they started banging their utensils and chanted, "If we can't eat, we can't work!"

The guards passed around their riot gear and started to surround the hall when a loud, melodic note of *"Allahu Akbar,"* or "God is great," cut through the cacophony. Everyone stopped. An imam began the Islamic call to prayer. The trailing note echoed off the cavernous walls, reverberating in their souls.

One of the Russian guards trained his sights on the imam when a Kazakh guard yanked the rifle right out of his hands. All the Muslim zeks got down on their knees and placed their head and hands on the ground, in Muslim fashion, as the imam continued the ceremony. Christians, Jews, and atheists alike were moved by their zeal. The Muslim Kazakh guards lowered their rifles and got down on their knees, joining in the prayer. The non-Muslim guards rushed out of the hall for reinforcements.

After the *adhan*, the zeks cheered their victory. They began talking animatedly among themselves—Muslims and Jews, Russians and their Ukrainian, Polish, and Baltic comrades. Historic grievances were pushed aside to share in this small but significant fight for dignity.

The good times ended when more guards swarmed in, encircling the zeks. A young *nadziratel*, trying to prove his mettle, started fumbling with a large acoustic megaphone. He mumbled incoherent proclamations when, one by one, the men started jumping back. The Wart had arrived. He grabbed the megaphone from the young guard and put it to his big mouth.

"We're in it now," said Leonid.

"*Vnimaniye, vnimaniye,*" said Belyaev. "Just what in the hell do you damned zeks want?"

"Justice!" shouted one *zek*.

"Freedom," said another.

The cohesion of the zeks was disintegrating. Their whole demonstration was threatened. Sokil stepped in to restore order.

"We demand adequate rations in order to work," said Sokil in clear Russian. "Stalinist policies of collective punishment are defunct according to the articles of the Twentieth Congress." The zeks roared with approval. The guards were surprised by the zeks' unity. Belyaev raised the megaphone.

"If we give you the appropriate rations, will you stand down?" Belyaev asked.

Sokil looked to his comrades. They nodded in approval. He turned back to Belyaev.

"*Da.*" Belyaev turned to the other guards. They talked animatedly for several minutes. One could cut the tension with a knife. The zeks nervously eyed the guards' rifles and knew this could easily turn into a bloodbath. Finally, Belyaev turned around and picked up his megaphone again.

"Very well," he said, "and then you will work!"

The zeks could hardly believe it. One of the Russian zeks even began singing "The Internationale," the old Soviet anthem, perhaps to curry favor with the guards, or perhaps because they actually believed that they had begun another Russian Revolution. Others joined in, and the hall was soon alive with singing.

The regular urka kitchen staff went around passing out the food. These usually glum characters even managed to crack some smiles. They had to admit they were impressed with these new politicals.

It was the same smelly fish, balanda, and bread, but it was heavenly after tasting a small piece of freedom. It was a small victory, but they knew that for a fleeting moment they had shaken the system. Volodymyr happily slurped down his cabbage when he felt a hand grasp his shoulder.

"*Diakuyu,* Baran," said Sokil. "Thank you for having my back."

He then handed Volodymyr a large, fresh roll. Volodymyr stood up and saluted Sokil. Sokil saluted back.

They finished their breakfast and went off to the mines. This time, they walked with a purpose. They knew they were marching to more agony, but there was less weight on their shoulders. Some of the guards even seemed impressed by their show of solidarity and didn't harass or berate them.

As day turned into night and his bunkmates settled in for the night, Volodymyr quietly slipped away. He crept along the perimeter of the zona, counting the usual guards and their rounds, memorizing and timing their rotations. He timed it just right so that he could slip past them at the changing of the guard at the top of the hour. Volodymyr then slipped to the edge of the zona by the women's camp, waiting for his *kokhanna*: Kateryna Polonyna.

They had been meeting regularly the past few weeks. They worked out a system to meet twice a week, one hour after lights out during the change to the graveyard shift. He eagerly awaited her arrival, clutching his precious gift from Sokil. Volodymyr was sure she would appreciate it. It was rich dark bread from the fertile *chornozem,* or black earth, that made Ukrainian land so coveted.

She wasn't there yet. It was a little curious, but he nonetheless had faith. It got later and later. He covered up his bread, having shamefully taken a few nibbles in the biting cold, and was about to walk away when he heard a cough. He turned around, and sure enough there she stood.

"*Pryvit, kokhanna,*" said Volodymyr. "How are you feeling this lovely moonlit evening?"

"*Pryvit,* Vlodko. You look chipper," she said weakly.

Volodymyr was concerned about her tone. He thought sharing his good news would cheer her up, though. He brought out the covered bread.

"I have a gift for you," he said. "Get ready, I'm going to toss it over!"

Kateryna opened her hands. Volodymyr looked over his shoulder, making sure it was clear, and tossed the bread. She caught the towel, unraveled it, and did manage a small smile.

"*Diakuyu kokhanna*," she said, tucking it into her coat.

"You're not going to try any?" Volodymyr asked disappointedly. "I'm sorry about the bites, but it's good dark bread like back in *Ukraina*."

"It's not that," said Kateryna. "There's somebody else that needs this more."

Volodymyr looked closer and realized she was making an effort to hide part of her face.

"What happened?" he asked.

"Nothing, don't worry about me," she said quickly.

"But I must," he said. "I'm tired of worrying about myself."

She was silent.

"Just let me see the rest of your beautiful face," he said.

She relented.

"Alright, but don't make a scene." She slowly turned her face to reveal a large swollen black eye. Volodymyr covered his mouth, but she could see the whites of his furious eyes. She quickly covered her eye back up.

"That was how far it got," she said gravely. "My dear friend, whom you saw on the train, was not so fortunate."

Volodymyr listened.

"One of the brasher guards got fresh with me," she said. "I politely but firmly told him I wasn't interested. He struck me with such force, but he left. He found my friend on the way back from dinner and forced his way with her . . ."

She trailed off. She wiped away a tear. Volodymyr hadn't seen her so shaken up before.

"Oh, it was terrible, Vlodko. And the other guards watched on and laughed, drunk on vodka. There was nothing I could do. I still hear her screams!"

She covered her mouth and looked over her shoulder, making sure nobody else heard. Volodymyr was speechless. They stayed quiet for a while, until they heard the gates open and close. It was the next shift.

"It's time," said Volodymyr.

Kateryna barely nodded.

"I know." "Same time later this week?" he asked.

"Next week," she replied.

"Whatever it takes," said Volodymyr. "I will be here when you're ready."

"I know. Please forgive me. I do appreciate you and your gift. *Dobranich*," she said, bidding him good night.

"*Dobranich*, Kateryna z Polonyna," he said.

She smiled weakly, disappearing into the night. Volodymyr sat for a little while longer. It seemed every time something good happened, something equally awful also had to happen. It was like a cruel dance of the universe they were all trapped in. The whole place acted like a great pendulum, swinging back and forth between the extremes of man and nature. Volodymyr quietly got up. He waited for the guards to part ways for the night. In the quiet, reflective night, he wondered what the guards were feeling, if they were capable of feeling.

When he got back to the barracks, he went right to the broken floorboards by his bed. He made a painstaking effort to cover up his handiwork with a sawdust paste to mask the cracks in the wood. UUncle Yurko would be proud.

Volodymyr lifted the boards one by one. They were just about large enough for him to fit through. He knew Kateryna and he might need to escape.

5

MID-MARCH 1954:

THE UKRAINIAN CENTRE

THE TRAIN SCREECHED to a halt. The loudspeaker blared its messages and the dogs went wild. The train door rolled open and a cascade of disoriented zeks tumbled down. Volodymyr and Stas shuddered, remembering their same experience just a month ago.

"Do you two understand your task?" asked Jerzy.

"*Tak, Kapitan,*" said Stas. "We are looking for the brightest *sharashka zek.*"

Sokil and Stas's Polish commander Jerzy, who had recently arrived on a separate train, had assigned them to an "infiltration task force" with the mission of orienting the new arrivals and recruiting potential zeks for their growing resistance. They got word that there was a particularly prized arrival of *sharashka* prisoners. The *sharashka* was a special prison devised by Beria in 1938 for scientists and technicians rounded up in Stalin's purges. These special zeks had created weapons during the war and included the founder of the Soviet space program, Sergei Korolev, a Ukrainian rocket engineer.

The technology race was heating up in the new Cold War against the West. These skilled zeks were in high demand. Many had been freed, but many were still stuck in the grind of the sprawling Gulag system. Volodymyr and Stas knew these zeks were too smart for their own good and wouldn't last long without their protection.

"*Davay zeki!* Welcome to Kengir University," a guard sneered.

The other guards laughed maniacally. They kicked and prodded these special new zeks through processing like any other. It was twisted egalitarianism at work. Volodymyr and Stas followed them along through the same ringer they had gone through. They were stripped and searched. They choked on the same delousing powder. One zek, however, stood out. He actually struck back!

He was swiftly reprimanded with the butt of a rifle.

He crumpled to the floor. The other zeks implored him to stay down. He ignored their pleas and stood up. He limped forward to further processing. Volodymyr and Stas turned to each other and smiled: "That one!"

After getting their profiles and finger prints taken, the new arrivals were finally released. Volodymyr and Stas slowly followed the feisty *sharashka* zek. They waited until he was alone.

"*Privyet! Dobri udry, tovarishch,*" said Volodymyr, speaking Russian, as a test.

"I don't have any money, urka," he said in accented Russian, though not enough to tell.

He pulled out his *bushlat* and shook out his *ushanka* angrily. Volodymyr and Stas chuckled. They were happy his antics were not just a show for the guards.

"What's so funny?" he asked.

"We're not urka," said Volodymyr.

He was confused. He looked them over. The man's face turned white as snow.

"I don't know anything about counterrevolutionaries, *tovarishch*" he said quickly.

Volodymyr and Stas laughed even harder.

"We're not KGB," said Stas.The man's face turned red. He threw his hands up in disgust. His anger was raw.

"Then leave me the hell alone."

He stormed off.

Volodymyr and Stas caught up to him, and Volodymyr stuck out his hand.

"Perhaps we started off poorly," said Volodymyr. "I'm Volodymyr, and this is Stas."

"We are also zeks," said Stas.

The man was puzzled. He pursed his lips, thinking hard. Then, he had it.

"Oh my, you're politicals," he laughed.

Volodymyr and Stas weren't amused now. They scoffed at the wimpy label. They were proud, fierce enemy combatants.

"I'm in UPA," said Volodymyr.

"I'm in Armia Krajowa," said Stas.

The man stopped laughing. He rubbed the back of his neck, blushing. He nodded.

"Oh, I see," he said. "I have a lot of respect for you men taking these monsters head-on. This place is the devil's playground. I'm Valeriy Pavlovich. I'm also Ukrainian, from Kharkiv."

Volodymyr liked him already.

"It's always a pleasure to meet *nashi*," said Volodymyr.

"*Pryjemno*," said Valeriy. *A pleasure.*

"Now that we've properly met, let's walk and talk," Stas suggested.

They would eat those words.

Volodymyr and Stas started to discuss their backgrounds when Valeriy began to talk, and talk, and talk. Like a man starved of food, he was a man starved of meaningful conversation. He was more than happy to tell his life story. He was proud of his special status too.

"The communists want to colonize space before the imperialists do," Valeriy laughed. "It's a miracle we have the great Korolev. I knew him from the *sharashka* in Kazan during the war. What a man!"

"What did you do during the war?" asked Stas.

"I was in Stavka telecommunications," said Valeriy proudly, referring to Soviet high command. "I was on the first Soviet team to use radar from England."

"How did you end up here?" asked Stas.

Valeriy's expression soured. "Well, after the war, I let my true feelings be known about our government's conduct."

Valeriy then lifted his shirt, revealing a large red mark on his ribs where the guard had just struck him in line.

"I guess some things never change," he said, wincing.

"Would you like to get back at them?" asked Volodymyr.

Valeriy lowered his shirt and raised his brows. Volodymyr and Stas looked behind them to make sure there weren't any guards nearby. Then Volodymyr leaned in.

"Would you like to work with us? We are a large, strong, and organized multinational force, just like in the war."

Valeriy was shocked. He was silent for a while. Volodymyr and Stas were wondering if they had just made a big mistake when he finally smiled.

"Well, what the hell, I'm already in jail," said Valeriy, rubbing his aching ribs. "Marx said, 'Workers of the world, unite!' So, what do I have to lose but my chains?"

"That's the spirit," said Stas.

"Come with us. We'll introduce you to my commander, Sokil. He appreciates people with talent like yours," said Volodymyr.

Valeriy agreed, although he was still a bit jumpy. He kept a few paces behind them, looking over his shoulders every so often. Finally, they reached Sokil's barracks. Volodymyr was about to knock on the door when Sokil opened the door, quickly looking side to side, and beckoned them to come in. They shuffled into the barracks and Sokil quickly shut the door. Sokil then went back to the small window to look around before rejoining them.

"Sorry about all the cloak-and-dagger, but you can't be too careful," he said. "I've been under increased surveillance." Valeriy was standing nervously, tapping his foot. He was still riled up from the trip and the guards. Sokil looked him over.

"Who is this?" asked Sokil.

"His name is Valeriy. He's *nashi*, from Kharkiv, and he has some very impressive skills," said Volodymyr.

"Really?" "Why don't you tell him," Volodymyr said to Valeriy.

Valeriy hesitated, looking at the door, but he relented.

"I was in telecommunications during the war." "Go on," said Sokil, his eyes widening.

"Well, we intercepted enemy communications, and I was on the first Soviet team to use radar," said Valeriy.

Sokil nodded his head approvingly. "I have to say, I'm intrigued."

Sokil patted Valeriy on the shoulder. "We'll get him adjusted in due time. Now let's step back outside, as I'm not allowed many visitors these days."

Just as they were about to leave, Sokil turned to Stas.

"Stas, my Polish comrade, why don't you show Valeriy the mess hall? You can tell him about our demonstration there."

Stas agreed and took Valeriy along. Sokil waited until they were out of earshot. He then leaned into Volodymyr.

"This is very important, Volodymyr. We're having a special meeting today—Ukrainians only, not even Stas can know. Not yet. And we can't have any of your Russian roommates be aware either. Understand?"

Volodymyr nodded. Sokil reached into his pocket. He unfurled a small piece of paper. Volodymyr leaned in and realized it was a rudimentary map.

"Take this and memorize it, then destroy it," said Sokil. "There is an abandoned supply house on the edge of the zona. Our contact Lylyk works night shifts in the warehouse, and he told us it's clear. Meet us there at the changing of the night shift."

"I've heard of him," said Volodymyr.

"*Tak*, his name precedes him. He's an excellent spy. I think he can really see in the dark like a bat." It was a lot to process, but Volodymyr agreed.

"I'm counting on you being there, Volodymyr," said Sokil. "You've been doing an excellent job around here."

Sokil looked around again and went back inside. Volodymyr didn't know what to feel. He hadn't heard Sokil call him by his real name since the war. The loudspeaker shook Volodymyr out of his swirling thoughts. It was time for dinner. He quickly folded up the map and tucked it into his *bushlat*.

After dinner, he lay in his bunk staring at the ceiling. He went over the map again and again in his head. He looked around to make sure nobody was looking and tore up the map, gently hiding the shreds under the floorboards. One couldn't be too careful. He gingerly opened the door and disappeared into the night and into the unknown.

He didn't know what to expect when he got there. His mind was racing. He quickly stopped and took a deep breath. He knew he couldn't afford to get nervous and make a mistake. He kept his head and moved forward.

Volodymyr's outings with Kateryna had become an unexpected advantage. He knew the different shifts of the guards and which pitfalls to avoid. The dangers were still great, however, and any wrong move could easily become his last. He had memorized the map as best as he could. The most dangerous part would be the final stretch, where he would have to make a break across an open courtyard.

Volodymyr weaved his way through the maze of barracks to the perimeter of the zona. His adrenaline was pumping. He stopped by the gate and waited for it to close for the second shift. He carefully crept out when he heard something.

"What was that?" asked a voice.

A bolt of panic shot through Volodymyr. He felt sick with terror. Another guard showed up. Volodymyr searched frantically for an escape when he saw a garbage bin. He knew it was a long shot, but he had no choice.

He jumped in the smelly trash and hoped for the best. He closed the lid tight. The smell was something awful, like the train *parasha*. The muffled voices got louder. Volodymyr realized they were right next to him. He held his breath.

"What did you hear?" asked a voice.

"I don't know, maybe nothing, but—""Alright, we'll check the other side of the fence," said the other guard.

Volodymyr heard their footsteps trail off. He waited several minutes before finally opening the lid. He took a deep breath and coughed.

He looked around and quietly made his way to the courtyard. After his close call, he knew he couldn't afford to mess up. The courtyard wasn't all that big, perhaps twenty yards to the closest cover, but to him at that moment it felt like a kilometer. He took a breath, said a quick prayer, and off he went, making a mad dash to the warehouse.

He ducked behind a wall. His heart was beating hard when he heard something. It was footsteps, getting closer. Volodymyr closed his eyes, waiting for the hot lead to send him to hell, when he heard those beautiful words.

"*Slava Ukraini*," said a voice. *Glory to Ukraine.* "*Heroyam slava*," said Volodymyr. *Glory to Ukraine's heroes.* "Call name?" asked the man.

"Baran," Volodymyr replied.

"Ah, we've been waiting for you, Baran. I'm Lylyk." "*Pryjemno*, Lylyk, I've heard good things about you." "Likewise." They shook hands, and Lylyk's face contorted. He started to sniff the air.

"What is that smell?" he asked.

Volodymyr was happy it was dark. His clothes were surely mired in muck. He blushed.

"Well, it figures, this whole place stinks to hell," said Lylyk, covering his nose. "Whatever it is, at least it will keep the *vovki* from poking their noses around."

Lylyk knocked on the door. "*Nashi*."

Several locks clicked and turned, and the door opened. Lylyk motioned for Volodymyr to enter. He walked in and the door was quickly shut behind them. The room was dimly lit, but Volodymyr could make out all the faces of UPA.

"Welcome, Baran," said Sokil, walking over to

extend his hand when he started to cough.

Volodymyr was caught. He tried to say something quickly to save face.

"I was forced to take evasive maneuvers when I was almost spotted by some guards. Unfortunately, the only hiding place was a waste receptacle."

The room was silent. Volodymyr looked to the door. Sokil burst out laughing.

"Many would've retreated, but Baran was never afraid to get into the muck," said Sokil.

Volodymyr breathed a sigh of relief. There were several dozen men crammed in the old supply house. They'd had plenty of practice maneuvering tight spaces in the trenches and in their many cramped train rides. Sokil went to the center to address the room.

"Well *Kozaky*, welcome to the first official meeting of the Ukrainian Centre," said Sokil, referring to them fondly as *Cossacks*. "Everything that takes place here must be kept here, or face the consequences."

They all turned to each other soberly, taking in the magnitude of what they were doing. They were rebels again. If they were discovered, it could easily mean their death.

"Now, this is only a temporary meeting place as our ranks grow, but remember: The great oak starts out as a tiny acorn," Sokil continued. "We have connections with Armia Krajowa and the Baltics, and we have the respect of the Chechens and Tatars. We have even made inroads with disgruntled Russians, including some high-ranking former Red Army. As for the urka: We have come to an understanding. A type of détente. They will not harass us, and we will not go after them."

Lylyk stood up. "I propose to the council that in lieu of our traditional command structure in these extraordinary times, we vote to promote *Sotnyk* Sokil to *polkovnyk* of the camp to consolidate all our *kurins*."

They all started murmuring loudly. This didn't seem like part of the plan. Sokil was composed, but he was fidgeting. Another UPA lieutenant stood up.

"*Tak*," he said.

"I second that," said another.

It continued down the room with only one UPA *sotnyk* hesitating, but eventually agreeing.

"Then it is agreed," said Lylyk.

"*Diakuyu, brattya,* I will use all the powers invested in me to uphold the laws our organization. *Klyanus*," said Sokil. *I swear.*

The room nodded approvingly. It was a big test for their organization to promote Sokil to colonel of the camp. Sokil continued with the various other pressing issues.

"Now, as for our female combatants in Camp No. 2, whom we briefly saw on the train ride: Our contact Soloveyko has done good work rounding up intelligence on her end," said Sokil, using their contact's code name, Nightingale.Sokil revealed a small grainy picture, but Volodymyr could tell right away it was Kateryna. He was shocked. Sokil kept talking, but Volodymyr wasn't listening. He thought he was immune to surprises by now, but this hit him hard.

"Now, to conclude our meeting," said Sokil, turning to Volodymyr, "Volodymyr Andriyovich Zaluzhniy, stand."

Volodymyr's eyes widened, and his hands began to sweat. He was certain they had figured out his secret rendezvous with Kateryna, or Soloveyko. He awaited some sort of public scolding. Sokil pulled out a small book.

"Raise your right hand and place it on this Bible," said Sokil.

Volodymyr was confused, but did as he was commanded.

"Volodymyr Andriyovich, do you swear to uphold the laws and discipline of our organization to protect and serve our great Ukrainian nation?" asked Sokil.

"*Tak, klyanus,*" said Volodymyr. *Yes, I swear.*"Then by the power invested in me by God and country, for your brave and loyal service to the Ukrainian Insurgent Army, you have been promoted to *poruchnyk. Slava Ukraini,*" said Sokil. Volodymyr was now a lieutenant.

"*Heroyam slava,*" they all replied.

"Now, gentlemen, let's return to our quarters lest the guards get suspicious," said Sokil.

The men quietly got up and went out the door one by one. Just as Volodymyr was about to leave, someone grabbed his shoulder. He turned around to see Sokil standing over him.

"I know you won't disappoint us," said Sokil, squeezing Volodymyr's shoulder.

"*Klyanus*," said Volodymyr.

"Congratulations, Baran. It's a big day for both of us. We have to watch each other's back because nobody else will. I appreciate what you did at the food hall. You're going to do big things."

Sokil finally let Volodymyr go and they parted for the night. Volodymyr knew his world had just got more complicated. He knew his promotion would be tested soon enough, but the main issue at the moment was how to deal with Kateryna. Their scheduled meet was tomorrow, and he didn't know what to say.

He returned to the barracks, quietly opening the door and slipping into bed. He didn't know exactly what time it was, but it was somewhere between midnight and dawn. He fell asleep wondering about his next move, praying nobody had noticed his absence.

The next day went as well as hell on earth could. They worked themselves to the brink of death, and then worked some more. Volodymyr's promotion the night before and his imminent meeting with Kateryna kept him going.

Dinner was the usual slop. There was a fight between some zeks and urka and the subsequent beatings by the guards, but otherwise it was routine. No one seemed suspicious.

Stas raised a few strange questions, but didn't pursue them. Leonid was quiet. He was still shell-shocked by the death of the Evangelist.

Later, when the other zeks retired for the night, Volodymyr went out to meet the Nightingale. He made his way past the usual guards and checkpoints. He arrived earlier than usual to figure out his move, only to find Kateryna already perched on her typical spot. She smiled when she saw Volodymyr. He was still brooding, and she sensed his unease.

"How are you, *kokhanna*?" she asked.

"*Dobre*," Volodymyr said quickly.

There was an awkward pause. Kateryna waited for more. Volodymyr was mute.

"Aren't you going to ask how I am?" she asked.

"Well, how are you, then?" asked Volodymyr bluntly.

"Is something wrong, Vlodko?""You tell me Agent Soloveyko," he blurted.

Kateryna's eyes widened.

"How did you find out?""So it's true," said Volodymyr, exasperated.

"Oh, Vlodko, I was going to tell you. I was just waiting for the right time," she said.

"Did you know who I was all this time?" asked Volodymyr.

Kateryna was silent.

"Well, did you?" asked Volodymyr, a little too loudly.

"Shhh," said Kateryna, quickly looking over her shoulder. "*Tak*, I recognized you on the train from a photograph."

"So this was just some intelligence-gathering operation the whole time?" he asked. "You didn't have any feelings for me at all!"

"How can you say that?" Kateryna asked angrily.

She leaned into the fence. Her hands gripped the cold, steel wire dividing them. Volodymyr leaned back.

"I really do care about you, Vlodko."Volodymyr looked into her eyes. She was on the verge of tears. He was at a loss.

"I don't know what to think," he said. "I've been betrayed so many times."

Kateryna reached her hand through the fence. Volodymyr reached his out. Though they were nowhere near touching, this small gesture moved mountains. This act was risky, as any breach of the zona would be seen as attempted escape and they could be shot if seen.

"Do you know my call name?" asked Volodymyr.

"Baran, I believe?" she asked.

He nodded.

"Do you know how I got that name?" he asked.

She shook her head. He then told her the story. She burst out laughing.

"He never knew what hit him," Kateryna laughed.

"How did you get your name, *Soloveyko*?"Kateryna suddenly was quiet.

"Oh, I'm sorry, you don't have to tell me if you don't want to," said Volodymyr.

"No, it's just that no one has asked me about that in a long time," she replied. "It was years ago, on a night patrol. I thought I was alone and began to sing. My commander heard me. I thought he would reprimand me, but he liked my singing. He even had me sing for the unit. It lifted our spirits when the Germans and Soviets had us pinned down."

"What did you sing?" asked Volodymyr.

"Oh, Vlodko, it's been so long," she said.

"*Oh in the glen by the Danube a nightingale chirps,*" Volodymyr sang, beginning an old Ukrainian folk song.Kateryna answered. "*The base hums, the violin cries, my beloved wanders.*"Those few stanzas were enough to warm their hearts in the freezing night. Volodymyr would sing that song with his former wife. Volodymyr's thoughts of greener pastures escaped him, and his words flew out of his mouth.

"Would you ever think of getting out of here?""Escape?" Kateryna asked nervously, looking over her shoulder again. "How?"

Volodymyr looked over his own shoulder and then leaned in close.

"I carved out a hole under the floorboards of my bunk. My good friend Stas was a miner. We can hide shovels and wire cutters in there and then we can dig out, perhaps even cut out a hole in the wire right here."

Kateryna was silent. Volodymyr was nervous he had said too much.

Eventually, she leaned in.

"Spring would be best," she said. "The steppes aren't as cold and windy, and the grass begins to grow, like in *Ukraina*."

"*Tak*, spring it is," said Volodymyr.

"Well, Vlodko, Baran, *mylyj miy*," said Kateryna "*Dobranich*."

"*Dobranich*, Soloveyko," said Volodymyr.

Volodymyr's heart was singing. When he entered the barracks, he didn't even realize he was humming. Someone put their hand over Volodymyr's mouth. His heart leapt into his throat.

"It's me, Vlodko," said Stas, removing his hand from Volodymyr's mouth.

"What are you doing scaring the life out of me?" said Volodymyr.

"Quiet, you'll get us caught," said Stas, looking over his shoulder. "I know about your little night trips, but nobody one else does, yet."

Volodymyr was shocked.

"Is it the girl from the train?" Stas asked.

Volodymyr nodded.

"I figured," he smirked.

They both quietly chuckled. Volodymyr looked to Stas seriously. He leaned in close.

"Stas, you and I have been through hell and back together, *tak*?"

"*Tak*, but I'm afraid you're about to pour gas on the fire," said Stas.

"What say you, me, and the girl, Kateryna, get out of here?" asked Volodymyr.

"How?" Volodymyr quietly lead Stas to the floorboards. He gingerly lifted them up, carefully revealing his hiding space. Though it was dark, Volodymyr could feel Stas's shock.

"We can hide supplies here and cut a hole in the wire," said Volodymyr.

"On one condition," said Stas.

"What's that?""You charge headfirst."

6

APRIL 18–25, 1954:

OTETS JUDAS

"SLAVA ISUSA KHRYSTU," said the priest. *Glory to Jesus Christ.*

"*Slava Naviki,*" the Ukrainian congregation answered. *Glory Eternal.*"Be careful about him," Sokil whispered to Volodymyr.

It was Easter Week on the Julian calendar used in Eastern Christian traditions. More specifically, it was Palm Sunday, known as *Kvitna Nedilya,* or Flower Sunday to Ukrainians who used pussy willows instead of palm leaves for its celebration. The Soviet Union's official ban on religion meant that all services had to be done clandestinely.

The Ukrainian Greek Catholic priest Otets Julian was new to the camp. His past was murky, and there were rumors that he had some nefarious connections. The Ukrainian Centre had asked him to perform the Easter ceremony so they could test him.

"Now on this blessed Sunday, during the holiest time of year, let us take communion so we may honor the entrance of our Lord and Savior *Isus Khrystos* into Jerusalem," said Julian.

The Ukrainian congregation lined up to meet the new priest. The first few went by without incident, until it was Lylyk's turn. He stared at the priest. The priest began tugging nervously at his collar.

"*Slava Isusa Khrystu,*" said Otets Julian. "*Slava Naviki,*" Lylyk replied. He

continued to stare at the priest.

"Will you take communion?" asked the priest nervously.

"In time," said Lylyk.

"Do you have something to say?" asked the priest, trying to save face.

"I have a clean heart, Otets Julian," said Lylyk, genuflecting.

He finally opened his mouth for the scavenged bread and rough prison wine made by some Georgian zeks.

"*Vnimaniye, vnimaniye,*" said the loudspeaker.

They quickly packed up and hid their religious icons lest the guards come raining down on them with biblical fury. Lylyk volunteered to help Julian, who begrudgingly agreed.

"Remember what I said, Baran," said Sokil.

They emerged out of the stuffy supply house into the spring air. Nothing in this acrid place reflected the holiday, but the weather was at least better than when they arrived. Yet, the sun didn't shine on Volodymyr.

New walls had sprung up where he used to meet Kateryna. He only heard from her sporadically now. They used to toss notes over the walls when they were being built, but now that was impossible with an influx of new guards.

Conditions in the camp had deteriorated even further after a new, stricter regime was appointed from Karaganda to "correct" the situation with the zeks who were only demanding their rights. Even the once relatively untouchable urka hadn't been spared. That development was an unexpected asset to the politicals.

"Happy Orthodox Easter," said Stas.

"*Diakuyu,* Stas, but I explained I am Catholic too, but of the Byzantine Rite," said Volodymyr.

"Well you're still a Christian, right?" Stas laughed, secretly passing Volodymyr some improvised Polish *paska,* or Easter bread.

"Well, I can't refuse good food from my Christian brother," said Volodymyr.

Leonid approached.

"Happy Easter," said Leonid. "I know you Roman Catholics just finished, but us Orthodox just started today."

"I'm celebrating now too," said Volodymyr.

"I thought you said you were Catholic?" asked Leonid.

"Yes, but of the Byzantine Rite," said Volodymyr.

"Well, no matter, we're all sinners here," he replied.

They looked at the imposing new walls, barbed wire, and watchtowers.

"Jesus wept," said Stas.

"Amen," said Leonid solemnly.

"Get moving, zeks, or I'll have you sent to the SHIZO," a guard barked.

The three of them hurried forward, knowing that they could end up like the Chechen.

"Where is God on this holy day?" asked Volodymyr.

There was no day of rest for the zeks. Volodymyr had even been put on extra punitive duty for "improperly addressing" a guard by forgetting to say "comrade." He limped by long after most had headed in for the night, including Stas and Leonid. He was nearing Sokil's barracks when he saw two guards.

Volodymyr instinctively turned the corner and waited. They were dragging something large. When he looked closer, he realized, to his horror, it was person.

"Off you go, fascist scum," said a guard, dropping the zek like a sack of potatoes.

They briskly walked away. Sokil appeared when it was clear. He cautiously approached the zek, and then ran over and collapsed next to him.

"Lylyk," he cried.

Volodymyr ran out of his hiding space. Nacham and several other Ukrainians were not far behind. Sokil picked up Lylyk and held his ear to his mouth.

"He's still breathing," he said.

"I didn't tell them a thing," Lylyk whispered.

"I know you didn't brother," said Sokil, brushing aside Lylyk's bloody hair.

They had all seen some terrible injuries in the war, but the amount of trauma shocked even these veterans. Lylyk's eyes were swollen shut, and blood poured out of a gash in his head. Volodymyr looked closer and realized several of Lylyk's fingernails had been pulled out.

"We don't have the proper supplies," said Nacham, shaking his head. "We have to take him to the infirmary."

Lylyk grabbed Nacham with great exertion. "Where do you think they did this?"

He then collapsed from exhaustion.

"I'll get my field kit," said Nacham.

"Hurry, Nacham," said Sokil, propping up the injured man. "Alright, now somebody grab his legs and let's bring him out of the cold!"

Volodymyr and another Ukrainian grabbed Lylyk's legs and they carried him inside. They found a table and splayed him out. Sokil put a pillow under his head.

Volodymyr had never seen Sokil so distraught, stroking and patting Lylyk's face. He and Lylyk went way back. They had fought together on the Carpathian Front in the First World War.

Nacham came back with a black medical bag. He produced a clear bottle and unscrewed the top. The fumes were overwhelming. Lylyk was going in and out of consciousness.

"He'll need this for the stitches," said Nacham.

It was a bottle of strong *samohonka*, or moonshine. Sokil lifted Lylyk's head and carefully tipped the liquid into his mouth. Lylyk immediately spit it out.

"Are you trying to kill me?" he Lylyk.

"It's the only antiseptic or anesthetic we have right now," said Nacham, digging furiously through his bag.

"So be it," said Lylyk, grabbing the bottle and nearly finishing it.

"Brace yourself," said Nacham.

Sokil put a rag in Lylyk's mouth. Lylyk weakly nodded. Nacham poured the burning alcohol on Lylyk's open head wound. Lylyk writhed in pain. After about half a minute, Lylyk relaxed somewhat. Nacham then went to work stitching up the wound with a needle and thread from the textile workshop.

"Can you remember anything?" asked Sokil.

"Otets Julian," said Lylyk, angrily taking another sip of *samohonka*. They were shocked.

"*Tak*, it appears our otets is a wolf in sheep's clothing," said Lylyk, wincing. "Easy, Nacham."

"I'm sorry, the damned guards confiscated my best needles," said Nacham.

"Anyway, between interrogations, I learned there was another *nashi* in the cell next to me," said Lylyk. "He knew Otets Julian, whose real name is Ivan Stepanovich, from the Kolyma camp. He said he's assumed many names to protect his identity, but they called him Otets Judas."

They still couldn't believe what they were hearing.

"I didn't believe it either, at first, but this man was credible," Lylyk continued. "This Judas was a priest once somewhere in Volyn but was defrocked after he betrayed his congregation's UPA connections to the Soviets after the war. He had to have turned me in for the way I leaned on him during the service."

"So it's true, then," said Sokil, woefully. "What has our world come to that we can't even trust our otets? We need to silence this traitor to God!"

His words hung heavy in the stuffy air. Volodymyr felt a pain in his heart. Western Ukrainians were particularly religious. His soul was shaken.

"We can't do anything tonight," said Sokil. "I'll take Lylyk myself to the head urka, who still has some connections to the guards. They will provide him with medical care. Everyone else, go back to your barracks so we don't raise suspicion."

The night was even darker now, with clouds having rolled in. The higher walls and towers also blocked out more of the stars that first captured Volodymyr's and Kateryna's eyes. He wondered what she was doing now, if she was looking up at the same moonless night as him and sighing. He quietly made his way back to the barracks with a heavy heart.

The next day's morbid morning routine dragged him down further. They lined up outside and marched to breakfast. Volodymyr didn't even look up to greet Stas. Then, about halfway to the mess hall, they noticed commotion outside one of the barracks.

"Halt," said a guard.

He was also wondering what was going on. They all watched the strange scene. The guards were completely ransacking a barrack.

A distraught young man stood nearby under armed guard.

Volodymyr looked closer at the young man and recognized him as a young Ukrainian from Easter communion. Pillows, covers, mattresses, even chairs were flying out the door. A frazzled guard ran out.

"I found it," he said excitedly.

He then disappeared back into the barrack. The suspense was too overwhelming to their armed escort, who joined in the excitement. Volodymyr, Stas, Leonid, and their lot carefully crept closer out of morbid curiosity. It was hard to tell at first, with everyone crowding around the door, but soon they realized what was happening.

"It's all here, sir," said the guard. "I have to admit, I'm impressed by the sophistication of this particular tunnel."

The guard was not exaggerating. It was a fairly spacious hole, with no trace of dirt anywhere near it. It was placed precisely under the cooking stove, with an airtight cover above that matched the surrounding floor. Nobody could've found it unless they were told where to look.

Again, Volodymyr was faced with the horrible reality that Otets Julian was the only one outside of gulag officials and zeks allowed in the barracks. He had seen the religious young man seeking the otets's guidance.

Then, like a waking nightmare, the zeks trembled as the dreaded Wart emerged out of the darkness. He turned to the zeks, smiling fiendishly, and then back to the cowering Ukrainian boy. The Wart relished their fear.

"Well, I've seen everything I need to," said Belyaev. "Take him to the SHIZO!"

"You heard him: Off you go," said the guard.

"No!" the young zek cried.

He took off with an unexpected burst of energy to the zona.

"No, please God, no," the other zeks cried out desperately.

The young zek ignored their desperate pleas and ran into the barbed-wire fence, into no man's land. He desperately clawed at the wire like a trapped animal. The watchtower guards quickly turned their guns on him and *bang bang bang!* It was over. The young man slumped over, still clinging to the wire, and collapsed, along with any lingering faith in humanity.

"Get these zeks out of here," said Belyaev.

Their overseers snapped back to attention and began corralling the zeks to feeding.

"You heard him, there's nothing to see here," said their guard.

More guards and orderlies appeared, one pushing along a battered old cart. The guards quickly went to work prying each of the young man's fingers from the wire to which they still clung. His face was frozen in pain, inhaling his last breath so close to freedom. They hauled him up and threw him onto the cart. The guards handled him with the callousness of a slaughtered hog. , and

they carted him off to the mass grave.

Volodymyr felt ill. The zeks paid their respects with their long, silent, passing glances, remembering the young man's contorted face, and their growing anger boiling inside.

They solemnly marched forward to breakfast. They entered the mess hall like a funeral procession. Nobody talked. They hardly moved, only shuffling forward to receive their meals.

Volodymyr sat down and stared at his plate.

He was starving, but he had no appetite. He couldn't shake the horrible feeling about the new priest being responsible. He kept thinking about what Lylyk had said in his torment, but he still couldn't come around to believing it. The sickening sight of the young man being stuffed onto the cart kept swirling around his head, making him nauseous.

"Alright, move out," said a guard.

Breakfast was over. It was too much for Volodymyr to swallow. He gave his meal to a *dokhodyaga*. Volodymyr stared at the floor, barely moving. He eventually looked up and realized he had been left behind. The guards probably thought he was also a *dokhodyaga*. He felt like he was dead. He then heard some voices behind the mess hall.

Volodymyr quietly got up and snuck behind the hall. He carefully peeked around the corner, and nearly vomited. There was Otets Julian with a KGB officer. Volodymyr looked closer and realized to his horror it was not any officer, but the Wart himself.

"Well done finding that tunnel, *tovarishch*. We will remember that," said Belyaev, handing Julian a pack of *makhorka* and some bread.

Julian looked uncomfortable, but he still took his payment. Volodymyr felt his despair turn into rage. He watched in utter contempt as Belyaev patted Julian on the back and led him inside.

Volodymyr marched forward with renewed purpose. He knew what he had to do. He blended into another shift of zeks to the mines. Volodymyr took his task and went to work to find Sokil. He found Sokil at the edge of the pits unloading iron ore. "Baran?" asked Sokil, surprised. "Take a shovel or the guards will give you hell."

Volodymyr took the spade and stabbed the pile of rock.

"I will do it," said Volodymyr.

Sokil quickly covered Volodymyr's mouth. "Not here. Come with me. We're about to change shifts."

A loud whistle blew.

"Fresh meat," yelled a guard.

The zeks in Sokil's gang quickly parted for the new arrivals, lest they get sucked into a second shift. They made their way out of the pits and to the barracks. Sokil grabbed Volodymyr and they ducked out of line. Their absence in the sea of zeks didn't cause a stir.

They reached Sokil's barrack. Sokil made sure they were all clear and quickly ducked inside. Sokil looked out the window one more time before heading to the corner of the room.

"One can't be too careful," he said.

He moved his hand along the corner of the wall and stopped. He then pried open a loose floorboard, revealing a cavity. He reached in and pulled out a long, thin wire with two pieces of wood wrapped around the ends.

"If we're going to do this, we have to do it right," said Sokil. "No sound, no witnesses, no blood."

He handed the wire to Volodymyr.

"Wait until after *Velykden* services, when he's all alone. I will let you know the route he takes," said Sokil, referring to Easter Sunday, aptly named the "Great Day."

Sokil's voice faded away. The thin wire started to feel like a heavy chain in Volodymyr's hands as the adrenaline wore off and the full weight of his decision dawned on him. He absently nodded to what Sokil was saying.

Sokil grabbed his shoulder.

"You'll be made *sotnyk* for this," said Sokil. "*Davay*, Baran! Make haste, lest we be strung up instead!"

Volodymyr quickly tucked the wire into his *bushlat* pocket and scurried toward the door.

"Good luck. We will be in touch soon," said Sokil. "And remember: Be grateful it is you with the wire for him, and not the other way around."

Volodymyr shuddered. He just wanted get out as fast as he could. He made his way to his barracks just before Stas and his bunkmates came back from their shift to get ready for dinner. Volodymyr frantically pulled up the wood planks under his bed and tucked away the wire.

After a long week of preparation and trepidation, the Great Day finally arrived. The tradition of fasting before Velykden was easy to maintain in Kengir. The suspense was killing Volodymyr, having lost several pounds in the short time. He practiced every rare free moment and even in his sleep for the dreaded task. He kept his distance from everyone.

Volodymyr went to the clandestine mass with the other Ukrainians laser focused. Sokil covertly greeted him. They all waited silently, solemnly, for Judas to appear. It took a while, so long in fact that they were beginning to worry that he wasn't going to show, or even worse that it was some kind of trap. Finally, after over an hour, Judas arrived.

"*Khrystos voskres,*" said Julian. *Christ is risen.* "*Voyistyno voskres,*" the congregation answered. *Indeed he has risen.* Volodymyr mouthed the words. He couldn't even hear Julian. He was trying his hardest to keep his composure. He didn't even realize the service was over until Sokil patted his shoulder.

"Go on ahead and wait by the meetinghouse," said Sokil.

Volodymyr nodded instinctively. He was on autopilot. He only briefly looked behind and saw Sokil speaking with Julian. He then marched forward into holy battle.

He went straight to the prearranged meeting point and waited on the side of the meetinghouse, stalking his prey. The volatile April weather began to turn and it started to rain. It was a miserable wait. He grasped the wire, wondering, hoping it wouldn't be as awful as he thought. He said a prayer, which he knew was bitterly ironic.

Finally, judgment day had arrived. Julian was walking towards him. The rain was falling harder. Volodymyr knew it was time: Sink or swim. He kissed Slipyj's crucifix, genuflected, and unfurled the wire. The pattering rain subdued his footsteps. He was right on top of the priest when he paused and whispered desperately, "God forgive me."

Volodymyr swooped his arms over Julian and wrapped the cord

around his neck, pulling tight. Julian slipped and dropped down like a lead brick, pulling them both down into the muck. The heavens opened up and all hell broke loose. Julian clawed desperately at Volodymyr's face and arms. The muck was sucking in their souls. Volodymyr pulled with all his strength. Julian kicked and squirmed for a few more seconds and, after one last gasp, it was over. Julian's arms fell to his sides and he went limp. The heavens hung low and Volodymyr lower.

Sokil, Lylyk, and two other UPA men ran out. One grabbed Julian's legs and the other his arms and they carried him off. Sokil bent down next to Volodymyr.

"Baran, can you hear me?" he asked.

Volodymyr sat motionless, getting soaked in the pouring rain.

"Vlodko," said Sokil.

Volodymyr looked up. Sokil had never called him that before. Sokil wiped Volodymyr's face.

"It's over," said Sokil. "It was an awful thing I asked of you, but it had to be done!"

Volodymyr could just barely make out what Sokil was saying.

"You gave him one last sermon," said Lylyk, behind them. "It's better than he deserved."

Volodymyr felt paralyzed. Sokil and Lylyk, still bruised and swollen himself, helped him up. He felt unsteady, like a lamb first learning to walk.

"You have to be strong, Volodymyr, now more than ever," said Sokil. "We will deal with the rest; now you just have one more mission, and it may be the toughest, but you must go on living normally."

"How?" Volodymyr whispered.

"You will learn to live with it in time, but now you just need to survive until we get out of here," said Sokil. "*Davay, kozak!*"

Volodymyr marched forward to the barrack, never lifting his head.

It was a long slog, like one of the arduous marches in the closing days of the war. He opened the door and realized he was alone again with his thoughts. He slumped down, hitting the hard wood floor. He felt lower than the mud caked around his soles.

He closed his eyes and heard the priest's horrible, inhuman squealing as the life had left his mortal body. Volodymyr thought about his first battlefield kill in the spring of 1944, when he had shot a German soldier. Though he'd felt terrible at first, it was cut and clear: That was war, and the man he killed was the hated enemy.

Otets Julian reminded Volodymyr of something more personal, and painful. It had happened in spring of 1941 when Volodymyr turned sixteen. It was only a few months before Germany invaded, and food was becoming scarce after the borders closed. They had several lambs born that year.

Volodymyr's father solemnly summoned Volodymyr to the barn one day. Volodymyr opened the door to two scrawny lambs. His father told him to be very quiet. Andriy waited several moments before swiftly plucking the lamb and snapping its little neck.

"Quickly and painlessly," said Andriy. "No blood."

It was then Volodymyr's turn. He hesitated. Andriy picked up the lamb and put it in Volodymyr's hands. His father insisted that he had to do it at least once.

Volodymyr closed his eyes and grabbed the lamb's neck. He held his breath and pulled, but it didn't work. The lamb started squirming. Volodymyr then pulled hard and the lamb squealed and writhed, eventually going weak after several agonizing seconds. Volodymyr was so shook up, he vomited afterwards. Luckily, his father never made him do it again, but that day Volodymyr knew he was not so innocent anymore.

Otets Julian had felt like that hapless lamb. He was a traitor and had to be dealt with, but he was also a civilian, not an enemy combatant. He'd been so helpless, squirming and squealing. He had no idea what was going on or how to even fight back. It was a tragedy, not a heroic struggle.

Volodymyr went to his bed and knelt down. He lifted up the floorboards. He pulled off Slipyj's crucifix and buried it beneath the slats, sealing it shut.

"God is dead," he said.

The next day Volodymyr never fully awoke. He felt like he was still in some kind of dream. He went through the motions of the day, but was never fully conscious. He was walking in a fog.

"Vlodko, you're eating with your whole face," teased Stas.

Volodymyr realized he had dozed off and gotten food on his chin and nose.

"I don't know . . ." said Volodymyr, trailing off.

"Are you alright?" asked Stas.

The work bell rang before Volodymyr could answer, which was just as well, because he could barely talk or move at all.

"Come on, son," said Leonid.

Volodymyr looked up and thought he saw Julian. He jumped back, spilling his bowl and spoon. Stas quickly picked them up.

"What's going on over there?' asked a guard.

"Nothing, *tovarishch*," said Leonid, turning to Volodymyr. "I'll try to get you on light duty."

Stas was trying to hold up Volodymyr, who was shaking all over.

"Are you sick?" asked Stas.

"Only God knows," Volodymyr mumbled.

"Come on, we're getting you to the infirmary," Stas replied.

"No, no, I can work," said Volodymyr, rushing out the door.

He remembered what they did to Lylyk. Maybe he would die in the mines, but perhaps that would absolve his sins.

The release of death did not come.

Volodymyr nodded in and out of consciousness the entire time. One moment he would be raising his pick, and the next he was bringing his arms down around Julian's neck. He went back to the barracks and stared at the ceiling all night. He watched while the room turned from dark to light, wondering if he was still breathing. Even the announcements taunted him.

"*Vnimaniye, vnimaniye, Slava Isusa Khrystu. God, forgive us our sins and those that have trespassed against us. Amen,*" Volodymyr heard, in Julian's voice.

"*Slava Naviki,*" Volodymyr answered, to nobody.

The next few days got worse and worse. Stas and Leonid hand-fed him like a baby. Sokil, Nacham, Lylyk, and the main UPA were in hiding after Belyaev started asking about their missing informant priest. All Ukrainians were suspect.

"You can't go on like this," Stas whispered to Volodymyr. "People are starting to get suspicious."

He leaned into Volodymyr.

"Did you do something?" Volodymyr didn't answer, couldn't answer. He didn't even know how to answer. He stumbled along to work.

The simple act of standing took great effort. He nearly collapsed waiting in line. It felt like he was drunk. Everything was blurry and muffled. It felt like the room was spinning.

He looked at his waist, or lack thereof. He had cut more holes to buckle his belt, and it still barely held. He placed his hands around his waist and his fingers nearly touched. Slowly, Volodymyr looked up and met the gaze of a *dokhodyaga*. Now he understood.

Volodymyr entered the mines after two weeks of starvation. He picked up his spade and, with one mighty swing, broke through the earth's crust. He spiraled down into the center of the earth.

Volodymyr woke up in the infirmary. A cold sweat went down his back. He was sure they had found him out.

"Hey, are you alive in there?" someone asked.

Volodymyr didn't know if he imagined it.

"I can see you're awake," the voice said again. "Turn your head."

Volodymyr slowly turned and saw an orderly standing over him. He was a stout, stocky Asian man with piercing dark eyes. He wondered if he was one of the brutal Kazakh guards that would strangle him to death.

"I'm Ondar," said the man. "I'm the one that's been keeping you breathing. You're one tough bastard. A lot of people wouldn't have survived a tumble like that; you fell right off the mine shaft, over six meters!"

Volodymyr looked down and saw his bruised body. A self-fulfilling prophecy. He had been so convinced he would go to the infirmary to be tortured that he went and did it himself. He started laughing, and then sobbing.

"Are you mad?" asked Ondar, looking over his shoulder.

He covered Volodymyr's face with a towel while one of the guards walked by.

"Is there anyone you can talk to?" Volodymyr stared blankly.

"There's a man, an old Tuvan shaman," said Ondar. "He may be able to help."

He scribbled on a piece of paper.

"Can you read?" Volodymyr nodded.

"Good, this is a map to his hut," said Ondar. "You must bring him a personal item, and fast for a day to purge all impurities, but I see you've already done the latter. He has an assistant named Kongar. He wears an eagle's claw necklace. He's a little grumpy, but he's just protective of the old man."

Ondar handed Volodymyr the note. "I'll give you your discharge papers."

Volodymyr gathered enough strength to grab Ondar's arm.

"*Spasiba*," said Volodymyr. *Thank you.* "I don't know your language."

"*Proshu*," Ondar replied. *My pleasure* in Ukrainian. "Our suffering is universal, my Ukrainian friend."

After leaving the hospital, Volodymyr found some strength in a new sense of purpose for his new mission. He made his way back to the barracks. It was their working shift and he knew nobody would be there.

He made his way to his bed and knelt down. Carefully, he felt along the boards of his hiding space and lifted them. He felt like something would jump out of the hole and attack him. He breathed a sigh of relief seeing Slipyj's crucifix still resting in its tomb. He still felt uncomfortable, looking at the image of Christ suffering on the cross. Or maybe, he realized that was how he was supposed to feel. He scooped up the necklace and quickly made his way out.

He zigzagged through the barracks and warehouses, avoiding the *vakhta* and watchtowers. He kept along blind spots near the outer *zona*, following the map Ondar gave him. Finally, he saw a middle-aged Asian-looking man smoking a cigarette by a shack.

He wore an eagle's claw necklace. It had to be Kongar.

Volodymyr didn't know how to approach. He suddenly remembered old caricatures of bowing Oriental monks. He didn't know how accurate they were, but he didn't have anything else to go on. He clasped his hands together and bowed to Kongar. Kongar stared at him menacingly.

"Are you Kongar?" asked Volodymyr.

He stayed silent.

"Ondar sent me," said Volodymyr, hoping that would illicit a response.

"Are you here to see the shaman?" asked Kongar in accented Russian.

"*Da*," said Volodymyr, straightening up, embarrassed.

"Did you bring your personal totem?" Kongar asked.

Volodymyr nodded and patted his *bushlat*.

"Then come with me," said Kongar, stamping out his cigarette.

Volodymyr followed, a little uneasily. Kongar led him into an increasingly isolated area of the camp. He thought it might be a trap when he saw a lowly *zemlyanka*, an earthen dugout hut with smoke emanating from a small chimney. They stopped at a small wooden door adorned with beads and an eagle's talon with feathers, emblematic of the renowned eagle hunters of Central Asia.

"Wait here," said Kongar, disappearing into the darkness.

After a while, Kongar reemerged in a cloud of smoke.

"You may enter," he said.

Volodymyr looked behind him uneasily. He entered the dark hut. Kongar closed the door behind them. The air was thick with incense. It was so overwhelming that Volodymyr almost fainted. His starvation diet added to his dizziness.

"Careful, or you'll fall into the fire," said Kongar, catching Volodymyr's arm.

Volodymyr then noticed a small, ashy fire in the center of the room. The light was disorienting, shining in through wood slats in the roof and turning the room into something like a kaleidoscope. Kongar eased Volodymyr down onto a small rug. Volodymyr felt the fluffy, pleasantly familiar texture of sheep's wool that he had all but forgotten about.

"This is the shaman," said Kongar.

Volodymyr's eyes adjusted, and he saw a small old Asian man hunched over the fire. He wore large eagle feather earrings and a flowing red robe that glowed with the coals. He looked at Volodymyr curiously.

Kongar nudged Volodymyr.

"Your item." The shaman slowly unfurled his ancient hand. Volodymyr reached into his *bushlat* and pulled out Slipyj's chain. He placed it into the shaman's hand. The shaman closed his eyes and brought it to his chest. He said something in Tuvan, and placed it on his prayer rug. He then held up a cup. All his movements were methodical, like he was moving in a different pace of time.

"Drink this *chifir*," said Kongar.

Volodymyr took the cup and hesitated. He'd heard about *chifir* being a very strong tea that could produce a type of narcotic high. He finished the cup and handed it back to the shaman.

"Now the ceremony begins," said Kongar.

The shaman poured water onto the coals and the room was enveloped with vapor, becoming like a *banya*, or sauna. The shaman began to sing *khoomei*, the traditional throat-singing of the Tuvan and Mongolian peoples. He produced a low rumbling drone that seemed to vibrate the entire room. Then he switched to an eerie, high-pitched whistle. Volodymyr had never heard anything like it. He began to feel numb in his face and limbs. He started to fidget nervously when Kongar steadied him.

"This is normal, just relax," he said.

Volodymyr slowly inhaled and exhaled the smoky air. He looked back at the shaman. Perhaps it was the smoke, lighting, or malnutrition, but it appeared to Volodymyr that the shaman was glowing. The shaman kept up his *khoomei*, and Volodymyr eventually drifted off into a deep, dark sleep.

He was floating back to the Carpathians. He was on a small raft paddling frantically against a rough current in the middle of a furious summer storm. The maelstrom grew rapidly until it was too great for his tiny raft. The tree beams broke apart on some large rocks and he was tossed over into a raging whirlpool. Volodymyr struggled and screamed, but nobody could hear him. The water gurgled into his mouth and he was sucked under, yet he did not drown.

He opened his eyes and realized that he had been transported to the train car shooting through the Kazakh steppes. Kateryna appeared in the other car. He reached out to her, but she was too far away. The train stopped and she disappeared into the distance. Volodymyr jumped out of the train car and chased after her, but his legs didn't work right.

Huge walls and wire suddenly sprung out of the earth around him. Then watchtowers and barracks appeared, and he realized he was back at camp. The sky turned from dark to a hellish red, fire and screaming enveloping him. The earth then ripped open and he tumbled to the bottom of the mineshaft with Kateryna and Stas and all his comrades. The sky opened up and a bright figure in the form of Saint Michael the Archangel descended to Volodymyr, handing him a spear with a tryzub tip.

Volodymyr ascended from the pit, and he was back to the bright blue sky above a golden polonyna in the Karpaty, where he saw a lamb perched atop a peak.

Volodymyr woke up in a cold sweat. He forgot where he was, at first. The shaman patted Volodymyr's face and placed Slipyj's chain back around his neck. He smiled and gave Volodymyr some water.

"How do you feel?" asked Kongar.

Volodymyr was silent for a few moments, trying to process the most vivid spiritual experience of his life.

"I feel like a great storm has parted in my mind," said Volodymyr, staring into the coals, "but I see dark clouds gathering on the horizon for us all."

7

MAY 16, 1954:

THICK AS THIEVES

"Stalin is dead, Beria is dead," said Sokil, "so why are we still paying for their crimes?"

The diverse congregation listened restlessly. The camp regime was out of control. Discipline and oversight of the guards had completely unraveled through further isolation and cuts in funding. It had gotten to the point that no one, not even the urka, was safe. Guards were simply shooting people for fun.

Such was the case when a poor old Chinese *zek*, who barely knew a word of Russian, was lured to a guard tower in the zona to retrieve a pack of *makhorka* when a guard winged him. A poor girl named Lida was shot for simply hanging out stockings on the boundary fence. Then there was the great incident when the guards opened fire on a column of zeks returning from the ore-dressing plant, seriously wounding several men.

Something drastic had to happen, lest they all eventually be wounded or killed in another "accident." The Ukrainian Centre had called a meeting of representatives of the different camp groups on Sunday, the day of rest, on what would become a fateful day—May 16, 1954. Volodymyr and Stas sat side by side among their UPA and Armia Krajowa comrades and the allied Baltic partisans.There was one significant addition to this meeting: urka. They were represented by a tough former Soviet first lieutenant named Gleb Sluchenkov. He was rumored to be a Vlasovite, a member of the anti-Soviet army of Andrei Andreyevich Vlasov, who was executed in 1945 by the Soviets after being handed over by the Americans. Sluchenkov was an imposing figure, still clinging onto his old uniform. He scowled at the politicals with his fearsome dark eyes. Sokil was up to the challenge.

Their tenuous truce with the urka these past few months had finally borne fruit. By working together, the politicals and urka were able to form a large and organized network that had infiltrated the camp regime. Most, if not all, of the camp regime informants were either dead or in hiding. Sokil had the floor at the moment for the Ukrainians.

"As we all know, there is only one outcome for escape," said Sokil, running his thumb across his neck, signifying death.

"So what do you suppose we do?" asked Sluchenkov.

"Something the camp regime would never expect," he replied. "We take the camp!"

The room was silent. Even the partisans were stunned. Volodymyr and Stas looked at each other in disbelief.

Sluchenkov smirked.

"And just how do we do that?""Together. All zeks, all nationalities," said Sokil.

"You really think we can unite all these different peoples, many of whom have been at war for generations?""What choice do we have?" asked Sokil. "The powers that be already tore us from our motherlands, threw us together, and expected us to thank them, hold hands, and sing the Internationale into the sunset!"

The zeks laughed. Sluchenkov fidgeted in his seat. He was clearly used to being the center of attention. "All kidding aside, this is a tall order, considering everyone involved," said Sluchenkov.

"I thought someone in charge could manage that," Sokil replied.

"I'm in charge," said Sluchenkov firmly.

Everyone began talking at once. Yammering tongues in dozens of languages were overwhelming the meeting when Sluchenkov stood up. Everyone quieted down.

"I'm in," said Sluchenkov.

"*Davay tovarishch*," said Sokil, extending his hand to the head urka.

"You're lucky I hate these bastards too," said Sluchenkov.

Everyone knew, no matter their own opinions, the matter was settled. They were all in. Finally, after decades of shared misery, the politicals and criminals were working together to improve their circumstances. It was Marxism at its finest.

"Right, let's get to work," said Sokil, unfurling a large map. "Our first objective is to capture the service yard. From there, we can spread out to the supply houses."

"What about the guards?" asked Sluchenkov.

"There are too few guards inside to get all of us. If we can create some sort of diversion, we can split up and move to liberate the women's camp before they get reinforcements."

"Leave the diversion to us," said Sluchenkov.

They hashed out a plan over the next hour. They would split up and divide and conquer the camp. They knew they greatly outnumbered the understaffed guards.

The urka would begin the assault in the afternoon after lunch, when the guards were less alert. The urka would be less severely punished than the politicals should things go wrong. They also had more freedom of movement in the camps and the guards paid much less attention to their barracks.

There was a spirit of comradery in the air they hadn't felt in years. They felt like free men. All of the men there knew the risks, but it was worth it. They figured they were dead already, so at least they would die free.

"So, it is agreed: From now on, we are politicals and urka no more, but one multinational army," said Sokil.

"*Da, tovarishch*," Sluchenkov agreed.

They dispersed and went back to their barracks to prepare for lunch and just desserts. Everything went by normally. The guards were not wise to their intentions, which meant that everyone had kept their mouths shut. Then, once the zeks departed for their barracks, the urka split off from the politicals to the storerooms and women's camp.

Scouts leapt up on the huts and roofs like nimble mountain goats guided by their commanders. They communicated with whistles and hollers in a well-coordinated formation to surround the *vovki*. The politicals, especially the former partisans, couldn't help but admire their skills in unconventional warfare.

"Oh, what could've been had we worked together earlier?" Volodymyr thought out loud.

There was no time to reflect, though. In one fell swoop, the urka leapt off the huts and clambered up the camp walls to the women's camp. With pipes and clubs in hand, they strode right up the main road to the service yard. The politicals were shocked by the lack of response from the guards, who normally seemed so eager to shoot anything that moved. Then, something even more outrageous occurred. The warders finally appeared and started running to the political. "*Davay tovarishchi*," said a frantic guard. "The thieves are in the women's camp! They are going to rape your wives and daughters!"

Some of the politicals who weren't in on the plan started to come forward, taking the bait, when they were stopped by the others who were wise to what was happening.

"Have you lost your minds?" asked the guard, flabbergasted.

He soon gave up and ran off. The urka *were* doing their job beautifully—too well, in fact. Eventually, the Wart emerged with a platoon of hastily organized guards to meet them. Rather than risk an unnecessary bloodbath, the urka retreated back over the walls with scouts covering their retreat by throwing rocks and firing slingshots at the guards.

If it had been the politicals—especially the anathema western Ukrainian, Polish, and Baltic trinity—there would almost certainly have been bullets flying rather than curses. For the class-allied urka, however, the incident was deemed overzealous mischief. The rest of the day went by without much incident.

Dinner was served and, amazingly, there was a movie shown afterwards about the Russian dissident composer Rimsky-Korsakov. It was a mild May night and the film was being played outside by the mess hall. Several large spotlights illuminated the perimeter around the zona. Volodymyr, Stas, and Leonid were seated near the edge of the screen by one of the spotlights. The lights were so bright they could barely see the screen.

"Why do you think they're treating us to a show?" asked Stas, using his hand as a visor.

"I think it's more to calm their nerves," said Volodymyr, checking out the guards.

A *vovk* was nervously tapping his foot, a *nadziratel* kept checking his rifle chamber, and the *naryadshchik* from the mines was drenched in sweat from chain-smoking. The movie went on for a while without much commotion, but between the blaring lights and poor film quality, the zeks also started getting restless.

Someone in front stood up.

"Hey, why don't you turn down the lights?" "*Da*, we can't see the screen," said another *zek*.

"Sit down and shut up, or we'll stop the film," said a guard.

Rimsky-Korsakov started playing the piano.

"*Davay tovarishch!* Sing us a tune, any tune," said a *zek*.

"If you don't shut up, I'll sing you a funeral hymn," said the guard, pointing his rifle at the man.

One of the lamps by Volodymyr popped and went out. They were startled, but the light was ignored. Such malfunction was not unusual. Then, another light went out, and another, and another. It was clear this was no coincidence, but sabotage.

High-pitched whistles broke out from all directions. They knew the urka *were* back working their magic. At the crescendo of the movie, when Rimsky-Korsakov is expelled from the tsarist conservatory, the lights went out. They heard a low rumbling and then a mighty crash.

"They're breaking into the service yard," said a *zek* excitedly.

It was the catalyst that ignited the zeks' fury. Pent-up years of rage overflowed and burst their banks. One by one, the zeks leapt out of their seats, their fists raised to the guards. The moment they had all been waiting for had finally arrived: The Kengir Uprising had begun!

"For the Motherland!" screamed Leonid.

"*Allah birdir! Allahu akbar!*" the Tatars and Chechens screamed. "-*Makhmadera!*" Others cheered the Kazakh war whoop.

"*Slava Ukraini!*" the Ukrainians roared.

Whatever the language, the zeks unanimously decreed they had had enough! Animosity between the urka and politicals was brushed aside. Their mutually hated floggers were the targets for retribution.

The guards fired a few shots, but they were overwhelmed and retreated. The zeks rushed forward like a great rogue wave to meet their comrades trying to break down the service yard gate.

"I can't believe it, brother," said Stas.

"Believe it," said Volodymyr. "Let's help our other brothers and sisters!"

They charged forward to the service yard. Dozens of zeks grabbed a large beam, using it as a battering ram and smashing the gate to pieces. They then turned to the women's camp.

"I'm coming, Kateryna," said Volodymyr.

Volodymyr and Stas saw a growing contingent of zeks at the entrance to the women's camp. They were all on the same wavelength. Men and women stood together.

"*Davay brattya!* Let's liberate our sisters," a man said.

Volodymyr and Stas could hear the women shouting and knocking on the wall. There was a zek crew handling a section of railway line. Volodymyr and Stas grabbed each end. The poetic justice of using the same train line that brought them to bondage to liberate their comrades was not lost on them.

"Stand back, ladies," a man shouted.

"All aboard, gentlemen," said a Ukrainian. "Last train to Kengir!"

The men charged full steam ahead with the huge metal beam and rammed the brick and mortar wall. The force of the impact sent shockwaves through all their bodies. The wall crumbled and sent a plume of dust and debris flying in all directions.

At first, they didn't know if they had been successful, but when the dust settled, they saw the glorious sight of their women emerging to embrace them. The men embraced their sisters. Some men were being reunited with their actual sisters, daughters, and wives. Volodymyr looked frantically through the rubble when he saw the angel.

"Kateryna!" Volodymyr cried.

She turned and screamed with joy, "Volodymyr!"

They ran through the rubble and embraced, crying tears of joy into each other's arms.

"I thought I'd never see you again," said Volodymyr.

"But I knew you would," Kateryna laughed, then cried.

They held each other in their arms, trying to make up for two long months. Volodymyr looked back. He turned to Stas, who was keeping patient vigil just behind.

"I don't believe you two have met yet, but this is my good Polish *tovarishch* Stas," said Volodymyr.

Kateryna turned to meet Stas, standing in the rubble while others darted past.

"*Pryjemno*, Stas," Kateryna smiled. "I've heard so much about you."

"As have I," said Stas, blushing.

Volodymyr was brimming with joy—his best friend and lady finally meeting—but the chaotic events around them didn't allow much time for sentimentality. In the ensuing chaos, they heard sporadic bursts of fire. They looked over to realize their worst fears. A platoon of armed soldiers had broken into the service yard.

"Stand down or face the consequences," Belyaev bellowed through a megaphone.

"Go to hell, you *Chekist* bastard," said a *zek*, referring to Lenin's Soviet secret police.

Belyaev nodded to one of the soldiers.

"*Ogon*," said the soldier. *Fire.*

The soldiers opened fire on the unarmed zeks. Urka and politicals alike fell in droves. Their screams and the endless, horrible puttering of the machine guns sent them all into a panic. Zeks were running in all directions.

"We have to find my friend Kasia," said Kateryna. "Follow me to my barracks."

She grabbed Volodymyr and Stas and lead them into the women's camp. They weaved their way through the maze of barracks, dodging frantic zeks and stray bullets. Finally, they reached her barrack.

"Come on!" she yelled over the deafening gunfire.

They threw open the door and ran inside.

"Kasia! Kasia!" Kateryna called frantically in the darkness.

Volodymyr and Stas went to the window and watched the ensuing scene. The zeks had erected a huge barricade between camp sections two and three, which divided them from the guards in the service yard. They could hear the exchange between the guards and zeks. The guards fired several volleys into the air.Nobody knew what to do. It appeared that both sides were at an impasse. Then, they noticed somebody climbing up the barricade. Slowly but surely, an emaciated *dokhodyaga* scaled the piles of logs, rubble, wire, and steel. Everybody looked on in shock, including the guards. After an excruciating climb, he went over the top. Belyaev put the megaphone to his mouth.

"If you do not cease, we will enter by force!" The man tore open his shirt, revealing his protruding ribs, and roared, "Then you will have to go through me!"

His words rallied the zeks, who cheered wildly. His bravery showed the zeks that even a man with one foot in his grave could stand up to the Soviet behemoth. More climbed up to join him. The zeks began hurling rocks, bricks, and finally one man threw a Molotov cocktail that exploded by some guards, igniting a supply house.

The guards were outnumbered and were forced to retreat. They turned their ire to the more lightly defended women's camp. Volodymyr and Stas ducked under the window. Kateryna was still upset about Kasia.

"Oh, Kasia, where are you?" Kateryna moaned.

"The guards are coming," said Volodymyr.

"We have to get out," said Stas.

"No," said Kateryna. "We're going under!"

She ran to a corner of the room and started stomping on the floor. They assumed she had gone mad with grief. She then bent down and lifted up a huge wooden pallet and slid it over.

"Get inside," she commanded.

Kateryna slipped into a large dugout in the floor. Volodymyr and Stas were hesitant, but they had little choice. They could hear the guards closing in. They held their breath and leaned back. Kateryna pulled the large board over, sealing them in.

They were pressed shoulder to shoulder with less than a foot between them and the floor above. It felt like they had dug their own grave. Kateryna turned her head to Volodymyr.

"I got the idea from you," she said.

Volodymyr was both flattered and horrified. He didn't have much time to think. They heard the door swing open and several stomping boots rush in.

"Check every bed," said a gruff Russian voice.

The guards began completely ransacking the place. Their boots were right on top of them, cracking and crunching the old wooden boards. A bed frame came crashing down, shaking the whole barrack.

"Keep looking," said the guard.

Dust and dirt flew into Volodymyr's nostrils, and he sneezed.

"Stop," said the voice.

Everything stopped, including the three of their hearts.

"Oh God, I deserve to die, but not my friends," Volodymyr prayed.

Something outside attracted the guards' attention. They rushed out the door. The three hideaways breathed a sigh of relief, but they knew it wasn't over.

The guards left the door open in their haste. They could hear the horrors unfolding outside. The moaning of the countless wounded was horrible enough, but then worse. They heard bloodcurdling screams followed by grunts and shouts, and then silence. The warders and Red Guards were going around finishing off the wounded. It was something out of the darkest episodes of the war they had all thought was behind them.

They sat there in stunned silence. All night long they heard the moans turn to screams and then into deafening silence. At one point, the cabin turned an eerie reddish hue and they could smell smoke, but they felt no heat. They were still too afraid to leave the relative safety of their spider hole. Eventually, dawn did rise.

8

MAY 17, 1954:

SCRATCHES ON A

PRISON WALL

"I THINK IT'S OVER," said Kateryna.

Slowly, they opened their crypt. It was eerily quiet. They crept through the empty barrack, expecting the guards to rush at any time, but no one came. They mustered the courage to look out the door. They had seen much, but they were shocked by the damage.

The barracks were scorched and strafed with bullet holes from the ferocious firefight the night before. They turned and saw they hadn't imagined the strange sights and smells. The cabin right next to them had burned to the ground. They each genuflected.

They inched out the door. Feeling some breathing room, they walked several paces when they saw three dead zeks right by the gate and a few further away just beyond the wire. Most of them had been killed by the indiscriminate hail of bullets, but some bared marks of blunt-force trauma and bayonet wounds.

The zeks' expressions ranged from contorted agony to strangely serene, depending on how they had died. Some of them reached out to each other. It didn't matter if they were urka or political; their bonds were sealed in blood now. The three of them wanted to get out of there as quickly as possible and make it to the zeks' barricades in Camp No. 3. There was no turning back after this bloodbath. They ripped a piece of white cloth and attached it to a singed beam from one of the barracks. Then, they slowly approached. Someone appeared over the barricade.

"Halt, who goes there?" asked a young *zek*.

Volodymyr and Stas nudged Kateryna. They thought a woman would be less threatening. She coolly approached the nervous young zek with her hands raised at her sides.

"We're *zeki*," said Kateryna.

"I'm just supposed to believe you?" he asked.

"Let them in, Nazar," said a familiar voice.

To their great relief, they saw Sokil. The young zek hesitated but eventually relented. The three of them quickly rushed into the barricades should the jumpy young zek change his mind. Sokil patted Volodymyr and shook his and Stas's hands. The young guard still stared.

"Don't mind, Nazar. He's a good boy," said Sokil. "Glad you could make it, Baran, Stas."

Sokil paused, turning to Kateryna. "Ah, Soloveyko!"

Kateryna saluted. Volodymyr smiled now. Stas looked confused. Volodymyr leaned toward him.

"She's a soldier too.""Now I see the attraction," said Stas, playfully nudging Volodymyr.

"We can talk inside the barricades," said Sokil. "The guards are sure to return."

They entered the gates of the large barricade, like passing through the great walls of ancient Kyivan Rus. They only hoped their walls would not share the same fate as when Batu Khan sacked Kyiv. History still weighed heavily on all of them.

Despite the tension, there was a sense of comradery born out of their terrible ordeal. They were at war again, and they knew they were on the right side of history. Zeks of all sexes and backgrounds were busy at work, but this time of their own free will. Politicals and urka, side by side, manned the barricades with improvised weapons as diverse as they.

"Make way for the wounded," said a zek, followed by more zeks brought in on makeshift stretchers.

"This way to the hospital. I think Nacham could use our help," said Sokil.

They saw carnage and chaos out of the First World War. Volodymyr remembered such harrowing stories from both his grandfathers. There was a makeshift field hospital set up in a series of improvised tents. Tables were set up in rows with blood-soaked rags laying helter-skelter among the wounded and dying. Zeks were running frantically, trying to wipe down the blood from the tables before placing another patient down.

They noticed a young Polish woman, judging by a makeshift sweatband in the Polish colors, scrubbing down a table. She turned around, wiping her perspiring forehead. Volodymyr was struck by something familiar when Kateryna screamed, "Kasia"! The woman looked up, and her whole face smiled.

"Kateryna," she cried.

They hugged each other tenderly.

"Oh, *diakuyu Bozhe*," said Kateryna. Thank God. "I thought the worst when you weren't at the barracks!"

"I'm so sorry, Kateryna," said Kasia. "They changed my shift to the infirmary at the last moment when this whole thing blew up. The bodies started pouring in by the minute!"

"We had to hide from the guards," said Kateryna, turning to Volodymyr and Stas. "Vlodko and his friend Stas helped me."

"Ah, the famous Vlodko," Kasia smiled. "And Stas you said? Is he . . ."

With a smile, Stas said in Polish, "*Dzien dobry.*" *Good day.*

"*Dzien dobry, dzien dobry,*" Kasia laughed. "So good to hear our mother Polish!"

"I-I remember you from the train," Stas stuttered.

"Oh, *tak*, that's right," said Kasia excitedly.

She shook Stas's hand. He shook hers, blushing. She turned back to talk to Kateryna.

"You said *I* was too shy with the ladies," Volodymyr whispered to Stas.

"I haven't had much practice these past few years," said Stas.

They carried on in their own world when reality came knocking. Nacham appeared in a blood-soaked smock trying to make sense of the madness. Sokil ran up to him.

"Nacham," he called.

Nacham kept on giving incoherent commands.

"Nacham," said Sokil, louder.

Nacham jumped.

"Oh sorry, I didn't know you were there," said Nacham, wiping his face.

"Is there anything we can do?" asked Volodymyr.

Nacham just stared out at the scene blankly before finally replying.

"We could use some disinfectant and stitching equipment from the shops. And any kind of food and water."

"We'll see what we can do, brother," said Sokil, patting Nacham on the back. "Hang in there. You're doing God's work, just like during the war."

"I don't think this is God's work," said Nacham, exhausted.

A flustered zek ran up to them and saluted Sokil. Volodymyr recognized him from the UPA meeting in the fall. His call name was something about being light on his feet.

"Ah, Shvydko," said Sokil. *Quickly.* "What's the news?"

"The guards are approaching," he said.

"We'll be back, Nacham," said Sokil.

Nacham didn't react. They quickly followed Shvydko to the barricades, where there was a flurry of activity. Sokil made his way up over the top. Volodymyr, Stas, Kateryna, and Kasia followed just behind.

Outside, they saw army construction battalion soldiers known as "black tabs," judging by their uniforms. They reluctantly approached the bodies still lying on the yard. The camp guards were overseeing them. The zeks were furious, but none more so than Sokil. He stared at fallen Ukrainians that he felt personally responsible for overseeing.

"Halt," said Sokil. "What are you doing to our fallen comrades?"

The guards and workers froze. They didn't realize anyone had seen them. A few of the workers ran, but the guards stayed put and reluctantly faced the zeks.

"We are removing the deceased for processing," said a guard.

"You mean to hide your crimes?" challenged Sokil.

The guard was stunned. Even the zeks were surprised by Sokil's bluntness. The guard nervously wiped his perspiring forehead.

"We have orders," he replied. "We are not the ones responsible for killing these men."

"You're all responsible," said Sokil sternly. "At least show them some respect in death!"

The fury of the zeks was palpable. The guards did something

surprising, perhaps out of respect, or more likely fear. They removed their caps and held a moment of silence. It was a small albeit important gesture. They gently carried off the bodies and retreated beyond the zona.

A zek scaled up the barricade. They recognized him as a newly arrived Ukrainian priest. This time, he had been properly vetted by UPA with confirmed credentials as a combat veteran. His name was Otets Mykola. He removed his own cap and began the Ukrainian-Slavonic funeral hymn: "*Vichnaya Pamyat*," or "Eternal Memory."

His rendition was extra poignant, especially in the hospital tent. One by one they began singing, and it got louder, so loud that the guards and soldiers in the zona surely heard it. Their united voices echoed through the camp in homage to all their fallen.

The non-Christians also solemnly paid their respects, each saying a short prayer in their respective faiths. Religious differences were set aside while they extolled their dead. It was the great irony that tolerance found a place in their tyrannical society among their recidivists. When the singing was over, Shvydko clambered back up the barricade like a mountain goat. He pointed excitedly in the distance.

"Valeriy picked up a signal.""*Davay*," said Sokil.

They clambered down the parapets. Zeks ran back and forth trying to figure out what to do next. They had forgotten about their exhaustion and terror; they were running on pure adrenaline. Shvydko lead them over to a humble wood shack.

"Careful of the wires," said Shvydko, gingerly opening the door.

Only then did they notice the tangle of wires jutting out from the door and roof. Slowly, they tiptoed in and saw Valeriy back at what he knew best. He was listening intently to the radio, frantically turning various dials and knobs. The radio was a large hunk of metal surrounded by a mesh of wires and antennae protruding from every angle all throughout the room. It felt like they were in a spider's web.

"Valeriy has been listening all night," said Shvydko. "He said there's a lot of radio chatter. News of our revolt has reached the brass in Karaganda, Alma-Ata, and even, very possibly, Moscow!"

Valeriy lifted his finger into the air. "I hear something!"

Other zeks started crowding around the tiny hut, eagerly craning their necks to hear what their tormentors had to say. There was a lot of static at first; all they could hear was mumbling. Valeriy adjusted a wire and it came in crystal clear: "Repeat: Zek revolt in Kengir Steplag, stop. Casualties reported, stop. Request assistance from Moscow, stop."

They were stunned.

"So, it's finally happened," said Sokil. "We've reached the Kremlin."

Outside, they heard commotion again.

"We have control of the mess hall," said the young zek guard from the barricade.

They knew their hold on the camp was tenuous, and that if they were to consolidate their control, they had to act quickly. They also realized it was a great opportunity to help Nacham and the patients. Sokil turned to the group.

"Alright, let's send a team out." He eyed Volodymyr.

"Of course," Volodymyr saluted, turning to his friends.

Stas, Kateryna, and Kasia agreed.

"Godspeed," said Sokil.

They quickly left the hut and made their way to the barricade. The young zeks trusted them now, eagerly letting them through. They quickly and quietly made their way to the mess hall. They treated it as a reconnaissance mission. Volodymyr knew three of them had military training, but he wondered about Kasia.

Kateryna was confident in Kasia's abilities. She kept pace with them and didn't make a sound. They kept to their side of the camp for as long as they could and then rushed through no man's land between them and the zona, carefully trying to keep out of range of the watchtowers still under the camp regime.

They reached the mess hall and beheld another surreal scene. There were zeks freely milling about without a care in the world. Just above them, anti-Soviet slogans and banned flags and banners fluttered outside the hall in the May breeze. Two zeks stopped them.

"Who are you?" one asked.

"We are zeks," said Volodymyr.

This was the first time in Gulag history that such an identity was advantageous. The two other zeks looked them over skeptically when someone called out, "Let them in; they are *tovarishchi*." "Greetings, comrades," said Leonid.

"Leonid!" Volodymyr laughed. "We thought the worst when we got separated. What are you doing at the mess hall?"

"I'm in charge of distribution," said Leonid proudly. "Apparently I'm one of the most trustworthy *starostas* here, and least likely to steal!"

He led them inside. The atmosphere only got stranger. It started to feel more like a carnival than a revolt. Countless banners and flags hung from the rafters and walls with outlawed slogans and symbols. The Lithuanian, Estonian, Latvian, and Polish flags flew proudly alongside the banner of the Sultan of the Crimean Khanate. The skull and crossbones flag of the Ukrainian Makhnovite anarchists was draped over the food court, along with the national blue and yellow Ukrainian flag and the red and black flag of Bandera. Several zeks then unfurled a large pre-communist Russian national flag.

Various messages were scratched into the prison walls in all the different languages of the camp. Their words of defiance read: *Arm Yourselves as Best You Can, Attack the Soldiers First, Bash the Chekists, Boys!* Perhaps the most threatening of all: *Down with the Stoolies, the Cheka's Stooges!* Leonid went into the kitchen and came back with a large bowl of fresh soup and bread for them.

"Like I said, we are in charge now," Leonid laughed, plunging a large ladle into the bowl.

The zeks were boisterous with good cheer. Several circles had formed, different nationalities intermingling. Such comradery was unheard of in the Gulag. One of the older politicals, a professor from Leningrad, was giving a lecture.

Volodymyr was finally happy, laughing with his woman as his best friend talked it up with his woman's best friend. He was lapping up the soup and scenery. Nobody knew how long it would last. Volodymyr turned and saw Sokil had finally made it. He picked up some black bread to give to Sokil when he saw him whispering animatedly with Lylyk and Shvydko. Sokil turned to the room.

"*Uvaha*," he called.

Volodymyr's stomach sank. Everyone quieted down. Sokil had gained quite the reputation, even among the non-Ukrainians. He continued, "We have intercepted a message about the highest delegation from the camp regime coming to meet us, including General Bochkov of Gulag Headquarters and his deputy General Vavilov, who oversees Kazakhstan. They will report what they find to Ivan Dolgikh, head of all the Gulag."

The zeks were stunned. This was real now. They had to figure out what to do next.

"Who will speak for us?" asked a young Russian.

"Well, definitely not one of these Banderists and the like," said another Russian.

"Oh, like you Vlasovites are any better?" said a Ukrainian.

"What about the Tatars and Chechens?" asked a Muslim zek.

"Don't make me laugh," another cackled.

Everyone started shouting at each other. Sokil hurled a large ceramic bowl. It sounded like a gunshot reverberating off the cavernous walls. Everyone froze.

"Now that I have your attention, we can stop behaving like zeks and act like men. Many of you are veterans of the Great Patriotic War, and the enemy is once again knocking at our gates. Now rise up together like you did before!"

Sokil cleverly used the Soviet name for World War II to get the Russians onboard. Indeed, many of the urka were veterans of the *shtrafbat*, Soviet penal battalions inspired by the Nazi *strafbataillon* that had fought in the war.

Shvydko ran into the middle of the room. "They have arrived."

"It's time," said Sokil.

The zeks rose up and marched forward like good soldiers again. Many of the urka had actually taken up their former roles as officers, rallying their men behind them. The politicals were pleasantly surprised. They marched alongside them. Their fates were one.

They approached the barricades when they noticed the women marching right along. They met up, creating a united front to the zona. It was a scene out of the 1917 Revolution. The zeks approached the zona and were cautiously optimistic about the lack of soldiers. The gates opened and the delegation entered. There were several dapperly dressed men in clean uniforms and, unbelievably, they saluted the zeks. Times had changed.

"Greetings, *tovarishchi*," the lead man said. "I am Kapitan Vinovich from the general staff of General Bochkov. We are here to discuss your concerns."

There was an audible gasp among the zeks. *Concerns? Comrades?* They weren't calling them rebels or fascists? The men mulled about, nervously trying to figure out what to say when a shout came from the women.

"Murderers!" "What's this?" asked Vinovich.

"We want justice for all the killings of men and women," said another woman.

"Who?" asked Vinovich. "Which killings, *tovarishch*?"

"The same beasts that beat and rape us," cried other women.

"It can't be," said Vinovich, exasperated.

"*Pravda*," they said. *It's true.*

The zeks grew bolder. Anything seemed possible. They kept up their momentum.

"We want the new walls torn down," a man said. "Men and women together!"

"Take our numbers away. We are people with names and families," shouted another. "And we should be able communicate with our families like any other prisoners!"

"We want Belyaev out," Volodymyr shouted, surprising even himself.

This was met with thunderous cheers and applause from the zeks.

People wondered who was brave enough to come forward and represent them. Kateryna appeared.

"*Pryvit, tovarishch Kapitan*," said Kateryna. *Greetings, comrade captain.* "I am Kateryna Petrovych Zemlya."

"*Privyet, tovarishch* Kateryna Petrovych," said Vinovich. "Who is Belyaev?"

"Kapitan Belyaev is in charge of this camp," said Kateryna. "We demand his removal for gross abuse of authority, and the release of all zeks wrongfully detained in the SHIZO."

"It will be done," said Vinovich.

9

MAY 18, 1954:

THE WALLS COME DOWN

"VICH-NA-YA PA-A-AMYAT" tolled solemnly through the procession making its way through the camp to the morgue. In Eastern Slavic tradition, many zeks kneeled before the passing coffins, although many were just too weak or injured to stand properly. The zeks had gathered the imprisoned priests of Kengir, of which there were plenty, to perform the full traditional funeral ceremony for all the deceased prisoners still in the camp compound. The bodies taken by the guards two days before had been buried in haste to hide their crimes. The zeks were allotted this one token for their dead. Religious ceremonies were banned under Soviet law, but the zeks were adamant, and the guards didn't have enough reinforcements.

Christian clergymen of various denominations led the procession. It was quite an accomplishment. Whether they made the sign of the cross right to left in Orthodox fashion, or left to right like the Catholics and Protestant Lutherans, they were Christian brothers nonetheless, extolling their dead.

The guards stood by with their weapons drawn, yet, here and there, a guard would quickly genuflect when the procession passed. The morgue was a damp, cold, and foreboding room packed to the brim with emaciated corpses. Volodymyr passed by a fallen Ukrainian comrade he recognized from Mordovia.

"I'm sorry, brother," he said. "We did not forget about you."

Behind him, the Muslim imams were washing the feet of their dead, side by side with the Jews and their rabbis reciting the Kaddish, the Hebrew prayer for the dead. The Soviet state's atheism made religious authorities readily available in the Gulag. In some ways, it was easier to find a priest in Kengir than outside the wire. Volodymyr was still uneasy being around clergy since his Easter ordeal.

The guards had promised to leave the zeks alone for the day, so long as they got back to work. After the ceremony, the zeks had their lunch and went off to the mines and workshops. Volodymyr and Kateryna were about to part ways for the first time since the uprising began.

"You were incredible, standing up to the guards like that," said Volodymyr.

"I got strength knowing you were behind me, my dear, brave Vlodko," she replied.

She leaned in and kissed him. He grabbed hold of her, feeling her every curve, absorbing every fiber of her being. He hadn't felt so good in years.

"I'll see you soon, *kokhanna*," said Volodymyr.

They laughed and kissed again before heading off. It didn't feel like they were in prison, more like they were normal people again going off to work. There were no *nadzirateli* or *vovki* breathing down their necks. When they reached the mines, they didn't see any guards at all, not even a *naryadshchik* setting inhuman quotas to fulfill.

Each nationality chose representatives as foremen. They set their own pace and worked with pride. In fact, they even sang while they worked, breathing life into their lost homelands. The Ukrainians made up a popular song that all the zeks had come to know by heart:

"We will not, we will not be slaves,

We will not carry the yoke any longer . . .Brothers in blood, of Vorkuta and Norilsk,

Of Kolyma and Kengir . . ."

At the end of the day, they may not have extracted quite the same level of material, but there were no serious injuries or deaths, and no machinery, men, or women broke down. They marched back to the main camp with energy never seen before—until they reached the zona. The *nadzirateli, vovki,* and warders had returned.

They surrounded the workers.

"Move, you damned zeks," they said, pushing them along to the mess hall for dinner.

The zeks certainly didn't trust the camp regime, but they were genuinely surprised by how suddenly they had reverted to their old ways. Volodymyr strained to see the camp interior and saw guards, soldiers, and even officers donning work clothes and frantically working. He then realized the wire they were traversing had been refitted and the broken lamps repaired. Something was dreadfully wrong.

They corralled the zeks through the doors of the mess hall. The guards were edgy, quickly and roughly prodding them along. When they entered the dining area, the zeks became even more unnerved. Guards were behind the counter with the staff, like back in March. Volodymyr looked over at a guard. He didn't recognize him.

"What're you looking at, *zek?*" the guard asked mockingly.

They moved forward to the counter. The staff looked nervous and sweaty. Their eyes were darting back and forth between the zeks and the guards. Volodymyr held out his plate. The urka plopped down an old potato. He quickly tried to give Volodymyr some more, but the guard would have none of it. He smacked the cafeteria staffer's ladle to the floor. It fell with a sharp crash, rattling the whole line.

"Move it," said the guard impatiently.

They sat down and quickly slurped down their slop. The guards were constantly checking their watches. The whole routine was off. The loudspeaker then came on.

"*Vnimaniye, vnimaniye*," the loudspeaker crackled. "There will be early bedtime tonight. Head straight to your barracks, and do not leave for any reason!"

"You heard the man upstairs. Dinner's over," said a guard.

They all quickly gathered up their belongings and shuffled out the doors. The guards hastened them along to their barracks. One of the zeks protested and was quickly taken away. More began to protest, and they too were promptly whisked off. Volodymyr and Stas looked again to the compound and saw the walls had been partially repaired in haste. They all realized what was going on. They had been tricked, and now they were being trapped! Shrieks and whistles started breaking out among the urka. The politicals knew what it meant.

"We have been lied to," said a *zek*. "Revolt!"

The zek then struck a guard. That was the end! Two guards pounced on the brave *zek*, but the other prisoners, having tasted freedom, would not have it stolen away again. Volodymyr and Stas grabbed hold of one of the guards and pulled him off. Several more zeks came to their aid. The guards were outnumbered.

"Retreat!" called a guard.

The guards and warders took fright and fled to the zona. The zeks saw their chance and stormed the barricades once again. The urka archers took aim and took out the lights. This time, however, the guards were more prepared. The soldiers fired flares and lit up the camp. Everyone's faces glowed with an eerie, ghostly aura. They saw several flashes from the watchtowers, followed by a series of popping sounds. They realized to their horror what was happening, yet again.

"Incoming," said the zek that first struck the guard.

It would be the last thing he ever said. He jerked back and fell to the floor. Volodymyr and Stas ran for cover. Flares were raining down all around them.

"We have to find Kateryna!" Volodymyr yelled.

"And Kasia," said Stas.

Volodymyr nodded firmly in agreement. They charged through the mayhem to the workshop where many of the women worked. Flashes from the flares illuminated the frightened zeks and guards running frantically in all directions. Nobody could tell who was who. Bullets and slingshots ricocheted off the lampposts.The workshop was finally within reach when a zek tossed a Molotov cocktail over their heads. It burst into flames, igniting the *vakhta*. The guards ran back to the zona. Volodymyr and Stas dashed through the door. A group of women inside screamed. They calmed down when they saw the men were fellow inmates. Volodymyr looked around the room and called to Kateryna. She ran happily into his arms.

"*Diakuyu Bozhe*, we thought you were guards," she said.

"Kateryna, what should we do with the prisoner?" asked Kasia.

"Prisoner?" asked Volodymyr.

The group of women parted to reveal a young guard bound to a chair with a sock stuffed in his mouth. He thrashed in the chair. Volodymyr and Stas were shocked. The man was mumbling something. Volodymyr pulled the sock out of his mouth.

"You could have given me a clean sock, at least," the guard gasped.

"Who are you?" Volodymyr demanded.

"I am First Lieutenant Quartermaster Medvedev, and if you don't let me go, we're all dead.""We'll be the judges of that," said Kateryna.

"You Banderists won't get away with this," Medvedev spat.

Volodymyr shoved the sock back into his mouth, then he walked to a nearby table. There was a small razor on the table. He grabbed it and went back to Medvedev, who jerked back in fright.

"I'll cut you loose, but you're coming with us," said Volodymyr, cutting the rope holding him to the chair.

He then put the razor to Medvedev's throat.

"You try and run, you better hope you get shot." Medvedev solemnly nodded. Volodymyr pulled the sock out of his mouth, but they kept his hands bound. Volodymyr and Stas grabbed hold of his arms and brought him to the door.

"*Davay zek*," Volodymyr sneered. "Now you'll have a taste of your Soviet justice."

They marched out into the night. The eerie lights from the flares sporadically lit up the chaotic camp. All of the women kept a steady pace toward a large crowd gathering in front of the zona. They knew women were less likely to be shot at.

"Make way," said Kateryna. "We have a prisoner!"

Everyone immediately parted. They stared at Medvedev like he was from Mars. They had never seen a guard so vulnerable. The other zeks began getting uncomfortably close.

"You bastard," said a man.

"Fascist," said a woman.

"You'll get what you deserve, you devil," said another.

Luckily, some of the veterans got between them so they could pass through. Eventually, after some cajoling, they made it to the front of the angry crowd. There were several guards on the barricades above shining flashlights.

"Who goes there?" asked a guard, shining a flashlight into Volodymyr's eyes.

"We have one of yours here," said Kateryna. "Let our people go, and we'll give yours back."

"What are you hens clucking about?" asked the guard.

They then produced Medvedev. The guard was stunned. He started swinging his flashlight wildly.

"You got held up by a bunch of *suki*, Medvedev?" the guard cackled.

"At least I stayed at my post," Medvedev retorted.

"We demand safe passage for our wrongfully detained comrades as promised by our earlier agreement," said Kateryna.

"What agreement?" asked the guard.

"From Kapitan Vinovich," said Volodymyr.

"I never heard of any Kapitan Vinovich," said the guard mockingly.

The zeks were at a loss. They knew then and there they had been duped. The situation was deteriorating. They debated whether they should give up their one ace.

"Give us Medvedev, and we'll see what we can do," said the guard.

"We want to see our comrades," countered Kasia.

"They are incarcerated for their own protection at the moment," said the guard. "Give me Medvedev, and I will release them."

"How can we trust you?" asked Stas.

"Do you have a choice?" the guard replied.

They reluctantly agreed and cut Medvedev loose. He walked through the gates to the relative safety of the guards.

"*Ogon!*" yelled the guard.

They then opened fire over the zeks and retreated to the zona.

"Charge!" one of the zeks yelled.

So began the second zek revolt. The four friends were swept up in the maelstrom of prisoners. They crashed into the walls kicking, screaming, and clawing at the wood and steel.

Someone started passing around picks, axes, and shovels. Volodymyr hacked at the wooden support beams with an axe. He'd honed his lumberjacking skills from a lifetime of hard living in the dense Carpathian forests. Stas tore into the earth with his pick like a mad Polish miner. Kateryna and Kasia dug furiously with their shovels.

Their ranks grew by the minute. Soon enough, there was a hole just wide enough for a slender person to pass through. Kasia slipped in. There were a few tense moments of silent dread, thinking the guards had gotten her, when she poked her head back in.

"The coast is clear. The towers have stopped shooting," she said.

Stas sunk his pick into the ground and dug in with his hands. Volodymyr and Kateryna followed right behind. They emerged on the other side, uniting all the camp divisions and the service yard. The guards had indeed stopped shooting, and they'd left plenty of tools in the service yard in their haste to retreat.

There was a mighty eruption of hurrahs from the zeks.

It was not over yet, though. There were still the SHIZO prisoners. The four friends picked up their tools and rushed forward to join their comrades charging the SHIZO.

"Volodymyr, Stas, Kateryna," they heard.

They then saw Leonid with a group of *starosta*. He was running like a young man holding a large pick and an even bigger grin. They embraced.

"I thought you all were goners," said Leonid, looking over the unfolding scene. "Can you believe it?"

"It's not over yet," said Volodymyr.

"Of course not," said Leonid, turning to the rest of them. "*Davay tovarishchi!* Let's free the rest of our comrades. Storm the Reichstag!"

The sound of their fury was deafening. Thousands of feet pounded like thunder rumbling through the steppes. It was like a mass cavalry charge by one of the great Khans. The steppes were on fire. They put the fear of God into the guards.

It was the first time in Kengir's history that zeks tried to break into the SHIZO. They approached the SHIZO zona, and paused. They still feared the guards could come back any moment. They stared at the maze of barbed wire and watchtowers surrounding the imposing brick building. Little by little, the zeks started hearing strange sounds. They soon realized they were coming from inside the SHIZO.

"*Davay tovarishchi*, you're almost there," their incarcerated comrades cried.

Volodymyr grabbed a rock and started pounding on a lock. Others soon followed. Stas started hacking at the beams. They charged at the SHIZO. The floodgates of humanity had been breached and the wave of zeks crashed against the gates.

"*Davay* Baran, is that all you got?" he heard.

Sokil was standing with Nacham and several other men holding a huge severed beam. Volodymyr called over Stas, who was also trying heroically but failing to open the heavy gate. They grabbed each end of the beam. They dug in and charged full steam ahead.

"Incoming!" Sokil yelled.

The zeks parted way for the demolition team and their battering ram. They slammed into the gate and it gave way. It fell with a thunderous thud. The zeks poured in.

"*Vpered brattya!*" a Ukrainian cheered. *Forward, brothers!*

They charged the steel doors and struck with all their might, but they fell back.

"Again," said Sokil.

They backed up and struck the doors again, to no avail.

"Look up!" someone yelled.

Lylyk was climbing in through a broken window with the help of Shvydko. After a few moments, they heard locks and bolts clicking and turning on the other side. Then, the door opened and there appeared a smiling Lylyk.

"This bat still has wings," Lylyk laughed.

"I knew they couldn't break you," said Sokil, lightly patting Lylyk's shoulders. "*Davay Kozaky*! Storm the castle!"

The zeks poured into the narrow, winding hallways, pressed shoulder to shoulder against the bars and walls. Their cheers and shouts mixed with those of their ecstatic SHIZO comrades. They broke into the cells, smashing the locks with whatever they could. They all embraced their released comrades with equal joy, no matter who they had been before. They were all aboard the same wayward ship.

Volodymyr kept moving forward. He saw some zeks trashing a clerk's office. They set a trash can on fire and started throwing papers into it. Nacham stopped them.

"Don't burn their documents," said Nacham. "This is proof of their crimes!"

They understood. The Nuremberg trials were only a few years before, and they knew every bit of evidence had counted against Hitler's war machine. The same mostly illiterate zeks stared helping Nacham gather up the papers.

Volodymyr saw an open cell door. He gingerly entered. Inside was mostly dark except a dim lightbulb suspended above a steel table with two chairs on either side. The room reminded Volodymyr of the *osobye lagerya* he'd spent some time in with Stas before they were shipped off to Kengir. It still gave Volodymyr chills thinking about the endless nights in solitary confinement after ceaseless interrogations. After a while, he hadn't known if it was day or night, or if he was even alive.

Volodymyr approached the table and saw a hammer. He looked closer and realized the hammer still had traces of blood on it. They knew people were tortured here, and disappeared. This bloody tool was yet another burden of proof.

Volodymyr saw something glinting in the corner of his eye. He saw a picture frame. When he looked closer, he was instinctively frightened at first, but his fear quickly boiled over into rage when he saw the smiling moustache of Joseph Stalin. He thought about his imprisonment, the destruction of his family, and the millions of his people murdered by this madman.

Volodymyr grabbed the hammer and, with all his strength, smashed Stalin's face into a thousand pieces. The frame crashed to the floor. He stomped on it, over and over. He then punched it until his fists turned bloody. Someone grabbed his shoulder. Volodymyr whipped around and saw several zeks.

"Easy, *tovarishch*," said the man in a heavy Lithuanian accent. "When you're done killing Stalin, can you bring your hammer to help us free our commander Knopkus?"

"*Tak, davay.*" "Follow us," said the Lithuanian.

Volodymyr wiped the broken glass off his knuckles. He turned around one more time and looked at the broken, bloody mess of Stalin's face on the floor. He spat on it.

"That's the last of my people's blood you'll ever take," said Volodymyr before following the Lithuanians out the door.

They started down the hall.

"My name is Gitanas. I'm from Vilnius," said Gitanas, referring to the capital of Lithuania.

"I'm Volodymyr, from *Ukraina*." "Hence the mutual affection for Comrade Stalin," Gitanas laughed. "We're almost there—the special ward."

The corridor narrowed significantly, and the cells were much farther apart.

"Here he is," said Gitanas.

Volodymyr saw a typically tall, lanky Lithuanian man with sharp pointed features adorned in a tattered uniform.

"We're back, sir," Gitanas saluted.

Knopkus saluted back, looking uneasily at Volodymyr's hammer.

"We can smash open the door," said Gitanas, pulling Volodymyr over.

He lifted up the giant metal lock. It looked like something from the Dark Ages. Volodymyr didn't know what to think.

"Unfortunately, the guards busted off the key in the lock, but if we strike exactly at the point of the door hinge, we can open it," said Gitanas.

The hammer started feeling heavier in Volodymyr's aching, swollen hands. He started sweating a bit. He knew he wasn't the best candidate for this task, but he knew someone that could be.

"My Polish friend Stas was a miner," said Volodymyr. "He could strike a pinhead on a needle. I'll find him!"

"Hurry back," said Gitanas.

Volodymyr turned to find Stas. It was pandemonium in the SHIZO. There was hardly any room to move. Volodymyr tried to listen for people speaking Polish, but there was so much noise it was hard to even hear himself. Luckily, he saw Stas's Polish commander Ignatius.

"Kapitan Jerzy," said Volodymyr.

"Ah, Baran!""Do you know where Stas is?" asked Volodymyr.

"*Tak*, he went to the special ward to help free a Polish officer and friend of mine," Jerzy replied.

"*Dziekuje*, Kapitan," said Volodymyr, turning back to where he had come from.

Volodymyr ran back and saw Stas with some other Armia Krajowa. He grabbed Stas. Volodymyr was huffing and puffing.

"What's wrong, Vlodko?" asked Stas.

Volodymyr had no breath to explain. He pulled Stas along, charging headfirst until they reached Knopkus. There, Gitanas was standing with a large spike. Volodymyr pointed to Gitanas.

"He'll explain," Volodymyr gasped.

"The lock has been jammed," said Gitanas, holding out the hammer. "We need someone to strike precisely and with enough strength at the hinge to open the door."

Stas grabbed the hammer.

"Who will hold the spike in place?" he asked.

For this task, nobody was eager.

"I will," said Volodymyr, catching his breath.

"You sure?" asked Stas.

"Just do it," said Volodymyr, grabbing the spike and pinning it against the door hinge.

"Alright, don't move a muscle," said Stas.

Volodymyr stared at the hinge. *Bang!* Stas struck the spike, and nothing happened. *Bang!* Ever so slightly, the hinge bent. Stas wiped his hands for the coup de grace. *Bang! Bang! Bang!* The hinge broke and the door fell down with a mighty thud. Knopkus emerged from his dank, dark cell like Dracula from his crypt.

"*Dziekuye, diakuyu,*" said Knopkus, thanking them in Polish and Ukrainian.

Down the special ward hall, they heard yet more commotion.

"Make way for Kapitan Kuznetsov," said a Russian.

There appeared an impressive, uniformed Russian officer. He was unwashed and unshaven, yet he was poised and confident. Volodymyr knew these men were important.

10

MAY 19, 1954:

A NEW DAWN

IT WAS A NEW DAWN. The loudspeaker crackled on. There was a low, ethereal humming.

"*Allah-a-ahu Akbar,*" the imam sang.

The barrack doors sprung open. The Muslim zeks poured into the open. It was time.

"*Hayya 'alas-Salah,*" the imam continued. *Come to prayer.*

Volodymyr, Stas, Kateryna, and Kasia emerged from their Christian barracks in disbelief. They beheld an otherworldly sight. The Muslim zeks got down on their hands and knees and bowed southwest to Mecca, many with tears in their eyes. Even the non-Muslims were mystified by the sound of the *adhan*. It was a clear sign that the camp regime had left.

The pain of the imam's people weighed on his quivering verse. The

Muslim communities of the Soviet Union had been struck multiple blows after the war amid Stalin's purges and then Khrushchev's anti-religious policies. They couldn't help but shed tears for these poor people.

"Now we ask for a moment of reflection for inmates of all faiths, especially our Tatar brothers and sisters that have perished on the tenth anniversary of the *Sürgünlik*, one of the great crimes committed by the Soviet regime against our Tatars by exiling them from their Crimean homeland," said the imam.

After the imam was finished, the Muslims stayed prone until they were ready. The entire camp was silent; even the steppes were still. The zeks waited intently for what seemed like more to come. Everyone held their breath.

"*Uvaha, uvaha,*" said a crackly voice.

Despite the static, Volodymyr recognized Sokil's voice. Kateryna, Stas, and Kasia were just as excited. Men and women had taken to the same barracks since the chaotic nights began. Not a single case of rape or assault had occurred in their sector, despite the guards' constant haranguing about mass debauchery.

"Please rise for the hymn of *Ukraina*," said Sokil.

They heard more loud murmurings. This was also impossible. In addition to the Soviet ban on religion, there was also a ban on nationalist songs. Soon enough, they heard a choir begin to play the outlawed Ukrainian national anthem. Originally written in 1862, the anthem had become popular during the Ukrainian War of Independence (1917-1921) and during WWII among Ukrainian patriots in Ukraine and its large diaspora, especially in America and Canada.

"*Shche ne vmerla Ukraina, ni slava, ni volya,*" the chorus sang. "*Ukraine has not yet perished, neither its glory nor its freedom.*"

Volodymyr and Kateryna placed their hands on their chests and sang from their hearts. Though their throats were choked with emotion, they belted out their glorious anthem. Even Stas and Kasia started getting teary eyed, seeing their friends so moved. The final stanza came and Volodymyr cried, thinking about his father and dido that first taught him this song.

"And we will show that we are brothers of Cossack mettle," they sang.

The four of them laughed with joy. Volodymyr and Kateryna kissed each other. They and the hundreds of recently freed SHIZO prisoners felt something they had all but forgotten: Hope.

"Please stand for, *'Jeszcze Polska Nie Zginela,'*" said Jerzy. *"Poland Is Not Yet Lost."* Now it was Stas's and Kasia's turn. Written in the late 1700s by exiled Poles during the Third Partition of Poland between Russia and the Habsburg Empire, the Polish national anthem had inspired the Ukrainian national anthem and many other Eastern European countries. They too sang it with passion and grace. Stas smiled while Kasia happily wiped tears from their faces.

"Today is the first day as free men and women," said Sokil. "Please report to the courtyard when you are ready for orientation."

"When we're ready!" Volodymyr laughed.

They walked out into the courtyard. The watchtowers were empty. Singed, broken lampposts were leaning against the mangled wire of the zona. It was surreal not having guards berating them every step of the way. The simple act of free movement made them all feel dizzy and giddy.

It was not unlike taking their first steps. They felt like new people. The inmates greeted each other as comrades, not miserable zeks. They were actually friendly without the threat of reprisals. The zeks laughed and cried, many strangers hugging each other. Inmates of all genders, ages, and backgrounds convened around the courtyard. There was great excitement in everyone's eyes.

Finally, the de facto zek delegation arrived. The imam led the way with Sokil, Nacham, Jerzy, Leonid, the other *starostas*, and Sluchenkov. Just behind them were the two mystery military men from the SHIZO.

"*Assalamu alaikum*," said the imam to the crowd. *Peace unto you.*

The Muslims touched their foreheads and bowed in an ancient gesture of respect. The imam then turned to Sokil. He bowed and touched his forehead in the same respectful gesture.

"*Assalamu alaikum*," the imam said to Sokil.

"*Wa ⊠alaykumu s-salam*," said Sokil. *And unto you peace.*

The zeks were stunned, especially the Muslims. Ukrainians and Tatars had also had a complicated relationship as both enemies and allies of opportunity. Historical barriers, like the camp walls, had also gone up in smoke.Tatars were among the original Eastern nomadic invaders that ravaged ancient Rus and the early Muscovy principalities after the fall of Kyiv in the mid-1200s and into the 1600s during the Khmelnytsky Uprising. They had allied with Khmelnytsky and the Ukrainian Cossack armies against the Poles for a heavy price of slaves and gold. The Tatars would continue to shift their allegiances back and forth throughout the war and the turbulent times to follow known as "the Deluge" in Poland, and "the Ruin" in Ukraine. Their greatest threat had always been Russia, which wound up devouring all three nations.

"Welcome to the dawn of freedom," said Sokil. "We have a lot of work to do to keep it."

"*Tak tovarishchi*," said Jerzy. "Today is a day of rest and reflection before we regroup to discuss our next course of action. Stay tuned for more announcements. God bless us all."

A Central Asian man, judging by his turban, walked out into the middle of the courtyard.

"Slaves no more," he said. "*Allahu Akbar!*"

He then ripped off his number patch. This seemingly simple act sent shock waves through the zek ranks. One by one the zeks began tearing off their own patches, reaching a feverish pitch. Volodymyr was only too eager to shed his shameful foreign attire.

"*Slava Ukraini*," said a Ukrainian. *Glory to Ukraine.*

"*Heroyam slava*," the other Ukrainians replied. *To her heroes glory.*

Yet more unbelievable outlawed slogans out in the open. It was almost too much to bear. The blinding light of day revealed just how long they had been in the dark. Kasia began stepping on her own patches. They all laughed and joined in.

Sokil and Jerzy saw the four of them and walked over. Stas shot up a salute. Jerzy happily returned it, but was more focused on Kasia.

"Ah, you have met our brave doctor Kasia," said Jerzy. Jerzy proceeded to shake her hand. She smiled and blushed. They were all surprised, even Kateryna. She turned to Kasia.

"I didn't know you were a doctor," said Kateryna.

"Well, not exactly, I mean I was in medical school when the war broke out," she replied.

"*Tak*, don't be bashful, and from my hometown of Przemyśl nonetheless," said Jerzy.

Volodymyr and Kateryna were even more surprised. Przemyśl had a painful history, including with the struggle between Ukrainians and Poles. The city had been devastated in both world wars and experienced widespread ethnic clashes between Ukrainians and Poles. They were surprised Kasia was so friendly to Ukrainians.

Sokil stood patiently waiting in the background. He looked tired but resolute. He was finally in charge again.

Volodymyr turned to him.

"That was a fine sermon, sir." "Perhaps I can be ordained if this doesn't all work out," Sokil laughed.

Volodymyr couldn't help but notice the two SHIZO men

accumulating their own admirers including, surprisingly, Sluchenkov. They were still in rough shape from their isolation, but they looked to be in good spirits. Sluchenkov was especially interested in meeting the former Red Army officer. There seemed to be a mutual intrigue.

"Who are those two men?" asked Volodymyr. "Stas and I helped free the Lithuanian."

"Ah, you mean Knopkus and Kuznetsov," said Sokil. "*Tak,* they are important men. Kapitan Kuznetsov is a former Red Army colonel. He was jailed because one of his men escaped to West Germany under his command. He was accused of 'slanderous accounts of camp life' thereafter during his imprisonment."

The three of them were a little surprised by Sokil's relationship with a Soviet officer. He must be important.

He continued, "The other man is indeed a Lithuanian commander: Yuriy Knopkus. He was involved in the Norilsk uprising. A brave man," Sokil said admiringly.

They understood this reaction. The Baltic peoples were well respected among the Ukrainians. These small nations had played an outsized role in the postwar order. They had also been brutalized by the Soviets, with hundreds of thousands of their citizens deported and imprisoned after the war, like the Ukrainians.

"We'll have to reconvene at some point; I must be off to plan our next moves with the others," said Sokil.

"*Tak,* until later, *tovarishchi,*" said Jerzy.

Sokil and Jerzy headed off to join the other leadership, including Kuznetsov, Knopkus, and Sluchenkov. The camp was swarming with activity. Despite their tragic losses, new life had been breathed into the browbeaten zeks.

Something else grabbed their attention.

They caught a flash of bright color and realized people were casting off their prison clothes and replacing them with their street clothes and traditional attire retaken from the storerooms. The Slavs had on their embroidered *vyshyvanky* shirts and puffy fur *kuchma* and *ushanka* hats. The Central Asians donned their turbans and bright robes. It was like a grand bazaar.

"*Dobri udry, dobri den,*" Leonid laughed. *Good day* in Russian then Ukrainian. "That was a fine speech from our *Otaman* Sokil, no?"

Leonid had a large puffy *kuchma* and a gray long-coat.

"I haven't worn one of these since the war," said Leonid.

Volodymyr had a flashback to his dido when he'd brought out a captured Russian soldier's uniform from WWI.

"There's my tailor," Leonid laughed, greeting an Asian man who came over carting a pile of colorful clothing. He was adorned in a large turban and orange robes. "*Davay,* let's get these zeks back into real clothes!"

Kongar then motioned to the cart.

Tucked away in back was a thick, colorful woolen Hutsul *kyptar* that looked nearly identical to Volodymyr's old one. Volodymyr snatched it up. He felt the thick, matted, layered wool and traced the latticed pattern down its sides. He thought of home and nearly cried. Kateryna caught his tears.

"We're not home yet, but it's a start," he said.

Kasia gave them both a *rushnyk.*

"Only tears of joy today," she said.

She then started off, turning impatiently.

"Come with me to our barracks, dear friends."

She grabbed Stas by the hand. He blushed, and they took off.

Leonid laughed.

"Well if that isn't a happy couple and my cue to shove off. I'll see you all in due time."

"*Kanyezhna,*" said Volodymyr. *Of course.*

"Ah *dobre, dobre,* my Ukrainian friend," said Leonid.

Kongar bid Volodymyr adieu in his subtle way before patting his chest rather strangely before he left.

"Did you know him?" asked Kateryna.

Volodymyr didn't need to say it out loud. Kateryna understood. She saw it in his eyes.

"Let's join our friends, shall we?" she said.

"I'll be right there," he replied.

Volodymyr felt something strange near his chest. He reached into his vest and pulled out an eagle charm necklace. Volodymyr looked around to see if the shaman was around. Although he couldn't see him, he knew he was watching. Volodymyr ran to catch up to Kateryna. It was surreal seeing the zeks moving freely about and intermingling. Men and women strolled along as if on a date in the park.

It was like a grand international bazaar with vendors and merchants. Although they had no money, an ad hoc bartering system had formed, along with many promises—"Hey, if you give me that coat, I'll be *dezhurnaya* for a week. The barracks will be spotless!" He saw a Tatar trading a Slav a turban for a *kuchma* with great fanfare.

Despite the comradely atmosphere, there was a significant portion that did not participate, mainly the SHIZO inmates. They were still wary about this strange "zek revolution" and its sustainability. Volodymyr understood them too. They had been so traumatized, so betrayed by previous promises that they did not even dare taste freedom again lest it be snatched away.

Imprisonment takes many forms, including that of the mind. Volodymyr had delved into that terrible void in Mordovia, when Slipyj had saved him from certain doom in the *psikhushka*. He still shuddered when he thought about how close he had come to the abyss.

Kateryna shook him out of his trance.

"Come on, *kokhanna*. We'll be late for Sunday lunch!""Of course, *druzhyna*," said Volodymyr, Ukrainian slang for *wife*.

"What was that?" she laughed.

He stopped.

"Are you alright?" she asked.

"*Tak*, I'm fine, let's see our friends," he replied.

Volodymyr wasn't sure, though. It was a slip of the tongue while he was caught up in the moment. It was what he used to say to his wife when they were first married. These were more intrusive thoughts that he knew he would have to tell Kateryna about. That was for another time though; everything was moving so fast.

"Here we are," said Kateryna excitedly.

Kasia ran out.

"Welcome, *Ukrainski tovarishchi!*" "If my grandparents ever heard that," Stas laughed.

They entered the barracks. Volodymyr felt like he was returning to a crime scene. There were still faint blood stains outside from the bodies of the first night of the revolt. He stepped on the creaking floor, and he immediately shuddered as he remembered the pattering of the guards over their heads.

Kasia had made up her side with the new embroidered *rushnyky*. He looked closer and picked up a picture of a young girl with two young men, an older man, and a woman dressed in traditional clothing. Kasia put her hand on their faces.

"That is my family: My mother, father, and two brothers: Jacob and Janusz. I haven't heard from them in a long time." Kasia sighed.

"Kasia, how did you wind up here?" asked Volodymyr.

She stopped.

"I'm sorry, it slipped out," he said. "You don't have to say anything you don't want to."

She was silent, but she relented.

"No, there shouldn't be any more secrets. Everyone here has suffered." She stared out the window for a moment.

"It was just after the war in the ruins of my village near *Ukraina*. The Russians were everywhere, and they appointed a real ogre of a commissar to our village."

She paused, gathering her thoughts. Stas sat beside her. She didn't seem to notice, lost in her thoughts.

"Well, this man, if you can call him that, took a real liking to me," she said bitterly. "I refused his advances. So he went to my father, who also refused, saying that I was already engaged, which wasn't true, but he didn't know what else to say. The commissar was furious and arrested us, claiming we were subversives! We were shipped to all corners of the East, and I haven't heard from anyone since."

She was shivering, staring at the guards' now-empty *vakhta*. Stas put his coat around her. "*Dziekuje*," she said. "The man who attacked me this winter was his brother, if you can believe it. They followed me all the way into hell."

There was a knock at the door. Kasia jumped. Stas and Volodymyr stood up.

"Is anyone home? *Tovarishchi*?" asked a man.

Only a prisoner would talk like that. Volodymyr gingerly opened the door. A *starosta* stood there smiling.

"*Privyet tovarishchi*," he said. "We are gathering together in the mess hall to elect representatives. We need everyone we can get."

"*Da*, we will be there," said Volodymyr. The man then looked to Kasia, who was quickly trying to dry her tears.

"Don't cry, child. All tears dry up and storm clouds disappear," said the *starosta*.

He then closed the door.

Kasia wiped her face and brushed herself off. She stood up and resolutely walked to the door. She paused briefly and then pushed open the door.

"Come on, then. We don't have time to wallow in self-pity."

11

MAY 19–22, 1954:

THE ELECTION

THEY FOLLOWED KASIA out the door. It had started to feel cramped in those barracks so choked with memories. They followed the growing contingent of zeks to the mess hall. Kasia led the way while Stas tried to keep pace. She wasn't the giddy girl they had met. Perhaps that wasn't really her at all.

"She'll be alright," said Kateryna. "She gets in these moods."

Volodymyr wasn't so sure. He knew what it meant to be in a mood, and it wasn't anything to laugh about. Their training kicked in in such moments and they had to soldier on. How long they could go on this way was another question. Everybody had a breaking point.

Soon there was a mess of men in front of the hall. Several young *zeks*, led by Nazar from the barricades, were trying to keep order. Nazar was flustered.

"*Bud laska, please*, one at a time," said the Ukrainian zek in front of the doors.

He saw Volodymyr and smiled at the familiar faces and let them pass. Eventually, the rest of the inmates settled down enough for them to enter. The cavernous halls echoed with a cacophony of dozens of languages. The entire hall was packed. Some of the recently freed SHIZO inmates waited cautiously in the rear, biding their time, perhaps to relay what transpired to their skeptical comrades.

Handmade flags of all camp nationalities fluttered in the twinkling overhead lights: Ukrainian, Russian, Polish, Lithuanian, Latvian, and Estonian. A banner of the light blue and yellow *tamga* emblem of the disbanded Crimean Khanate and the red, green, and white flag of the Chechen Republic of Ichkeria were also present.

The packed hall spilled into the courtyard. Anti-Soviet slogans were still scrawled on the walls from the previous days. It felt like the early days of the revolution. Then, the loudspeaker turned on. Everyone instinctively quieted down.

"*Uvaha, uvaha*," said Sokil. "The first election of zek representatives has begun."

"What the hell does that mean?" someone shouted.

Many in the hall started laughing. Jerzy appeared next to Sokil. He took the megaphone.

"It means it's time to take the initiative and create our own authority.""Who gave you authority?" asked another.

The laughing died down and the discussion became more heated. Who was in charge? The heady early days of their revolution were fading, and the hard truths of realpolitik were dawning on them. They wouldn't get much further without a solid plan. Sokil and Jerzy tried to regain control of the floor when the zeks at the door started parting.

"Make way for the kapitan," said a *zek*.

The hall quieted down again. It was Kuznetsov. He was escorted by several burly men including, surprisingly, a Ukrainian partisan Volodymyr recognized as Mykhailo Keller. Keller had once publicly axed a zek informer. He was no Soviet sympathizer. Kuznetsov entered the center of the ring. Sokil handed him the megaphone.

"Who the hell are you supposed to be?" asked the heckler.

"You will address me as Kapitan Kuznetsov.""You and what army?" the heckler sneered.

"The Soviet Army of the Combined Western Front," said Kuznetsov, "and if there is another outburst, it will be dealt with accordingly!"

The man knew he was serious and shut his mouth. The politicals were all naturally wary of any Soviet figures, even ones on the outs with the authorities. The Russians in attendance clapped loudly for him. The response from the others was noticeably muted, but they nonetheless understood his value, though cautiously.

"*Tovarishchi*, we must stop with these provocative nationalistic statements," said Kuznetsov. "Anti-Sovietism will be the death of us! We cannot permit such behavior on the part of a few provocateurs!"

The hall grew even more animated. Everybody had something to say, but didn't know how. They descended into name-calling and finger-pointing again.

"He's the provocateur!" said a Polish *zek*.

"Shut your mouth, dumb Polak," said a Russian.

Stas was visibly upset by the rude Russian. Another uniformed man stepped into the fray. Sokil and Jerzy looked relieved. Volodymyr did too when he saw the Lithuanian.

"What is this, a circus?" asked the heckler. "Who are you?"

"I am Kapitan Knopkus. I was involved in the brave but ill-fated Norilsk uprising, so I know how these events can turn out if we are not careful! Kuznetsov is the Soviet face that will give us legitimacy."

"That Chekist?" asked a *zek*, exasperated.

"Shut your mouth, Vlasovite," said another.

This outburst drew the wrath of the politicals. Volodymyr saw things were getting out of control. He started scanning the hall for a quick exit. Those in the hall were close to blows when Kuznetsov hurled a plate against the wall. The shattering ceramic sounded like a gunshot and the zeks froze.

"It is time to stop acting like sniveling zeks and be men," he said. "This ridiculous infighting will be the death of us! We must present a united front if we are to get anywhere."

"I concur, *tovarishchi*," a man said. "All of these frivolous nationalistic proclamations and infighting is exactly how we will be divided and fail!"

Volodymyr recognized him as one of those red-blooded Orthodox Soviets—not to be confused with the religious, but just as zealous.

"Who are you supposed to be?" a man asked.

"I'm Makeyev, just a humble, good Soviet citizen like yourself," he replied.

"I'll bet," Sluchenkov sneered. "That's why you're locked in here with us!"

The zeks laughed boisterously.

"Say what you will, *tovarishch*, but that is the truth," said Makeyev. "Let's not sink into slanderous accusation like in Beria's time!"

"*Da*, it's the Beriaites! Long live the Soviets! Bread! Liberty! Peace!" said a man, yelling slogans that harkened back to the early days of the Russian Revolution. The Russians and communists stood up. Someone began singing the Soviet anthem:

"*Soyuz nerushimyj, Rezpublikh svobodnykh,*

Splotila naveki, Velikaya Rus."

The Russians and communists all started singing along, including Kuznetsov. Volodymyr shuddered thinking about those opening lines—the "indestructible union of 'free' republics, united forever by great Russia."

The non-Russian politicals stood by, passively resisting by remaining silent. They begrudgingly knew that Kuznetsov was right about his strategy, though, at least for now. Once they quieted down, Knopkus took the floor again.

"My men are behind you. We will prepare defensive measures and a fallback position should heavy weapons be employed, but I highly doubt the camp regime have such capabilities," said Knopkus. "I think we are ready!"

This was met by thunderous applause from the non-Russian men.

"All this talk about what the men want," a woman called out. "What about us?"

The women in the hall started cheering and clapping, including Kateryna and Kasia. The men were a little surprised. The woman who called out was named Lyuba Shakhnovskaya, a former economist and communist party member.

"*Da, kanyezhna*, we hear you, Miss Shakhnovskaya," said Kuznetsov.

"Don't belittle me with bourgeois titles," said Lyuba. "Soviet doctrine grants all sexes equal rights, *tovarishch kapitan*."

"Then let us vote!" said Sokil.

It was an incredible act, to vote. After years of being told when to eat, sleep, even when to relieve themselves, they were now able to decide their futures, even if it was just for the next day. Several zeks went around with ballot boxes, paper, and pencils.

"Anyone who cannot read, please tell the pollster who you vote for," said Sokil.

Illiteracy was still prevalent in the Soviet Union, especially among the urka. It was these "class allies" that the Soviets so coveted, however. Volodymyr again remembered his dido's words about when slaves attained power, but he shook those words off. They had no other choice. After hours of counting, recounting, and a recess lasting through dinner, the results were in.

Sokil read out the results:

Supreme Commander: Kuznetsov

Agitation and Propaganda: Knopkus

Internal Security: Gleb Sluchenkov

Military: Oleksa Zalizniak (Sokil)

Technical: Valeriy Pavlovich

Food: Leonid Kotlin

Services and Maintenance: Lyuba Shakhnovskaya.

"Then it is decided," said Kuznetsov. "Now to the barricades, *tovarishchi!*"

The zeks disbursed to reinforce their positions. Volodymyr and his friends waited behind. They were among the more skeptical.

"You know how much Soviet promises are worth," said Volodymyr.

They nodded solemnly. "Time is up. It's up to fate now," said Stas, turning warily to Kuznetsov, "and Kuznetsov."

They exited the hall and heard a hearty "*tovarishchi!*" They turned to see an exuberant Leonid. He motioned for them to follow.

"*Idi i smotri,*" said Leonid. *Come and see.*

They followed him around the corner of the hall.

"Look up," said Leonid.

They looked up. High upon the hall flew a white flag with a red cross in the middle surrounded by a black border. Leonid saluted.

"The international maritime code for ship in distress," said Leonid, wiping away a tear. "The men of Kronstadt live on!"

Volodymyr looked at the fluttering flag and wondered, *would* they live on? Indeed, they all wondered where this was all headed. Who was the captain of this zek mutiny on the high plains? Much of the core Ukrainian Centre had not even attended the meeting, but they knew they all had to work together. Whether they liked it or not, they were all in the same miserable boat.

The next day they got to work. The Commission, as they became known, worked in the women's camp. The Military Department, where Sokil and the other zek brass met, had its command center near the bathhouse in Camp No. 2 near the SHIZO. They took advantage of the more heavily fortified walls.

The zeks got to work repairing the camp. Volodymyr and Stas were part of a construction brigade; their backgrounds in carpentry and mining were well suited of their new tasks. Kateryna and Kasia were in the same battalion making tools in the workshops. They were able to see each other during breaks. To think they even had breaks!

The progress was impressive. In the short amount of time since they had overthrown their tormentors, they had created a formidable defensive. There was much military and engineering talent. Ironically, much of the best and brightest of the Soviet Union were withering away in prisons. Now, they had purpose again.

The camp looked like a medieval fortress. The zeks dug trenches along the outer perimeters of the zona and reinforced the walls. They wrapped a sea of barbed wire just behind, should the walls be breached. They even created booby traps by rigging trapdoors and pitfalls and creating an assembly line of Molotov cocktails.

There were rows of *yizhaky,* or hedgehogs, crisscrossed iron beams created by the Czechs and used throughout WWII in urban defense. They were welded together from the myriad of scrap iron in the camp. There were even examples of psychological warfare, such as the proliferation of signs saying, *Danger! Mines!* With the number of capable scientists and engineers in the camp, the authorities would have to take these signs seriously. The zeks themselves were unsure if there were really mines or other explosives, so they stayed clear of those areas too.

There was some hesitancy against taking such defensive measures; many of the Russian military thought any resistance against a full-frontal assault would be futile, but the politicals and urka, especially Knopkus and Sluchenkov, insisted. Keller was in charge of organizing security, and he organized the zeks into *kurin* groups of up to twenty. Having been former combatants, many of the politicals were quite comfortable with this arrangement. The urka were more resistant, but with the thoughts of their dead comrades fresh in their minds, they too fell in line.

One curiosity was the creation of mixed-gender patrols, which had stemmed from the idea that men would act braver to protect their women. Most of the women were Ukrainian, and many of them were former partisans. They naturally fell in line and taught their comrades.

Volodymyr and Stas were working with a construction crew where they had broken through the wall the first night. Stas was stamping in the very hole he had dug. He wiped his brow and laughed.

"Looks brand new—the perfect crime."

"It seems strange, doesn't it?" said Volodymyr.

"What does?" asked Stas.

"Repairing our prison." "You're quite the character," Stas smirked. "A philosopher warrior."

"Is Vlodko the new Plato?" asked Kateryna.

Volodymyr and Stas turned around to see their Helens of Troy.

"We have fresh bread from the kitchen," said Kasia, handing it to a famished Stas.

They also passed them tea, something once reserved only for the camp staff and stoolies. Volodymyr looked at the swirling dark tea, thinking of the shaman's *chifir* and his visions. He noticed Kateryna looking at him curiously.

"Is everything alright, Vlodko?" "*Tak, tak,*" said Volodymyr, slurping down his tea.

He didn't realize it was still fresh and he burned his tongue, but held his composure. He didn't want to tell Kateryna about his doubts. He wanted to hold onto these precious moments.

"How's the work coming along?" asked Kasia.

"We've done a great job repairing the zona," said Stas.

"Baran?" a man asked.

They all turned and, to their surprise, saw Keller. He was an imposing figure with his stern gaze focused unmistakably on Volodymyr. He knew exactly who he was looking for, but he wanted Volodymyr to acknowledge him.

"*Tak*," said Volodymyr, a little hesitantly.

"Come with me," said Keller.

"What do you need him for?" asked Kateryna.

Keller shot a stern glance at her.

"That is not your concern, Soloveyko—yours or your Polish friends," said Keller, turning to Volodymyr. "There's no time to waste. *Davay.*"

Volodymyr followed him. He turned back to his friends with a brave face. They smiled back reassuringly, but they knew something serious was happening. He followed a little bit behind Keller.

Keller had an unmistakable gait. His right arm hugged his side when he walked. Most assumed his peculiar walk was a result of a war injury, but there were rumors that it served a more sinister purpose. They said Keller had learned much from his detention by the KGB. Their agents would often walk in such a way to quickly draw their sidearm. Whatever the explanation, Keller was a force to be reckoned with. They walked farther and farther into the zona. Volodymyr's stomach sank when he realized they were approaching the "minefield." Keller stopped.

"Follow me." "These mines aren't real, right?" Volodymyr laughed nervously.

Keller stayed silent. Volodymyr swallowed hard. There was a narrow pathway leading to a nondescript hut. Each step felt like a ticking time bomb. Volodymyr thought this was a pretty extreme way to keep a charade going, but he wasn't about to test that theory.

They approached the door. Inscribed in tiny print it read: *Technical Dept.* in Russian. There was a sign adorned with a skull and an electrical bolt along a large fence surrounding the hut that read: *High Voltage.* Volodymyr looked nervously at the imposing surroundings when Keller's sharp knock on the door startled him.

"*Khto tam?*" asked a voice. *Who's there?*

"Keller." There was a pause. Multiple locks turned. The door opened, and Volodymyr was relieved.

"Ah, glad to see you, Baran," said Sokil.

"You too, sir," said Volodymyr, eyeing Keller in his periphery. Keller was unmoved.

"Come in, Baran. Your Valeriy doesn't cease to amaze me." Volodymyr entered the hut. He saw Valeriy and some other men and women huddled around a network of wires and a large device. The setup was even more elaborate than the already-impressive system used to intercept the initial messages just a few days ago. The radio was blaring in the background. The cramped room felt like a bomb shelter. Volodymyr knew that was not just for looks.

"*Pryvit,* Baran," said Valeriy, not taking his eyes off a delicate wire he was soldering to a large metallic box fitted with a myriad of knobs and dials.

"Glad you got past the minefield," Sokil laughed.

Volodymyr also laughed, expecting to be let in on the joke, but Sokil did not elaborate.

"We want someone as trustworthy and brave as you to be part of the security apparatus," said Sokil.

Keller continued to stare ahead, stone-faced.

"What would I have to do?" asked Volodymyr.

"Nothing that you aren't capable of," Sokil replied.

Volodymyr felt a little uncomfortable, thinking suddenly about the priest. Sokil seemed sense his unease. He placed his hand on his shoulder.

"Nothing like that," he said gently.

Volodymyr felt slightly relieved.

"Eureka!" Valeriy exclaimed.

They rushed over to the beeping and flashing contraption.

"We've been trying to create our own self-contained communications system," said Valeriy. "We just received a message from the other hut!"

"What does it say?" asked Sokil.

Valeriy scrolled through it excitedly and then paled.

"It says they have reason to believe that the camp authorities are trying to sabotage the power in the camp," said Valeriy. "I'll just send them a message that we haven't seen any proof of that on our end."

Valeriy began furiously tapping out the message when there was a loud buzzing sound followed by a large boom. Their radio sparked and shut down. They opened the doors and realized, in the pitch-black night, that the lights had gone out in Kengir.

12

MAY 23–24, 1954:

THE ZEK ULTIMATUM

THE ZEKS HUDDLED around candles and lanterns in the dimly lit mess hall. They were trying to make out as much as possible of their "Prisoners' Manifesto" in the disappearing rays of the setting sun through the windows. Volodymyr and their group were straining to see what was being written.

They heard a humming noise, and everyone stopped. The lights above them began to flicker. One by one, the bulbs turned on. The lights shone on Kengir again. Everyone cheered another small victory. Over the past few days, there had been a flurry of diplomatic activity trying to reach out to the Gulag authorities after the Kengir camp regime cut their power.

Through their brilliantly engineered network, they had relayed to the camp authorities their election of a prisoners' commission and their demands. The camp authorities had, amazingly, agreed to parlay and discuss terms. General Bochkov had agreed to meet with them. The zeks gathered around were trying to hammer out the final details of their draft. Its major points included the following translation (the first point driven strongly across by Leonid):

We the Prisoners' Commission of Steplag, Kengir, Karaganda Sector, Kazakh SSR, bring forth the following demands:

Punish the murderer of the Evangelist, Aleksandr Sisoyev.

Punish the murders on Sunday night of 16 May in the service yard by Kapitan Belyaev.

Punish the abusers of the women.

Rehabilitate our comrades illegally sent to penal subdivisions for their right to strike.

No more number patches, window bars, or locks on hut doors.

Inner walls between Camp Divisions not to be rebuilt.

An eight-hour day, as for free workers.

An increase in work payment.

Unrestricted correspondence with relatives and periodic visits.

Review of cases.

So read the zeks' ultimatum. Meanwhile, in the clandestine operations of the Technical Department, there was another battle being fought for restoring the camp's power. Volodymyr had privileged access to their activities, though there were many operations Volodymyr didn't know about. Even Sokil was at a loss to explain some of the inner workings of these "mad scientists." Their ingenuity seemed limitless.

On the first day the authorities knocked out the power, the Technical Department managed a way to hijack the power from the main outside power cable running into the camp. Valeriy came up with the brilliant idea of hooking up a series of wires to steal the charge from the cable. The authorities figured this out and cut the wire entirely.

Then some enterprising hydroelectric engineers, who had worked on the grand Dnipro River dam in Ukraine—one of the largest in the world—figured out a way to siphon off the water from the tap to create a rudimentary hydroelectric power station. There was also a great breakthrough when they discovered an old truck engine in one of the workshops that they converted into a makeshift generator. With these ingenious contraptions, the scrappy zeks were able to keep their revolution connected to the outside world.

Had the prisoners not achieved such a technological edge, they would be in much worse shape for negotiations. Worse yet, they wouldn't have been able to contact the regime, and there would be no negotiations at all. They were able to hear all the background chatter between the bosses and knew that their demands were being taken seriously. Their resourcefulness, from adapting to years of deprivation, was one of their secrets to success, so far.

"Quiet, I'm getting a signal," Valeriy called out excitedly from the corner of the hall.

Everyone in the hut stopped what they were doing short of breathing; even their hearts seemed to skip a beat. They heard a series of beeps and harsh static followed by mumbling. Valeriy turned a series of dials, and then they heard loud and clear: "Special envoy has arrived, prepare proper security measures." It could only mean one thing: Bochkov had arrived. As one of the highest ranking members from Gulag headquarters, they knew this was big news. They could hardly believe their ears. Valeriy jumped out of his chair.

"Tell the rest of the camp!" "I'll let the authorities know we are ready," said Makeyev.

"I'll get on the loudspeaker," said Sokil.

Kuznetsov stood up. "It's time."

"Are you ready, *tovarishch*?" asked Stas.

"Were we ready in 1940?" asked Volodymyr.

"Stalin and Hitler were still alive back then," said Kateryna. "Bochkov can't be as bad."

"But he's still bad," said Kasia.

Whatever their scruples, they couldn't stop the rapidly developing events around them. They heard the loudspeaker crackle on. Sokil was getting out the message.

"*Uvaha, uvaha!* Prepare to meet General Bochkov. Prepare Cargo 200."*Cargo 200?* Volodymyr thought nervously. That was the Soviet code word for soldiers killed in action. The rest of them were also nervous.

"What do you think he meant by that?" asked Stas.

"God only knows," said Volodymyr. "Time to meet our fate."

They exited the mess hall. The camp was animated, with zeks running back and forth preparing for the grand entrance. Curiously, there was a lot of activity by the morgue. Several carts were lined up, and Keller was leading a contingent of zeks in various military regalia.

"Here he comes," said a zek on the watchtower.

"*Vnimaniye,*" said Kuznetsov. "Officer on parade!"

The gates slowly opened. There was a hushed silence. Nobody appeared at first. Bochkov appeared to be testing them. Finally, after receiving some kind of assurances, he entered.

Bochkov was dressed in his full military regalia, oversized epaulets, head and all. He carried a white flag. *Incredible,* Volodymyr thought. The fact that they had gotten a Russian general to raise a white flag to them was a victory in itself. Kuznetsov then did something completely unexpected: He removed his cap.

"Caps off for our fallen comrades," he said.

Bochkov was caught off guard. He stumbled a little, quickly removing his peaked cap. His MVD underlings (Soviet secret police in charge of jails and camps) fumbled to do the same. One of the younger MVD guards even dropped his cap to his great embarrassment.

Volodymyr was impressed by Kuznetsov's unexpected audacity. Even Keller saluted Kuznetsov as bodies of "Cargo 200" passed by. Their bruised and bloody faces were exposed for all to see. Bochkov was visibly stricken by their condition. He called to some other soldiers to cart them off to some cars waiting by the gate.

"Check him," said Kuznetsov.

Out came Kateryna with her mixed-gender security team. She did the "honor" of patting the general down herself. She was painstakingly thorough. Bochkov's face was turning redder by the second. After almost a full minute, she then turned back to Kuznetsov.

"He's clean," she said.

"Are we done with these ridiculous charades?" Bochkov exclaimed.

"One can't be too careful, *tovarishch* General," said Kuznetsov, slyly. "You may proceed."

Bochkov briskly brushed himself off and huffed forward. His entourage marched forward, dramatically goose-stepping the whole way to the mess hall. They tried to save face, but the zeks had seen enough. The true show was about to begin.

Bochkov's contingent marched up to the mess hall. They abruptly paused. Two opposing columns of organized zeks several rows deep lined the way to the doors. Bochkov's troops looked uneasy. They were not expecting such a show of force from the prisoners.

Bochkov brushed past them to the door. Two zeks blocked his path. Volodymyr recognized them from Keller's contingent. Bochkov raised his hand.

"Out of my way, this is official business," he said angrily.

The zeks stood firm.

"Not until we receive approval," one said in heavily Ukrainian-accented Russian.

Keller purposely waited some time before he gave the signal. "He may proceed."

Kuznetsov nodded in approval. They then stepped aside and let the breathless Bochkov pass. Knopkus, Sluchenkov, and Sokil followed right behind.

Bochkov's envoy was unarmed and unnerved. Each guard carried a riot baton, but little else that the zeks could see. They had forgone weapons in "good faith," but the more likely reason was tactical. They were greatly outnumbered. If they were to open fire, they would be quickly overwhelmed, and the prisoners would then have both hostages and guns.

Bochkov and his men proceeded down the corridor to the main hall. The entire way was lined with prisoners armed with their menacing homemade clubs. Keller winked at his MVD equivalent. The MVD officer tried to keep his cool, but his neck was glossy with sweat. The rest quickly shuffled by. Half of war is said to be psychological, and the zeks were setting the tone.

They entered the main hall and were greeted with a full house. Though Bochkov didn't say it, one could see by his widening eyes and flushed face he was also nervous. Kuznetsov appeared in front of him.

"If you'll follow me, General." He led Bochkov to a long table. Several nice cups of tea and cucumber sandwiches were laid out for them. Kuznetsov used the cordial display to show Bochkov the meeting could end sweetly or sourly. Bochkov had undoubtedly come in thinking he would be running the show, but the zeks knew how to play the game.

"The cooks prepared us tea," said Kuznetsov. "Sorry we don't have anything stronger."

"Never mind that," said Bochkov. "Let's get down to business."

"As you wish." Bochkov grabbed up a sandwich and unapologetically wolfed it down. He then grabbed a teacup and slurped it down. He was looking around the room at the vast array of foreign flags created by the prisoners.

"I see you have been busy decorating," he said sarcastically.

"You mean the flags?" asked Kuznetsov. "They were made by our different nationalities."

"I would be careful with such nationalist displays," Bochkov warned.

The zeks were growing impatient with Bochkov's politicking. None looked angrier than the supposed "class-ally Sluchenkov. His knuckles turned white with pent-up fury. Bochkov continued munching down their precious rations, adding insult to injury.

"We are one great Soviet people with the common goal of equality and justice under the banner of socialism," said Bochkov. "We shouldn't be preoccupied with trivial bourgeois ideas."

It was too much for Sluchenkov. He unclenched his fists and opened his mouth. "Cut the crap. We're not stupid *Komsomols*," he said, referring to the Soviet youth organization.

Everyone was shocked, not least Bochkov. He swung around, spitting out part of his cucumber sandwich. Sluchenkov had said what everyone was thinking but afraid to say. For the moment, he was Volodymyr's unlikeliest of heroes.

"I would like to remind you that enemies of the people hide under such guises as anti-Soviet attitudes," said Bochkov.

Kuznetsov tried to calm the situation down, but Sluchenkov was adamant.

"What enemies? You mean like Beria, Yagoda, Yezhov, Abakumov? They were on your side!" Each was a disgraced former head of the Cheka, NKVD, KGB, and the wartime paramilitary death squads known as *SMERSH*, respectively.

"Enough! There's no point drudging up the nasty past. We're talking about the future!" said Kuznetsov.

Sluchenkov continued glaring at Bochkov. Volodymyr saw Keller eyeing the MVD. Bochkov swiveled back to Kuznetsov. He was visibly shaken, but continued the meeting.

"At least some of us have level heads," he said.

Sluchenkov made a rude gesture behind Bochkov's back. Several of the prisoners laughed, unbeknownst to Bochkov, but Kuznetsov ignored them.

"Let us continue, General," said Kuznetsov.

He then produced their ultimatum.

Bochkov took it and began reading. The zeks and MVD were silently trying to read his reaction. Immediately his expression soured.

"Prisoners can only request, not demand," said Bochkov.

"A matter of semantics" said Kuznetsov. "We can work out the wording, but we 'ask' that you take our 'requests' seriously, respectfully."

Bochkov stared at the paper for a while, trying to figure out what to say. He crumpled up the paper and stuffed it into his pocket. He then wiped his large paws on the table.

"I'll tell you what I'm prepared to do," said Bochkov. "I will agree not to transfer prisoners to other camps, or see them abused. And I will review their case files, but only if you all agree to go back to work with a reasonable set of accommodations."

The zeks were stunned. They started murmuring loudly. Bochkov's guards were getting nervous. How could they expect them to go back to breaking their backs in the mines after all this? Kuznetsov was silent for a while, trying to read the room. There was no easy way, so they had to bite the bullet—or they would bite the dust.

"There would have to be significant accommodations," said Kuznetsov. "Firstly, we request that there be regular breaks and more frequent time between rotations."

Bochkov pondered. He tapped his large fingers on the table. Eventually he nodded.

"That can be arranged.""And no Belyaev," said a *zek*.

The rest of the room loudly agreed. Kuznetsov did not need to elaborate on that point. Bochkov looked a little uneasy about that outburst, but he begrudgingly relented.

"I will grant your *requests*, but only if you go back to work immediately, starting tomorrow morning." The room was getting restless again, but Kuznetsov made the decision.

"Agreed."

He stood up and extended his hand.

Bochkov leaned in and briskly shook it. The deal with the devil was done.

Bochkov got up and made his way out the door. Volodymyr was standing nearby.

He saw Bochkov pause for a moment and say something to one of his lieutenants before he left. The lieutenant then turned to his subordinates and seemed to pass the message along. Some of them laughed. One of the guards noticed Volodymyr and smiled fiendishly. He mouthed, *Katorga*.

"Alright, men, you heard the general," said Kuznetsov. "Let's get the word out to the rest of the inmates, including our recently freed SHIZO comrades. Dismissed!"

The meeting was adjourned. They still had a lot of work to do before the next morning.

Sokil came over to them.

"The four of you are a good team," he said. "We need you all to get the word out to our SHIZO friends, whether they like it or not."

Sokil then briskly left, shaking his head. Everyone dreaded going back to work, but they knew there was no alternative at the moment. Volodymyr tried to think about how they would go about it.

"Time to break the news," Stas said glumly.

"*Tak*, let's get this over with," said Kasia.

For the second time, they headed to the SHIZO. Volodymyr couldn't help but feel a little defeated. He hoped bringing the women along might help ease their message across, or at least keep tempers lower.

Everyone was on the move.

The zeks present at the meeting were trying to get the news out. They saw one group get a mouthful and a near thrashing after telling the others they had to go back to work first thing in the morning.

The four arrived at the first SHIZO hut. They saw someone inside. Kasia insisted on knocking. A skinny old man answered.

"*Pryvit tovarishch,*" she said.

The old man was silent.

"There is no easy way to say this, so I'll just get right to the point. We're going back to work in the morning. The general said—""You can tell that fat-head *Komsomol* to go to hell, him and the Kapitan Kuznetsov or whatever he calls himself," said the old man, slamming the door shut.

The reaction was about what they had expected. The next few didn't go much better. After all they had seen, watching the defeated faces of these recently freed prisoners cut them to their cores. The worst zeks weren't even the angry ones; at least they still felt alive. The ones that bothered them the most were the silent ones, who already had one foot in the grave. They shuffled back to their huts wondering what the next day would bring them.

"*Vnimaniye, vnimaniye,*" the loudspeaker blared. "Report for work!"

They begrudgingly pulled up their *valenki* and prepared for work. They shuffled outside. The *vovki* were waiting. They muscled their way into their column, pushing people around.

"Men to the left, women to the right," said a shrill guard.

"That was not part of the deal," said a woman.

"Take her out," he said.

Several guards swooped in and surrounded her. They grabbed her arms. She resisted.

"Get your hands off me, you fascists!"

"Where are you taking her?" asked Kateryna.

"Somewhere nice and quiet where she can think," he said. "Now move out!"

The guards prodded the zeks forward.

Nothing had changed. They went to breakfast, ate their old rationed slop, and went to the mines. The same bespectacled *naryadshchik* was there, chain-smoking and scouring nonsensical quotas. He didn't even lift his head to greet them.

"Move along," he said.

The guards handed them shovels and picks, and down they went. Volodymyr and Stas stared at their old miserable spades, taunting them. They saw the same miserable looks in their comrades' eyes. They hadn't seen Kateryna or Kasia since the morning. Their absence only weakened their plummeting morale. They worked nonstop. Eventually, it was time for an allotted break, or so they thought. A young zek started to walk away. The *naryadshchik* finally stood up and glared at the *zek*.

"Where do you think you're going?" he asked.

"It's time for our break," said the *zek*.

"What's your number?" asked the *naryadshchik*.

"My *name* is Ivan Denisovich," said the *zek*.

"We say when it's time for a break," said the *naryadshchik*. "Take him away!"

The guards grabbed Ivan, who struggled and thrashed. One of the guards hit him with his rifle butt.

The zeks got the message.

They kept on for hours when finally, on the verge of collapse, they were released for the day. When they returned to camp, they realized that nobody could be trusted. The camp authorities had already broken their promises by rebuilding the walls.

13

MAY 25–26, 1954:

RECKONING

THE ZEKS AWOKE to furious banging and hammering early the next morning. They heard heavy equipment dragging along. The loudspeakers were eerily quiet.

Although they didn't have clocks in the barracks, they knew it was near time when they would get up to work. Volodymyr sat up in his bed. He looked down from his bunk to see Stas was not there.

Volodymyr felt a brief wave of panic, thinking Stas had been taken in the night. He looked to the window and was relieved to find Stas crowded around it with several other zeks. He got out of bed and joined them.

"What's going on?" he yawned.

Stas didn't budge. He beckoned Volodymyr over with his one free hand, the other hanging onto the windowsill. Volodymyr craned his neck over the others to see the guards had already rebuilt much of the wall between the men's and women's camps. The camp authorities had brought in tractors, trucks, and bulldozers and a battalion of free laborers.

There was a knock at the door. Everyone jumped and ran back to their beds out of instinct. The knocking got louder.

"Time to get up," said an impatient guard.

They barely got their *valenki* on when the guards opened the doors. Several guards rushed in, prodding the men along. They weren't the usual guards.

"*Davay! Davay!*" the guard barked. "You have a very important visitor coming!"

Nobody knew who he was talking about. Volodymyr passed by the guard and his stomach turned. It was the grinning guard from the mess hall. They locked eyes. To Volodymyr's dismay, the guard also recognized him.

"There are lots of surprises in store for you," said the guard.

As soon as the zeks emerged into the open, they were surrounded by dozens of *vovki*. They eyed the zeks like fresh meat. The guard snapped his fingers.

"Eyes forward." They marched past the barbed wire into the zona and soon were making their way to the *vakhta*. Its cold facade sent chills down Volodymyr's back. They hadn't been there since their first day. He passed the dreaded delousing table, and felt the sting in his eyes and nostrils. He could see Stas also winced at its sight.

"Where are we going?" a man asked.

The guard stopped dead in his tracks. Everyone bumped into each other. The guard stormed down the line to the hapless inmate.

"You will find out soon enough, *zek*," said the guard menacingly.

He rushed back to the front of the line. "March!"

They were herded into the *vakhta*. It was cramped and dark inside.

Many other prisoners were there. Volodymyr was getting nervous. He was reassured when he saw Kuznetsov standing in front with Knopkus, Sluchenkov, Keller, and finally Sokil and Jerzy behind him. Nacham was also there among the fray.

Volodymyr tried to get Sokil's attention, but Sokil was too focused. This was certainly something important. The doors opened and everyone was quiet when they saw the MVD.

"*Vnimaniye*," said an MVD officer.

A uniformed man with large golden epaulets entered the room with an MVD lieutenant right behind him. The lieutenant saluted the man. He briskly saluted back.

"Deputy State Prosecutor Vavilov," said the MVD lieutenant.

Everyone started whispering. *Deputy State Prosecutor?* It was getting serious. They thought they had cleared the air with Bochkov, but as with the rest of the Soviet system, it was mired in endless bureaucracy. But this was not some lowly Politburo Soviet. This was an important man.

Vavilov sat down at the long table prepared for him. There was a stenographer and MVD troops surrounding the *vakhta* inside and out should things go wrong. He looked over the room and cleared his throat.

"I open the floor," he said in a stern tone.

The prisoners started shuffling about nervously. Kuznetsov even seemed a little surprised by Vavilov. He started to speak when Leonid stepped forward. Volodymyr and Stas looked to each other in disbelief. They hadn't seen Leonid in days. He walked right up to Vavilov, a man on a mission.

"State your name and identification number," said Vavilov.

"Leonid Ilyich Ponomarev #62323." Volodymyr saw a changed man. Ever since the revolt, Leonid had grown more serious. It was like he had finally found one last mission to make up for all the lost years.

Vavilov nodded.

"Proceed." "I wish to speak on behalf of all the wronged inmates in this camp, especially the *starosta* veterans," said Leonid.

"Take care of your tone," said Vavilov.

"How would you speak to an oppressor?" asked Leonid.

There was a hushed silence—even the stenographer stopped typing. They had expected an outburst like this from Sluchenkov or Keller, but not dotty old Leonid. Something had changed in him indeed. Vavilov sat up rigidly. The MVD looked nervous.

"I'm not the one on trial here," Vavilov shot back.

"Then who is?" asked Leonid.

"You tell me." "I sure will." Leonid then took a deep breath. Nobody knew what he would say. Vavilov waited with a scowl. Sluchenkov smiled, the only one reveling in this unexpected outburst.

"This whole rotten system is on the gallows, and the noose is pulling tight," said Leonid. "I fought and bled in the Great Patriotic War like too many of my brothers and sisters here, and this is the thanks we get! My father, a true Soviet patriot, didn't die in Kronstadt so a pigheaded Chekist like you could get fat of off the people's labor!"

"That's enough. Get him out of here before I lose my patience," said Vavilov.

Leonid was already walking away.

Kuznetsov walked to the center of the room. He pleaded his case to a fuming Vavilov.

"Our *tovarishch starosta*, a fine Soviet citizen, may have gotten emotional, but he made some important points. I would like to remind you, *tovarishch* General, that I, along with half the people here, had a hand in taking Berlin!"

The zeks roared with approval.

"Your past service has nothing to do with your present circumstance," Vavilov retorted.

"I think it does, at least as a means of earned respect," Kuznetsov replied. "We respectfully request fair working conditions and humane treatment without the use of excessive force, especially in regards to live ammunition, along with a timely review of cases."

Vavilov's face was turning bright red. He turned to one of his lieutenants and whispered something to him. Everyone strained to hear him; even the stenographer was leaning in. He whipped his big head back around.

"I will look into your requests, but you must return to work at once.""Agreed," said Kuznetsov.

The zeks begrudgingly agreed. They had no choice but to trust him.

Vavilov was done.

"This meeting is adjourned," he said briskly.

He stood up and stormed out the door. The MVD followed close behind. Volodymyr and Stas saw Leonid walking by them. Volodymyr grabbed his arm. "Leonid."

Leonid was so caught up in his thoughts that he didn't recognize him at first.

"Oh, Vlodko," Leonid laughed nervously. "I don't know what came over me! I guess I got carried away."

"You said what everyone was thinking," said Volodymyr.

"*Da*, I hope so. I'll catch up later; there's much to discuss. I'm sure plenty of people have some words for me. I hope I didn't muddle things up."

The zeks had mostly left. Volodymyr was one of the last ones out when he heard a crash. He turned around to see the stenographer had dropped his papers. Volodymyr went to help him. The stenographer was nervous; his hands were trembling, and his shirt was soaked in sweat.

"*Spasiba*," said the stenographer, quickly looking to see if the guards were watching. "Be very careful about what happens next. I will pray for you!" He then ran out.

Volodymyr swallowed hard. They were at the mercy of the Soviet state.

They woke up the next day to the old alarms and nasty guards. Breakfast was short and sour. Work was long and arduous. Everything ground to a halt when the loudspeaker came on.

"*Vnimaniye, vnimaniye! Zaklyuchennyi* report to mess hall! All available staff report as well! Gather in a timely manner! That is all."The zeks were baffled. Nobody moved. The guards swaggered over.

"Alright, you heard the man upstairs. *Davay.*" "Don't listen to them; it's a trap," said one of the Ukrainians.

"If they were going to do anything, they would've done it already," said a Russian.

"Ah, what do you know, *Moskal*?" asked the Ukrainian, calling him a Muscovite.

"I'm down here with you, aren't I?" the Russian man retorted.

"We're going up," said Sokil firmly.

The zeks were still unsure. "We have to come out of here at some point," said Sokil. "Better out of our own will."

"I'll tell you all what: If you don't come out now, we will be happy to accommodate you down there," the guard sneered, cocking his rifle.

The zeks begrudgingly agreed. They slowly ascended the walls. Everyone's heads were on swivels, wondering if they would be shot on the way up while at their most vulnerable. They emerged un-harmed—for now.

"Now move!" barked the guard.

They warily made their way to the mess hall together. The zeks kept a tight herd, keeping the strongest like Volodymyr, Stas, and the other veterans on the outside and the infirm tucked inside. The *vovki* were back on the prowl.

Packs of MVD and their *nadziratel* cohorts stood by, ready to pounce. Though the guards didn't display their weapons in accordance with their tenuous détente, the prisoners knew they were armed to the teeth. They could see the wayward stock and barrel bulge in the jacket or on the side of the hip, itching for a chance to fire. Columns of polished MVD waited in columns leading up to the mess hall.

"They look serious," said Stas.

"*Vnimaniye*," said the loudspeaker.

"Here they come," said a watchtower guard.

The inmates and guards turned to the gates. The gates opened, and a large armored car puttered in. This was an unusual display of force by the camp regime.

"They must be top brass," said Stas.

"Or a firing squad," Volodymyr gulped.

"Move in," said an MVD.

The zeks made their way down the lines with Kuznetsov, Knopkus, Sluchenkov, Keller, Sokil, and Jerzy leading the way. Makeyev was conspicuously behind. Volodymyr and Stas tried to read the stoic Soviet statues lining the way, but to no avail. The troops stared straight ahead rigidly. Stas shook his head glumly.

"Where do they come from?" "I don't want to know," said Volodymyr.

They entered the mess hall. A large contingent of Soviet brass was already waiting for them. An MVD lieutenant stamped his foot and saluted two men sitting at a large table.

"*Zaklyuchennyi* have arrived, sirs," said the lieutenant.

Kuznetsov marched up to them and saluted. The morose brass just stared at him. These men looked more impressive than Vavilov or Bochkov—or *Bochka*, *Barrel,* as the zeks now irreverently referred to him.

Kuznetsov puffed out his chest and began to speak, "I am Kapitan—""*Da,* we know who you are, Kuznetsov," said one of the men. "Your former rank has no merit here."

Kuznetsov was deflated. He stood firmly, but his neck was sweaty. It didn't look good.

"I am Colonel Sergei Yegorov of the MVD, and this is General Ivan Dolgikh, Head of the Gulag."The zeks were both impressed and unnerved. They had travelled all the way from Moscow, which was not easy, even for men of their stature. This meant that their prison riot had graduated to a Gulag revolt. They had to tread lightly now. They were in uncharted waters.

"Well, I humbly thank you both for taking the time to meet us after your long voyage," said Kuznetsov. "I have been elected by my fellow *tovarishchi* to deliver our requests."

There was an audible groan from Sluchenkov. Kuznetsov's flattery was beginning to agitate the brass too. Yegorov leaned into Kuznetsov.

"You don't need to remind us how much trouble we took to get here, so let's skip the formalities and get down to business, shall we?"

"*Kanyezhna,*" said Kuznetsov. *Of course.*

Sokil handed Kuznetsov their updated list of requests, since Bochkov had taken their original.

Kuznetsov held up their decree. "We, the inmates of Kengir, 're-quest' the following:

Criminal charges against guards and their superiors of the camp that opened fire on unarmed prisoners; reduction of all twenty-five-year sentences and a careful review of all cases; the liquidation of punishment blocks; communication with relatives; no exile for freed prisoners; uniting of men's and women's camps; that the MVD, respect-fully, be removed from the camp compound."

"What's the meaning of this? How can you not trust the MVD?" asked Yegorov.

"That part was a last-minute addition I was not aware of, Colonel," said Kuznetsov.

The prisoners smirked. Kuznetsov himself had put it there. Yegorov was still upset. The MVD looked even more nervous. Dolgikh calmed them down.

"We understand emotions are high, but we will look into your demands," said Dolgikh.

Yegorov begrudgingly nodded in agreement.

They had dodged another bullet.

Dolgikh continued, tucking the paper away in a small briefcase, "Then it's settled, we will take your requests to the Central Committee. We will contact your relatives in due time. Dismissed."

Dolgikh and Yegorov pushed away from the table and walked out of the mess hall followed by the guards. The zeks were stunned. *Their relatives?* Volodymyr didn't know how to feel. They didn't have time to dwell on it.

"Alright, you heard him, zeks: You're dismissed for the day," a guard jeered.

The zeks quickly left the hall lest they suddenly be forced back to the mines.

"Are you coming to the barracks, Vlodko?" asked Stas.

"I'll be there in a bit." Volodymyr went off by himself to a more secluded corner of the camp near the zona. He stared out over the vast, lonely steppes. A zephyr blew through the empty plains and his hollow heart. Volodymyr hadn't heard from Yurko in many years, not since his poor wife. He shook off his thoughts lest he be sucked into despair.

Volodymyr made his way back to the barracks and was surprised to see Stas still outside talking with Jerzy and Sokil. Volodymyr quickly made his way to them.

"Baran," said Sokil, beckoning him over. "We're having our own meeting before dinner with the others, including Sluchenkov."

They quickly headed to their meetinghouse at the far end of the zona near the SHIZO.

"What's going on?" Volodymyr whispered to Stas.

"I know as much as you," said Stas.

They knocked on the steel doors of the meetinghouse. A small door slid open. A pair of eyes looked through.

"It's us," said Sokil.

The door quickly closed, and an array of locks opened to reveal Keller.

"We're about to begin, sir," said Keller.

They walked in. Keller eyed Jerzy and Stas suspiciously. Keller was no fan of the Poles, or anyone that wasn't a vetted Ukrainian. His reputation and paranoia made him a force to be reckoned. The room was packed. Sluchenkov had the floor, and he was on a warpath.

"What in the hell is the point of all these meetings?" he asked. "I haven't seen a damn thing change since we let these bastards back in!"

"This was a very important meeting, with very important men," said Makeyev.

"They can bring in the ghost of Lenin if they want, but it's not going to change anything," said Sluchenkov.

"You have to trust the system and the chain of command," Makeyev replied.

"It's because of their damned system we're here in the first place," said Sluchenkov. "I'm getting mighty tired of your preaching, choir boy! I served my country with honor while you sat on the sidelines having tea and cakes with your *Komsomol* club!"

The room was getting agitated. Sluchenkov had a point. What was really being done?

"Are you quite done?" asked Kuznetsov.

"*Da*.""We have to give them the benefit of the doubt," said Kuznetsov. "Not because we should, but because, frankly, we have no other choice. Let's see what they do first."

The zeks somberly agreed. Volodymyr and Stas saw the general malaise despite their meeting with top brass. Everyone was mired in a daze, trying to discern who to trust.

"Let's have our dinner, and tomorrow will be another day," Kuznetsov suggested.

The zeks got up and made their way to the mess hall. Sluchenkov said something to Kuznetsov, eyeing Makeyev. Kuznetsov waved him off, and Sluchenkov stormed off.

"What do you think?" asked Stas.

"I think a reckoning is coming," said Volodymyr somberly.

They went to dinner without incident. Then, about halfway, the loudspeaker turned on, which was unusual. The sound was on full volume.

"Zeks, report to the courtyard for orientation." The guards quickly got them up and moved them to the courtyard. It was eerily quiet. More and more guards started to appear. Their hearts sank. What they saw was even scarier than guns or bombs. It was the dreaded Wart that haunted their darkest nightmares.

"Did you miss me, *tovarishchi*?" asked Belyaev.

14

MAY 27, 1954:

EXPULSION

BANG! THE ZEKS were jolted awake by what they thought were gunshots. Dozens of barking voices surrounded their barracks. They assumed they were under attack. Volodymyr sat up in a cold sweat. They awaited their fate. The doors burst open and the MVD swarmed in.

"Move, you old didos," a guard growled. "We have a busy day!"

Volodymyr was trying to gather his things when he was yanked out of bed. The guards howled and cackled. He saw Stas on the floor frantically moving about, trying not to get stepped on. None of them knew what was going on. They didn't even know what to ask.

"We're going for a little ride," one of the guards smirked.

A ride? That never ended well. Usually these things were dealt with secretly in the night, but this was a mass event being done in broad daylight. He could hear a lot of commotion outside. Belyaev was surely trying to prove something. The guards were extra jumpy.

"Time's up," said the guard.

Volodymyr had barely got his *valenki* on when the MVD rushed them and dragged them out the door, some literally kicking and screaming. Some of the older and sicker men didn't even manage to get all their clothes on. Volodymyr and Stas kept close. It was clear that nothing had been accomplished by diplomacy. These brutes only understood one thing: Force.

"*Davay! Davay! Davay!*" the guards cajoled.

"Is that all these mad dogs can say?" asked Stas.

They rushed along. It felt like they were being swept into a whirlpool. Everyone stared ahead blankly. It was like walking in a fog. Volodymyr had another flashback to his terrible state around Easter after the Judas incident when he was knocking on death's door. He realized there was little difference between them and the *dokhodyaga*. They were all dead men walking. They trudged past the zona, *vakhta*, and all the way to the railyard.

Hundreds of zeks *were* already there waiting on the platform. A large train was waiting for them. The loudspeaker was blaring, the dogs were barking, and the *vovki were* running wild. It looked and felt like those first hectic days on arrival. They now knew something else: Belyaev was on a warpath. Nobody was safe.

"Men to the left, women to the right," said the announcer. "Please board the trains in an orderly manner!"

That was one of the most cynical phrases. There was no "orderly manner," only madness. The guards prodded them along. Some of the zeks *were* screaming, some crying, and some staring blankly into space. At least one zek *was* unconscious, though the guards could care less. Another *feldsher* was tired of being quiet. He dared to ask,

"Where are you taking them?" "How about you find out?" the guard laughed.

He grabbed the hapless zek by his lapels and tossed him into a train car. The other guards laughed hysterically. The poor *feldsher* couldn't even let out a yelp before they slammed the steel door on him and dozens of others crammed inside. The rest knew not to ask again.

"You two," another guard said to Volodymyr and Stas, "help pull up the ramps!"

Volodymyr swallowed hard. Stas winced. They felt terrible, but they had little choice, lest they share the same miserable fate. Making the zeks aid them was a favorite tactic of the guards. It made them all complicit in the camp's crimes. Volodymyr and Stas helped two other zeks pull up a large plank. They all looked at each other in pain and braced for the oncoming storm. Dozens of zeks trudged forward with just as many guards and MVD following.

"Davay! Davay! Davay!" the guards cajoled.

They prodded dozens of zeks up and into the overcrowded cattle cars. Everyone was in shock. It was all the more unbelievable that a day before they were still negotiating, or so they thought, with the camp brass. They had felt like they could really change something by working within the system. They wondered what could possibly have gone wrong, or worse yet, if this had been the regime's plan all along. While Volodymyr was pushing people along, he happened to catch the eyes of a young woman. She looked too young, too innocent to be here. Her tears met his own. He pulled out a rag for her as a paltry gesture.

"Diakuyu," she said, wiping her face.

"I'm sorry," said Volodymyr.

"I know," she said, grabbing his hand.

"Davay, don't just stand there," said a guard, pulling them apart.

Volodymyr watched her get swept up in the churning sea of human suffering. She watched him too. Even though they didn't know each other, they felt each other's pain. Volodymyr couldn't help but finally give in to his aching memories. He was transported back to that horrible day, so many years ago, when he was pulled away from the love of his life.

It was the black summer of 1949. The rail station in Sambir was packed with hundreds of prisoners and their Soviet Army escorts. Emotions were still raw after a large ambush by Volodymyr's UPA Hoverlia unit on Red Army troops a week earlier. They were supposed to be treated as legitimate prisoners of war, but nobody trusted their Soviet captors. Volodymyr was hanging onto the outside of a railcar trying to find her.

His recently wed wife Marichka, whom he had married in his village only a few weeks prior, was desperately trying to get to him. They had been friends since childhood, and only now, after years of war, had they finally been reunited. After frantic fighting, she managed to reach him.

"Vlodko," she cried.

"Marichka!" he yelled.

He jumped off the train and ran into her arms. They embraced, crying into each other like so many other couples and families. Nobody knew what to do. She spoke into his ear, "Don't let go." Then, a gruff Soviet soldier grabbed her. Volodymyr wouldn't have it. He charged.

"Get your hands off of her!" He rammed the soldier. The soldier fell to the ground, the wind knocked out of him. He scrambled for his gun when a commissar intervened.

"I'll handle it," said the commissar.

The soldier brushed himself off and begrudgingly stormed off.

"Where are you taking him?" Marichka asked the commissar.

"He will be processed and placed into an internment camp, where he will receive proper rations and conditions under the Geneva Convention," said the commissar. "You may even write to him; we're not monsters."

Volodymyr was forced back onto the crowded train. He saw

Marichka standing by. She waved to him, and even tried to manage a smile through her tears.

"I'll take care of Yurko," said Marichka. "We'll be a family again! You'll be back!"

"No you won't," said Kolya.

The train door shut, and that was the end of that chapter of his life.

Volodymyr saw that train door close on the woman. Now he was where Marichka had stood. The train whistle blew and he bawled five long years of misery. The roaring steam engine drowned out his wails. The loudspeaker switched on.

"*Zaklyuchennyi,* report to the mess hall for lunch.""Let's go, brother," said Stas, gently patting his shoulder.

It was obvious Volodymyr had been crying, but Stas didn't ask. They were all traumatized. Volodymyr shrugged him off.

"*Davay,*" said Volodymyr.

There was nothing else to say. The train chugged away, leaving a large black cloud that hung heavy over the men. Volodymyr took one last look at the disappearing train and wondered what would become of that poor girl, or the rest of them? Would anyone care? Volodymyr looked to Stas and the rest of his comrades and realized that they cared.

They were his family now. Now, another great woman was waiting for him, whom he hadn't seen since the day before Belyaev came back. He couldn't help the past, or that poor woman, but he would be damned if he let Kateryna face the same fate. They made their way to the mess hall. They then made their way to the counter and received their rations when someone called out to them.

"Volodymyr, Stas!" It was Leonid.

They looked over and saw him quickly motioning for them to sit next to him.

"Leonid, what's going on?" asked Volodymyr. "What's with all these awful trains?"

"You haven't heard?" he asked.

They shook their heads. Leonid looked behind him warily, then he leaned in.

"That bastard Belyaev expelled over four hundred people." They couldn't believe it. Everything was falling apart so quickly. They had to know.

"What about Vavilov and Dolgikh?" asked Stas.

"Even Bochkov?" asked Volodymyr.

"Don't make me laugh," said Leonid solemnly. "No, my poor *tovarishchi*, we have been thrown under the train. We are alone."

They didn't know what to say. The bell rang. The guards prodded them. Lunch was over as soon as it began. The camp regime wanted the zeks moving to prevent them from organizing.

"*Zaklyuchennyi*, report for work duties," said the announcer.

"*Davay! Davay*," the guards barked.

"Is that all they can say?" asked Stas.

"Be glad they're just talking," said Leonid.

The zeks were herded along to the mines. It would be a grueling day. The MVD now stood by the guards. Many of the guards were also new, brought in from all over Kazakhstan. They were exceptionally nasty to their alien captives, especially the indoctrinated youth.

"Eyes forward, fascists," said a young Kazakh guard.

"I fought actual fascists when your mother was still wiping your nose," said an old *zek*.

"Shut your mouth, or I'll do it for you, dido," said the young guard.

"No respect for their elders," said Leonid angrily. "This is the thanks we get!"

They arrived at the mines. The same nasty *naryadshchik* awaited them. He lit up another fat *makhorka* and sneered at them with a toothy weasel grin.

"Your quotas have not changed," said the *naryadshchik*. "*Davay!*"

The zeks were handed picks and shovels and down they went. It was hell. The guards worked them like the same old slave drivers. Volodymyr wiped the sweat pouring down his face. He heard a loud bang. He felt the whoosh and heat of a whistling object by his head.

"Less sweating, more swinging, *zek*," barked a guard, cocking his rifle. "That was your only warning!"

Volodymyr swung his pick into the rock, imagining the guard's head. They heard a large crowd of higher-pitched voices overhead. It was the women. Volodymyr looked closer and his heart started fluttering. He could see Kateryna and Kasia. He grabbed Stas's arm.

"Stas.""Quit messing around," said Stas. "You want to get us both shot?"

"Just look up, you stubborn Pole."Stas turned his head. He looked up and nearly dropped his shovel. He started swaying.

"My God.""My angel," said Volodymyr.

The women were being taken to the sweatshops after backbreaking digging and clearing of shrubbery in the fields for more construction on the camp perimeter. Nobody was spared the authorities' wrath.

Kateryna and Kasia tried to see into the pits to see if Volodymyr and Stas were there, but they were rudely interrupted by some fresh guards.

"*Privyet, devochki,*" a *vovk* smiled. *Greetings, ladies.*

Kateryna and Kasia tried to ignore them. They walked faster, but the guards gave chase and stopped them. Kasia shuddered as the lead *vovk* combed his fingers through her hair.

"Playing hard to get, are we?" he asked.

"Leave her alone," said Kateryna."What do we have here?" he said, turning to Kateryna.

He got right in her face, smelling her hair. He looked her up and down, fanning himself with his cap.

"It's a real hot one today, boys," he laughed. "How about a kiss, sweetheart?"

His friends cackled. He tickled Kateryna's chin. She leaned back and spat in his face.

"I like a lady with some bite," he said menacingly. "Allow me!"

He grabbed Kateryna and forcefully kissed her lips. The men started laughing hysterically—at least until he started screaming hysterically. He pulled away. His lower lip was bleeding where Kateryna had bit back.

"You'll pay for that, you *khokhol suka*," he howled. "Hold her down!"

Kateryna thrashed wildly while his men covered her mouth. They turned her around while he unbuckled his belt. He grabbed her pants.

"No!" Kasia screamed when she was restrained in turn.

"Don't worry, honey, you'll get your turn," he jeered.

He turned back to Kateryna when his body went stiff and he fell to the ground. Volodymyr stood over the *vovk* with a large shovel, huffing and puffing. The other guards were so stunned they let go of Kateryna. Volodymyr looked to her. The initial smile on her face quickly recoiled in horror.

"Look out, Vlodko!" she yelled.

There was a loud bang. Volodymyr's body seized in turn. He saw a swirling sea of stars like on the moonlit prairie. He hit the ground next to the unconscious guard. There was no pain at first, only a dull throbbing, but very quickly his lower body was on fire and he was in searing agony. His ears were ringing and his vision was blurry.

He could only make out bits and pieces of what happened next. He saw Stas disarm and savagely beat the guard who shot him, while Kasia kicked at the guard's legs. The other guards ran when they saw several zeks come out to see what the commotion was about.

"*Davay tovarishchi*," said a *zek*.

He charged out of the pit with his pick raised. At first, a trickle followed, and then a human wave welled up from the mine. It was like a great infantry charge out of the First World War. Several MVD and *nadzirateli* opened fire. Several zeks went down, but they pressed forward. There were simply too many for the guards, and they were overwhelmed and retreated.

"Take out the watchtowers," he vaguely heard.

"Vlodko," said Kateryna.Volodymyr slowly turned his head. He looked around. Everything was warped and wavy.

"Vlodko, don't leave me," said Marichka.

"He's losing a lot of blood," said Kasia.

"Get him to Nacham," said Stas.

Volodymyr turned his head back toward the unfolding chaos. He saw the zeks disappear. *Beautiful sunflowers were waving in the breeze. He remembered them from when he visited the farm of a distant relative down below the Carpathians in Vinnytsia. He started floating.*

"Am I dead?" he asked.

His voice sounded like it was emanating from a deep well.

"No, Vlodko," said Kateryna.

He turned his head. Stas, Sokil, Kasia, and Kateryna were carrying him.

He sighed.

"Then take me home," he said, fading away.

Volodymyr looked down. He felt the thick woolen seams of his kyptar vest. He laughed while he played with the colorful fluffy tassels. It felt warm and snug like his mother's hug. It was funny he should think about just that.

"Vlodko," he heard someone call.

Only one person sounded like that. He excitedly looked up and saw his mother smiling. She was beckoning him over to their home.

"Mama!" he shouted.

He ran through their polonyna, feeling the tall spring grass run over his hands. The birch trees were in full bloom against the tall, bushy Carpathian pines. It was a perfect mountain day with the sun poking through huge white clouds like the grazing sheep. He ran into his mother's wide-open arms.

"You've been gone a long time, mamko," said Volodymyr.

"So have you, son," said Marusia. "We've been waiting for you."

"Who?" asked Volodymyr.

She turned to reveal his father, dido, and baba.

"Welcome home, son," said Andriy.

He hugged his father. His dido was smiling and patting his head like when he was a boy. Volodymyr tugged at his dido's sleeves like when he was a child.

"Dido, can you play us a song on your bandura?""Not right now. It's Peest." Lent.

Volodymyr then heard the rhythmic toll of his church's bells.

"I missed you all so much," said Volodymyr.

"So have we, my little Vlodko," said his baba.

"I'm staying here.""Not yet, son; you have others who need you now," said Andriy. "You must get up, son!"

15

MAY 28–EARLY JUNE:

A PROPOSAL

"GET UP, SON." Volodymyr slowly opened his eyes. His vision was blurry at first. There were a lot of lights. Once he adjusted, he saw Sokil standing over him. Sokil quickly turned around.

"He's awake," he said.

Nacham ran over. Right behind him were Kateryna, Stas, and Kasia. Sokil moved away while Nacham examined Volodymyr. He shined a flashlight into Volodymyr's eyes.

"That's good, his pupils are dilating. Volodymyr, can you speak?"

Volodymyr cleared his hoarse throat and everyone leaned in. "Get that flashlight out of my eyes," he said.

"*Tak,* sorry," said Nacham, quickly turning off the flashlight.

"I could use some water." Kateryna quickly left and came back with a glass of water.

"My angel," he said.

He tried to sit up, but the pain in his lower back prevented him. Kateryna tilted his head and poured the water slowly into his mouth. He dribbled some on his chin, like a child. She wiped the drops that spilled with a small rag. He felt a little embarrassed, but didn't say so.

"How do you feel?" asked Nacham.

Volodymyr grimaced. He tried to sit up again, but failed. Kateryna wiped his perspiring forehead. He felt helpless, although he didn't want to alarm them.

Nacham understood.

"I'm sorry, again, but I have to ask." Volodymyr saw his bloody *bushlat* and moaned. He felt sick. Stas tucked in the sheet.

"You don't need to look, everything is still there," said Stas.

"Was I shot?"

"*Tak*, we removed the bullet, but you lost a lot of blood. Sokil helped save the day there," said Nacham.

Volodymyr turned to Sokil, who revealed a bandage on his arm.

Nacham continued, "Luckily for you, Sokil is a universal donor. Now rest up, and you can try to walk around in the next few days. I'll check up on you later."

Nacham left to help the other patients coming in. Sokil leaned in and patted Volodymyr.

"You gave us a real scare, Vlodko," said Sokil. "I almost lost one of my best *sotnyks!*"

"*Diakuyu*, sir," said Volodymyr weakly.

Though Volodymyr was the one in the hospital bed, Sokil looked pained.

"Are you alright, sir?" asked Volodymyr.

Sokil sighed. "I guess I never told you."

"Told me what"—Volodymyr coughed—"sir?"

"At ease," said Sokil, breathing deeply. "I know I ask a lot of you,

Vlodko, but I really care about what happens to you, perhaps too much so. You remind me of my son, Vitaliy. He was killed in Brody."

The Battle of Brody in 1944 was a largescale engagement near the western Ukrainian city of Brody between Ukrainians, Germans, and Soviets. Though UPA had been firmly anti-German since 1943, they had kept their Ukrainian brethren in the German army from being encircled by the Soviets at a high cost for all sides. It was a legendary battle amongst many Ukrainians for the fact they had survived such insurmountable odds.

Volodymyr was genuinely surprised. Sokil kept his life private from the men; perhaps only Nacham knew. Volodymyr lifted his arm with some effort and patted Sokil on his shoulder. Sokil grabbed his hand, and they sat there silently, breathing life into their dead.

"I want you to have something," said Sokil.

He reached into his pocket and pulled out two UPA *Sotnyk* epaulets and an insignia and placed them on Volodymyr's chest.

"These were my son's, and now they are yours, *Sotnyk* Volodymyr Andriyovich.""I can't.""You must. As a *Sotnyk*, you must have the proper insignia, and they are no longer appropriate for me after my promotion."

Sokil stood at attention and saluted Volodymyr, as did Kateryna. Stas and Kasia admired and understood their devotion. Many of those outside the walls thought they were mad, but their rights and rituals and devotion to duty were all they had left."Well, I'll let you get some rest," said Sokil, then turning to bid the rest of them adieu.

Kateryna pulled up a free chair and sat next to Volodymyr. She put her head on his chest. Volodymyr closed his eyes and stroked her hair.

"I thought I lost you," she said softly.

Volodymyr kissed her head. "I'm not going anywhere."

They smiled. Stas came over and rubbed his head. He smirked, trying not to cry.

"You did well, you crazy Ukrainian. You had me worried sick."

"You saved us," said Kateryna, then turning to Stas. "Both of you."

"*Heroyam slava*," said Kasia. *Glory to Ukraine's heroes.*

Over the next few days, Volodymyr convalesced in bed while the hospital grew more and more crowded. He contracted a fever from the influx of patients. Perhaps it was the illness, the heavy cocktail of painkillers, quite probably both, but Volodymyr felt like his dreams were real, trying to break though into their dimension.

The train whistle shrieked. The vovki *howled. Volodymyr was falling.*

"*Vlodko! Vlodko!" Marichka cried.*

"*Where are you, Marichka?" Volodymyr cried into the void.*

He woke up in a cold sweat. Kateryna patted his head down with a sponge. She sighed.

"You had another bad dream," said Kateryna wearily. "Who's Halya?"

"My mother," said Volodymyr quickly.

Kateryna wasn't convinced, but she didn't have time to persist. Nacham entered the room, saving Volodymyr from himself. He put a thermometer into Volodymyr's mouth.

"*Dobre*, your fever has gone down," said Nacham. "You're a strong one, Baran."

"I need to get out of this bed.""Well, you can try to walk around if you'd like; your wound is healing nicely." Nacham pulled off Volodymyr's bandage. "You're very lucky to be alive. Only a few centimeters to the left and your femoral artery would've been severed."

"Lucky me," Volodymyr scoffed.

"I'll be back with fresh bandages," said Nacham.

Volodymyr looked at his wound. It was still raw, but not infected. Kateryna looked concerned. She was about to ask something when Stas and Kasia arrived.

"How's our *Hetman* feeling?" asked Stas, referring to the Cossack equivalent of a general.

"Nacham said he's doing much better," said Kateryna.

"Oh, we're so glad," said Kasia, hugging her.

Stas slyly slipped Volodymyr a small flask while their women's backs were turned. Volodymyr took a swig and winced. Stas smiled and winked. "It's the good stuff."

"Well I'd sure hate to taste the bad stuff," Volodymyr coughed.

Nacham came back. He sniffed the air and saw Stas smirking with Volodymyr, conspicuously quiet. He gave them a stern look but didn't ask. He pulled out a cotton swab.

"Hold still."Stas held Volodymyr's arm. Nacham proceeded to pat down the wound with some disinfectant and clean it out. Volodymyr gritted his teeth. Nacham then wrapped up his wound.

"Are you ready to try and move?" asked Nacham.

Volodymyr looked down at his leg. He didn't want to admit he was nervous. He nodded.

"You've been in bed awhile. You're going to be a little weak," said Nacham, handing Volodymyr a cane. "This will help."

Volodymyr reluctantly took the cane. It felt heavy in his hands. Nacham nodded.

"Ready?""*Tak.*""*Dobre,* let's hold him steady," said Nacham, holding Volodymyr's side.

Stas wrapped Volodymyr's other arm over his neck. Kateryna lifted his leg while Kasia stood by ready, should he fall. Volodymyr put his legs over the side of the bed.

"On three," said Nacham. "*Ras, dva, try!*"

Volodymyr's feet hit the ground. He was indeed very weak after a week in bed. He wobbled, grasping his cane with both hands. Kateryna and Stas steadied him while Kasia held out her hands.

"Are you ready for us to let go?" asked Nacham.

Volodymyr let one hand go and nodded. He tried to bend his leg, but pain shot up his leg. He felt like he had been shot all over again. He got dizzy and stumbled. Luckily all of his friends picked up the slack and kept him from wiping out on the floor.

"I wouldn't do that," said Nacham. "Keep it straight for a while."

Volodymyr grudgingly nodded. He didn't like being told what to do. He felt helpless.

"*Dobre,* now if you will excuse me, I have to get to my other patients," said Nacham.

"I'll help," offered Kasia.

"There she goes, my trooper, and so I must follow," said Stas. To Volodymyr he added, "Keep moving!"

He bid them adieu and followed Kasia, leaving them alone where they had left off.

"You want to keep going?" asked Kateryna.

"Wherever you want," said Volodymyr.

They slowly walked forward. Volodymyr grabbed onto the cane. He couldn't help but feel like his poor old dido. Kateryna sensed his pain, seeing his strong hands tremble.

"How are you feeling?" she asked.

He was about to gripe when he saw a patient lying in his bed covered in bandages from head to toe, blood still oozing through.

"I'm alright," he said, gritting his teeth.

Sokil walked in. He saw them and hurried over, waving a paper. He was smiling.

"Baran, you're up!" Sokil laughed. "You saved me the trouble of getting you out of that bed. Kateryna, I'm glad to see you too."

"What's in your hand?" asked Volodymyr.

"I was getting to that," said Sokil excitedly. "*Nashi* inmates have put together a production of *Zaporozhets za Dunayem* for tomorrow night in the courtyard. Can you believe we even have live theatre now?"

It was being performed by the plethora of actors and artists in the camp who had been swept up in Stalin's purges. How thoughtful it was for that madman, like the surly sultan in the play, to give them such talented actors.

"We'll be there," said Volodymyr.

Kateryna was surprised.

"*Dobre,* I will see you there," said Sokil. "Tell Stas and Kasia to come too!"

"So is that a date?" Volodymyr asked Kateryna.

She smiled and stroked his cheek, but Volodymyr saw sadness in her eyes.

They arrived the next evening with Stas and Kasia. It took some effort for Volodymyr to get there, but he was determined to show Kateryna everything was alright. He still sensed uneasiness in her. When they got there, they were pleasantly surprised.

"It's a pretty good turnout," Stas remarked.

Rows of seats were spread out around the yard with an opening in the center for the actors. Although the Ukrainians made up the majority of the attendees, just about all of the ethnicities in the camp were in attendance. They heard the chattering of dozens of languages.

"Let's get a good seat," said Kasia excitedly.

She locked arms with Stas, who merrily made his way down the rows near the front. Kateryna followed right behind. Volodymyr hesitated and looked around. He was disappointed to see all his comrades except Leonid.

"I knew he was just a damn *Moskal,*" Volodymyr sighed.

It was getting too dark to see when the camp spotlights turned on, illuminating Sokil, who was standing in the center of the ring. The zeks quieted down.

"*Uvaha,*" said Sokil. "Welcome to this evening's extraordinary presentation of the Ukrainian opera *Zaporozhets za Dunayem.* For those of you who don't know, the opera is about exiled Ukrainian

Cossacks trying to adjust to their new life in Ottoman territory. The characters in this play are not too unlike all of us here. They are also strangers in a strange land, trying to readjust as best they can to their even stranger hosts. Please enjoy!"

The lights dimmed and the musicians started playing in the background. They played a slow, old Ukrainian ballad while the actors appeared on stage. Volodymyr looked over to his friends. Stas and Kasia were giddy in each other's company. Kateryna looked on, but her mind seemed to be somewhere else.

The old Cossack protagonist, Karas, came out with his wife, Odarka. There was something oddly familiar about the old Cossack. Volodymyr looked over the old man adorned in a turban and embroidered shirt and belt, his face lighting up when he finally figured it out.

"It's Leonid!" he laughed.

Leonid, or Karas, argued with Odarka about why he was staying out and acting so strangely, at one point retorting:

Now I'm a Turk, not a Cossack, and I'll dress as such,

*From Ivan I'll become [Sultan] Orhan . . .I'll have so many women around, you won't recognize me!*Stas laughed extra loudly. Kasia responded with a firm slap on his chest. The audience around them laughed even harder.

It was like a great catharsis. Out of the miserable darkness came light. Even the usually morose urka looked on in childlike wonder. They hadn't been exposed to any type of real entertainment in years, save the occasional grainy Soviet film. The play went on without a hitch, save for a malfunctioning light that caused the "Sultan" to lose his way and stumble.

Leonid cleverly exclaimed, "When the Sultan goes down, so does the light in our sky!"

The crowd loved it. At the end, the cast bowed to a standing ovation, even from Volodymyr.

"Well done, Leonid," Volodymyr cheered, leaning on his cane.

Leonid looked in their direction and winked.

"*Diakuyu! Spasiba! Dziekuje! Aciu!* A great many thanks to everyone here tonight," said Sokil. "*Dobranich!*"

The audience began to depart. Stas was talking animatedly with some Poles. He rushed over to Volodymyr and Kateryna. He was flushed with excitement—and some vodka.

"They say there's an after-party," said Stas. "Everyone's invited!"

"Maybe later," said Volodymyr.

He was still concerned about Kateryna, who was conspicuously quiet.

"Alright, but I can't make any promises about who or what will be left afterwards," Stas laughed.

"Who do you think you are, *Pan* Sultan?" asked Kasia.

"I like that," Stas laughed. "Call me that from now on!"

Kasia stormed off and Stas ran after her. Volodymyr smirked. Kateryna was still staring at the empty stage. He hobbled over to her.

"Did you like the show?" asked Volodymyr.

"*Ta-tak,*" said Kateryna quickly. "Everyone loved it."

"Well, it's just us now," said Volodymyr, extending his free hand.

Kateryna took it and they walked into center stage. The rows of empty seats surrounded them. They looked around, taking in the sudden quiet of the night.

"It's funny how quiet it always is after a big event," said Volodymyr.

Kateryna nodded.

"Are you alright?" he asked.

"Why don't we sit down?" she replied.

She pulled up two seats and eased Volodymyr into his. She then pulled her chair in front of him and sighed.

"I'm afraid I haven't been completely honest about my past." Volodymyr took her hand, but she pulled away.

"I was married before," said Kateryna.

Volodymyr was silent."His name was Bohdan. He was a good man, but also hardheaded. Perhaps I have a type." Kateryna smirked. "He was also the love of my life."

She trailed off.

"What happened to him?" asked Volodymyr, wiping a tear from her cheek.

"He was severely wounded during a firefight with the Germans. I stayed by his side for weeks past when the medics said he was supposed to have already died. I told him there was no other, and I didn't know if I could go on without him. He died in custody after we were captured when the *Moskali* overran our position. Yet, here I am. I never did meet anyone else worthwhile, until you came into my life. Then, seeing you lay there in that hospital bed, so helpless, churned up all those painful memories. I'm sorry, Vlodko, I'm just so mixed up. You must think I'm so selfish."

Volodymyr pulled his seat closer to her.

"Look at me," he said gently.

Kateryna turned her face. Although it was dark, he could see her pretty, puffy cheeks. He looked into her tearful eyes.

"All I see is a beautiful, caring woman."She smiled and kissed his hand.

"I haven't been totally honest either," said Volodymyr. "Marichka's not my mother."

Kateryna nodded. "I didn't think so."

It was a few weeks before Volodymyr's dreaded departure in 1949. After years of fighting in the mountains, Volodymyr descended back into Pechenizhyn to find his childhood sweetheart, Marichka, waiting for him. They wasted no time. Yurko organized the wedding.

It was a beautiful Carpathian day. The birch trees were in full bloom. Marichka's golden hair and pine-green eyes twinkled in the sun. The birds sang and the church bells tolled for them. They made their procession around the altar in Ukrainian tradition, with Yurko holding the ceremonial crowns over their heads. They really felt like the king and queen of the world that day, and that they could conquer anything. Then, the Russians returned, and the dreaded trains.

"After those doors slammed shut, I never heard from her again," Volodymyr sighed. "I don't even know if she's dead or alive."

Kateryna leaned in and tenderly kissed his cheek. She then laid her head on his lap. They stayed like that for a while. They listened to the chirping crickets in the still, late-spring night. Perhaps it was the season, or the heady days of the revolt, but Volodymyr felt a surge of strength. He slowly stood up, leaning on his cane. Kateryna offered to help. He grabbed her hand and they stood up together.

"You see, we lift each other up," said Volodymyr. "I don't know what will happen next, or even if we'll survive this all, but I do know one thing: I love you. Kateryna *z Polonyna*, will you marry me?"

16

EARLY JUNE 1954:

THE PINE WAS BURNING

Weddings sprang like wildflowers out of the steppes. Everyone was overcome with a beautiful fever. These were the heady days of late spring. New life was breathed in Kengir. Volodymyr was getting ready for his big day along with dozens of other couples. It was amazing how quickly people came together when things fell apart. Perhaps that was the secret strength of human nature. Stas was helping him tie the tassels on his embroidered Ukrainian *vyshyvana sorochka* and wool *kyptar*. Volodymyr was sweating heavily in the June heat.

"If you sweat anymore, you'll melt," said Stas.

"I can't help it," Volodymyr replied. "It's been a long time."

Leonid was preparing a strong batch of *samohonka*, or moonshine, in the kitchen. The smell was overpowering. Volodymyr wouldn't have been surprised if the Soviet Air Force was missing a drum or two of fuel. Leonid picked up the pot and carried it over to them.

"This might help," Leonid winked.

He carefully passed Volodymyr the ladle, and Volodymyr took a swig. He started gagging.

"Are you trying to kill me?" he asked.

"You can't take any liquor with you to heaven," said Leonid, passing it to Stas.

Stas took a large gulp and nearly fell over. "Good stuff, Karas!"

"It's for the Sultan," Leonid laughed.

"But Muslims don't drink," said Stas.

"Thank God we're Cossacks," said Leonid, taking a hardy swig.

Volodymyr tugged at the tassels wrapped around his neck. He was starting to feel the pinch. It was a bittersweet moment for him. He wondered if this was the right thing to do.

"What a beautiful night," said Marichka. "I wish it would never end."

She was resting against Volodymyr's shoulder. It was the night before their wedding. They had only appeared back in each other's lives a few days prior. The Russians were closing in, and their future was uncertain. They were living on borrowed time.

"But tomorrow is our wedding day," said Volodymyr.

"I know," she said, "but I don't know where we'll be afterwards."

"Well, I'm here now," said Volodymyr.

"Promise me one thing, Vlodko. Whatever happens, just don't forget about me, about this night."

"Then let's make it a night to remember," said Volodymyr, kissing her tenderly.

Oh Marichka, wherever you are, please forgive me, thought Volodymyr. *You will always have a place in my heart.* "Is the groom ready?" asked Mykola.

Otets Mykola had become the unofficial bishop of the Ukrainians in the camp. He had earned his frock. He still bore the battle scars etched across his face from facing down the guards with the rest of them on the parapets. Volodymyr took a moment to think. He was ready.

"*Tak*," said Volodymyr, finally.

"Then follow me," said Mykola.

"Let's go headfirst, Baran," said Stas.

They made their way to the new chapel the zeks had created by converting a *vakhta* in the women's camp. There was already another wedding on the way out when they arrived. It was a Lithuanian couple they recognized. Their Catholic priest finished the ceremony in Latin and then Lithuanian to great cheers. Just across the way they heard a Muslim ceremony, and then the breaking of a glass followed by a hardy "*mazel tov*" from a newlywed Jewish couple.

They even saw Kuznetsov sneaking around with a Ukrainian woman by his side. He was still flanked by his two burly Ukrainian guards, which everyone found quite amusing. They were said to be there for his protection, but everyone knew they were there to keep him in line.

Kateryna and her maid of honor, Kasia, stood beneath the largest tree in the camp. Kasia had weaved Kateryna's hair into traditional braids, called *kosy*. Any Slavic bride-to-be wore them until her wedding day, which had finally approached again after so many years of misery.

"You look beautiful, Kateryna," said Kasia.

Kateryna still wasn't sure. She looked at her reflection in a small cracked mirror Kasia had found. They had no choice but to laugh at her distorted smile. Kasia nudged her.

"A great woman can make anything beautiful.""*Dziekuje*, my sister," said Kateryna, hugging her tightly.

Kasia's own struggles had given Kateryna the strength to move forward. She felt some reservations, even though she knew better. She gathered herself, making final adjustments to her *kosy*. Kasia smiled and patted her hand.

Volodymyr, Stas, and Leonid followed Mykola to the Ukrainian congregation. Sokil, Nacham, Keller, Lylyk, Shvydko, and other Ukrainian veterans stood at attention. Sokil came up to greet Volodymyr, taking the traditional place of the father.

"How are you feeling, son?" asked Sokil.

"He's a little sweaty," said Stas.

Volodymyr elbowed him, and Sokil laughed. He patted Volodymyr on the back.

"Oh that's natural. It means you picked a good one." He winked. "*Davay tovarishchi*. Let's take our positions!"

Stas and Leonid followed Sokil. Volodymyr approached the altar. Mykola waited with a small Bible he'd snuck into Kengir. Stas patted Volodymyr reassuringly on the back while he waited for his bride. Volodymyr was lost in his thoughts, thinking about his family and Halya, feeling ashamed again.

"Volodymyr?" asked a woman.

He turned, and his icy heart melted. The light caught Kateryna's eyes like on that magical moonlight prairie night. Volodymyr quickly touched her face.

"Are you alright?" Kateryna smiled, patting his hand.

"I'm sorry, I was just making sure I wasn't asleep," said Volodymyr, "because before me stands the woman of my dreams."

She kissed his hand. They looked into each other's eyes and knew they were ready. Mykola took his place at the altar. He fixed his collar and waited for everyone to settle down.

"Are we all ready?" asked Mykola.

"*Ta-tak*," Volodymyr stuttered, just like that first moment they met off the train.

Kateryna laughed and nudged his arm. Volodymyr had to laugh too. Stas behind him.

"*Dobre,* then we will begin the ceremony," said Mykola. "Do you have a ring?"

"I have this," said Volodymyr, reaching into this pocket and producing Slipyj's cross. He had secretly pulled it out from under the floorboards only the night before. "For you," said Volodymyr, "a blessing for my angel."

He placed the cross around her neck, and Kateryna hugged him. Mykola approved.

"Lovely," said Mykola, turning to the audience. "We are all gathered here today to bear witness to this extraordinary act of love in the face of the evil that surrounds us, showing that love, indeed, conquers all."

"Amen," said Kateryna.

"Now we will bind their hands with the traditional *rushnyk,*" said Mykola.

Kasia came up to them with a finely sewn red, black, and white embroidered *rushnyk* made in their textile warehouse. She bound it firmly. She had tears in her eyes as she said, "Congratulations." She then turned to Stas, who winked. She smiled and blushed. She then sauntered back to her place beside Kateryna. Things were going surprisingly well so far.

Mykola continued, "This *rushnyk* signifies the bond between this couple. Now we will perform the procession around the altar. Will the best man and maid of honor come forward with the crowns?"

Stas and Kasia came forward with two metal crowns welded in one of the warehouses. They held them over Volodymyr's and Kateryna's heads. Three Ukrainian singers accompanied by a Ukrainian zek with an accordion abandoned by the guards began to play the ancient

Ukrainian wedding song, *"Horila Sosna Palala,"* "The Pine Tree Was Burning." The song melded aspects of ancient pagan and Christian traditions referencing a great *vatra*, or bonfire, which would accompany such an event, symbolizing the allegory of rebirth in fire. All the Ukrainians sang as Volodymyr and Kateryna made their way around the altar with Mykola blessing their path to signify their place revolving around heaven and earth.

Kateryna started to cry when she sang, *"Oh my braids, my braids, how you've served me well."*

Volodymyr wiped her tears with one hand while trying to hide his own with his other. She couldn't have imagined getting married again, especially in this godforsaken place. *Love is a strange thing.* They both knew that. Once they finished the procession, Kasia placed another larger embroidered carpet, or *kylym,* at their feet.

"Once these two step onto the blessed *kylym*, they will have been elevated to holy matrimony," said Mykola, "then they will drink from the cup of life."

"Ready?" asked Volodymyr.

He extended his hand like on that quiet night when they were center stage. Kateryna grabbed his hand and they stepped onto the altar. Mykola brought out two cups. He handed them to Volodymyr and Kateryna.

They crossed arms and drank. Everything was going down smoothly until Volodymyr spilled some of his wine on Kateryna. That was a bad omen, but Kateryna shrugged it off.

"You can't believe all these silly rituals," she whispered.

Volodymyr wasn't so sure. He thought about the dark clouds that followed him. He forgot where he was for a moment, thinking about his shamanic visions.

"I now pronounce you two, Volodymyr Andriyovich and Kateryna Petrovych, man and wife," said Mykola. *"Slava Isusa Khrystu!"*

"*Slava Naviki*," they answered.

They kissed each other tenderly. The crowd went wild. The musicians started playing even louder trying to be heard over their cheers. They walked down the aisle and the audience followed right behind; now it was time for the *zabava* wedding reception, which was famously raucous. The musicians continued playing in the background.

They made their way to the courtyard, where other couples had gathered. Their songs and music mixed with the various other songs being sung in a grand zek symphony. They repurposed the long table they had used for the futile meetings with the camp authorities for the Slavic couples to sit at the head of the wedding party, as is tradition. The Jews and Muslims sat at other ends of the yard, creating another stage. Volodymyr and Kateryna sat down next to the Lithuanian couple.

"What a sight, eh?" the Lithuanian man asked them.

"I couldn't have ever imagined such a thing," said Volodymyr.

"By the way, how is Stalin doing?" the man asked Volodymyr.

Volodymyr looked closer. He had to think a bit. He laughed embarrassedly.

"Ah, Gitanas," Volodymyr laughed.

"The one," Gitanas replied.

"How is Knopkus?" asked Volodymyr.

"Well, to be honest, there's something big brewing," said Gitanas, a little hesitantly. "Let's try to enjoy ourselves while we can."

Volodymyr nodded soberly. Perhaps his paranoia was not unfounded.

Kateryna leaned in.

"What was that about?" Before Volodymyr could answer, Stas stumbled over to them with a large bottle.

"Cup runneth over," he giggled, overfilling the two couples' cups.

"*Dziekuje*, you crazy Pole!" Volodymyr smirked.

"How does your people's chant go?" asked Stas. "Oh right. *Budmo!*"

"Hey!" said Volodymyr and Kateryna, followed by three more *budmo*'s and three more hey's. It was an old Ukrainian Cossack cheer meaning "we will be." They all drank the bitter brew, wincing and coughing to varying degrees, except Gitanas's wife.

"Good stuff," she said, burping and quickly covering her blushing face.

"Now that's a woman," Stas laughed.

"Wait a second," said Gitanas, "I remember you! You're the mad Polish miner that freed our Knopkus!"

"I take some offense to that, sir," Stas smirked. "I'm not a miner anymore!"

They toasted glasses. Kasia came over and grabbed Stas's sleeve. She smiled and bowed to them all politely in tradition, and quickly turned back to Stas.

"What are you doing harassing everyone?" she asked.

"I'm entertaining them!" "You're acting like a fool," said Kasia.

"The tsar's royal clown was the envy of many, because he could always speak his mind without repercussions," Stas replied.

"Well the tsarina was not as forgiving," said Kasia, slapping Stas on the chest.

"Ah, I remember you two from the play," said Gitanas's wife, a little heady from the drink. "Now that was a show!"

Everyone started to quiet down. Sokil, Mykola, the imam, and a rabbi walked into the center of the congregation. Mykola made the sign of the cross.

"*Slava Isusa Khrystu,*" he said.

"*Slava Naviki,*" the Ukrainians answered, and other varying forms from the other Slavs.

"*Assalamu alaikum,*" said the imam."*Wa �alaykumu s-salam,*" the Muslims answered.

"*Dobri lyudy*, I'll make this short and sweet," said Sokil. *Good people.* "Let's all remember what a blessing it is that we're all here today, together now as one people. We are a beacon of light and hope in this cruel, dark world. *Nazdorovya!*"

"*L'chaim*," said the rabbi.

Both wished them universal good health in Ukrainian and Yiddish.

The tables were not as full of food as traditional weddings would dictate, but they made the best of it. Their carefully chosen dishes made each plate more special. They brought in plenty of the camp's canned preserves from the mess hall. Meats were in short supply, but there was a decent amount of military surplus rations, and the occasional precious pickled herring. There were, however, plenty of cucumbers and potatoes from their humble gardens.

They knew their supplies were limited, but they were tired of starving. They figured their food would run out no matter how much they conserved, so they might as well die full. They passed around a large loaf of black bread and dipped it in salt. In eastern Slavic traditions, this act symbolized both the sweetness and bitterness to be expected in life and, therefore, marriage.

Volodymyr and Kateryna looked at the thick black earthen loaf, remembering the bittersweet moments in winter when they were still confined to their different camps, dreaming about someday being in each other's arms. They remembered when Volodymyr had tossed the bread over the wire to Kateryna. It was a great treasure. Kateryna passed the bread to Kasia. She took the bread and remembered tenderly, and bitterly, how Kateryna had given her that humble, precious gift to try and assuage her anguish after being assaulted by the guards. Stas stroked her hair while she wiped away a tear. The evening went on and the accordionist started to play *"Horila Sosna Palala."*

"Vlodko," said Kateryna, motioning to the other couples taking the dance floor, including Gitanas and his swaying, tipsy wife. "We'll go slow."

"*Davay, kozache,*" said Stas. *Let's go, Kozak.*

Stas stood up with Kasia, and Volodymyr reluctantly agreed. His leg was still not great. The three of them helped him up, and he hobbled over to the other couples.

Volodymyr and Kateryna wrapped their arms around each other. They swayed slowly to the lulling rhythm of the accordion. They hardly moved, but that didn't matter because the world moved around them. They sang the ending stanza with particular tenderness: "*The boy liked me from afar, the boy liked me forever, the boy is now my husband.*" They went in for a kiss when the accordion sprang to life.

"*Hopak!*" a Ukrainian shouted.

The Ukrainians started clapping and whistling. They formed a circle around the center of the courtyard and the accordionist in preparation for the vivacious Hopak. The Hopak is considered the national dance of Ukraine. It originated from old Slavic village dances and evolved under the Cossack times into a kind of showcase of physical prowess.

Two of the younger couples began spinning and doing a fast-paced polka around the circle. A young man then jumped into the center doing *prysyadki,* squatting up and down, kicking his legs side to side into a mighty split jump to great fanfare. Another man rolled and did the iconic *povzunets,* squatting down and kicking his legs forward one by one. Everyone went wild. The dance continued until a flurry of wild drumming took over.

A Chechen man leapt into the center and started spinning wildly up and down. It was time for the Caucasian answer to Hopak: Lezginka. The faster he spun, the faster the drummers pounded, when another man started spinning and jumping around the entire perimeter on his toes. Had the guards been watching, they wouldn't have known whether to be impressed or intimidated.

Eventually, when the dancers and drummers had worn themselves down, a Jewish fiddler came into the fray with a stolen violin they had rescued from the guards. Nacham and another man brought out two chairs. A Jewish couple sat in the chairs and they were hoisted into the air. The Hora was in full swing.

"*Hava, nagila hava,*" Nacham sang.

They had never seen Nacham smile so much.

The festivities were a great burst of nervous energy from the camp. They feared what would happen if they stopped. Eventually, though, the wild evening began to wind down.

Volodymyr and Kateryna had separated from the fray and headed to a more secluded portion of the camp. Every once in a while they smirked hearing loud kissing from a couple in the barracks. They sat down at the very edge of camp. Kateryna rubbed Volodymyr's leg.

"How does your leg feel?" "It's fine," said Volodymyr. "Being with you, I know I'm alright."

Kateryna kissed his cheek and leaned on his shoulder.

"I love the nights on the steppes in this strange land," she said. "It's like we're floating in space."

"Just like that night we first saw each other," said Volodymyr, "when I saw an angel in this hell, and knew we belonged to each other."

Theirs was the moon and the stars. They gazed into each other's eyes like on that cold, dark February night. Kateryna undid her dress. Her elegant curves were silhouetted against the moonlit sky. She helped Volodymyr with his clothes. They set the night ablaze with their passion. The rest was written in the stars.

17

EARLY JUNE 1954:

A ZEK'S TESTAMENT

THE BLADE TORE at the earth. The harsh Kazakh sun beat down on them. Sweat poured down their faces and hands. Swarms of hungry flies obscured their vision, yet they kept digging.

Volodymyr, Stas, and Nacham had the unfortunate task of identifying the untimely grave of the murdered inmate from the winter whose leg was crushed by the excavator and then finished off by the cruel guard. Sokil and several other zeks helped in the morbid task. The zeks smoked constantly to mask the smell of death. Volodymyr was suddenly reminded of the unfortunate engineer, passing them his final smokes. He wondered if he too had joined the dead. Nacham plunged his blade in the ground and immediately stopped, coughing heavily.

"I found him," Nacham gagged.

One of the zeks looked in and immediately turned and vomited. The stench was overwhelming. The bag was still intact, but the contents were surely a nightmare. Only poor, brave Nacham was remotely qualified to document and clinically verify his fatal injuries.

They had matched the man's mugshot to a young Armenian man named Hayk Nigoyan. It seemed like a small conciliation to put a body to a name, but they hoped his sacrifice would breathe life into their cause as evidence of the regime's crimes. With rags wrapped tightly around their noses, they pulled Nigoyan out of the ground and onto a cart, trying to breathe as little as humanly possible. It seemed like a sacrilegious act, but the guards had retrieved all of their victims from the spring massacres and winter assassinations, including the poor old Evangelist. Yet, they forgot, or tried to forget, their mass graves.

Mykola solemnly chanted *"Vichnaya Pamyat,"* tossing water on the martyred Christians, including the poor girl who was shot for hanging her clothes on the wire. She lay in limbo, forgotten in the morgue. They documented her gunshot wounds and properly laid her to rest in the mass grave with Nigoyan and the dozens of other victims of the Soviet regime.

The Slavs kneeled as the deceased passed by in Eastern Christian tradition. The imam and rabbi sent their dearly departed off in turn. Nacham was a tough man, but he was visibly shaking and smoking heavily, which he didn't normally do. Sokil was trying to console him. Volodymyr and the others were worried. After the ceremony, Kuznetsov appeared.

"Vichnaya Pamyat," said Kuznetsov. "This has been a difficult day for everyone, but thanks to our engineers, we have a chance to tell the outside world what we witnessed here."

Everyone started murmuring loudly, wondering what he was talking about.

"*Da, tovarishchi,*" said Kuznetsov, "we will begin interviews after lunch in the SHIZO."

"How can we possibly eat?" Kasia murmured.The zeks shuffled to the mess hall. They lined up and received their food. Already their rations had gone down since their grand banquet. Nobody had much of an appetite, though. The four friends sat down. Leonid saw them and sat down without touching any of his food. There was a hushed silence. Though there were no guards, people spoke in whispers, thinking about what to say.

"What are you going to say?" Kateryna asked Volodymyr.

"The truth," he replied, pushing away his food.

The five of them made their way to the SHIZO with a group of about a dozen other nervous zeks. Volodymyr didn't know exactly what he would say, but he knew he would have to tell the truth. They walked up to the steel door. A Ukrainian guard was waiting, smoking a *makhorka*. They couldn't help but think how quickly the zeks themselves had started replacing the camp guards' positions.

"Enter," he said.They entered the damp, dark corridor. There were still scattered papers, desks, and chairs with burn marks on the walls from their revolt just a few weeks prior. It was eerily quiet until the door opened at the end of the hallway. A woman came out, shaking and sobbing. They thought about turning around when they saw Valeriy inside the room beckoning to them. Volodymyr decided to go first.

"Good luck," said Stas.

Kateryna kissed Volodymyr's cheek.

"We'll be right here," Kasia added.

"Come on in, Volodymyr," said Valeriy.

Volodymyr entered and they closed the steel door shut behind him. He could feel the air leave the room. It was dark inside, with a single twitching lightbulb suspended above the ceiling.

"Please have a seat," said Valeriy. "I'm sorry about the location, but unfortunately the SHIZO was the only place in camp with the correct recording equipment left."

Valeriy had an assistant fiddling with a microphone. He was no doubt another "mad scientist" from the Technical Department. "This is a Dictaphone," Valeriy explained, placing a small metallic box and microphone in front of Volodymyr while he wound up the roll on a huge tape recorder.

"Testing, *ras, dva,* testing," said Valeriy.

"We're ready to go," said his assistant.

"One of the Siberian zeks thought this was a type of torture device, poor devil," said Valeriy. "Begin with your name, number, and the rest is up to you. We're here to tell your story, the ones the regime doesn't want people to hear."

Volodymyr nodded and cleared his throat. "My name is Volodymyr Andriyovich Zaluzhniy, zek 22422."

He looked to Valeriy, who nodded and encouraged him to continue.

"I was captured after an ambush against Soviet troops in Sambir in 1949 as a member of UPA's Hoverlia battalion. I was promised proper treatment under the Geneva Convention"—Volodymyr became increasingly agitated—"but what happened afterwards, after being ripped away from my family and wife, was anything but."

Valeriy was listening intently.

"I was first brought to Mordovia," Volodymyr continued. "It was my first long train ride, and I thought it was a nightmare, but little did I know my nightmare was just beginning. The guards constantly harassed us, calling us 'fascists' and 'Hitler's *Khokhly.*' At this point, I hardly had any clothes on after an officer had taken my mother's *kyptar,* but that hardly mattered because they robbed us blind anyway. The first weeks were really tough, as I wasn't used to such confinement, having lived mainly in the woods for years. What saved me was my friendship with Archbishop Josyf Slipyj."

Valeriy told Volodymyr to hold while he adjusted the volume on his recorder, then, "Go on." "I first met Slipyj in line at dinner. I noticed the crucifix around his neck, the one that would eventually become mine. I asked if he was a priest. He smirked and said he was the Archbishop. At first, I thought he was joking, but others overheard us and confirmed his identity. Although I wasn't religious at that time, my Uncle Yurko was, and I asked Slipyj for a blessing to give him when I still thought I would go home. He wrote it down on a note and I sent it to Yurko the only time I was given the opportunity to send a letter. Lord knows if it got to him. What happened next would bind our fates forever. A real pompous little urka tried to rob Slipyj, of all people. I let that little *Moskal* have it!"He coughed. Valeriy gave him a glass of water and he drank the whole glass.

"*Diakuyu*," said Volodymyr. "And because I was UPA, I wasn't punished the usual way, but thrown into the dreaded *psikhushka*. That's where the real madness began . . ."

"Let's go, killer," the vovk sneered, dragging Volodymyr along by his lapels. "Now you'll see some real monsters!"

Volodymyr could barely see through his swollen eyes. The guards had savagely beaten him. Through the sliver of his barely better eye, he could see he was being taken to a large brick building within the zona, surrounded by its own watchtowers and wire.

What kind of place is this? *Volodymyr thought.*

He was brought into a large white room with blinding lights. There was a long corridor with people running around in white lab coats. They brought him to a long table where a morose, doctor-looking type was flipping frantically through a stack of papers."What is it now?" asked the "doctor," still looking at his papers.

"This zek assaulted another zek, and I think he is unsound," said the guard.

"But I was defending—"The guard smacked Volodymyr. The pain in his still-raw face felt like fire.

The doctor waved his hand.

"Take him to processing," he said, not once acknowledging Volodymyr.

"Come on, you," sneered the guard.

They took him to an even larger, barren room. He was stripped naked, doused with delousing powder, and put in an oversized jumpsuit. The guard hurried him on.

"Davay," the guard cajoled.

He took Volodymyr down a long hallway. There was a sign that read: Criminally Insane. *The screams of these tormented souls echoed down the halls. Many of these poor people walked around in their own excrement, some chained to their beds. He was brought to a small cell with flimsy bunkbeds.*

"Meet your new cellmate," the guard snickered.

He pushed Volodymyr into the cell and closed the door.

Volodymyr couldn't see at first, but once his eyes adjusted, he could see a ghost of a man curled up in his bed. Volodymyr didn't know what to make of this statue when an alarm sounded and the man sprang to life, wailing and screaming, banging on the walls and bars like a wild animal. Volodymyr was petrified."I don't think I slept more than a few hours while I was there," recalled Volodymyr. "After a week I was starting to go mad myself, when Slipyj personally intervened and had me transferred to another camp. He gave me his crucifix and a promise to keep in touch with my family.""Incredible," said Valeriy, "in the most awful way."

Volodymyr nodded in agreement.

"I'm so sorry this all happened to you, Volodymyr, but you have done an invaluable service. Please let your friends know they can speak just as freely here."

Volodymyr got up and shook Valeriy's hand. He then returned to his friends. Leonid's foot was tapping nervously.

"How did it go?" asked Leonid.

"I told the truth."Leonid nodded and went in. He talked about his service, and barely surviving Sachsenhausen, only to be thrown into the Gulag. Kateryna talked about the guards' constant sexual harassment and the death of her husband in Soviet custody. Stas spoke about his arrest and betrayal and his father's murder in Katyn. Poor Kasia spoke of her false imprisonment and how the guards sexually assaulted her with impunity. Finally, Nacham appeared after his grisly work, still caked in muck. Volodymyr nodded to him, but Nacham was someplace else, someplace deep in his mind. He entered the room without saying a word.

"Nacham, welcome," said Valeriy. "If you could just say—"Nacham cut him off. "This isn't my first interrogation.""I understand. You can proceed."

"I am Nacham Abramovich Lemberg, zek 10723. I am the senior *feldsher* of Steplag 3, Kengir. I have treated many victims of numerous crimes and documented their injuries, along with the bodies of the deceased. Digging up the dead today dredged up many dark memories that I have suppressed for decades for fear of my own life. I realize now that was selfish. I want people to know the truth of these hidden Holocausts. I have experienced things no man ever should, but I want the world to know so it will never happen again."

He paused, catching his breath.

"I barely survived the Babi Yar massacre in Kyiv, when the Germans massacred thousands of my people, but the world now knows of these horrors," said Nacham haltingly. "Seeing those emaciated corpses today reminded me of something else: My shame in promoting Soviet lies as a young *de-kulakizer* during the Holodomor in Ukraine. I must tell this story because not many people have this chance. You will then understand the viewpoint of a once-ardent communist and know that I have no bias, only truth as I have witnessed."

It was winter of 1932. Nacham was a young Komsomol attached to an international unit of so called "de-kulakizers." Their task was mainly to spread propaganda promoting collectivization to the land-owning peasants known as "kulaks." The Ukrainian peasants had fiercely resisted Stalin's efforts at expropriating their lands, and the Soviets had come down on them hard. Stalin's grand plan had gone beyond any economic or ideological goals of communist theory and descended into mass murder on an industrial scale. He and his Soviet henchmen had decided to collectively punish the Ukrainians by systematically starving millions to death.

Nacham had heard rumors, as they all had, of bodies of men, women, and children strewn on the roads, rotting like harvested wheat stalks. They thought such rumors were overblown, perhaps even counterrevolutionary propaganda. One day they arrived at an officially selected village where they were given an official welcome by the "re-educated" townsfolk. Nacham knew something was wrong when they were greeted by the children—or what looked like children. These little skeletons began singing with their hoarse, pained voices, struggling to make any sound at all. He noticed one child sneak away and pick up some discarded seeds on the ground and run it to his unconscious baba. The authorities saw things weren't going well and shooed the children away.

The Komsomols were given orders to go to designated villages to spread the "good word" of the Soviet system. They were given directions and an unusually stern warning about not veering off the path, and not to go out at night. Though Nacham was a little unnerved, he nonetheless went to fulfill his duty. He walked down the long, lonely steppe road. It was taking him much longer than he thought.

It was starting to get cold, and dark. He saw from the map he had kilometers to go on the endless rural road, but realized there was a shortcut through some pine woods. He cut through the forest and eventually he saw a small village. It was nearly dark now, so he thought he could stay over in someone's house, or at least get better directions.

His stomach was growling furiously. He thought it was strange that he hadn't eaten much since he'd entered the heart of what was known as the "Breadbasket of Europe." Nacham walked into the village and was stunned by the complete silence. He knocked on a door.

"Pryvit, is anyone home?" he asked in Ukrainian.

Nobody answered, but the door creaked open. He gingerly entered.

"Pryvit?" he asked once more.

He looked all around, but all the rooms were open and empty except for a closed door to what he assumed was the bedroom. Something was creaking inside. Slowly, he opened the door and saw a pair of muddy feet dangling from the door frame.

He shut the door and ran out into the night. He didn't know where he was going; he just wanted to get away from this terrible place. Not knowing where he was going, Nacham ran toward a large hill on the outskirt of the village. He recoiled in horror. He didn't know if it was his imagination, but it appeared that the hill was moving. Like a waking nightmare, a little hand emerged from the earth. Nacham grabbed the hand, and pulled out a little boy from a pile of emaciated corpses. His wide, saucer-like eyes were frozen in terror.

"I'll come back with help," said Nacham.

He then ran back to the road, where he saw some soldiers riding on a cart.

"Tovarishchi!" Nacham yelled.

They stopped their cart and he told them about the boy.

"What exactly did you see?" asked a lieutenant. "I think you should come with us."

"But what about the boy?" asked Nacham.

"Now," commanded the lieutenant, brandishing his pistol.

They threw him on the cart and rushed to a party headquarters. He realized the back of the cart was filled with large sacks that read PSHENITSA, or wheat in Russian. Nacham now understood he had seen something he wasn't supposed to see. They took him to an interrogation room for debriefing. They questioned him for hours through the night until finally they threw him into a dark cell.

Though he couldn't see them, he could hear others around him. They told him that everything he had seen weren't isolated incidents, but were happening throughout the country. Nacham couldn't believe it. He had known things were tough, but not this bad.

They tossed in a young inmate who was beside himself with terror. He revealed that they were all to be shot at dawn to hide what they had seen. The prisoners devised a plan to run for the hills when the guards took them out. They figured at least one of them would survive to tell their tale.When the hour of judgment came and they were taken outside, they all broke off in different directions. The soldiers started shooting. Several men and women went down around Nacham, but he couldn't stop. He ran until his legs gave out and he jumped into a river. He floated on a log until a boatman picked him up.

"Whether they were shot and gassed or starved and worked to death, it was the same crime against humanity and God, in which neither the Nazis nor this regime believe," finished Nacham.

The tape clicked to a stop. Valeriy wiped away his tears. Nobody spoke.

"I was the only one to escape," Valeriy's assistant said quietly.

They turned to him.

"Half my village was wiped out. I barely escaped after I heard my parents talking about how they would cook me," he said.

"You may go now, Nacham, if you so wish," said Valeriy.

"Go where?" Nacham asked bitterly.

18

JUNE 10–11, 1954:

A BREACH OF CONFIDENCE

"Vnimaniye! Spasy nas! Come in! May Day!" said Sokil, typing SOS in the background. "If anyone out there can hear us: We are the inmates of Steplag, Kengir, and we need your help!"

The camp regime had tightened the noose, and the zeks were feeling the pinch. They got together all the radio power and rudimentary generators they could to send out a signal into the void in a desperate attempt get their messages out to the wider world. In an attempt to appeal to a wider audience, Sokil had invited an accomplished Russian cohost to his daily broadcasts.

"Proshu, welcome to my cohost, Slava Politkovskaya," said Sokil.

"Spasiba! Diakuyu," said Slava. "We the proud people of the Soviet Union request fair treatment as prescribed by law. Our pleas for decency have fallen on deaf ears, and we are being punished for requesting

to be treated like human beings. I implore our Kazakh *tovarishchi* to heed our rightful calls for justice. Long live the Soviet Union!"

They played the Soviet anthem at the end of each transmission. It was a savvy move devised by Slava to curry favor with any of the KGB intercepting their broadcasts. Volodymyr was listening in the background on Valeriy's radio. He wasn't pleased about the Soviet remark.

He certainly wasn't thrilled about being called a "proud Soviet," but he understood that was important to get their message across without sounding too radical.

Volodymyr had become more interested in the inner workings of the Technical Department. He was also still recuperating and couldn't do his usual security details, which annoyed Keller. Valeriy was showing him the ropes and allowed Volodymyr to sit in on the radio show and some of the less sensitive projects. He also preferred Volodymyr's company to icy Keller, who was more interested in keeping security. They did have some agreement on the sensitive issue of Russian influence on radio.

"*Assalamu alaikum,* our Kazakh *tovarishchi.* We will be back with more news. *Spasiba,* signing off," said Slava.

"You have been listening to Radio Kengir," Sokil added.

"Radio Kengir was a nice touch," said Slava.

"Spur of the moment," Sokil laughed.

Valeriy nodded and ended the transmission while Volodymyr listened in on the small transmitter on his desk. Sokil and Slava walked out. Sokil looked chipper. Slava smiled broadly. The two of them seemed to be sending their own messages. Volodymyr coughed, reminding them they were not alone. They received the message.

"Vlodko, glad to see you've taken a liking to broadcasting," said Sokil.

Volodymyr smiled and nodded politely while keeping a wary eye on Slava.

"This is Slava, my cohost. She worked in radio during the war."She smiled and extended her hand. Volodymyr shook her hand lightly. Volodymyr was still skeptical, but he relented for Sokil's sake.

"How nice of you two to formally meet," Sokil beamed. "Well, it's about lunch, I'm famished. We've been up since dawn."

Sokil was smitten. He looked over his cohost fondly, nodding with everything she said. Volodymyr hoped she was everything she said. They walked away, hand and hand. He whispered in her ear and she giggled and blushed. Volodymyr didn't know what to think.

He made his way to the mess hall. It was packed with hungry zeks. Volodymyr looked down at his half-empty plate. Their rations were going down, but the zeks kept their heads up. He made his way to Kateryna, Stas, and Kasia.

"There's our radio man," said Stas.

Volodymyr smirked. He placed his meal down at the table. His ears were still buzzing.

"Radio Kengir was a nice touch," said Kateryna.

"I liked the opening segment in all the languages, including Polish," added Kasia.

"You were up that early?" asked Stas.

"You've just gotten lazy," Kasia teased, "up over an hour past sunrise."

They picked at their increasingly measly meals of old vegetables and canned fish.

"It can't be a honeymoon forever," Stas sighed.

Volodymyr was tapping his spoon, still thinking about Slava.

"What's on your mind?" asked Kateryna.

"This new cohost is good," said Volodymyr. "A little too good."

"What do you mean by that?" asked Stas.

"I'm not sure, probably nothing," said Volodymyr. "Call it paranoia, but I have a strange feeling that there is dishonesty in our ranks.

I remember how spies did us all in before."

They all nodded solemnly. They finished up what was left of their lunches and went outside. They were used to strange occurrences in Kengir, but they couldn't help but notice people running about, pointing at the sky.

They were hesitant to look up. They were still traumatized by years of bombings. They didn't hear any aircraft. Kasia finally picked her head up, squinting a bit, and then smiled.

"Birds?" asked Stas.

"Kites," She laughed.

They thought her mind had gone to the birds, when indeed they looked up and saw dozens of kites flying in the sky. They dangled over the walls. The four of them joined the growing crowd, cautiously making their way to the zona to get a better view. Several kite flyers lined the perimeter. They were mainly Chechens. It was a surreal sight to see these burly, bearded men with strings wrapped elegantly around their fingers.

While the great powers were launching satellites around the earth, Kengir initiated its own primitive space race. A zephyr picked up and flew the large kites over the walls. Small fuses underneath the kites started sparking, and then exploded. The kites dispersed a torrent of letters onto the ground. They heard people outside speaking Kazakh and Chechen. They realized it was the brave villagers of Kengir.

"*Makhmadera*," they heard from outside the walls.

This was followed by a torrent of bags flying over the walls. One of the zeks opened the bags and cheered. They started running with the bundles like great trophies.

"Food!" they yelled.

Everyone ran to the walls. Everyone expected the starved zeks to beg for more food, but there was a greater hunger for knowledge. The zeks started asking about news from the outside world. They even started asking these strangers about their relatives in faraway lands that these villagers couldn't have even dreamed existed. Surprisingly, the villagers answered as best they could.

The zeks had not had contact with anyone besides the dreaded guards for God only knew how long. The villagers themselves—perhaps out of curiosity, pity, or both—answered back. The Caucasians and Asians translated for the Slavs. They knew families were present when a Chechen man laughed and said, "No, dear boy, we were not born in this camp!"

They heard faint booms and cracks in the distance. They knew the guards were watching. The zeks started tossing over parcels and letters for the villagers to take with them in a desperate attempt to tell their stories.

"*Allah birdir,*" a man said. *God is great* in Tatar.

The Tatars answered back, "*Assalamu alaikum,* brothers and sisters!"

"*Wa 'alaykumu s-salam.*"

They very well may have been their actual relatives. The villagers made promises that they would be back, but God only knew when or if that would happen. Volodymyr and the others smiled and sighed, knowing their fate floated on the wayward zephyr and these Kazakh villagers. Kateryna kissed Slipyj's cross.

The next day Volodymyr came early to the Technical Department. He approached the door and was stopped by an unfamiliar *zek.*

"Pull out your pockets," said the *zek.*

"It's alright, *tovarishch,* I'm in the radio department," said Volodymyr nonchalantly.

"Your pockets," the zek said.

Volodymyr begrudgingly pulled out the pockets in his trousers.

"Your *valenki,*" said the guard.

"What about them?" "*Proshu,* remove them." Volodymyr pulled off his boots and handed them to the impatient *zek*. Volodymyr knew this was all being done under the watchful gaze of Keller. The zek guard turned over and shook Volodymyr's boots. He then handed them back to Volodymyr. He turned back to the door.

"Clear," he said. Turning back to Volodymyr, "Proceed."

Volodymyr grabbed his boots and defiantly walked over barefoot. Keller opened the door. Neither he nor Volodymyr said anything. Volodymyr walked over to Valeriy, who was frantically turning dials and knobs. He stopped to look at Volodymyr's exposed socks.

"Barefoot and naked," Valeriy smirked. "I see Keller's not taking any chances."

"What's going on?" asked Volodymyr.

"There's been a huge influx of radio interference," said Valeriy. "I can barely hear myself, let alone send out a message. The Poles came up with an interesting idea to get out or message manually—a sort of update to the Chechen kite fleet. Stas and Jerzy can say more."

"Stas too?" asked Volodymyr.

"*Tak*, Vlodko, it looks like you have competition," Valeriy teased.

Valeriy got up, stretching his cramped limbs, and guided Volodymyr over to the back of the radio tower. Sure enough, there were Stas and Jerzy along with other Slavic zeks and a thick-bearded, Chechen-looking man standing around what looked like a large bubble. Volodymyr didn't know what to make of it all. Stas turned and smiled.

"It looks like you're not the only one that can play with the mad scientists," he laughed.

Volodymyr was more interested in what the rest of them were looking at.

"Has Valeriy told you what us devious Poles are up to?" Stas asked.

"Only that you were inspired by the Chechens," said Volodymyr, trying to elicit a response from the stoic Chechen.

"*Tak*, that's Mansur Dudayev," said Stas. "He was the mastermind behind the kite armada."

Volodymyr shook his head, still trying to figure out what alien object had befallen them.

"Fire it up," said Jerzy.

"*Davay*," said Stas excitedly.

Everyone held their breath, some started to pray. Then, as if to answer their desperate pleas, a swift zephyr oxygenated the burning bucket of coal beneath the giant bubble. The huge mass inflated, and Volodymyr now realized what he was witnessing and laughed just as excitedly.

The huge hot air balloon inflated. Along the side was written: *Copernicus*. The balloon was aptly named by its Polish creators after the famous Polish astronomer and mathematician, Nicolaus Copernicus, who had proposed the then-revolutionary theory that the earth revolved around the sun. The balloon set off over the walls toward the residents of Kengir. Everyone laughed and cheered. No doubt the rest of the inmates saw the astounding maiden voyage. The *Copernicus* sailed gallantly over the Technical Department. Keller ran out with his pistol drawn, thinking they were under attack by flying saucers. They heard a sharp bang, followed immediately by a loud pop. Their hopes were deflated when a sniper bullet ripped right through the canvas. The balloon sputtered and crashed back down to earth. They knew a well-positioned sniper could have shot the large target from eight hundred meters. They picked up the pieces of *Copernicus*. Even Keller looked upset.

"Oh, the humanity!" Stas cried.

That evening, Keller picked up the patrols along the perimeter. All hands were on deck, including Kateryna's battalion. Volodymyr was working late with Valeriy. The background noise was deafening. The Soviets had invested heavily in electronic warfare as an asymmetric advantage in the Cold War with the West.

Valeriy was completely entrenched with his gadgets. Volodymyr was falling asleep at his post when he heard a large bang and crash. The whole room shook. It was followed by even more booms from the front gate. Volodymyr went white.

"Kateryna," he cried.

Volodymyr hobbled as fast as he could to the door. His leg still wasn't completely healed. He opened the door to chaos. The zeks were charging the walls, fighting a still-unseen foe. There was so much noise, it was hard to tell who or what was making it. Volodymyr was struggling with the pain in his sore legs when someone grabbed his side and propped him up. Volodymyr turned and was relieved to see that Stas was also staying late.

"Easy does it," said Stas. "There's no need to rush. We'll meet those *vovki* head on!"

The zeks stormed the gates. They heard the boom of the guards trying to break in. More guards were trying to scale the walls, but the inmates were ready. They fired large slingshots and arrows. Several of the guards let out wild yelps before they fell back down to the ground.

Volodymyr looked around frantically for Kateryna when he finally saw her. She was on the parapets with other men and women trying to beat back the guards. It was like a medieval castle breach.

"Stay here. I'll get her," Stas said to Volodymyr.

Stas climbed up to meet Kateryna. Volodymyr was still weak, but he never took advice before, and he figured he wouldn't start now. He started to climb slowly and carefully up the crates, barbed wire, and debris. The zeks tossed anything that wasn't bolted down—and some things that were—against the gates. He could hear the guards struggling.

"What is this, the Middle Ages?" a guard yelled before plunging into their improvised mote.

"Kateryna!" Volodymyr cried.

She turned to meet him when they heard a loud crash. Kateryna went flying. The guards rammed the gates with a truck, but the zeks' defenses held. The injured driver stumbled out of the flaming wreck and was pelted by rocks and bricks. Volodymyr clambered down with Stas right behind. She lay face down on the ground with a large smoldering log on top of her.

"Somebody help us!" Volodymyr cried, but nobody stopped.

He bent down and turned her head to the side. He put his ear next to her mouth. She was still breathing. He turned back to Stas, trying desperately to be heard over the chaos.

"She's alive, *diakuyu Bozhe*, but she's hurt bad.""I'll lift and you pull on three," said Stas. "*Ras, dva, tri!*"

Stas jostled the log, but it was too heavy. Volodymyr was still too weak from his own injuries to help. Out of the darkness, hearing their plight, a burly zek came to help.

"*Davay*," he said.

After a harrowing push, they lifted the log. Kateryna was freed. Volodymyr knelt down.

"We'll take her to Nacham and Kasia in the infirmary," said Stas, lifting her up. She and Volodymyr both moaned. "Can you walk?" Stas asked Volodymyr.

Volodymyr nodded vigorously. He would try anything for Kateryna. He meant nothing.

"I will help," said the *zek* in Caucasian-accented Russian.

Volodymyr realized it was Mansur.

"I saw you take out that guard that day and survive, *tovarishch*," said Mansur. "It must be written."

They carried her to the infirmary, trying to ignore the mayhem around them. More and more zeks came out of the woodworks to the scale the parapets. The guards were increasingly being drowned out by the roar of the inmates. They had no time to speculate on these historic events while their world was closing in. Kateryna was turning paler by the minute.

"Where are you taking me?" she moaned.

"Home," said Volodymyr.

They charged into the infirmary desperately calling out for help.

"Medic!" Stas yelled. "Nacham! Kasia!"

They found a table and splayed Kateryna out. They realized the seriousness of her injuries in the light. Volodymyr looked down and saw her blood on his hands.

"Kateryna!" Kasia cried, running over.

She examined Kateryna's heavily bleeding arm. A large chunk of metal was sticking out of it. Kasia turned away.

"We need to stop the bleeding," she said. "I'll get Nacham!"

"Nacham's busy," said another nurse.

"What do you mean?" asked Kasia.

She looked at Nacham, who was desperately holding down a writhing man.

"I-I've never done a surgery myself before," she stammered.

"You can do it," said Stas.

"*Tak,* we know you can," said Volodymyr.

Kasia was still unsure when she felt a wet hand grab hers. They all looked down to see Kateryna's bloody hand grasping her. Kasia agreed, knowing they had no other choice.

"Then we'll have to move fast," said Kasia. "Grab me some forceps!"

"Right away," said Mansur.

"Volodymyr, Stas, apply pressure to her wounds."Mansur returned with the forceps. Kasia clamped her wounds. She then got out stitches and a needle and went to work sewing up the wound. Kateryna bit down and took it. After another agonizing minute, the bleeding finally stopped. They all breathed a sigh of relief. Stas gave Kasia some water.

"You did it," he said, hugging her.

"I need a minute," she said, wiping her perspiring face with her shaky hands.

"Take all the time you need," he replied, wiping her bloody fingers.

Kateryna was very pale, but stable. Volodymyr stroked her head. He then looked to Mansur. He was also distraught, not the usual stern Chechen face they put on for the others.

"*Spasiba, tovarishch*," said Volodymyr. "We couldn't have gotten her here in time without your help."

"A Chechen must help fellow warriors," said Mansur. "You have all proven your worth."

"*Assalamu alaikum*," said Volodymyr.

"*Mir vsi*," said Mansur. *Peace to all* in Ukrainian.

An out-of-breath zek charged into the infirmary. Volodymyr realized it was Shvydko. He saw them and rushed over.

"Good news," Shvydko panted. "The guards have retreated!"

Volodymyr looked at poor Kateryna and the other injured patients and wondered, *For how long?*

19

JUNE 12–13, 1954:

THE MISHA INCIDENT

THE INMATES OF Kengir spent the next day licking their wounds and repairing their breached walls. Their confidence was shaken and their psyches battered. Kateryna was recuperating under the watchful care of Kasia and Nacham while Volodymyr and Stas surveyed the damage from the fiery night before. They could hardly believe their eyes.

Keller and Sokil were inspecting a hole in the wall that a small truck could drive through. That's most likely what had happened. The guards even tried to set up a machine gun post before the zeks chased them out. Volodymyr saw the singed beams that had pinned Kateryna down and shuddered. They realized in the light of day how close they had actually come to being overrun. The burnt truck was smoldering just outside the gate.

"It's good they didn't have any heavy armor," said Stas.

Volodymyr remembered his ghastly visions of doom and wondered what they would try next. Then Keller abruptly stormed right past them. Behind him Sokil muttered several curses, not realizing Volodymyr and Stas were there.

"What was that about, sir?" asked Volodymyr.

"Oh, sorry, boys. I didn't know you were right there. How's Kateryna?"

"She'll be alright," said Volodymyr.

"Nacham told me that Kasia rose to the occasion," said Sokil, looking to Stas.

"*Tak*, she really pulled through for us." "*Tak*, we'll need her," said Sokil forebodingly. "What a mess."

"It could've been worse," said Volodymyr, trying to reassure Sokil.

"I know," Sokil sighed, "and I'm sure it will be next time." He walked off.

Volodymyr and Stas looked to each other and back at the smoldering truck at the gates. The whole camp was in a daze. It was hard to believe that the wedding had only been a week ago. The guards tried to crash their party, and they nearly succeeded. The honeymoon was over. The last few weeks of relative peace had been shattered in an instant. Although the guards were beaten back, the zeks knew they would return. Their next moves were critical.

"Well, there's enough people here for now," said Volodymyr. "Unfortunately I'm still not much good lifting my weight. I'll go help the best I can in the infirmary and see how Kateryna is holding up."

"I'll go too," said Stas. "Kasia needs just as much help as anyone out here."

There was a palpable sense of dread and growing paranoia among the zeks. More people were looking suspiciously at one another. Volodymyr and Stas even found themselves looking over their shoulders. It was starting to feel like those dreaded Purge days.

They made their way to the infirmary, and it was busy as ever. More patients had arrived. It wasn't the absolute bloodbath like in those chaotic May days, but it was no joking matter. Kasia already looked like a hardened veteran. She was now giving orders.

"I'm going to need more bandages and antiseptics," she said to some younger nurses. "We're running low on iodine and chloroform, so use them sparingly—only for severe cases."

She was exhausted but looked more confident of herself after performing Kateryna's surgery. Her posture had even changed, and her expression looked more determined. She was so consumed by her duties that she didn't even notice Volodymyr and Stas walking up to her. Stas touched her shoulder. She jerked away.

"Oh, I'm sorry, guys. I haven't stopped since last night."

"You should pause. You'll burn yourself out otherwise," said Stas. "We're here to help."

"I just don't know where to begin," she sighed. "But Kateryna is stable. She's resting. Go see her, Vlodko."

"*Tak*, I'll help with Kasia and Nacham," said Stas. "She doesn't need a blabbermouth like me around right now."

"*Dziekuje*," said Volodymyr.

They parted ways. Kasia and Stas went to find supplies for the other patients. Volodymyr went over to see Kateryna. He weaved his way through the maze of hospital beds until he saw hers, covered by a curtain. He went to pull it open when he paused, suddenly filled with a strange dread. *What if she's worse than yesterday? What if she's a different person? What if I'm a different person?*

He chased away his irrational thoughts as he gingerly moved her curtain over. He breathed a sigh of relief. She looked pale but was otherwise alright. Her eyes were closed, and she was breathing a little hard. That was to be expected after such a traumatic night. He pulled up a chair next to her.

He watched her breathe. Though she was battered and bruised, she still looked like the angel to him. He placed his head on her chest. While listening to her heartbeat, he started to doze off himself when he felt fingers combing through his hair.

"How are you feeling?" Kateryna asked.

Volodymyr opened his eyes. He saw her big green eyes staring back. He kissed her hand.

"After all you've been through, you're wondering about me?"

"We're married now, aren't we?" she smiled weakly.

He had nearly forgotten in all the mayhem. He kissed her and stroked her hair. He tried to think of something to say, but his brain wasn't working right.

"What did I do to deserve you?" he asked.

"We deserve each other," she smirked.

Volodymyr stroked her leg. She winced. Volodymyr jerked his arm back. He felt terrible forgetting her injury in the heat of the moment.

"No, it's alright, look," she said.

Kateryna pulled up her blanket, revealing the burns down her leg. She was putting on a brave face, but Volodymyr saw the fear in her eyes. He then pulled up his pant leg to show the bullet wound. He placed her hand on the raised scar.

"All wounds heal," he said.

Kateryna understood. They knew they needed each other now more than ever. For this short moment, they were able to steal some time to themselves. Their moment of relative peace was interrupted by the crackling speakers. "There will be an important meeting for everyone available at the mess hall," said Kuznetsov. "I stress, *every-one*; only seriously injured patients, medical staff, and those on guard duty are excused. That is all."

He sounded serious.

Volodymyr looked to Kateryna. She looked worried, but she nodded her head. They knew he had no choice but to go. He started to get up when she grabbed his hand. She looked at him sincerely, ruffling his hair with her good arm.

"Just promise me, whatever happens, don't lose your head," she said.

"A *baran* never loses his head," said Volodymyr.

Kateryna smirked nervously. Everyone who wasn't staff or patients started leaving the infirmary. Volodymyr kissed Kateryna and turned to leave. Before he left he looked back one more time and saw Kateryna looked nervous. He wondered if he should be too. His intrusive thoughts were taking over again. He saw Stas outside pacing.

"Are you alright?" he asked Stas.

"What do you think the meeting is about?" "I told Kateryna not to worry, but I'm not so sure," said Volodymyr.

"You have quite the bedside manner," Stas smirked.

"I say what I think," said Volodymyr.

"Me too," said Stas. "I guess that's why we're here."

They walked to the mess hall. People were whispering in small groups, looking at the influx of armed zeks. There was a pervasive feeling of being watched.

They entered the crowded mess hall. It felt like walking on eggshells. Everyone was on edge. Multiple zeks armed with batons and bats were posted at the doors. Volodymyr saw Keller staring ahead coldly. Again, he didn't acknowledge Volodymyr or Stas, though he clearly saw them. They sat down at the long tables. Sokil, Sluchenkov, Kuznetsov, Knopkus, and other high ranking zeks stood front and center. Sokil lifted the megaphone to address them.

"*Vnimaniye! Uvaha!*"

Everyone quieted down. He handed the megaphone to Kuznetsov. Kuznetsov paused, looking over the crowd before speaking. There was an ominous tone to the room.

"*Tovarishchi,* we have a pressing issue," said Kuznetsov. "After the recent assault, which we barely managed to win, we have come to an uneasy conclusion."

Everyone started murmuring animatedly. *What could it mean?* He sounded like Bochkov.

"Stop speaking to us like a bureaucrat, *Kapitan,*" said Sluchenkov. "There's a simple *blatnoi slovo* for what you're trying to say."

"Then why don't you tell the men?" asked Kuznetsov.

"*Kanyezhna.*" Sluchenkov smiled fiendishly. "*Tovarishchi,* there's a *krysa* in our den!"

The whole hall erupted. *Could it be? A rat?* It felt like a giant lid had been removed from a boiling cauldron. Zeks leapt up like lemmings. One man waved his hands wildly in the air.

"How could this be?" a man exclaimed.

"Who would do such a thing?" another woman wailed.

They all let steam loose. Sluchenkov looked amused. He'd happily coaxed them on.

"*Da,* how, indeed?" asked Sluchenkov. "The proof is in the pudding, as our former British allies would say."

"Where's your proof?" another man asked.

Many started nodding in agreement. Kuznetsov was trying to control the crowd, but it was becoming impossible. Sluchenkov's accusations weren't making things any easier.

"Well, *tovarishch,* we can't confirm anything yet, but there was a lot of strange activity within our zona reported by our security apparatus," said Kuznetsov.

Volodymyr turned to see Keller firmly nodding his head in agreement.

"More precisely, they attacked at our weakest points," said Sluchenkov. "They even managed to set up machine gun posts right under our noses."

"I agree something smells rotten, but let's not turn this into a purge," said Sokil.

"Nobody mentioned anything about purges," said a Latvian man, "but I think you've been getting too close to that new communist cohost of yours."

Many in the crowd, especially the non-Russians, started nodding vigorously. Even Volodymyr found himself swept up in the moment. He slammed his fist down.

"I'm no 'proud Soviet'," Volodymyr proclaimed.Volodymyr turned and saw Keller finally acknowledge him with an approving nod.

"We're not on trial here," said Sokil firmly.

"This is exactly what we have to avoid," said Kuznetsov. "These kinds of dubious accusations that can't be put back once they're out!"

"I may know who it is," said a woman.

Everyone turned to a feisty little old woman. Her name was Masha. She was an Old Russian teacher from the Urals. Her reputation as a fiery tsarist-turned-dissident preceded her. She was adamant.

"His name is Misha Ilyich. I saw him sneaking around just before the guards attacked, looking directly over the walls," she said.

"Is he here?" asked Sluchenkov.

"No," said Keller, breaking his icy silence.

Everyone started looking around, practically tearing apart the walls for this phantom.

"Check the infirmary," someone said.

"Alright, we'll send a representative," said Sokil.

It was too late. Pandora's Box had been opened. The mob was on the move.

Sokil moaned.

"What have we done?""What needed to be done," said Sluchenkov.

Volodymyr and Stas were swept up in the moment. They were also looking for blood. They all wanted retribution for the greatest sin of betrayal. The Soviet Union's infamous purges, especially under Stalin, had warped a generation. Volodymyr and Stas were finding it harder to find their footing, or their consciences. They had forsaken their better angels.

"I hope we get this bastard," a man said.

"Amen," Volodymyr agreed.

"Hell is too good for the Hun," said Stas, referencing an old anti-German WWI slogan.

The crowd swelled as it reached the infirmary. Many new zeks joined in, not even knowing what the mob wanted—they just wanted to vent. Hell hath no fury like an angry zek mob. Nacham was standing outside in front of the door. Sluchenkov came up to him.

"Step aside, *feldsher*. We have important business to attend to."

"My patients are my business," said Nacham sternly.

"Then join us," said Sluchenkov.

"Nacham," said Sokil, moving his way to the front.

"What in the name of God is this?" asked Nacham.

"I'll keep things under control," Sokil replied.

"This is what you call 'control'?" asked Nacham.

Volodymyr hadn't seen Sokil and Nacham at heads like this in a long time.

"We're coming in sooner or later," said Sluchenkov.

"We just have some questions for a man inside," said Kuznetsov.

"You can tell me what you want, and I'll ask him," said Nacham.

"Nacham, I can handle it," said Kasia.

They all stepped back. Kasia stood firmly beside Nacham. Nacham looked pale.

"The patients like me, sir," she added.

Nacham was silent. He turned back and then reluctantly parted before the seething red sea.

"Only questions," said Nacham, looking at Sluchenkov, "and only those in charge. This isn't a circus."

"*Kanyezhna, tovarishch,*" said Sluchenkov. "Where is the man called Misha Ilyich?"

Nacham and Kasia lead them over to the end of the infirmary. Volodymyr and Stas were part of the selected group. Kasia pulled a curtain aside, and there sat a lowly old man.

"Are you the one they call Misha Ilyich?" asked Sokil.

"*Da,*" he said quietly.

"Why weren't you at the meeting?" asked Sluchenkov.

Misha stared at the floor. His silence spoke volumes. Sluchenkov was not someone to relent. He leaned in.

"Deaf are you?" asked Sluchenkov, louder. "Why weren't you at the meeting?"

"You won't accept my answer," said Misha.

"Why not?" "Because you've already made up your mind." "Now listen, dido, don't play games," said Sluchenkov. "If you give us a truthful answer, we will accept it. Now I'll ask one more time: Why weren't you at the meeting?"

"I was visiting my wife," said Misha.

They looked around. They wanted to give him the benefit of the doubt, but they only saw him. They heard a commotion, and saw Masha tearing down the hallway. She was on a warpath.

"He doesn't have a wife," she sneered.

"What do you know about me?" he asked.

"I'll get you, old fool," she said.

"She wants revenge for an old country gripe," said Misha, "something my family did to hers a long time ago that has nothing to do with what happened here."

"He speaks lies with a forked tongue," Masha said.

"He isn't lying," said Kateryna.

Everyone turned to see Kateryna slowly getting out of her bed.

Volodymyr quickly went to help her. She shrugged him off. He saw the disappointment in her sad eyes. It felt like a knife in his side. She made her way over to them.

"What's all this?" the woman asked. "Go back to your bed, young lady."

"You're the one who needs to lay down your arms, baba," said Kateryna. "His wife was in her death throes of cancer. She gave me this just before she died."

Everyone keenly watched Kateryna, especially Misha, while she pulled out a small photo. She handed it to Sokil. He looked at it and passed it to Misha. Misha looked at it and started to cry. Volodymyr leaned in and saw a youthful, vibrant version of this sad old man with a young beautiful woman in a wedding dress in front of a village church. His tears dripped down their happy faces. They all looked just as defeated; even Masha frowned.

Sokil sighed hard.

"I'm sorry for your loss." The old man just sat there and cried. Nobody dared move or console him. They were powerless at that moment. Volodymyr saw the whole sad scene and shriveled up inside.

"A master is not as cruel as a servant would be in his place," said Kateryna.

Those words never felt truer. His dido certainly wouldn't have been proud of him at that moment. Volodymyr felt ashamed. Worse yet, he understood very well what it was like to be on the receiving end of misguided justice.

It was that black summer of 1949. Volodymyr's Hoverlia Battalion launched their last large ambush on the NKVD in a thickly wooded mountain pass. It was a heavy firefight with large numbers of causalities for both sides. Volodymyr's kurin, under the command of Sokil, was separated from the main group. They were eventually surrounded and forced to surrender by a lack of ammunition. They would've used their teeth, but they had too many wounded. Even Nacham was over-whelmed. They reluctantly realized their time had come and they would have to leave their fate to the mercy of the merciless Soviet Union.

"Lay down your arms," yelled the NKVD polkovnik.

They complied and laid down their weapons. The NKVD gradually came out of the thicket. They too were bloodied and bruised, brandishing their rifles and machine guns. Their captors approached them with fear and disdain. They heard "Khokhol fascists" muttered over and over. Then the polkovnik came out, joined by his entourage. They formed a disparate troika. Volodymyr was unlucky enough to be picked first in line for Soviet 'justice'.

"You are now zaklyuchennyi of the Soviet Union," the polkovnik proclaimed. "You have been deemed terrorists by this lawfully designated troika and thus ineligible to be treated as prisoners of war under the Geneva Convention."

Volodymyr was trapped between these beasts. He started to panic when he remembered the big, stubborn old baran named Taras that they used to have on their farm. He used to guard their flock. One day Taras was cornered on a mountain ledge by a pack of wolves. Volodymyr and his family watched in horror, unable to intervene, when they saw a remarkable turn of events. The old baran backed up. They assumed he would leap to his death, but instead he charged forward and rammed the head wolf, sending him tumbling. The others ran in shock. Volodymyr took Taras's lead. He backed up and rammed the polkovnik so hard he tumbled down the side of the mountain. Sokil and the rest rushed the other NKVD, and they also ran in turn.

The guards may not have broken through the gate, but they had shattered the zeks' sense of security. It was a breach of confidence that opened a schism within their ranks. It was a harbinger of events to come.

20

JUNE 14–15, 1954:

CARROT AND STICK

"Zaklyuchennyi who surrender will be treated fairly," the loudspeakers outside the zona blared. "For those who resist, the boats await you in Magadan!"

Magadan, that dreaded eastern Siberian city, was the last stop before the mines of Kolyma that sealed the fates of thousands. The zeks found it amusing that they were supposedly in the harshest camp regime, yet the guards still threatened them with someplace worse. It is said that the grass is always greener. So, conversely, the regime must also be harsher. What infuriated the zeks most was the unfortunate fact that some zeks had actually crossed the zona and joined Kengir's propaganda machine. Volodymyr and Stas were helping clean up near the gates when they heard the sniveling pleas of one of their supposed comrades.

"Come join your *tovarishchi*. Be the good Soviet people that you are and be on the right side of history," said the announcer. "If you don't believe us, then listen to one of your own!"

"They are good to us, *tovarishchi*. They will treat you fairly! Don't let the extremist Banderists and Vlasovites in the camp lead you to destruction," said the *zek*.

Stas wiped his dripping forehead, glistening under the scorching June sun.

"I'm offended by that last part," said Stas. "What about Armia Krajowa?"

He turned toward the camp loudspeakers and yelled,

"Don't forget about the damned Poles!" He managed to get some chuckles from the nervous zeks. The camp regime was relentless. Their tirades lasted through the night. They could hear the announcers gradually get hoarse as the endless hours went on and they had to switch off. The zeks knew they were at a crossroads.

After exhausting the "stick" to beat the zeks into submission, the camp regime tried the "carrot," coaxing the weaker zeks back into their strangling arms. One particularly cruel line would announce how much food the guards had waiting for them. Volodymyr's stomach would growl on cue when he heard how many hot cauldrons of *borshch* they had to serve. Most of the "carrots" in the Soviet Union went to Moscow and some to the soldiers, so they could beat the people harder with their sticks.

"All available men and women, please gather in the mess hall for an important meeting," said Sokil.

"Go ahead and hide," the guard's loudspeakers taunted. "We'll get you sooner or later!"

Volodymyr and Stas were just happy to get some respite from the harsh Kazakh sun and guards' haranguing. Volodymyr had reopened a portion of his wound trying to prove his mettle. He was put on light duties, mainly handing out water to Stas and the others repairing the walls.

He was also trying to forget about the ugly "Misha Incident," as it was known among those who'd taken part. They all were. After all that, Misha turned out to be the loyal zek and stayed, while Masha got disgusted and ran off to the guards. Kateryna was still bitter. It all weighed heavily on his mind.

"How are you holding up, Vlodko?" asked Stas.

"By a thread," Volodymyr sighed, "like all of us."

"She'll get over it," said Stas. "Kasia isn't happy with me either."

He handed Volodymyr his water. Volodymyr guzzled down the cup. He hadn't realized his thirst. He was so confused and exhausted, he felt like he was outside his own body at times. They were all trying to pull themselves together. Slowly, but surely, they made their way to another meeting. Hunkered down in the mess hall, the zeks decided what to do.

"Well, *tovarishchi*, shall we resist or surrender?" asked Kuznetsov.

"We can hold out if we organize properly and fortify our positions," said Knopkus. "We held them back. We'll assemble teams and assign manned rotations to guard the perimeter."

"You can't run an army of *dokhodyagi*," said a man. "We haven't had a decent meal in weeks, and now you want us to take on the Red Army?"

It was a fair point. Volodymyr poked at his concave stomach. Their supplies were running low. The guards had created an effective siege. One of the zeks had been shot dead trying to scavenge just outside the zona. His lifeless body was still slumped over the barbed wire as a warning. The sympathetic villagers couldn't get close anymore. Leonid, as the elected official of the Food Department, took the floor.

"I won't sugarcoat the situation," he began. "Our rations are running down, but if we conserve we should have enough for at least a few more weeks."

"How much more can we conserve?" a woman asked. "I already see people chasing mice like hungry cats."

"We can do it, *tovarishchi*," said Leonid. "Remember our martyrs of Leningrad."

"Or the *Holodomor*," Volodymyr muttered.

"Whatever we do, we must make sure we're all on board," said Sluchenkov. "What say you, Makeyev?"

Makeyev was conspicuously in the background. He hadn't been around much since the Misha Incident. He was caught off guard.

"About what?" he asked.

"Oh nothing, just our lives," Sluchenkov snapped.

Sluchenkov was still bitter about the Misha Incident. Sluchenkov wanted to get the weight off his back. He felt like he had to save face, and Makeyev was an easy target.

"*Tovarishchi*, please," said Kuznetsov, "let's not let personal quarrels get between us."

"This isn't personal," said Sluchenkov. "I think we all deserve to know that our leaders have our backs when the shit hits the fan."

Everyone started eyeing Makeyev, who looked uncomfortable as he took the floor.

"I have nothing to prove," he said. "I've been with you from the very beginning."

"*Dobre*, then you'll be on first patrol," said Sluchenkov.

"*Kanyezhna*," said Makeyev.

"I'll tell you what," said an Estonian partisan, "I'd rather die free than surrender!"

"So we'll vote," said Sluchenkov. "All in favor of continuing our resistance, say, *ura!*"

There was a resounding hurrah. The debate was over. Makeyev stayed quiet. Volodymyr and their group firmly agreed. They weren't crazy or suicidal, but they knew there was no more reasoning with their mad dog guards. Talking to them was like talking to a cold hard rock, which is something they knew painfully well about after all these years of backbreaking toil. They were stuck between a rock and a hard place, and all they had left were themselves and their sledges.

Volodymyr was reminded of a famous poem by the beloved Ukrainian poet, Ivan Franko, called "Kamenyari," or "Stonecutters." Franko's epic was about a condemned chain gang breaking through a literal and allegorical cliff to win their freedom, though they knew most of them wouldn't survive. Volodymyr wondered how many of them would tell their story.

"Then it's settled. We move out," said Kuznetsov.

"*Kurin marsh*," said Sokil.

The Ukrainians rose up, formed ranks, and marched forward. They were in lockstep out the doors to the parapets to give the guards their answer. One of the men started singing the UPA anthem, "*Oy u Luzi, Chervona Kalyna*," or "Oh in the Meadow, a Red Gelder Rose," referencing the European berry tree that has ancient roots in Ukrainian folklore. The tune was adopted by UPA from the veterans of the earlier Ukrainian War of Independence, like Sokil. Sokil sang along.

They signaled to a guard with binoculars on the other side of the zona. Volodymyr and the rest of the zeks watched in awe while a large black banner adorned with an intimidating skull and crossbones was unfurled that read, "Freedom or Death." The flag was instantly recognizable as the banner of the infamous Ukrainian anarchist leader Nestor Makhno. Even many of the Russian zeks respected the Ukrainian firebrand of the steppes.

Makhno was a Ukrainian revolutionary anarchist leader during the Russian Civil War that created his own independent state in southeastern Ukraine known as Makhnovshchyna. His army had inflicted mass casualties on both the Red and White Russian armies before Makhno was defeated by the consolidated Russian forces in 1921. Wounded and desperate, he escaped through Romania to France, where he died in Paris in 1934 of tuberculosis.

Kuznetsov was not thrilled by their brazen display, but he allowed it. "Your fate has been sealed," the camp authorities said ominously. "Because of your insolence, I regret to inform you the following inmates who would have been otherwise pardoned will no longer be considered."

The camp officer went on to rattle off a list of names. It was a surprising tactic. They droned on and on, making sure now to take patronymics and full names into effect. Volodymyr didn't recognize any of the names as being part of their main resistance. They would soon realize the cold calculus behind the chosen names.

"That's a lot of names," said Stas. "You think they're all real?"

"Even if half are, there's going to be trouble," he replied.

The announcer abruptly finished after several minutes. The men looked dazed. It appeared some of their ranks' names had been called after all. They saw the despondent look in their eyes. Some prisoners stared at their feet looking sick; others walked in circles like lost sheep. Not more than fifteen minutes later, they saw Shvydko running up.

"What's going on, Shvydko?" asked Sokil.

"They've started a revolt," Shvydko panted. "We've already revolted," said Sokil, confused.

"Follow me to the SHIZO." They followed close behind. They didn't even make it halfway when they heard screaming and smelled smoke. There was commotion coming from the SHIZO cells. They all feared the guards had broken in again, but they soon realized it was the zeks themselves bringing the house down.

"You've doomed us all," said a wild-eyed old man emerging from the abyss.

The majority of the zeks called were ones known not to have taken part in the uprising. The guards had masterfully stoked internal strife between the zeks. They had started a miniature civil war. A woman came running up to them from the opposite direction.

"They're taking hostages," she said.

"Where?" asked Sokil.

"The infirmary.""Come on, men," said Sokil. "We have to help our *tovarishchi!*"

Volodymyr and Stas didn't have to be persuaded. Sokil was intent on saving Nacham too. Kuznetsov and Knopkus could deal with the SHIZO rioters. The rest of them would take forces to the infirmary.

Zeks ran helter-skelter throughout the courtyard like during the guards' attacks. This time it was a disaster of their own making. They had no time to answer the desperate pleas of prisoners when their closest friends and relations were in trouble. They also knew that without the infirmary, they were all doomed. They reached the infirmary and were greeted by a troubling sight. A ring of armed zeks surrounded the building.

"They're definitely not *nashi*," said Sokil.

There were too many, too close to the patients. It appeared to be a hostage situation. They had encountered hostage situations during the war, and they rarely ended well. The rescues that did succeed often had a man on the inside. They thought about what to do, when Volodymyr's leg started acting up again. His pain struck him with inspiration.

"I can get in," said Volodymyr.

"How?" asked Sokil.

Volodymyr rolled up his pant leg to reveal his bruised leg. They understood. Volodymyr would be their Trojan horse. He wouldn't even have to feign an injury. They would signal to each other from the windows.

A burly, wild-eyed man was animatedly giving orders.

"I know him," said Sluchenkov bitterly. "His name is Dima, a petty thief from my hometown. He acts tough, but he's full of it. You'll be alright."

"You sure you want to do this?" asked Stas.

"Kateryna and Kasia are in there," said Volodymyr, swallowing hard.

Volodymyr and Stas slowly approached Dima. He had two burly zeks beside him. Volodymyr didn't even really need to exaggerate his limp.

"Stop! That's enough," said Dima. "We'll take him from here!"

Stas carefully let go. Volodymyr wobbled. Stas whispered to Volodymyr before he left, "Don't worry, brother, just stick to the plan and we'll get you all out."Stas moved his eyes to the rear of the building. Volodymyr could see Shvydko, Sokil, Sluchenkov, and Jerzy moving in while Dima and his guards had their backs turned. They grabbed Volodymyr and jerked him away from Stas. Volodymyr winced.

"He's injured," Stas said angrily. "What's wrong with you?"

"He's a Banderist; he'll take what he gets," said Dima.

Volodymyr was rushed to the door. Dima and his guards stopped, checking around the corner. Luckily, the rest of the men had successfully disappeared behind the building.

"Clear," said one of Dima's boys.

"*Davay*," said Dima, pushing Volodymyr inside.

"You're lucky I'm injured," said Volodymyr.

"What are you going to do?" Dima taunted. "Hit me with your cane, dido?"

I'll get even with you, if it's the last thing I do. Volodymyr was fuming, but he knew he had to control his anger for now. He had more important things to do. He had to find Kateryna, Kasia, and

Nacham. They moved him along. Volodymyr scoured the room when he saw Kasia and Nacham. They saw him and smiled, but he shook his head, not to give him away. They understood and walked over professionally.

"I can take him," said Kasia.

"Not him," said Dima. "He's a special case."

"A wolf in sheep's clothing," one of Dima's boys teased.

"Then I'll take him," said Nacham.

"Oh no, not you, *feldsher*," said Dima. "We know you're UPA. We're taking him to the special ward."

They moved him to the secluded part of the hospital and shoved him onto an old mattress.

"Sit, stay, *khokhol* dog," Dima laughed.

Volodymyr stayed quiet for a while, trying to get his bearings in the dim light, when he heard, *Vlodko!* He turned to see Kateryna in a bed just beside him. He happily hobbled over to her. They embraced tearfully, but not too long should Dima get suspicious.

"How did you get in here?" Kateryna whispered.

"Well, we told them I was injured and needed medical attention, which wasn't a complete lie," said Volodymyr, wincing. "How did you wind up in the special ward?"

"They started separating the partisans, especially the Ukrainians, for when 'the camp returns to normal,'" said Kateryna bitterly.

"Don't count on them being here," said Volodymyr.

"You have a plan?" Volodymyr pointed out the small window. They could see a small flashing mirror by a barrack. Volodymyr looked behind and carefully approached; producing his own small mirror and flashing it back. They could make out Stas. He flashed out in Morse code: *How many?* Volodymyr turned to Kateryna, who confirmed: *3 Inside; Outside Unknown.* Stas signaled they would get reinforcements.

So, they hunkered down. Time passed slowly. It's always calmest inside the eye of the storm. Dima didn't come around; only one of his cronies checked in long enough to give them a dirty look and take off. After nearly an hour, Nacham was able to see them.

"How are you, Baran?" asked Nacham. "I hear your leg is giving you some trouble."

One of Dima's men was overseeing them. Nacham leaned in and slowly pulled up Volodymyr's pant leg. "What's going on outside?" he whispered.

"They're coming back with more people," said Volodymyr. "Stas, Sokil, Sluchenkov, Jerzy."

"Hmm, even Sluchenkov?" Nacham grunted. "He's got nerve, I'll give him that."

"There will be a signal; a diversion," said Volodymyr. "They said there would be no mistaking it, so be ready."

"Time's up," said Dima's henchman.

Nacham nodded and left, lest Dima get suspicious. Kasia came in with some water and old bread. They were happy to see each other nonetheless.

"I'm sorry, but this is all we have," said Kasia, handing them the measly bread. "How's Stas?" "You'll see him soon enough," said Volodymyr, wolfing down the bread.

"Rescue?" asked Kasia.

Volodymyr nodded. He swallowed hard. He opened his mouth when there was a loud explosion. The whole infirmary shook. The shockwaves knocked Volodymyr out of his chair. They were followed by more explosions, followed by shouts and scuffles outside.

"Get off your asses!" Dima screamed. "Get out there and fight!"

The windows were broken by rocks, one by one. Smoke started pouring in. It was the geniuses of the Technical Department at work. They had smoke bombs and flash grenades. Volodymyr was still trying to find his way in the dark. He called for Kateryna, but there was no answer. Dima's people went wild, howling in the dark. Several of their comrades had entered. Stas broke open the front door and in came Sokil, Sluchenkov, and Jerzy. When the smoke cleared, Volodymyr's greatest fears were realized.

"If any of you tries anything stupid, I'll kill her," Dima seethed. "I mean it."

Dima held a knife to Kateryna's neck. Nobody moved. They knew he was serious. Volodymyr tried to find something, anything that could take Dima out. He saw his cane, and his opportunity to strike back. He carefully grabbed it. Stas caught his eye, and

Volodymyr nodded. He made a slight dipping motion with the cane, indicating his intention to strike down Dima. Stas blinked twice, agreeing to the plan. Sokil, Sluchenkov, and Jerzy caught on and tried their best to distract Dima.

"Don't do anything rash," said Stas, approaching Dima. "Nobody needs to get hurt here."

"That's what you think, Polak," said Dima. "Now stay back, all of you!"

Kateryna was in shock. She didn't utter a sound lest the knife pressed to her throat slip. Dima was getting more erratic by the minute.

"We can talk this through," said Sokil. "We're reasonable men."

"I don't think you really want to hurt a helpless woman," Jerzy added.

The carrot wasn't working. It was time for the stick. Sluchenkov was up.

"You talk big, but you're the same little weasel we left behind in the Urals, Dima. I'd say you give Russians a bad name, but you're not even Russian, you Mongol half-breed!"

"You shut your damned mouth, Sluchenkov, or I'll shut it for you,"

Dima exclaimed. "Don't you tell me who's a real Russian, hanging around with these fascists, you Vlasovite!"

Sluchenkov's taunting had worked. Dima now pointed the knife at him and away from Kateryna. Volodymyr was within striking distance. Stas nodded.

"*Davay.*" Volodymyr struck Dima's arm and the knife went flying. Volodymyr then struck Dima across the head with all his might. Kateryna ducked away, and Dima fell to the floor.

"Always watch out for dido's cane," said Volodymyr.

The rest of them charged. Despite being struck, Dima was tough, and they still struggled to control him. Eventually, they overpowered him. They dragged him out of the infirmary, despite his injuries. Keller and his team were waiting outside after taking out Dima's cronies. They decided what to do next with the defeated, yet still dangerous, Dima.

"What should we do with them?" asked Stas.

"Feed them to the dogs," said Sluchenkov, referring to the *vovki* waiting just outside.

They prodded them along to the edge of the zona.

"You're at the mercy of fate now," said Sokil.

"Better than the likes of you, Banderist scum," said Dima.

The loudspeaker turned on and the voice sent shockwaves throughout the camp.

"*Tovarishchi*, please be reasonable. The jig is up. The only way out of this alive is to surrender," said Makeyev.

"I'll kill him if it's the last thing I do," said Sluchenkov.

21

JUNE 21–22, 1954:

THE MASTER AND MOLOTOV COCKTAIL

AFTER A WEEK, the zek riots subsided. Dozens of zeks had been seriously injured and scores were expelled once the combined forces of Kuznetsov and Knopkus closed in on the SHIZO and turned them over to the camp authorities outside. The ashes were not even cold yet when another inflammatory proclamation came over the airwaves. Valeriy and the technical team brought their equipment into the mess hall for all to hear. All of the zek top brass and security apparatus were present. The signal came in with the usual static at first, but the unbelievable words started coming through.

"*Zaklyuchennyi* of Kengir, if you are listening, we have important news from our most gracious and merciful leaders in *Moskva*," said the announcer. "Your demands have been accepted and a member of the Presidium of the Central Committee is on his way!"

They were dumfounded. At first, they thought they had misheard the announcement. Volodymyr and the group had only recently left the infirmary after the Dima debacle. Volodymyr didn't have time to talk to Valeriy before the big announcement. Everyone looked to each other for answers.

"What could it mean?" asked a man.

"It's clearly some kind of trick," said another.

"I don't know what it means," said Kuznetsov warily.

"I agree," said Sluchenkov. "I say it's bullshit!"

The zeks got more animated. Kuznetsov looked exhausted. He didn't answer definitively.

"I didn't say that per se. I just don't know," said Kuznetsov. "It would be a pretty big feint, and I don't know what they would get out of it."

"I don't think we should let our guard down," said Knopkus.

"*Tak,* I agree, we keep regular guard rotations, and reinforce the perimeter," said Keller.

Keller had taken up a more active role in discussions. His crucial role in liberating the infirmary had pulled him out of the shadows. Kuznetsov absentmindedly nodded. They hadn't seen him so despondent. It was a disconcerting sight. Whether they liked it or not, they needed Kuznetsov. The gulag regime still wouldn't deal with the Ukrainians, Poles, or Baltics directly, and Sluchenkov was too much of a hothead to be diplomatic.

"We will reconvene in the morning after a good rest. I will join first watch," said Sokil, picking up from Kuznetsov. "Dismissed."

The inmates of Kengir picked themselves up and retired for the night. Volodymyr looked over and saw Kuznetsov and Sluchenkov were having a serious conversation in the background. Makeyev's betrayal, coupled with the zek revolt, weighed heavily on all of them.

It was a long walk back to the barracks. Despite not having regular work, the past few weeks had left them nonetheless physically and mentally exhausted. The whole camp had been turned upside down yet again. People mulled about throughout the night and day. The circadian rhythm of the camp was thrown off. The four friends sat up in their bunks brooding.

"What are we supposed to do?" asked Kasia.

"Getting some sleep is all we can do right now," said Stas.

"*Tak*, we have watch in the morning," said Kateryna.

Volodymyr was too tired to even say *dobranich*. They crawled into bed and passed out. It would prove to be a restless night.

Volodymyr was back in the infirmary staring down Dima. He clutched Kateryna to his side and raised his cane for the fateful blow. Everything was in slow motion, and then sped up double time. Volodymyr slipped and fell, missing Dima and striking the ground. The entire earth shook.

Volodymyr was shaken out of his sleep. They all woke up. They crept out of their barracks and met other nervous onlookers. The zeks popped their heads out of the barracks one by one, like prairie dogs, to investigate the strange noises.

"My God, another attack?" asked Kasia.

"No, I don't think so," said Stas.

They waited several long seconds. They were about to go back inside when a large thud shook the whole barrack. The miniature earthquake was followed by the rumbling of creaking and grinding of what they could only guess was heavy machinery just beyond the zona. It sounded like the excavator from the mines. Whatever it was, they couldn't see it from there.

"Let's see what's going on," said Kateryna.

"We'll go to Sokil. He should still be on watch," said Volodymyr.

They made their way to the watchtowers. The phantom construction continued. They were stumbling in the dark when they were approached by a neighboring *zek*.

"What's going on?" their neighbor asked them.

"Your guess is as good as ours," said Stas.

The man nodded and quickly scampered off. They made their way to the gates and approached Sokil. He was standing by one of the towers conversing with the sentries. A jumpy young zek leapt out of his post, scaring all of them.

"*Khto ty?*" he asked in Ukrainian. *Who are you?* "That's *Sotnyk Baran*," said Sokil.

"Oh, sorry, sir," the young man said, saluting Volodymyr.

Volodymyr quickly saluted back, almost reluctantly. He still wasn't used to his promotion. He felt more comfortable as a combatant. Sokil waved the young zek off.

"What brings you all here?" asked Sokil. "Your shift doesn't start for about two hours."

"We were wondering about the noise," said Kateryna.

"We don't know what it is either," said Sokil. "They started about an hour ago. It sounds like some heavy equipment. They must have received reinforcements from Karaganda."

"You think they're getting ready for this Central Committee official?" asked Kasia.

"I'm not even sure there is such a person, quite frankly," said Sokil.

They heard a heavy engine fire up, followed by another loud crash outside the walls.

"It sounds like excavating equipment," said Stas. "I recognize it from my mining days."

"Your guess is as good as mine," said Sokil.

Everyone was guessing at this point. The Soviets were masters of psychological warfare. The sound got louder and closer. The young guard ran up to them. He looked ghost white.

"There's something happening by the gate," he said.

They could hear strange metallic clinking and clanking. They looked around and didn't see anything happening on their side. The gates then swung open. Their hearts sank.

"Breach!" a zek screeched on the watchtower.

Everyone nearby ran to the gates with weapons drawn. They gathered anything they could: shovels, picks, pikes, and spears. People from other barracks followed suit. Everyone's heart was beating, waiting for the onslaught. They were met with deafening silence.

"Close the gate," said Sokil, quickly breaking everyone out of their trance.

The zeks quickly closed the gates. They wondered what nefarious strings the guards were pulling. They waited until dawn broke to look closer. Volodymyr and the others carefully approached. They thought they had imagined it all, but a sentry spotted something.

"Look at the size of those tracks," he said.

Sure enough, they spotted huge caterpillar tracks cut through the dirt. The depth of the treads suggested heavy machinery. Whatever it was, they knew they had to prepare for the worst. Even though it was their shift, the whole camp was on guard.

Everyone in camp was getting ready to fight to the death if needed. Men and women of all ages were sharpening spears and swords. Volodymyr imagined this is what it was like when Kyiv was under siege by the Mongols centuries ago, but now they were in the khan's realm. The Technical Department had decided to spare some of their nefarious supplies, including an array of caustic and flammable substances, including what was left of their diesel and kerosene.

A Finnish man named Simo was teaching them all about the art of the Molotov cocktail. The name was derived from a joke about being a "gift" for the infamous Soviet Foreign Affairs Minister Vyacheslav

Molotov. Simo was a veteran of both WWII and the Winter War against the Soviets (1939-1940) in which the vastly outmanned Finns had inflicted catastrophic losses against the poorly led Soviets in the months leading up to WWII. Their brilliant tactics and asymmetric warfare became legendary. The Finns then continued to fight the Soviets in what became known as the Continuation War on the side of the Nazis. The Finns were forced to pay heavy reparations, including ceding even more territory to Russia. Simo was among the thousands captured and never returned after the wars.

The zeks were situated around the courtyard with Simo and his assistants in the center. They had all of the ingredients: Kerosene, bottles, and rags spread around several of the large tables they had used for their unsuccessful meetings with the Soviet regime. Those diplomatic endeavors had gone up in flames. They were ready to return the favor.

People were carefully pouring the precious kerosene into glass bottles made in their shops. Simo watched over them, carefully inspecting their malicious handiwork. Although Finns were generally reserved, he couldn't help but smile mischievously, no doubt thinking about his own personal exploits using the deadly concoction during the wars.

"Twist the rag and stuff it in, turn it upside-down, and light," said Simo rhythmically.

He lit up a Molotov cocktail and threw it at an old mattress placed in the courtyard. Direct hit! It exploded and combusted in a brilliant display. The mattress was instantly engulfed in flames and it burned down to the coils in less than a minute.

"There you have it: The best brew in Helsinki," said Simo.

The zeks laughed. Volodymyr and his friends were head of the class. They'd had some experience with the concoction in the waning days of the war when they were low on ammunition. Leonid joined them and was also surprisingly adept at making this devil's drink.

"I learned from other Finns during my time in the far north," Leonid smiled. "I give them credit where it's due. It's a hell of a brew!"

Simo smiled, but he had taken more of an interest in Kasia. She was having some trouble with the rag. Simo quickly came over. He was happy to oblige.

"Twist it like it's the neck of one of these *vovki*," said Simo.

Kasia scowled and twisted with all her might. She shoved it into the bottle with ease now. Simo smiled. Stas shuddered.

"I won't stick my neck out for a while," said Stas.

The bell rang. It was time for dinner. Leonid put down his bottle and smiled.

"Well, we've had our fill of cocktails for today. Let's eat!"

"What's on the menu?" asked Volodymyr, trying to keep the game up.

"Three course *balanda*," he laughed.

They took their food outside. They didn't know who or what would come through the gates, so they didn't want to take a chance and let their guard down. They slurped down their soup and stewed about their situation.

"What do you think about this latest announcement, Leonid?" asked Kasia.

They all turned to him; he was the *starosta* after all. Leonid was quiet for once.

"I've heard about these kinds of tricks before, especially under Stalin, to tame the situation before they would rush in, but not like this; we would've been dead already. To tell you the truth, I think the rank and file are just as confused as we are."

It wasn't the answer they were hoping for.

They heard a low rumbling in the distance. Their plates and tins rattled on the tables. It felt like a miniature earthquake. Their loudspeakers turned on.

"*Tovarishchi,* head to the gates," said Sokil.

They threw down their ladles and picked up their arms. There was no time to second-guess anything now. They ran to the gates, expecting the worst. They looked up to the sky, expecting a bombardment.

"What do you think this is?" asked Kasia.

"Only *Boh* knows," said Kateryna.

More zeks emerged from the mess hall and barracks. The gates swung open yet again. They held firm, their knees were locked, and their grips were tight around their clubs, spears, and picks. Kasia twisted the rag in her Molotov cocktail. Her knuckles were white. They gritted their teeth and planted their feet. They divided their defenses according to their means. During the war, with conventional weapons such as rifles, each soldier was responsible for roughly ten meters. Their limited arms meant they could only be responsible for about a third of that distance. They packed themselves in a tight formation like that of a Roman legion.

Minutes ticked by. Their nerves were fraying. Again, they were met with nothing but eerie silence. They quickly closed the gates. They lowered their weapons and started to walk away when they heard a loud bang on the other side of the camp walls. They turned their attention to one man on the walls: Misha. He was frantically motioning outside the walls.

"They're trying to break in," he said. "I don't have anything to stop them!"

Everyone looked for something to answer Misha's desperate pleas. Their spears and clubs were useless for oncoming attackers in vehicles. They didn't have time to bring out any of the catapults that they were experimenting with in the Technical Department. Volodymyr saw their tables of half-full bottles and was struck with inspiration. He quickly concocted a Molotov cocktail for Misha. He ran back and threw one up to him. Misha just barely caught it with his fingertips. There was an audible gasp. Misha lit up the rag and looked dead ahead at the enemy. He threw the Molotov cocktail with all his might and a little bit of blind faith.

They could see the flaming projectile fly over the fence and strike a large bulldozer attempting to ram the tower. The bulldozer went up in flames and the driver jumped out. A wave of cheers ran through the line. People shouted, *Misha! Misha! Misha!* Volodymyr and Misha looked each other in the eyes for the first time since the incident. Misha nodded appreciatively. Volodymyr returned the favor. They thought that was the end of their troubles when a young zek cried out, "Look out!" The flaming bulldozer was barreling forward like a ballistic missile without its driver. It was too late for Misha to react. The bulldozer rammed into the tower where Misha stood. The impact made a terrible crunching and cracking, like breaking bones. Misha tumbled down right onto his head. Volodymyr moved in. Other zeks ran in with water to extinguish the blaze before it caught onto the watchtower and the rest of the wall. They formed a human chain for an old bucket brigade. Volodymyr, Stas, and Leonid pulled Misha away from the scorching flames. Sokil finally ran up with a fire extinguisher. Kasia and Kateryna followed suit and brought in more extinguishers from the warehouses.

They fought the blaze for nearly half an hour before it finally died down. It appeared to have been enough of a show of force to prevent more of the camp guards from moving in. Nacham finally appeared from the infirmary to see Misha. Volodymyr turned him over. Misha's face was black and blue. Nacham patted his face, but he was unresponsive. He checked his pulse.

"What time is it?" he asked solemnly.

The next day at dawn, they tolled a bell over the announcements. Everyone who was able amassed in the courtyard. All faiths were in attendance. Sokil lowered his head.

"A moment of silence for our brave Misha," he said.

They brought out his body to the courtyard. He was covered in a finely woven *rushnyk* in a wooden coffin made in the woodshop. A Russian Orthodox priest performed the ceremony. They all sang "*Vichnaya Pamyat.*" Everyone kneeled for Misha's passing body. It was a tragic end to a heroic last deed for the unfortunate Misha, victim of both the Soviet regime and mob violence. Volodymyr couldn't help but still feel ashamed. He looked at Stas, who looked pale. He undoubtedly felt some similar internal turmoil. Keller stared ahead stoically, but he lowered his head when Misha passed. A young Russian clergyman held up a small icon of the Virgin Mary. Volodymyr looked closer, and realized it was the same icon from the pit. It was fate.

They saw Sluchenkov looking uncharacteristically morose. He was even singing along with the solemn lament of the Russian priest. He genuflected dramatically when Misha stopped by him. Even more amazingly, he touched the coffin and mouthed, "*Forgive me.*" He looked up and briefly met Volodymyr's gaze. Volodymyr averted his eyes out of respect, but for that fleeting moment he saw a broken man peeking out from his tough shell.

"It could've been worse," said Stas.

"It will be," said Leonid.

Volodymyr solemnly nodded. He looked over the charred vehicle and watchtower. Nothing good was coming for them now. They weren't waiting for any representative, only judgment day.

22

JUNE 23–24, 1954:

BIRDS OF THE SAME FEATHER

"**THE END IS NIGH**," an old zek screamed. "Repent or face damnation!"

His name was Glaza, Russian for *eyes*. He was a supposed mystic from one of the fundamentalist Orthodox sects in Siberia. Rumor had it that his vision was taken from him at a young age, and then he received the gift of foresight. Glaza had not been very active during the early days of the revolt and only appeared recently from his humble *zemlyanka* near the SHIZO.

A curious crowd gathered around him. There seemed to be a new prophet every hour. Much of the camp had reverted into a kind of religious hysteria. People were naturally looking for answers, but they were searching in questionable places. Otets Mykola looked dismayed.

"It was a matter of time," he said. "False prophets always appear in man's despair."

They were wading into uncharted waters. Nobody responded to the attempted break-in. Valeriy checked the airwaves but only picked up jumbled signals. Volodymyr wondered what it all meant. He was receiving his own mixed signals. He was plagued by increasingly disjointed thoughts and dreams. It all started to feel like his days as a *dokhodyaga* back around Easter. He looked at a man in the crowd and saw Otets Julian's face staring back. Volodymyr recoiled in quiet terror.

"Are you alright?" asked Kateryna.

"*Ta-tak*," Volodymyr stammered.

Volodymyr also saw in his periphery Sokil's concerned expression. They all looked worn down. Those early days were also rough, but they'd still had hope. Conditions were deteriorating fast, and they wanted to prevent a freefall. Misha wasn't in the ground a full day when another died of unknown causes.

"We should hold a meeting with all the clergy," said Mykola. "We need to talk some reason into people before we all go mad."

After what they still called "lunch," they gathered in the courtyard with their religious representatives. Along with Mykola and other Ukrainians there was the imam, rabbi, and the Russian Orthodox priest from Misha's funeral, along with Polish, Lithuanian, Latvian Catholic, and Estonian Lutheran clergy. Mykola came to the center and genuflected to those gathered.

"*Slava Isusa Khrystu*," he said.

"*Slava Naviki*," the congregants answered.

"We know you all have questions and concerns," Mykola began, "but that's no reason to give into hysteria."

"Charlatan," a woman hissed.

Everyone turned to an old Russian woman named Yelena they also knew from the religious circles swirling around the camp. She pointed her old craggy finger at Mykola. The crowd grew restless.

"*Proshu, tovarishchi*," said Mykola. "I turn my cheek and open the floor for our friends."

"They're not our friends," someone said.

"Only he who has never sinned may cast stones," said Mykola.

"The Old Testament also said an eye for an eye," said a woman.

"You see, even among their ranks there is division that will break us," said Glaza.

He then walked forward with his congregation in tow. He felt his way with a long staff and two burly Russian zeks by his side. They walked up to Mykola.

"*Pryvit, tovarishch*," said Mykola.

"That is not how you view me or us 'true believers,'" said Glaza.

"You see how they mock us?" said Yelena.

"We don't mock you. We just think everyone should be careful making proclamations," said Mykola.

"God talks through me," said Glaza.

"Through prayer, *kanyezhna*," said Mykola.

"No, directly as his vessel," Glaza replied.

"You can't possibly mean that.""Though I have lost my earthly vision, you are the one who is blind.""Shut your blasphemous mouth, warlock," said a woman.

Nobody knew who cast the first stone, but they descended into literal mudslinging. Mykola and Glaza were forced to retreat by their congregants for their own safety. The meeting was a disaster. They retired to their separate sides of the camp even more divided than before. They went to sleep with more questions than answers.

It was raining heavily. Volodymyr was sinking into the mud. He struggled to break free, but he was weighed down by layers of chains. His hands were covered in blood. He then looked up and saw Otets Julian standing over him, condemning him. His face was death.

"You will pay for what you did," said Julian. "If not with your blood, then that of your lamb."

Volodymyr then heard the bleating of his slaughtered lamb. It made his ears bleed. He screamed and cried, but nobody heard him; nobody cared.

He woke up drenched in sweat. It felt like he really had been in a downpour. He looked over and Kateryna was still sleeping. Stas and Kasia were also sound asleep on the other side of the room.

Volodymyr's thoughts were racing around his head. He genuflected and said three Hail Marys. Then, he recited all his family members' names alphabetically in rapid, monotone succession, making sure not to stumble, or he would have to start all over. It didn't work. It never did. It was worse when Volodymyr was younger, or in times of trouble during the war. Some in his village thought he was mad, but his mother understood. She said Volodymyr had the "Thinker's Disease." His obsessions and compulsions were getting the better of him again in these desperate times.

Volodymyr found himself alone and afraid, like on that fateful Easter day. He knew again that if he couldn't find absolution in Western religion, he would head East to the arms of the shaman. He had no choice, lest he descend into the depths of madness.

He gingerly got out of bed so as not to wake Kateryna. He looked over her, his sleeping angel. Volodymyr tried his best to keep strong for her, but he was losing it. He carefully opened the door, making sure none of his new family were disturbed.

Volodymyr quietly made his way to the shaman's hut. He looked up at the starlit night sky and sighed. All the bright, pretty stars were surrounded by darkness like the zeks of Kengir. He remembered cute sayings as a child about how the darkness made the stars "shine all the brighter" or about a "diamond in the rough," but they didn't sound right anymore. They never saw war or the Gulag. He wondered how—like the heavens above—such a beautiful world could hold such darkness. If they were created in the image of God, or even the product of nature, where had they gone wrong? He felt so small. They were living on borrowed time, and he had no chance to do things differently. Like many of his generation, he had been robbed of so many opportunities. How he wished poor Ukraine could be free and he and his countrymen develop like a normal country instead of constantly being invaded and tortured. He wanted to fly away among the stars, but he was nonetheless stuck here on this miserable plot of earth like everyone else. He wasn't any different, which was their strength. They had nothing except each other. He would've never met Kateryna, Stas, Sokil if he wasn't captured, wasn't forced to fight, but he wouldn't have left Halya and his family either.

He was so lost in his thoughts he nearly gave himself away. He looked around to make sure nobody else was watching. Volodymyr was surprised to see Ondar conspicuously waiting by the shaman's *zemlyanka*. Volodymyr was about to call out, but Ondar already knew.

"Are you alone?" asked Ondar.

"*Tiimee medeej*," said Volodymyr. *Yes of course*, in Mongolian.

"Are you sure?""*Tak*, what are you talking about?"Ondar pointed behind him. Volodymyr turned to see Kateryna waiting in the wings. He was shocked.

"What are you doing here?" he asked.

"I was worried about you," she said. "You didn't say anything, or leave a note. What was I supposed to think?"

Volodymyr turned back to Ondar and asked for Kateryna with his eyes.

"We said you and you alone," said Ondar firmly.

"They both may enter, if they are willing," said the shaman.

They all turned, surprised to see the old shaman poking out of the *zemlyanka*.

"On the condition that she can keep a secret," said Ondar.

"*Tiimee*, she was a partisan like me," said Volodymyr.

That seemed to satisfy Ondar enough. They parted the beads in the old *zemlyanka* to enter. Volodymyr waited in the doorway for Kateryna.

"Agent Soloveyko strikes again," Volodymyr smirked.

"I'm only following the lead of a hardheaded Baran," she said.

Volodymyr looked around, having a flashback to his previous visions before regaining his bearings. Ondar was preparing the fire. The shaman leaned forward inquisitively.

"Does she know the ritual?" asked the shaman.

"No.""Good," said the shaman, surprisingly. "There will be no barriers to her mind."

Ondar handed her the *chifir*. She turned to Volodymyr, who nodded.

"Are you ready, my daughter?" asked the shaman.

Kateryna warily nodded. Volodymyr drank first. She followed right behind. The shaman began his *khoomei*. Ondar placed some herbs and wild steppe grass onto the fire. The room filled with incense. They were transported to another realm of consciousness. Kateryna was completely silent. Volodymyr started to worry when she started to smile.

"What do you see?" he asked.

"I'm floating," said Kateryna. "I'm light as a feather, entering the clouds. It's so peaceful up here, *kokhanna*. I don't see you though, Vlodko?"

Volodymyr saw a red sky at dawn, meaning a storm was coming. Then, like clockwork, he heard a great screech like thunder. A great sokil descended. It picked up Volodymyr in its talons and carried him over flames and destruction. It held him tightly, and he bled, but he knew that meant he was still alive. He didn't see Kateryna.

The chant lasted for over an hour before they came down. Ondar handed them some regular tea. They drank it slowly. Volodymyr and Kateryna looked into each other's eyes with newfound resolve, but also some trepidation. They knew their different visions would be answered soon.

"*Z Bohom*," said Ondar.

Volodymyr and Kateryna emerged from the *zemlyanka*. It was very late. The moon was starting to set. Volodymyr was stargazing again when Kateryna tapped his shoulder.

"Do you think we'll survive this?" she asked.

Volodymyr was silent.

"I thought so," Kateryna sighed.

"Whatever happens, we'll be together," said Volodymyr, pulling her close. "We'll be among the stars."

They made their way back to their barracks. They gingerly opened the door and tiptoed inside. They sat down on the bed trying not to wake up Stas and Kasia.

"Where were you?" asked Kasia.

"Stargazing," Kateryna replied.

They slept as late as they could and went to breakfast the next day. Everyone was forced to cut down on meals. They ate as much as they could before a tiny dinner. The four of them were eating when Volodymyr saw Valeriy sit down behind them. He looked worried.

"I just don't understand it," Valeriy mumbled.

The bell rang. It was funny that nobody had ever turned off the automatic bell for mealtimes. It was almost as if they expected, somehow, things would go back to normal, but they knew that there was nothing normal for them—not anymore, not for a very, very long time.

"Are you coming, Vlodko?" asked Kateryna.

"*Tak*," said Volodymyr, watching Valeriy, who was now talking with Sokil and Keller.

Volodymyr figured he would go to the Technical Department to figure out what was going on. There was an unusual uptick in activity. The wind picked up and Volodymyr smelled a powerful mix of gasoline and sulfur. He approached the gates and was patted down by Keller himself. He didn't persist though. He and Volodymyr were on much better terms since the "Dima Debacle."

"Valeriy may need a hand," said Keller.

"I'll try my best," said Volodymyr.

Volodymyr opened the door and saw Valeriy listening intently.

"What do you hear?" asked Volodymyr. "Nothing," Valeriy replied.

"They're jamming our signals?" "I don't know what they're doing. Your guess is as good as mine."

That's not what Volodymyr wanted to hear. He was trying to think of what to say when he was startled by a tap on his shoulder. It was Stas.

"Stas, you startled me." "That may just be the beginning," said Stas.

"What do you mean?" Stas pulled him aside, away from Valeriy's earshot.

"There's a meeting tonight between the Ukrainian Centre and Armia Krajowa." So Stas knew. Volodymyr had never told him about the Ukrainian Centre by name, so it was legitimate. Volodymyr went back to the barracks when he saw Kateryna waiting by the door.

"*Sotnyk* Baran," Kateryna saluted.

"At ease, Agent Soloveyko," said Volodymyr. "I should've known you were one step ahead."

"Lead the way," she said.

They made their way to the Ukrainian Centre headquarters. Even though the guards weren't around, they still kept quiet out of habit. Spies were everywhere.

"*Sotnyk* Baran, Soloveyko," Shvydko saluted. "Follow me."

They approached the door when a trap door slipped open.

"*Slava Ukraini*," said the man inside.

"*Heroyam slava*," they replied.

The locks inside tumbled, and there stood Lylyk all healed up.

"You look good, sir," said Volodymyr.

"Welcome back," said Lylyk.

They entered the cramped quarters. Sokil, Nacham, Keller, Stas, and Jerzy were already inside. Some of the Poles started getting agitated. One Pole crinkled his nose.

"It figures these Ruthenians would find an old barn like this, fit for the pigs that they are," he said, using a defunct Austro-Hungarian term for Ukrainians.

"We don't have to take your shit anymore," said a Ukrainian, "and what makes you so high and mighty? Your Polish Empire is no more!"

"At least we had one," said the Pole, "and now we have our great Poland back, and we'll get the *Kresy* too!"

"Over my dead body," said the Ukrainian.

"That can be arranged," said the Pole.

"*Tovarishchi! Proshu*," said Sokil.

"*Tak*, this infighting won't get us anywhere," said Jerzy.

"He's not my *tovarishch*," said the Ukrainian. "Not after they burned my village and threw my whole family in Jaworzno during *Akcja Wisla!*"*Akcja Wisla*, or "Operation Vistula," was the code name for the mass deportation of ethnic Ukrainians by Poland in 1947. In just a few months, over 140,000 Ukrainians had been expelled from their ancestral homelands in the eastern Polish border regions and scattered throughout central and western Poland. Whole families were crowded onto cattle cars, like the zeks, and held in squalid conditions in the former German Jaworzno concentration camp in Poland, where diseases like typhus ran rampant.

"What else could we do to stop your terrorist attacks?" asked the

Pole. "Your people are certainly no angels after they wiped out my village, among countless others in Volyn!"

Recalcitrant formations of UPA, encouraged by the Germans, had launched a punitive expedition in western Ukraine, which culminated in the 1943 Volyn Massacres. Estimates vary widely, but Polish civilian deaths likely ran into the tens of thousands. The Poles committed thousands of reprisal killings in the following years even after the war ended."What did they do in Pawlokoma?" asked a Ukrainian, referring to an infamous Armia Krajowa massacre of Ukrainian civilians in 1945."I'm not saying any of that was right, but you should have treated us like human beings between the wars, especially after we fought together against the Russians, instead of your 'pacification,' which did anything but," said another Ukrainian. "All because we had a portrait of Taras Shevchenko in our little *Prosvita* room."

That statement struck Volodymyr, thinking about his poor father and dido. He also remembered how they would fondly recite the great Ukrainian poet, artist, and activist, Taras Shevchenko, who'd risen from serfdom to great international renown only to be thrown in the tsar's prisons and die just before serfdom was officially abolished.

The man was specifically referring to the "Pacification of Eastern Galicia" in 1929.

During that year, thousands of Polish police and civilian mobs had descended into the western Ukrainian countryside in a mass punitive operation against the Ukrainian populace. It was a culmination of anti-Ukrainian Polish policies targeted against the supposed Ukrainian resistance movement, specifically the Organization of Ukrainian Nationalists (OUN). These brutal policies had radicalized the largely apolitical Ukrainian peasantry, giving rise to UPA. The event was reported globally and even brought to the attention of the League of Nations. The Poles were not severely reprimanded, largely because the new world order was more preoccupied with propping up Poland to defend against Bolshevik Russia.

The room was brought to a fever pitch. Sokil and Jerzy were powerless. Volodymyr, Stas, and Kateryna looked helplessly to each other. Volodymyr was struck by the image of the falcon from his vision. He then remembered the beloved Ukrainian-Polish song, *"Hej Sokoly,"* or "Hey Falcons."

"Hey there by the black waters, a young Cossack mounts his horse," Volodymyr sang in Polish.

"A young girl weeps, the Cossack rides out from Ukraine," Stas sang in Ukrainian.

"Hey, hey, sokoly, fly above the mountains, forests and valleys," Sokil sang in Polish.

"Ring, ring, ring my bells, ring throughout the steppes," Jerzy sang in Ukrainian.

The room started catching on. Even the original instigators stopped to listen. When the chorus refrain returned, the whole room was singing together, birds of the same feather. By the time the meeting ended, their spirits were soaring.

Volodymyr, Kateryna, and Stas practically skipped back to their barracks. Kasia saw them after coming back from the infirmary. She was about to ask what was going on when Stas took the words right out of her mouth with a hearty kiss. They retired to their beds. The mysterious construction outside had ceased. Volodymyr and Kateryna stared into each other's eyes as they lay in bed.

"Dobranich, kokhanna," said Kateryna.

Volodymyr kissed her tenderly. They peacefully went to sleep that night. If they never awoke, they would be just fine with that.

23

JUNE 25, 1954:

THE TANKS ROLL IN

THE TRAIN SCREECHED *to a halt. Volodymyr was tossed about. The heavy steel doors rolled open. The sun was blinding. Volodymyr gingerly peeked out. He was all alone on the train again. He stepped out and was greeted by a warm hug. Kateryna kissed him tenderly.*

"We made it, Vlodko." "Where are we?" asked Volodymyr.

They were at a strange platform in the middle of the steppes surrounded by saiga. A wayward zephyr blew. Volodymyr turned around to see Kateryna when he realized she had blown away. Out of the ground came Otets Judas. He pointed behind Volodymyr. Somebody grabbed him and pulled him back onto the train.

"Last train to Kengir," said Belyaev.

They sped off, hurtling into the abyss. Volodymyr was holding on for dear life. The train stopped and a plank was rolled out. He was kicked down the plank, tangled in heavy chains. The train disappeared. Volodymyr was now in a grand stadium dressed like a gladiator from Slipyj's stories about ancient Rome. Belyaev stood before him. He dangled Slipyj's cross in Volodymyr's face before tossing it out into the lions' den.

Volodymyr knew he would have to fight to the death. He saw the poor young girl from the train crying in the stands. He raised his sword to Belyaev. They started fighting savagely when the sky opened up and fire poured down from the sky.

Volodymyr woke up in a cold sweat. It took him a few minutes to realize he was still in the barracks. This dream had felt so real. He looked at his palms, and they were raw red like he had been swinging a sword. He could still feel Belyaev's cold steel. He saw sweet Kateryna was still asleep. Volodymyr gingerly got out of bed and made his way to the window. He looked out at the still, night sky. Something caught the corner of his eye—a shooting star! It hovered in the air, slowly descending, which was strange. Volodymyr then saw another, and another.

Thud! Thud! Crash! Boom! The whole barracks shook. They were all woken up by strange, loud noises outside the gates. The tractors and machinery rumbled like thunder. Stas and Kasia embraced each other while the bed shook. Their bones rattled. It felt like they were back on the train to Kengir.

"They must be beginning construction again," said Volodymyr, trying to calm them, but he wasn't so sure. Kateryna got up and made her way to the window to join him. They heard a distant wailing sound. It grew louder, and before they were able to react, a huge explosion blew out the windows. Shattered glass flew around the room. They were knocked to the floor. The world turned upside down.

"Is everyone alright?" Volodymyr yelled.

"*Tak,* some cuts and scratches, nothing serious," said Stas.

Volodymyr heard their voices fading in and out. The shock of the explosion had blown out his hearing. The oxygen was sucked out of the room. They could barely catch their breaths. They hadn't experienced an explosion like that since the war, and maybe not even then. Kateryna cupped her hands and talked directly into Volodymyr's ear.

"We have to get out of here. The roof might collapse." Volodymyr looked up and saw the twilight sky through several holes in the roof. The rafters were teetering. Volodymyr nodded. They all grabbed hold of each other and crawled their way out the door, feeling their way in the dark, making sure not to cut themselves too bad on the broken glass from their window.

They got outside and were greeted by what looked like daybreak. It was too early though, and the light glowed iridescently. They looked up and saw the entire sky filled with flares raining down on them like falling stars. They had never seen so many flares. It would've been rather pretty in any another circumstance. They had no time for stargazing. Zeks were running wild. The sirens wailed, and the announcements came on.

"*Vnimaniye! Vnimaniye!* Report to battle stations," said Kuznetsov. "I repeat—"He was cut off mid-sentence. The power was cut. The whole camp went dark. The world was on fire and their time was running out. Volodymyr had to think fast.

"The barracks are a target," said Volodymyr. "We must move!"

They barreled out the door, half-expecting to meet their end right there. Had they waited a few more seconds, they would have received just that. They started off not a moment too soon when the barracks next to them were hit, then theirs. The entire facade collapsed. Kateryna and Volodymyr held onto each other for dear life. None of them knew where to move. They stared in shock at the burning wreckage when, to their horror, they saw a hand reach out.

"*Spasy nas,*" they faintly heard.

They rushed over. It was a young Russian woman they knew as a kindly neighbor. Volodymyr and Stas moved a beam that was pinning her leg. Kateryna and Kasia pulled her out. Kasia knelt down next to her mouth and checked her pulse. She solemnly shook her head.

"She didn't have a chance." They quickly genuflected and laid the young woman's hand down. She didn't have anything to worry about anymore. They turned to see somebody running to them. They didn't know whether to run themselves. The figure got closer, and they saw a frantic Shvydko.

"Come with me," he gasped.

The explosions were getting closer, and louder. Smoke was billowing out of the *vakhta*. Their sentries were screaming frantically from their towers. One of their sentries was waving wildly when he suddenly fell from his perch. The tower collapsed on top of him. He was dead.

"They're correcting fire," said Shvydko.

"How many?" asked Volodymyr.

"I don't know, but I think this is the big one," said Shvydko.

They ran to the SHIZO. With its reinforced walls and extensive barbed wire, it was one of the safest places. Many other zeks seemed to feel the same way and ran into the depths of their collapsing fortress. They found Sokil desperately crying out orders over the deafening explosions.

"What do you mean we're cut off?" asked Sokil.

"*Tak*, they're coming through the wire," Keller replied.

"What can we do, sir?" asked Volodymyr.

Sokil turned. Volodymyr didn't recognize him at first. He was caked in dirt, and his entire face was black with soot except for two blazing eyes. He grabbed Volodymyr and yelled into his ear, "Baran, we need all our sotnyks at the walls. We need all of you! *Davay!*"

Keller was manning a post. He ignited a Molotov cocktail and hurled it at some oncoming troops. The glass shattered and rained burning gas on the surprised soldiers, who turned back in a panic. The zeks didn't hesitate. They didn't have time to dwell. Everyone was running on pure adrenaline like during the first revolt in May, but even that had its limits.

While they were running, Volodymyr felt his legs slowly freezing. After a few more agonizing steps, he couldn't move his limbs. His heart was racing and he could hardly breathe. He was sweating bullets and shaking uncontrollably. He sat down. Kateryna noticed first and turned to him. She sat down beside him. She held his head, trying to look into his eyes.

"What's wrong?" she asked.

Volodymyr could hardly speak. His lips were trembling. Stas and Kasia quickly intervened. Kasia instinctively checked his body for wounds. She looked at his pupils.

"What's wrong?" Kateryna asked again desperately. "Is he hit?"

"No, I don't see anything," said Kasia.

Volodymyr's eyes wildly darted around. Every horrible noise was amplified. He couldn't catch a hold of his breath or mind.

Kasia leaned in.

"Vlodko, do you have any pain or pressure in your chest? Any numbness in your arms?" Volodymyr shook his head. He still couldn't speak. His lips were trembling too much.

"He's having a panic attack," said Kasia.

"What do we do?" asked Kateryna.

"That's up to him," said Kasia. "Poor, brave Vlodko."

Kateryna stroked and patted his cheeks trying to elicit a response. She looked into his eyes, but he was a world away. Everything was numb. Volodymyr couldn't even hear them over the chaos enveloping him inside and out. Everything was happening in slow motion. Everything had finally caught up to him, at once. All these years of suppressed trauma and nerves had bubbled up to the surface, and he couldn't react.

"Then I'll be his legs," said Stas. "Vlodko, brother, if you can hear me, we have to move, just like you said!"

Stas wrapped his arm around Volodymyr and slowly lifted him up.

Volodymyr instinctively imagined he was someplace else. He tried to think about his home, his family, even Marichka. He fought with all his might, but he couldn't see them anymore! That thought made him panic even more, until his father's words from his near-death vision came to him. *You have others who need you now. You must get up, son!* Volodymyr finally had the permission to let go.

He was free.

Like a burst of light, he realized something. He didn't need to see them right now. His family was right there in front of him. *Diakuyu tato, I'll see you in my dreams. Mamko, Dido, Baba, Marichka . . . They need me now.* He leaned into Kateryna and kissed her tenderly. He then turned to Stas.

"*Dziekuje,* my brother," said Volodymyr. "*Davay!*"

He shook out his legs, stumbling at first. After a few steps, he found his strength and charged the parapets to meet the oncoming storm. The three of them could barely keep up now. Stas was laughing and panting with Kateryna and Kasia close behind.

"Our Baran is back," said Stas. "God help them!"

Volodymyr charged his way through the herd of scrambling zeks. The Red Army gunners were trying to move into the breaches in the wall, but the zeks stood their ground with their crude weapons. Several of the stunned MVD stumbled into the freshly dug mote and were pelted with stones from the urkas' slingshots.

Somebody else came running out of the fray straight at them. It was Simo. He was holding a large, clear bottle. He handed the bottle to Volodymyr.

"Grab a Molotov and throw," he said. "There's no *tovarishchi* out there!"

Volodymyr looked at the bottle, swishing around its contents. For some strange reason, he thought about the Taras Shevchenko portrait destroyed in the *Prosvita* room. He then started to think about his family and how they had fought so hard for Ukraine. He knew if his poor father and dido were still alive, they would give their lives up all over again to be in his place, just to strike back one more time at their oppressors. Volodymyr heard his dido's voice reciting the famous Shevchenko quote that he'd drummed into his head as a child: "Learn what others have to offer, but do not forsake yourself." He mouthed the words in Ukrainian like a battle cry.

He didn't even pay attention to the live rounds exploding all around him. He was flying. He went over the top with his Molotov cocktail and ignited the rag. He called out to his ancestors, feeling their strength pumping in his heart.

"*Opryshky!*" Volodymyr roared.

The zeks unleashed a hailstorm of flaming cocktails onto the unsuspecting soldiers. There was another great roar over the steppes. The scene reminded Volodymyr of Ivan Franko and his famous epic:

I saw a vision strange . . .
Each one held tightly gripped a mighty iron sledge,
And sudden from the sky a voice like thunder cried:
"Break through this granite wall!" Some zeks managed to strike an armored personnel carrier barreling toward the gates. Several soldiers jumped out on fire. More zeks unsheathed long spears into the breaches of the wall. One of the MVD guards was impaled and let out a bloodcurdling scream. It took four other MVD men to pull him off. The inmates of Kengir had brought a knife to a gunfight and were holding, for now. Everyone's mettle was shining through.

Volodymyr was grateful. With his friends' help, and by recalling his ancestors, he channeled his inner strength. The guards retreated beyond the zona. Shouts of *ura!* rang down the zeks' ranks. Volodymyr was still in attack mode and initially didn't realize the soldiers and guards had retreated. He jumped when Stas came over and patted him on the back.

"Don't worry; it's me, brother," Stas laughed. "You sure gave them hell!"

"Well done, my brave *Hetman*," said Kateryna, kissing his perspiring cheek.

Stas and Kasia embraced. Volodymyr was relieved to get a breath in, but he wasn't celebrating yet.

"I don't think they're done yet."Almost on cue, the "construction" outside picked up in force. The entire camp shook. It felt like a thousand wild horses charging over the steppes. Kateryna grabbed hold of Volodymyr. Now he was trying to steady her trembling hands. The terrible noises sounded like they were coming from everywhere. It gradually dawned on them that it was a diversion for something even more devastating.

"Look," cried a zek from the watchtower, "I think I see—"He was cut off mid-sentence. There was a loud crack. He fell from the watchtower.

"Snipers!" another zek screeched before he too was cut down.

Volodymyr felt a bullet whizz right by him. He wasn't about to tempt fate twice. He grabbed hold of his friends and dragged them down, shielding them from the barrage of bullets. Several more zeks went down. They were forced to flee from the gates. The sky opened up with another barrage of parachutes carrying flares.

They then heard a low whirring sound. Before they knew it, a reconnaissance plane was practically on top of the camp. The plane swooped so close they could see the pilots snapping pictures. The plane's wing nearly clipped a watchtower. Snipers were picking off zek spotters left and right. Nobody knew what to expect.

They then heard multiple heavy engines firing up. These disconcerting noises were followed by a low rumbling, culminating in a mighty crash. They turned around and couldn't help but scream in terror. The infamous T-34 tanks rammed through their gates and rolled full steam ahead. Soldiers poured in through the breaches in the walls. Panic spread throughout the camp.

Stas grabbed Volodymyr tightly in dismay.

"They called in the whole goddamned Red Army!" he screamed.

Zeks were desperately firing their slingshots, spears, and cocktails, but they bounced right off the T-34s' armor. One tank turned its turret in the direction of the zek archers and blew them to pieces in a massive explosion. The whole scene was a purposeful display of Russian might. The zeks were all exhausted and panicked. The four friends retreated with the steady stream of inmates. Kasia tripped and fell, and Volodymyr picked her up.

"I'm just returning the favor," he said.

They moved forward, frantically running for cover. It was a terrible sight, even worse than those first bloody days of the Kengir Uprising. Volodymyr watched in horror as a man and woman stood hand in hand in front of a T-34, which proceeded to mercilessly run them over. Their bones crunched like bloody twigs beneath its tracks. The driver tossed out an empty bottle of vodka as he crashed into a barracks. Another tank swerved, narrowly missing the other tank.

The friends barely reached the SHIZO where the zeks had erected a fallback position. The walls there were the strongest. This would be the location of their last stand. Everyone was there: Sokil, Leonid, Nacham, Jerzy, Keller, Kuznetsov, Knopkus, Sluchenkov, the Ukrainian Centre, and countless others now only known to those who served beside them and survived. This would be the blood bond that sealed their fate.

"This is worse than Brody," said Sokil. "At least there we had guns!"

"Maybe we should finally escape, the four of us, like we said back in spring, remember?" asked Kateryna.

"We're completely surrounded. They'd cut us to pieces," said Volodymyr. "This is the only way now!"

Simo was gathering as much combustible material as he could. Leonid was helping carry a box of clear glass bottles. The four of them went to help.

"*Spasiba! Diakuyu! Dziekuje,*" said Leonid. "I believe I said that first day we all met that I wouldn't join UPA or Armia Krajowa. I guess a crazy old *starosta* like me will eat his words."

"Well, you *were* elected head of food and provisions, Karas," said Volodymyr.

In the spur of the chaotic moment, Volodymyr hugged Leonid.

"I learned there are some good Russians," he added.

"Don't get all sappy on us now! They're pouring in by the second," said Keller. "Load up the catapults!"

"Catapults?" asked Volodymyr.

"*Davay Kozaky,*" said Sokil, grabbing Leonid and Volodymyr.

Sure enough, a row of wooden catapults were lined up in front of the SHIZO gates. It was the 1950s vs the 1590s. They went to load up. They were handed torches and told to light up on Kuznetsov's command.

Kuznetsov raised his hand.

Sweat was pouring down Volodymyr's brow.

"*Ogon!*" screamed Kuznetsov. *Fire!*

The zeks unleashed a hailstorm of Molotov cocktails and other flaming debris. It rained down on the columns of MVD and Red Army soldiers. Several went down and up in flames, but more kept coming. Volodymyr lit and launched another cocktail at an oncoming armored column. They had formed an assembly line: One zek poured gasoline in the bottle, then handed it to another who put in the rag, who handed it to another who ignited it and launched it from the catapult. It was a true marvel of socialist engineering that would impress any of the supposed communists killing them.

They smelled the unmistakable stench of sulfur from the incendiary component when the projectiles exploded. The crude concoction of various salts, alloys, and petroleum had been used extensively by the Red Army during WWII as rudimentary napalm. All of this was courtesy of the Technical Department, comprised of the discarded scientists that had created it for the army in the first place. The surprised and terrified guards scattered while their vehicles caught fire.

"Lenta za lentoyu na boyi podavay," Lylyk started singing, a Ukrainian partisan song about gathering *"ammo for the battle."*

Everyone started singing along. They were all dirty Banderists and Vlasovites and every other Soviet slur and proud of it. The camp soon brought in more vehicles. While the zeks were trying to rebuild their forces they heard a loud boom, and their party came crashing down. Several of the zeks went flying when a T-34 crashed through their barricades. Soldiers poured in. Volodymyr put one oncoming man in his crosshairs. Fortunately, he realized at the last moment it was Valeriy.

"You almost got yourself killed!" Volodymyr yelled.

"Cover your mouths," Valeriy coughed.

Volodymyr realized Valeriy had a cloth around his mouth. He looked up and saw a thick cloud coming towards them. He frantically pulled out a Molotov cocktail rag and put it against his mouth. He turned to warn the rest of them, but it was too late. The acrid chemicals burned their eyes and nostrils. It was something out of WWI. Nobody could see anything. The whole battlefield quieted down. Volodymyr could only see sporadic flashes of gunfire from the watchtowers and walls. He called out but couldn't hear his own voice over the cacophony of terror. He was separated from Kateryna, Stas, and Kasia. The wind picked up and the gas started to dissipate. When the smoke cleared, Volodymyr saw the devil.

Belyaev had returned in fully fury. He was wildly waving a pistol and shooting at unarmed men and women. He was coming closer. Volodymyr finally saw Stas stumbling through the smog. Belyaev saw him too. He raised his pistol to fire when Volodymyr charged headfirst into him, knocking the pistol out of his hands. They locked eyes with pure hatred.

"So, you think you can take me, altar boy?" Belyaev taunted.

Volodymyr head-butted him. Blood dripped out of Belyaev's nose. Belyaev laughed and head-butted him back, knocking Volodymyr flat out on his back. Now Belyaev was on top. They were locked in a fight to the death.

"Vlodko!" Kateryna screamed.

Kateryna, Stas, and Kasia ran to help. Stas grabbed a log and knocked Belyaev off of Volodymyr. Belyaev crawled for his pistol. Kateryna and Kasia grabbed his legs, and he kicked Kateryna in the face. Volodymyr lunged at Belyaev. Belyaev grabbed his pistol and turned when they heard the wailing of incoming artillery. Everything went white.

Volodymyr was tossed like a rag in the breeze. He was losing consciousness along with his blood. He accepted his fate. He closed his eyes for the final time when he was lifted into the air over the devastation, just like in his vision. He figured he must be severely hallucinating on death's doorstep. He turned and saw Sokil carrying him away. He mouthed something to Volodymyr, but Volodymyr couldn't hear him. It was the last thing he remembered.

24

JUNE 26, 1954:

THE SHEPHERD

*"**Where are you, Vlodko?**" cried Kateryna. "I can't see you!"*

Volodymyr couldn't see a centimeter in front of his face. The phosphorus cloud enveloped the whole camp. Volodymyr was stuck, trying desperately to find his friends.

"Where are you?" asked Volodymyr. "I can't get to you!"

"Follow my voice," said Kateryna. "Hurry, Vlodko, something's coming!"

"I'm trying, kokhanna. I don't know where to go!"

A strong zephyr picked up and cleared away the smoke. He saw the bodies and the horror of the devastated camp. There was a loud screech. He looked up and saw something swooping toward him. It was the sokil! It screeched and opened its large, sharp talons. Volodymyr closed his eyes, bracing for the pain, when he felt something warm and fuzzy instead. He opened his eyes and saw a lamb resting by his feet. He recognized the lamb. He was home!

He was dressed in his church clothes. Two large gravestones stood before him. His mother and baba were crying. Yurko placed his hand on Volodymyr's shoulder. The epitaphs were jumbled, but Volodymyr understood they were his friends' graves. The priest chanted, "Hospody Pomyluy," "Lord Have Mercy." Volodymyr realized it wasn't their village priest, but Otets Slipyj. He pulled out his crucifix and placed it around Volodymyr's neck.

"Vichnaya Pamyat," said Slipyj.

"He's coming to," said Nacham, dabbing Volodymyr's face with a cotton swab.

"Diakuyu Bozhe," said Sokil.

"Where am I?" Volodymyr asked weakly.

"You're in the infirmary, son," said Sokil.

Just like back in June. This time, there were conspicuously fewer people around in spite of the horrific causalities. Volodymyr quickly felt his arms and legs. Although he felt like he had been hit by a train, he was intact. He then looked to his left, then his right, and started to panic.

"Where's Kateryna?""Take it easy," said Nacham. He wrapped a bandage around Volodymyr's head, obscuring his vision. Volodymyr stopped him. His injuries could wait. He sat up. He was adamant.

"Stas? Kasia?""You're lucky we got to you when we did," said Sokil. "You're lucky to be alive."

"Where are they?" Volodymyr asked desperately. "Why aren't you answering me?"

He was still woozy. His recent visions were fresh in his mind. Sokil and Nacham looked unusually nervous. They were both trying their best to humor him. He felt just as helpless as when he was a young boy in that bleak winter of 1937.

It was a bitingly cold day in Pechenizhyn. Although they were far up in their Carpathian stronghold, news travelled surprisingly fast. No Ukrainian was a stranger to suffering, but what they heard happening just over the border in the Soviet Union was unbelievably awful, even to these poor people. The whole village was lined up outside the church. The bells tolled solemnly. Volodymyr and his family were at the front of the procession out of the church. Volodymyr was still a young boy and wasn't told what was happening. His baba was beside herself with grief. Andriy, whom Volodymyr had never seen cry before, was crying along with her and Yurko. Volodymyr's mother hugged him, although he still didn't understand why.

"Hospody Pomyluy," *their otets solemnly chanted.* "Vichnaya Pamyat . . ."

His voice was also cracking. Volodymyr's dido had been gone awhile. They'd last heard that he was helping a relative in their village in Vinnytsia in Soviet-occupied Ukraine. Volodymyr remembered all the sunflowers from pictures his dido had sent them. Some of the other children in the village would whisper behind Volodymyr's back pityingly. He was starting to put things together in his young mind, and it hit him all at once, like a silver bullet to the brain.

"Mamko, *where's dido?*""With the angels, my brave son," *she said haltingly.*

The Vinnytsia Massacre was officially covered up by the Soviet Union, along with their multitude of crimes against humanity, including the Holodomor only four years prior. The Nazis, in a bitterly ironic twist, uncovered the massacre during their own genocidal march across Ukraine in 1943. Both Soviet and Nazi massacres took place there. Adding insult to injury, his family never received his dido's body, or later his poor father's body, because they were deemed "enemies of the people." Volodymyr began his arduous march into man's madness that day.

A man burst through the infirmary door. All three of them were shocked into their senses. The KGB bear of a man loomed large over them. Two young Kazakh guards stood beside him. The three zeks looked closer and could hardly believe it. They were the very three men that had escorted them on the last leg of their journey to Kengir. The KGB man recognized them too.

"Well, well, I knew you would all make trouble," he taunted. "I should've ended it all on the train when I had the chance."

Nobody knew what to say. They were all still in a daze, likely concussed. They were visibly injured, but the KGB man was adamant.

"Don't just stand around like sheep," he shouted. "*Davay!* Get out! General's orders!"

"He's injured," said Sokil firmly.

"If he can walk, he must go." Sokil and Nacham stood in front of Volodymyr. The Kazakhs raised their rifles. Volodymyr sat up and grasped their shoulders. His was determined.

"I can walk," he said. "I just need some help."

"You don't have to," said Sokil.

"I must. I must know what happened to my brother and my wife."

Volodymyr swung his legs over. He was still woozy, but he planted his feet and shakily stood up. He stumbled like a newborn lamb. Sokil and Nacham caught him.

"Alright, alright," said the KGB man mockingly. "Genghis! Tamerlane! Help them!"

The two Kazakhs pivoted to the KGB man in shock.

"I just need them out of here," he sneered. "They'll get what they deserve."

The two Kazakhs gruffly picked up Volodymyr.

"Easy," said Nacham.

"You're lucky we're helping at all," said one.

They carried Volodymyr out of the infirmary. Volodymyr looked up and was nearly blinded by the light. The embers of the previous day's battle were still smoldering, adding to the scorching heat. The two guards dragged Volodymyr along while Sokil and Nacham tried to keep him level. The camp was unrecognizable. The battle had continued for several more hours after Volodymyr was taken out. Most of the watchtowers were lying in heaps, and the walls hadn't fared much better. Half the barracks had been reduced to rubble. The smell of death permeated their singed nostrils. Sokil sighed.

"Just like our poor *Ukraina* after the war." "Less talking, more walking," barked the KGB man.

"Vengeance is mine, I will repay," Nacham muttered.

Eventually, they brought him out onto the steppes with the rest of the camp. The three of them were surprised to see hundreds of their fellow zeks splayed out on the ground, many seriously injured, in the scorching Kazakh sun. MVD, *nadzirateli,* and *vovki* patrolled the perimeter. It was a sad sight.

"Down you go, *zek*," said one of the guards, dropping Volodymyr like a sack of rocks.

"Now sit, stay, you zek dog," said the other guard.

They walked away laughing. Sokil and Nacham tried to cushion Volodymyr's landing as best they could. He still took the brunt. He let out a quick yelp, but held his tongue. The only thing keeping him together was his hope for finding his wife and friends. He scoured the bloodied and battered zeks, but there was no sign of them. Sokil and Nacham tried to shield him from the sun as best they could. Nacham padded Volodymyr's head. Volodymyr thought he was hallucinating, but sure enough, he saw a zek carefully crawling over to them. It was hard to tell at first through his swollen eyelids. Then he saw the toothy grin and smiled.

"Glad to see at least you all made it," said Leonid, handing them some leftover bread and water. "You just missed the feeding, but I won't let you go hungry. I'm still head of food security, don't you know?"

Volodymyr sipped the water and tore off a piece of the hard bread. He coughed heartily. Leonid covered Volodymyr's mouth.

"What's going on over there?" a *vovk* barked.

"Nothing, *tovarishch*," said Leonid.

"Keep it that way," he said before storming off to harass some new arrivals.

Volodymyr carefully chewed the bread. His jaw was still sore. Sokil patted Leonid.

"*Spasiba.*""*Proshu*," Leonid replied.

Two other figures slowly crept over. He made out what looked like a burly bearded bear and a long, lanky deer. Volodymyr realized it was Mansur and Gitanas. Gitanas smiled and leaned into Volodymyr's ear.

"*Pryvit,* my Ukrainian friend," said Gitanas, too loudly for Volodymyr's ringing ears.

"I'm not deaf," Volodymyr winced. "Glad to see you made it."

"Sorry," said Gitanas, "and glad to hear!"

"*Assalamu alaikum, tovarishch,*" said Mansur.

"Have either of you heard about Stas? Kateryna? Kasia?" asked Volodymyr.

"No, my friend," said Gitanas. "They separated the men and women anyway. My wife is somewhere there. The Poles are still being processed on the other side of the fence. I'm sure they're alright. The Chechens are also somewhere over there, but they're quite sneaky, as you can see, despite their demeanor."

Mansur managed a small smirk. He was learning their Slavic sense of humor. They were all still trying to adjust, yet again, to their strange new reality. Gitanas looked like something else was bothering him. He looked over his shoulder at the guards and whispered to all of them.

"Have any of you heard about our Knopkus?" asked Gitanas.

"No, we haven't seen our Keller since yesterday," said Nacham. "No Kuznetsov or Sluchenkov either."

"*Vnimaniye! Vnimaniye! Zaklyuchennyi* coming through," said the announcer.

A large motorcade rumbled by with armored cars at the front and back. There was a huge truck in the center fitted with a wire cage packed with zeks. Their hearts sank when they realized they had just discovered the whereabouts of their comrades. A morose Kuznetsov sat next to a battered Knopkus, Keller, and Sluchenkov. The zeks were silent.

"God help them," said Mansur.

Gitanas's expression changed dramatically. Volodymyr never imagined he could see such a fire in his eyes. Gitanas stared at poor Knopkus and decided he'd had enough. He slowly stood up, ignoring the guards, and saluted.

A passing MVD soldier noticed him.

"Get down, damn you, or I'll shoot!" Volodymyr was also tired of laying down for these beasts. He began to stand and they all helped him to his feet. Others around them started to notice and began to rise out of the steppes. It wasn't a vain gesture. Knopkus picked up his head and nudged the others. He sat up and saluted back. Keller, Kuznetsov, and Sluchenkov followed suit. Their driver noticed and tried to leave, nearly running into an armored car in his haste.

The MVD guard was furious.

"Get those men over here, now!" he screamed.

Several *nadzirateli* and *vovki* pounced on them, dragging them forward like fresh meat. The irate guard scoured them up and down. Their pistols and rifles were ready for the command. He was about to say something when he quickly stepped back and saluted.

"Kapitan Belyaev.""I hear we have some troublemakers," Belyaev taunted.

Belyaev was also fairly bruised up and bandaged from the previous day's fight. He looked particularly grim. He looked them over. Volodymyr prayed Belyaev wouldn't notice him, but hope only gets you so far in the Gulag. Belyaev locked eyes with Volodymyr. Volodymyr felt his heart in his throat. Belyaev smiled fiendishly and pointed at him.

"Make this one clean up the bodies." "Alright, you heard him, *zek. Davay*," said a guard.

Volodymyr didn't move. He looked helplessly to his friends. There was nothing they could do. Several guards grabbed him. The rest got between Volodymyr and his *tovarishchi*. They were outmanned and outgunned, yet again. They were too weak to fight this time. Volodymyr was ripped away once more from the only family he had left. He turned to Sokil and mouthed, *I'm sorry.*

"*Marsh, Polkovnyk* Baran," said Sokil. "Show them what Ukrainians are made of!"

"*Klyanus*," said Volodymyr.

"Get him out of here quickly, before they start a scene," said Belyaev.

More people noticed what was going on. It was getting hot again in Kengir. They threw Volodymyr onto a truck and sped off. All of the Ukrainians nearby stood up. He saw Shvydko, Lylyk, and Valeriy. Others joined in. Gitanas and Mansur beckoned the Chechens and Baltics. The Poles marched in, and he saw Jerzy salute.

"*A Cossack rides out from Ukraine,*" Jerzy sang.The Poles and Ukrainians started singing, "*Hey! Hey! Hey Sokoly!*" The guards fired into the air. The zeks sang louder. Others started shouting. *Liberty! Justice! Freedom! Down with the regime!* Just like that first day in Kengir, they marched triumphantly to meet their fate. There is an old Chinese idiom, made popular by the Chinese communists, that says, "A single spark can start a prairie fire." After the raging inferno that had engulfed Kengir, the Soviets were adamant about stamping out this incident before it spread. Despite Soviet efforts, they would not be forgotten.

Volodymyr bounced around the cart, wincing in pain, but his people—all their people—gave him strength. He caught a glimpse of Belyaev sweating nervously. They weren't done just yet. There was a young Kazakh in the back with Volodymyr. He looked at him curiously, and then reached into his pocket. Volodymyr braced for another beating when he felt cool water running down his face. The young Kazakh patted him down.

These small acts of human decency in the face of so much suffering stood out the most. Volodymyr had met so many bad people, but that made the good ones so special. He remembered Valeriy teaching him about a fundamental law of physics: Every action has an equal and opposite reaction. He thought that might apply to people also. "There is nothing bad that doesn't turn into good," Volodymyr's baba used to say.

After about ten minutes, the car came to an abrupt halt. The doors slammed. The driver and his passenger guard came over and dragged Volodymyr out of the cart and over to a burnt mess of timber and debris. Volodymyr realized it was where he had fought Belyaev and last seen Kateryna, Stas, and Kasia.

"Time to clean up your mess," said the driver.

They then sped off, leaving Volodymyr alone. Volodymyr saw three bodies lying together: Two women and a man. He slowly approached, filled with dread. His heart was racing and his palms were sweaty. There laid a young woman with singed blonde hair and a necklace. He turned her over and collapsed in horror when he saw Slipyj's cross. Stas was lying on top of Kasia. They were covered with shrapnel wounds. Volodymyr realized they had taken the brunt of the explosion that should have killed him and Belyaev. At that moment, he wished it had. He felt like his heart had been ripped out of his chest. He tore at his hair, his clothes, and his mind!

Volodymyr grabbed Kateryna's cold hand and instinctively tried to warm it up, only to realize she would never warm up to him again. He buried his head in her chest and wailed a primordial cry. He dug into the earth, trying desperately to escape his reality. His fingernails broke and bled.

He let the horror of it all roll over him, and he suddenly became very still. He finally let go, and lost everything. Now he had nothing left to lose. Volodymyr gently kissed Kateryna's forehead. He calmly sat up and found a piece of broken glass from one of the barracks glistening in the sun.

"You're with the angels now," Volodymyr whimpered. "I will join you soon my beloved, and my brother!"

Volodymyr put the glass to his wrist. He closed his eyes, accepting his fate. He then heard metallic clinking and footsteps. They abruptly stopped.

"*Davay, zek*," barked an arrogant guard.

He stood over Volodymyr with his rifle drawn. He reeked of liquor. Volodymyr's despair turned to fury. He grasped the glass and decided he would at least take one more of these beasts down with him. He was about to lunge when another man came over.

"Private," said the other man.

It was another Soviet officer. He was dapperly dressed in a crisp uniform. He had likely just arrived from headquarters in Karaganda. The soldier saluted.

"Why don't you help your *tovarishchi* get that tank out of the mud," the officer suggested.

"*Da,* Kapitan," said the soldier, marching away.

The captain looked at Volodymyr and his friends pityingly.

"Did you know them?" he asked.

Volodymyr blankly nodded. The captain pulled out a flask and handed it to Volodymyr, who just continued to stare in shock.

"I'm Kapitan Alexei Anatolyevich," he said. "And you?"

Volodymyr was silent.

"I don't blame you," said Alexei, taking a sip.

He continued staring curiously at Volodymyr. He then perked up.

"You look familiar, somehow, like a ghost from so many years ago."

Volodymyr was now a little curious himself. He slowly looked up. Alexei was still studying him when his face turned white. He dropped his flask.

"My God. Were you ever in Sambir?"

Volodymyr was startled. He didn't know how to answer. "Did you have a wife named Marichka?""*D-Da*," Volodymyr stammered.

"I can't believe it . . ." said Alexei. "How hard we try to escape ourselves."

"Is she alright?" asked Volodymyr. "Marichka?"

Alexei thought hard. He nodded.

"I was transferred from western Ukraine years ago, but last I saw she was. I took her home after you were taken away. I met your Uncle Yurko. A good man. He said he built that old house with his own hands. I gave them some money and told them you were most likely headed to Mordovia, but that's all I knew. I made sure Marichka was alright."

Alexei shakily lit up a *makhorka* and took a long drag, looking out over the devastation.

"What a mess," he said. "Was it worth it?"

The question took Volodymyr by surprise. He was still alive.

Everything changed in an instant. He had been ready to die, but he suddenly had a reason to live. If there was even a remote chance that Marichka was alive, he would stay alive. He could keep them all alive, if he could just get back to them.

"All I know is that I am a shepherd," said Volodymyr, "and a shepherd always returns to his flock."

EPILOGUE

IMMEDIATELY AFTER THE uprising, over a thousand zeks were shipped to other camps. The Ukrainians were dispersed as much as possible, but the last Volodymyr heard, Sokil and Nacham were still together, raising a ruckus in nearby Rudnik Gulag. Leonid was sent to a camp near Finland and was rumored to have been released and spending his retirement just over the border overlooking Kronstadt. The bodies of Kateryna, Stas, and Kasia were secretly buried in a mass grave on the steppes with the other victims. The official Soviet figure—thirty-seven killed during the revolt—was a gross underestimate, with most independent estimates in the hundreds.

In 1955, closed trials were held for the organizers. Keller, Knopkus, and Sluchenkov were executed. Kuznetsov was given a reduced sentence of twenty-five years and released early in 1960 in exchange for what was most likely help in identifying fellow "instigators." Although their rebellion was eventually crushed, the "Forty Days of Kengir" was instrumental in speeding up the liquidation of Steplag, which was closed in 1956. Dolgikh was unceremoniously stripped of his command that same year. Volodymyr was transferred to a Ukrainian gulag, where he was eventually released in 1964. After fifteen long years, he was finally coming home.

Volodymyr took one last long train ride from eastern Ukraine to a military railyard depot outside of the recently renamed city of Ivano-Frankivsk (formerly Stanislav) in western Ukraine, one of Ukraine's gateways to the Carpathians. He spent little time at the station, trying to put as much distance between him and the authorities as quickly as possible. He made his way from the big city avenues up to the winding mountain meadows of his Carpathian home. It was late June at just about the ten-year anniversary of his last train ride from Kengir. He didn't know if that was fateful or not. All he knew was that he had to get back to where he belonged.

Volodymyr made his way down the village road etched in his memory through the *polonyna* flush with the summer grasses and wildflowers to Pechenizhyn. The pines and birch leaves rustled in the summer breeze before the darkening clouds in the distance. It felt like he had been transported back in time. Nothing here had changed, or so he thought. He saw the domes of the village church and excitedly ran forward. Villagers should've been out and about, but it was eerily quiet. He passed by several houses. He happily waved at a neighbor. They quickly shuttered their door. Volodymyr was starting to regret his decision to come back when he heard a strangely familiar voice call out,

"Vlodko!" Volodymyr looked around but didn't see anybody else.

"Behind you," the man said.

Volodymyr turned and there he was, though older, his beloved uncle and father: Yurko. Volodymyr ran to him. They paused, looking over each other, surely thinking how much older the other looked. It didn't matter. They laughed and embraced like no time had passed.

"Yurko, you don't know how happy I am to see you." Yurko smiled and put his finger to his lips.

"As am I, Vlodko, but some things changed while you were away," he whispered.

Volodymyr followed Yurko into their home. The walls and roof were weathered like them all, but it was still home. Yurko quickly shut the door, which was unusual for such a close-knit community as theirs. He went into the kitchen and fetched some *horilka* and *borshch*.

"Slipyj said you were released, but I didn't expect you so soon," said Yurko.

"Slipyj?" asked Volodymyr, surprised.

"*Tak,* who do you think had you transferred to *Ukraina*?"After fifteen years in the gulag, Volodymyr was still in the dark. Yurko reappeared with a pot of *borshch*. Volodymyr smelled the sweet broth of his baba's recipe, on the verge of tears.

"*Smachnoho,*" said Yurko. *Bon appetit.* "You must be starving!"

"You have no idea," said Volodymyr.

He grabbed a ladle, still reflexively looking for his prison-issued tin and spoon, and dug in. He wolfed down the stew in sync with a no-longer-existent gulag time frame. He looked back at Yurko's thin frame and felt guilty about suggesting that he had "no idea" about hunger. The silence around the village was weighing on Volodymyr, especially the barn.

"The sheep are unusually quiet," said Volodymyr.

"Oh, they're gone, Vlodko," Yurko sighed. "The state took nearly everything."

"What happened to everyone?"Yurko leaned back and stared at the ceiling.

"Well, after you were taken, they got this real bastard as our village commissar since we were considered a 'hostile' village.' He really had it out for poor Marichka."

"Is she alive?" Volodymyr asked nervously.

"*Tak,* we'll get to that," said Yurko. "Tell me a little about yourself."

Volodymyr was silent. He didn't know where to begin. It is never harder to speak than when there is so much to say.

Yurko blushed and quickly added, "I'm sorry, you don't have to say anything. I was just babbling."

"No, it's alright." Volodymyr took a shot. It went down hard. Their family recipe was not for the faint of heart.

"Did you hear about the Kengir Uprising?" The stories flowed out with the steady stream of Ukrainian liquor. Yurko hung on every word. They talked into the night when Volodymyr asked Yurko about Alexei.

"*Tak*, Alexei was one in a thousand," said Yurko. "He helped Marichka and the baby escape their certain doom in the Gulag!"

"Baby?" asked Volodymyr.

Yurko stopped. He poured Volodymyr and himself another drink. Then he leaned in.

"Vlodko, this is hard to say, so I'll just say it. Your daughter Marusia, named after your dearly departed mother, just celebrated her fifteenth birthday in Rzeszów."

Volodymyr heard and saw just about everything, but he couldn't have foreseen that in his wildest vision. He was overcome with both joy and guilt. Joy that Marichka was alive and that for once he was responsible for life instead of so much death, and guilt that he hadn't been there for any of it. Yurko sensed his dueling emotions. He got up and hugged him.

"It's not your fault," he said gently. "She knows what a hero you are!"

For the rest of the night, they caught up on old times and time still left to live. In the morning, Yurko gave Volodymyr Marichka's address and another warm embrace. Volodymyr hugged his uncle tightly. He didn't want to let go, but he had one last great journey ahead of him.

"*Z Bohom,*" said Yurko. *God be with you.* "Marichka and Marusia are waiting for you!"

Volodymyr waved a tearful final goodbye to his homeland. He would have to sneak into Poland under the cover of darkness through one of the old partisan paths to avoid the border guards. Before all that, he made his way down the winding *polonyna* to the secluded mountain overpass he would visit as a child to be alone with his thoughts and figure out his next move.

He sat down on a large thinking rock by the cliff edge. He stroked the hard rock face, like an old friend, looking out at the winding Prut River valley below. He felt so small. In his breast pocket, he pulled out the eagle's talon he kept from Kengir and Slipyj's singed crucifix. He knew what he had to do first.

"Forgive me, Marichka, and my dear new daughter Marusia, but wait just a little longer," he said, looking east. "I'm coming, Kateryna."

The wind blew through the *polonyna,* answering his call. He stood up when he heard rustling in the underbrush. His heart dropped. He didn't know who or what could be out here in such a secluded place when he saw a little white cloud emerge. It was a lamb. He picked it up.

"So you also escaped?" asked Volodymyr. "Would you like to join me?"

The lamb let out a hardy *baa!* He felt redeemed. Now he thought about what his brave commander Sokil would do in his place. Volodymyr stood at attention, staring straight ahead.

"*Uvaha,*" said Volodymyr. "*Kurin, marsh! Ras dva, ras dva . . .*"

GLOSSARY OF TERMS

ADHAN: Islamic call to prayer

ARMIA KRAJOWA: Home Army; main Polish resistance movement during WWII (1942-1945); peak 400,000 (1944)

BABA: Grandmother; old woman

BABI(YN) YAR: Largest massacre of Jews in Soviet Union by Nazi forces in Ukraine, Sept. 1941; over 30,000 killed

BALANDA: Prison soup

BALTICS: Lithuania, Latvia, Estonia; under Russian rule until 1991; anti-Soviet partisan movement (1944-1956)

BANDERA, STEPAN: Main Ukrainian nationalist leader during WWII; assassinated in Munich, 1959; see *OUN, UPA*

BARBAROSSA, OPERATION: Nazi invasion of Soviet Union in June 1941; largest invasion in history; ended in failure

BARAN: Ram

BERIA, LAVRENTY: Head of Soviet security apparatus from 1938-46; executed 1953; See *Great Purge, KGB, NKVD*

BESKIDS: Section of Carpathian Mountains with ethnic Ukrainian population; see *Boykos, Hutsuls, Karpaty, Lemkos*

BLACK TABS: Colloquial name for Soviet construction battalion soldiers

BOLSHEVIK: *Bilshovyk;* radical communist-Soviet opposition party of Vladimir Ilyich Ulyanov (Lenin) from 1917

BRODY, BATTLE OF: Largest battle between Ukrainians, Germans, and Soviets near Ukrainian city of Brody in 1944

BLATNOI SLOVO: Thieves' talk; see *Urka*

BOCHKOV, V. M.: Boss of Steplag, Kengir; see *Gulag, Kengir, Kengir Uprising*

BOH: God

BOYKOS: Ukrainian ethnic subgroup of central Carpathian Mountains; descendants of ancient White Croatian tribes

BRATTYA: Brothers

BREZHNEV, LEONID: Leader of Soviet Union (1964-1982); reversed Khrushchev's liberalization; see *Thaw*

BUDMO: Cheers

BUSHLAT: Long-sleeved, cotton-lined jacket for prisoners

Carpatho-Ukraine, Republic of: Short-lived Ukrainian microstate in Carpathian Mountains (1938-1939)

Capitalism: Economic and political system in which trade and industry are controlled by private enterprise

Caucasian Mountains: Mountain range in south Russia, Georgia, Azerbaijan, and Armenia; highest peak 18,510 ft.

Central Committee: Highest body of the Communist Party; see *Communism; Soviet Union*

Centre, Ukrainian: Main Ukrainian gulag resistance group; see *Kengir, Kengir Uprising, Norilsk*

Chechens: *Noxciy*; Muslim-majority Caucasian ethnic group; live in clans known as *teip*; see *Lentil, Operation*

Cheka: Soviet secret police (1917-22); from Russian for *All-Russian Extraordinary Commission: VChK*

Chifir: Extremely strong tea that can produce a type of euphoric high

Cold War: Period of geopolitical tension between United States and Soviet Union and their allies (1947-1991)

Collectivization: Organization of private agriculture into state-run communes; see *Communism, Holodomor, Kulak*

Commissars: Political representatives of the Communist Party of the Soviet Union in the Soviet/Red Army

COMMUNISM: A socio-economic system where private property is abolished and industry is state-owned

CONCENTRATION CAMPS: Prisons that led to over five million deaths by Nazis, two million by Soviets; see *Gulag*

CRIMEA: Large peninsula in southern Ukraine on Black and Azov Seas; homeland of Crimean Tatars; see *Tatars*

CURZON LINE: Poland–Soviet Union border line proposed by British Foreign Secretary George Curzon in 1919

DAVAY: Come on; Let's go

DEZHURNAYA: Type of unofficial concierge in gulags who watched over living quarters and property; see *Gulag*

DIAKUYU: Thank you

DNIPRO: Dnieper River; largest river in Ukraine; third-largest fully in Europe through Ukraine, Belarus, and Russia

DOBRANICH: Good night

DOBRE: Good

DOPOBACHENNYA: See you later

DOKHODYAGA: Walkers; colloquial term for gulag prisoners on verge of death; see *Gulag, Zeks*

DOLGIKH, IVAN: Soviet general and commander of the Gulag (1951-1954); see *Gulag, KGB, MVD*

Dovbush, Oleksa: Ukrainian Hutsul Robin Hood-like figure (1700-45); see *Hutsuls, Opryshky*

Dzerzhinsky, Felix: Bolshevik revolutionary and first head of Soviet security apparatus (1917-26); see *Cheka*

Famine of 1947: Last major famine in Soviet Union; victims ranged in the hundreds of thousands; see *Holodomor*

Fascism: Far-right authoritarian, militaristic, ultranationalist ideology promoting the state and social hierarchy

Feldsher: Gulag medic; see *Gulag*

Franko, Ivan: Ukrainian writer considered national icon (1856-1916); city of Ivano-Frankivsk named in his honor

Great Purge/Terror: Mass murder led by Stalin/Beria/NKVD (1936-1938); over 700,000 deaths estimated

Greek Catholic: Catholics of the Byzantine/Eastern Rite after Union of Brest (1596); over five million Ukrainians

GULAG: Soviet concentration camps created by Lenin (1918) expanded by Stalin; two million died in camps

Halychyna: *Eastern Galicia*; population 6.5 million (1910); capital and largest city L'viv; ruled by many empires

Heroyam: Heroes

Hetman: *Otaman*; Ukrainian Cossack general; see *Khmelnytsky, Bohdan, Kozak, Petliura, Symon*

Hitler, Adolf: *Fuhrer*; dictator of Germany (1934-1945); started WWII by invading Poland in 1939; killed millions

Holocaust: Genocide of Jews during WWII; over six million died, including one million in Soviet Union

Holodomor: Soviet-Russian genocide of Ukrainians under Stalin (1932-33); killed over four million in Ukraine

Hopak: National dance of Ukraine originating as a festive Cossack dance; see *Kozak*

Hora: Traditional Eastern European and Jewish dance

Hutsuls: Ukrainian ethnic subgroup of eastern Carpathian Mountains; renowned artisans, warriors, and musicians

Ionov's Salt: Aluminum-based compound used as thickener in flammable weapons; used by Soviets since 1939

Iron Curtain: Metaphor used in Cold War to describe boundary between communist/capitalist states

Jaworzno Camp: German camp in WWII Poland; used by Soviets/Poland (1945-1956); see *Vistula, Operation*

Kaddish: Traditional Jewish funeral hymn

Katyn Massacres: Executions of over 21,000 Polish officers by Soviets in Katyn forest, Belarus, and other sites

Karaganda: City and region in central Kazakhstan covering 92,000 square miles; population over 300,000 in 1954

KAZAKHSTAN: Largest country by area in Central Asia; largest landlocked country in world; part of Silk Road

KARPATY: Carpathian Mountains; third-longest European mountain range; Ukraine's Mount Hoverla: 6,762 feet

KATORGA: Hard labor in Soviet-Russian penal system; used en masse since tsarist times, expanded in Soviet Union

KENGIR: *Steplag*; gulag for political prisoners and anti-Soviet combatants (1948-1956); peaked at 28,000 (1950)

KENGIR UPRISING: Largest gulag revolt May 16-June 26, 1954; officially thirty-seven deaths, thought much higher

KHMELNYTSKY, BOHDAN: Founder of Ukrainian Hetman State and Khmelnitsky Uprising against Poland (1648-57)

KHOKHOL: Crest; derogatory term for Ukrainians mocking the Cossack scalp lock; see *Kozak*

KHOOMEI: Mongol-Tuvan overtone throat singing

KHRUSHCHEV, NIKITA: Premier of the Soviet Union (1953-1964); brought period of some liberalization; see *Thaw*

KHRYSTOS VOSKRES: Christ has risen; said at Easter

KIEVAN RUS: Predecessor to Ukrainian, Russian, and Belorussian states (879-1240); fell to Batu Khan in 1240

KLYANUS: I swear

KOKHANNA: Beloved

KOLKHOZ: *Kolhosp*; collective farm; see *Collectivization, Communism, Holodomor*

KOLOMIYA: Major Ukrainian Carpathian city and ethnic center of Hutsuls; see *Dovbush, Oleksa, Hutsuls, Opryshky*

KOROLEV, SERGEI: *Serhiy Korolyov*; Ukrainian/Russian rocket engineer; first head of Soviet space program

KOLYMA CAMP: One of the largest gulags of the Soviet Union in eastern Siberia in Kolyma River valley near Japan

KOMSOMOL: Communist youth political organization created under Lenin; see *Commissar, Communism, Red Army*

KOZAK: Cossack; Farmer-warriors of the Ukrainian and Russian steppes from the Turkic word *Kazak*, or "free man"

KREMLIN: Fortified complex composed of cathedrals and walls in Moscow that houses the leaders of Russia

KRONSTADT REBELLION: Major anti-Bolshevik revolt in northern Russian city of Kronstadt March 1-18, 1921

KRESY: Polish name for western Ukrainian lands during interwar period (1918-1939); occupied by Soviets 1939

KULAK: *Kurkul*; wealthy peasant; see *Collectivization, Communism, Holodomor*

KURIN: Platoon; organization; see *Kozak, Sich Riflemen, UHA, UNR, UPA,*

KVITNA NEDILYA: Flower Sunday; Ukrainian term for Palm Sunday

Kyiv: Kiev; founded in AD 482 by Kievan Rus; Ukraine's largest city and capital; third-largest city in Soviet Union

Lemkos: Ukrainian-Rusyn subgroup of Carpathian Mountains; deported by Poland in 1947; see *Vistula, Operation*

Lenin, Vladimir: Russian revolutionary/founder of Bolshevik Party (1917-22); first Soviet Premier (1922-24)

Lentil, Operation: *Doxadar*; genocide of Chechens/Ingush from February to March 1944; see *Chechens*

Lezginka: Caucasian/Chechen/Ingush dance

L'viv Prison Massacre: NKVD executions of Ukrainian prisoners in wake of Operation Barbarossa in June 1941

Lyakh: Derogatory term for Poles from the "Lyakh" or West Slavic Lechitic tribes of ancient Poland

Lylyk: Bat

Malorossiya: Little Russia; defunct Russian colonial term for Ukraine

Makhmadera: Colloquial Kazakh-Russian expression roughly translated as, "stop asking and grab"

Magadan: Far-eastern Russian Siberian port city also used as major gateway to the gulag system; see *Gulag*

Makhorka: Rough tobacco

Molotov Cocktail: Incendiary weapon; named for Soviet foreign minister Vyacheslav Molotov; see *Winter War*

MORDOVIA: *Dubravlag*; major gulag labor camp founded in 1948 in Mordovia Republic in south-central Russia

MOSKAL: Muscovite; Ukrainian derogatory term for Russians

MVD: *Ministerstvo Vnutrennih del SSSR*; Ministry of Internal Affairs of Soviet Union (1946-1991)

NASHI: Ours; colloquially used by Ukrainians to refer to their countrymen

NADZIRATEL: Soviet prison camp guard; see *Gulag, VOKhR*

NARYADSHCHIK: Soviet prison camp clerk that assigns work; see *Gulag*

NA ZDOROVYA: To your health

NAZISM: National Socialism; extreme far-right ideology; official doctrine of WWII Germany; see *Hitler, Adolf*

NIMETS: Slavic slang for Germans from the word for *mute, Nimiy*, for their unfamiliarity with Slavic languages

NKVD: Soviet secret police successor to Cheka (1934-46) and predecessor to KGB (1946-91); see *Cheka, KGB*

NORILSK: *Gorlag*; major gulag in Siberia; majority Ukrainian inmates; major inmate uprising May-August 1953

OKHRANA: Tsarist secret police (1881-1917); see *Cheka, KGB, NKVD*

OPRYSHKY: Ukrainian Carpathian rebels of sixteenth to early-nineteenth centuries; see *Dovbush, Oleksa*

ORTHODOX CHRISTIAN: Eastern Rite Christians after 1054 centered in Constantinople; over thirty million in Ukraine

OSOBYE LAGERYA: Special Soviet camps created for dangerous political prisoners in 1948; see *Gulag; Great Purge*

OTETS: Priest

OUN: Organization of Ukrainian Nationalists; Ukrainian organization created in 1929 against foreign occupation

PARASHA: Waste bucket

PACIFICATION OF EASTERN GALICIA: Polish punitive operation against Ukrainians in Second Polish Republic, 1929

PARTISANS: Various guerrilla forces numbering in the millions operating in Europe during and after WWII

PAWLOKOMA MASSACRE: Polish massacre of hundreds of Ukrainian civilians in village of Pawlokoma in 1945

PECHENIZHYN: Carpathian hometown of Oleksa Dovbush; see *Dovbush, Oleksa, Hutsuls, Opryshky*

PETLIURA, SYMON: *Otaman* of Ukrainian National Republic (1917-21); assassinated in Paris 1926; see *Hetman*

PEREIASLAV, TREATY OF: 1654; joined Ukraine with Russia for tsar's aid against Poland; see *Khmelnytsky, Bohdan*

PILSUDSKI, JOZEF: Polish Chief of State (1918–1922); Minister of Military Affairs Second Polish Republic (1926–35)

Politburo: Lawmaking body of Soviet Union; members elected by Central Committee; see *Central Committee*

Pole: Field

Polkovnyk: Colonel

Polonyna: Mountain meadow; see *Beskids, Karpaty*

Poruchnyk: Lieutenant

Pravda: Truth; newspaper of the communist party of the Soviet Union (1912-91); privately owned since 1996

Proshu: Please; You're welcome

Prosvita: Ukrainian cultural organization founded in L'viv 1868-1939; shuttered by Stalin 1939; reopened 1988

Pryjemno: Nice to meet you

Psikhushka: Psychiatric ward for political dissidents, often used punitively; see *Gulag, Osobye Lagerya*

Rada: Ukrainian parliament; origins in seventeenth-century Ukrainian Hetman State; see *Hetman, Kozak*

Red Army: Army of the Soviet Union (1918-1991); largest army in history; over 34 million mobilized in WWII

Ruthenian: Defunct Austro-Hungarian colonial term for Ukrainians

Rzeszow: Major eastern Polish city near Ukraine and Carpathian Mountains; see *Karpaty*

Shaman: Spiritual healer in Asia and North America

Sharashka: Special prisons for scientists created by Lavrenty Beria in 1938; see *Beria, Lavrenty, Osobye Lagerya*

Shevchenko, Taras: Ukrainian poet and artist considered national icon (1814-61); former serf and tsarist dissident

SHIZO: *Shtrafnoi Izolyator*; punishment cell; see *Gulag*

Shpihun: Spy; see *Cheka, KGB, NKVD*

Shtrafbat: Soviet penal battalion inspired by the German *straftbattalion*; see *World War Two*

Shvydko: Quickly

Sich: Fort; base

Sich Riflemen: Elite division of Ukrainian army; formed from Ukrainians in Austrian army (1914-20); peak 25,000

Slava: Glory

Slava Isusa Khrystu: Glory to Jesus Christ

Slava Naviki: Glory forever (to Jesus Christ)

Slipyj, Josyf: Archbishop and cardinal of Ukrainian Greek Catholic church; inmate of *Dubrovlag*; see *Mordovia*

SLON: First gulag camp system set up in 1920s on Solovetsky Island in Russia's far north; see *Cheka, Gulag*

Sokil: Falcon

Soloveyko: Nightingale; significant in Ukrainian folklore and art

Sotnyk: Captain

Soviet Union: First communist state founded by Lenin's Bolsheviks in Russia (1921-1991); see *Communism*

Sploshnye nary: Plain wooden boards used as bunk beds

Stakhanovite: Soviet myth of miner Aleksei Stakhanov who allegedly cut hundred tons of coal in one shift in 1935

Stalin, Joseph: Longest ruler of Soviet Union (1924-53); Reign of Terror killed millions; see *Holodomor*

Starosta: Elder

Steppes, Great Eurasian: Vast fertile grasslands stretching from Mongolia to Ukraine with exclave in Hungary

Stavka: High command of Russian Empire and later Soviet armed forces including Ukraine and Belarus

Sürgünlik: Exile; genocide of Tatars to Central Asia by Stalin in May 1944; see *Tatars*

Stolypinka: Transport car irreverently named after Tsar Nicholas II's assassinated prime minister, Piotr Stolypin

Surzhyk: Ukrainian-Russian pidgin language spoken mainly in eastern and southern Ukrainian lands

Tak: Yes

Tatars: Turkic people of central Russia and southern Ukrainian steppes, especially Crimea; see *Sürgünlik*

Tatra: Western portion of Carpathians forming border between Poland and Slovakia; highest point 8,711 feet

Thaw: Period of some liberalization in Soviet Union by Khrushchev from 1956 until Brezhnev took power in 1964

Totalitarianism: Government in which the full power of the state is centrally controlled with full subservience

Tovarishch: *Tovarysh*; comrade

Troika: Groups of often three Soviet officials used to condemn prisoners in lieu of court; see *Cheka, KGB, NKVD*

Tryzub: Trident; national symbol of Ukraine from Kievan Rus royalty; see *Kievan Rus, Ukraina*

Tsar: Czar; title of East and South Slavic rulers derived from the ancient Roman imperial title *Caesar*

UHA: Ukrainian Galician (Halytska) Army; peak strength of over 75,000 men in June 1919; see *Halychyna, ZUNR*

Ukraina: Ukraine; largest country fully in Europe; population 40 million in 1954; see *UNR, ZUNR*

Ukrainian-Polish War in Galicia: War between the ZUNR and Second Polish Republic (1918-19); see *ZUNR*

Ukrainian-Soviet War: War between the UNR and Soviet Russia (1917-21); see *UNR*

UNR: Ukrainian National Republic (1917-21); independence declared in Kyiv January 22, 1918; see *ZUNR*

UPA: *Ukrainska Povstanska Armia*; Ukrainian partisans (1942-1956); up to 30,000 regulars; see *Bandera, Stepan*

URKA: "Professional criminal" class of the Soviet Union; see *Gulag, Zeks*

UVAHA: Attention

VAGONKI: Bunkbeds

VAKHTA: Guardhouse

VALENKI: Felt boots

VELYKDEN: Big Day; Easter Sunday

VERKHOVYNA: *Zhabie*; Ukrainian Carpathian settlement and Hutsul center near Romania; see *Hutsuls, Karpaty*

VICHNAYA PAMYAT: Eternal Memory; Traditional eastern Slavic funeral hymn

VINNYTSIA MASSACRE: Mass execution of 9,000-11,000 Ukrainians by Soviets (1937-1938); see *Great Purge/Terror*

VISTULA, OPERATION: *Akcja Wisla*; mass deportations of Lemkos/Ukrainians by Poland in 1947; see *Jaworzno Camp*

VLASOV, ANDREI: Soviet general who fought with Germans in WWII; executed 1946; followers known as Vlasovites

Volyn Massacres/Tragedy: Massacres of thousands of Polish civilians by Ukrainians and Germans in 1943

Vorkuta: *Vorkutlag*; Major gulag in north Russia 1932-62; peak 73,000 prisoners in 1951; major uprising July 1953

VOKhR: *Voenizirovannaya Okhrana*; armed gulag camp guards; see *Gulag, Nadziratel*

Vovk: Wolf

Vyshyvanka: Traditional embroidered shirt

Winter War: War between Soviets and Finland 1939-1940; 1941-44 when Finland joined Germany in WWII

World War I: WWI; second-largest war in history; over 20 million deaths globally; over 60 million mobilized

World War II: WWII; largest war in history; 50-85 million deaths globally; over 120 million mobilized

Yiddish: Ancestral language of Jews throughout Europe

Yizhak: Hedgehog; crisscrossed metal beams used as defensive barricades popularized by Czechs

Yegorov, Sergei: Soviet colonel and deputy chief of the MVD; see *MVD*

Z Bohom: Be with God

Zek: From Russian abbreviation *z/k* for prisoners, or *zaklyuchennyi*; see *Gulag, Urka*

ZEMLYANKA: Earthen dugouts used as rudimentary barracks in gulag, especially in early days; see *Gulag*

ZHYD: Jew; 12.7% of west Ukrainian population in 1910; 8.2% of Russian-controlled Ukraine in 1897

ZONA: Area within gulag camp barbed wire; see *Gulag*

ZUNR: Western Ukrainian National Republic (1918-19); united with UNR January 22, 1919; see *UNR*

BIBLIOGRAPHY

Abbott, Peter, and Oleksiy Rudenko. *Ukrainian Armies 1914-55.* Oxford: Osprey, 2004.

Applebaum, Anne. *Gulag: A History.* Anchor Books, 2004.

Applebaum, Anne. *Red Famine: Stalin's War on Ukraine.* New York: Anchor Books, 2018.

Chojnowski, Andrzej. "Ukrainian Polish War in Galicia, 1918-1919." In vol. 5 of *Internet Encyclopedia of Ukraine.* Canadian Institute of Ukrainian Studies, 2001.

Cipko, Serge, and Michael Palij. "Makhno, Nestor." In vol. 3 of *Internet Encyclopedia of Ukraine.* Canadian Institute of Ukrainian Studies, 2001.

Dolot, Miron. *Execution by Hunger: The Hidden Holocaust.* New York: W.W. Norton & Company. 1985.

Feifer, George. *Justice in Moscow.* New York: Simon and Schuster, 1964.

Gonzalez, Valentin, and Julian Gorkin. *El Campesino: Life and Death in Soviet Russia.* Translated by Ilsa Barea. New York: G.P. Putnam's Sons, 1952.

Grigorenko, P. G. *Memoirs.* W.W. Norton, 1984.

Komar, Luba. *Scratches on a Prison Wall: A Wartime Memoir.* New York: iUniverse, 2009.

Kubijovyc, Volodymyr, ed. "Concentration Camps." In vol. 1 of *Encyclopedia of Ukraine.* Toronto: University of Toronto Press, 1984.

Kubijovyc, Volodymyr. "Lemkos." In vol. 3 of *Internet Encyclopedia of Ukraine.* Canadian Institute of Ukrainian Studies, 1993.

Kubijovyc, Volodymyr. "Ukraine: A Concise Encyclopedia." In vol. 2 of *Ukraine: A Concise Encyclopedia.* University of Toronto Press, 1971, pp. 1059–1084.

Kubijovyc, Volodymyr, Vasyl Markus, and Ihor Stebelsky. "Union of Soviet Socialist Republics." In vol. 5 of *Internet Encyclopedia of Ukraine.* Canadian Institute of Ukrainian Studies, 1993.

Kushnir, V. J. *Polish Atrocities in the West Ukraine: An Appeal to the League for the Rights of Man and Citizen.* Prague: Gerald & Co, 1931.

Logusz, Michael. *Galicia Division: The Waffen-SS 14th Grenadier*

Division1943-1945. Atglen, PA: Schiffer Military History, 1997.

Magocsi, Paul R., and Geoffrey J. Matthews. *Ukraine: A Historical Atlas*. University of Toronto Press, 1985.

Morgan, Glenn. *Soviet Administrative Legality*. Stanford, CA: Stanford University Press, 1962.

Oleszczuk, Thomas. *Political Justice in the USSR: Dissent and Repression in Lithuania, 1969-1987*. New York: Columbia University Press, 1988.

Pavliuc, Nicolae, Volodymyr Sichynsky, and Stanislaw Vincenz. "Hutsuls." In vol. 2 of *Internet Encyclopedia of Ukraine*. Canadian Institute of Ukrainian Studies, 1989.

Rabii-Karpynska, Sofiia. "Boikos." In vol. 1 of *Internet Encyclopedia of Ukraine*. Canadian Institute of Ukrainian Studies, 1984.

Reshetar, John. "Lenin, Vladimir." In vol. 3 of *Internet Encyclopedia of Ukraine*. Canadian Institute of Ukrainian Studies, 1993.

Ripetsky, Stepan. "Partisan Movement in Ukraine, 1918–22." In vol. 3 of *Internet Encyclopedia of Ukraine*. Canadian Institute of Ukrainian Studies, 1993.

Rummel, R. J. *Lethal Politics: Soviet Genocide and Mass Murder since 1917*. New Brunswick, NJ: Transaction Publications, 1992.

Snyder, Timothy. *Bloodlands: Europe between Hitler and Stalin*. New

York: Basic Books, 2010.

"Stalin, Joseph." In vol. 5 of *Internet Encyclopedia of Ukraine*. Canadian Institute of Ukrainian Studies, 1993.

Solzhenitsyn, Aleksandr. *The Gulag Archipelago, 1918-1956: An Experiment in Literary Investigation*. Vol. 3. Translated by Harry Willets. New York: Harper Perennial, 1978, 2007.

Sprudzs, Adolf, ed. *The Baltic Path to Independence: An International Reader of Selected Articles*. Buffalo, NY: William S. Hein & Co., 1994.

Stech, Marko, and Arkadii Zhukovsky. "Franko, Ivan." *Internet Encyclopedia of Ukraine*. Canadian Institute of Ukrainian Studies, 2007.

Stevenson Callcott, Mary. *Russian Justice*. New York: Macmillan, 1935.

Struk, Danylo, ed. "Shevchenko, Taras." In vol. 4 of *Encyclopedia of Ukraine*. Toronto: University of Toronto Press, 1993.

Struk, Danylo, ed. "Ukrainian Insurgent Army." In vol. 5 of *Encyclopedia of Ukraine*. Toronto: University of Toronto Press, 1993.

Struk, Danylo, ed. "Vinnytsia Massacre." In vol. 5 of *Encyclopedia of Ukraine*. Toronto: University of Toronto Press, 1993.

Struk, Danylo, ed. "World Wars." In vol. 5 of *Encyclopedia of Ukraine*. Toronto: University of Toronto Press, 1993.

Subtelny, Orest, and Illia Vytanovych. "Cossacks." In vol. 1 of *Internet Encyclopedia of Ukraine*. Canadian Institute of Ukrainian Studies, 1984.

Thomas, Nigel, and Adam Hook. *Armies of the Russo-Polish War: 1919-21*. Oxford: Osprey, 2014.

Utracka, Katarzyna. "The Katyn Massacre: Mechanisms of Genocide." Warsaw Institute, May 18, 2020. https://warsawinstitute. org/katyn-massacre-mechanisms-genocide/.

Zawada, Zenon. "Ceremony in Poland Recalls Massacre of Ukrainians." *The Ukrainian Weekly*, May 21, 2006.

Zhdan, Mykhailo, and Arkadii Zhukovsky. "Crimean Tatars." *Internet Encyclopedia of Ukraine*. Canadian Institute of Ukrainian Studies, 1993.

Zhdan, Mykhailo. "Kyivan Rus." In vol. 2 of *Internet Encyclopedia of Ukraine*. Canadian Institute of Ukrainian Studies, 1988.

Zhukovsky, Arkadii. "Struggle for Independence (1917-20)." In vol. 2 of *Internet Encyclopedia of Ukraine*. Canadian Institute of Ukrainian Studies, 1989.

Zhukovsky, Arkadii. "Ukrainian–Soviet War, 1917-21." In vol. 5 of *Internet Encyclopedia of Ukraine*. Canadian Institute of Ukrainian Studies, 2001.

ABOUT THE AUTHOR

 **ROMAN GERUS IS** an active member of the Ukrainian-American community as a member of the Ukrainian National Association and his participation in Ukrainian schools, functions and festivals including touring the New Jersey-New York-Connecticut tristate area and Ukraine with his Ukrainian dance ensembles Barvinok and Yunist. Graduating from Rutgers University with a Journalism Major and Creative Writing Minor, Roman has written for various university and independent publications. He currently resides in New Jersey.

www.ingramcontent.com/pod-product-compliance
Lightning Source LLC
Chambersburg PA
CBHW030541190726
48283CB00006B/1962